Clare Connelly was ra[...]
among a family of avid [...]
her childhood up a tree, [...]
Clare is married to her [...] and they live
in a bungalow near the sea with their two children.
She is frequently found staring into space—a surefire
sign that she's in the world of her characters. She has a
penchant for French food and ice-cold champagne, and
Mills & Boon novels continue to be her favourite ever
books. Writing for Mills & Boon is a long-held dream.
Clare can be contacted via clareconnelly.com or her
Facebook page.

Lifelong romance addict **JC Harroway** lives in
New Zealand. Writing feeds her very real obsession
with happy endings and the endorphin rush they create.
You can follow her at jcharroway.com, Facebook.com/
jcharroway, Instagram.com/jcharroway and Twitter.com/
jcharroway.

If you liked
Unbreak My Hart and *Bad Mistake*
why not try

Sinfully Yours by Margot Radcliffe
Dirty Secrets by Regina Kyle

Also by Clare Connelly

The Notorious Harts

Burn My Hart
Harden My Hart

Off Limits
Burn Me Once

Also by JC Harroway

The Pleasure Pact

Bad Business
Bad Reputation

Billionaire Bachelors

Forbidden to Want
Forbidden to Taste
Forbidden to Touch

Discover more at millsandboon.co.uk

UNBREAK MY HART

CLARE CONNELLY

BAD MISTAKE

JC HARROWAY

MILLS & BOON

First Published in Great Britain 2020
by Mills & Boon, an imprint of HarperCollins*Publishers*
1 London Bridge Street, London, SE1 9GF

Unbreak My Hart © 2020 Clare Connelly

Bad Mistake © 2020 JC Harroway

ISBN: 978-0-263-27767-8

MIX
Paper from
responsible sources
FSC™ C007454

This book is produced from independently certified FSC™ paper
to ensure responsible forest management.
For more information visit www.harpercollins.co.uk/green.

Printed and bound in Spain
by CPI, Barcelona

UNBREAK MY HART

CLARE CONNELLY

MILLS & BOON

PROLOGUE

I'M HERE TO watch her. My closest friends in the world—men I think of more as brothers than friends—have sent me here to find out what I can about the half-sister whose very existence they only learned of a week or so ago.

I'm here to watch her but even if I weren't, even if that wasn't the express purpose for my flying from London to San Francisco, I would find it hard *not* to watch her.

Avery Maxwell is, in a word, mesmerising.

If I didn't know she was a Hart I'd never have guessed. Where her half-brothers are built like mountains, Avery is diminutive. Petite. She'd be about five and a half feet and her frame is slender, though there's a strength to her, arms that are elegantly sculpted, eyes that are intelligent and assessing as they scan the crowded bar, lips that—even when they smile—look somehow cynical. *That*, come to think of it, is a definite Hart trait.

She has dark hair, thick and long; it falls down her back with a hint of wildness and untameability.

I reach for my Scotch, cradling the glass for a moment, appreciating the feel of its fine shape in my hands, the elegant cut crystal half filled with amber liquid. She pauses, skimming the bar, and I wonder if she's meeting someone here. It seems as though she's looking for someone she recognises. Her eyes glance past me and I stiffen my spine, a hint of adrenaline flooding my system, as though she might—with one look of those dark, almond-shaped eyes—be able to discern my reason for coming to San Fran.

Her mouth forms a hint of a smile and then her eyes skate past me. I release a breath I didn't realise I was holding and narrow my gaze.

Suddenly, this favour doesn't feel so onerous—to find out what I can about the missing Hart and report back to her famous brothers. Their need to know what they can about her before working out the best way to make contact with her is completely understandable.

She could be any number of things that would make them want to steer clear. The fact she doesn't know she's part of one of the world's most successful dynasties is odd—but they could use that to their advantage and simply refuse to acknowledge her existence.

I shift a little in my seat, wondering why that idea offends me. It might be my inner British aristocrat—the fact I was born into a family like mine and raised, all my life, to believe in the importance of blood, lineage and birthright—even though on some level I reject that thinking, it's still a part of who I am.

And she's a Hart. Their blood runs through her veins—that counts for something.

CHAPTER ONE

THE MUSIC FORMS a pulse in my veins, the beat deep and throbbing. I look around the exclusive bar, mojito in one hand, clutch purse in the other. The thin strap of my dress drops a little over one shoulder; I don't bother to catch it.

The day has been a stinker. Baking hot, with barely a hint of relief coming in off the Bay. Even a dip in my infinity pool didn't cool me down, and here in this club the press of bodies, the tightness of space, combine to make my skin lightly sheened in perspiration.

But I'm not leaving, not yet. I look around, considering my options. A hot guy near the bar lifts his drink, silently inviting me to join him. He's gorgeous but a bit fussy, his hair a little too styled, his look a bit too contrived. Then again, there's the cowboy I was talking to earlier, straight out of Texas, all faded jeans and plaid shirt. It's unusual to find a guy like him in a place like this—but in talking to him I learned his dad's an oil baron. Makes more sense.

I continue to peruse the bar until my eyes skate

past someone—at first—and then shift back. A man is watching me. I narrow my eyes, trying to determine if I've met him before.

He's handsome so it's possible we've hooked up and I've forgotten, but no. I'm sure I'd remember him. His jaw is square, covered in stubble, his face autocratic and symmetrical, his skin has a golden tan and his hair is a light brown with a slight wave. He has an air of authority in his bearing, from the way he's sitting so straight and controlled to the breadth of his shoulders. He's wearing a suit, definitely bespoke, and hand-made shoes.

My lips curl with a hint of derision, because while there's a chance he's self-made there's also a greater probability he's some kind of entitled rich kid, living off his trust fund, wasting money on big boy clothes. Nonetheless, I'm intrigued enough to return his stare head-on, lifting my drink and draining it until it's empty.

I sashay towards the bar, not taking my eyes off him, and as I draw closer I lift my lips into a slow smile, loaded with sensual promise.

Rich kid or not, I'm not looking for anything more than one night. It's my tradition—how I mark this date every year—and he looks like he'd be decent in bed. Then again, that's hard to know for sure—lots of hot guys have been total disappointments in the sack.

'Hi there.' I flash him a megawatt smile now and I see the way his expression shifts, speculation in his eyes.

'Hi. How are you?' An English accent, very plum, very formal. Definitely rich kid.

'Let me guess,' I murmur. 'You're a lord.'

He shoots up one brow and my stomach twists because he's incredibly handsome and, up close, he's also very charming. His skin is tanned but he has some freckles across his nose, freckles that speak of a life spent outdoors. His hair is light brown with natural highlights at the side, and there's warmth in his features, a look of complete kindness that I can't help but recognise.

'Close. Earl.'

'Ah.'

'Earl what?' he prompts, expecting me to somehow intuit his title.

'Well,' I murmur in response, 'now, that's a little harder.'

'Have a drink and I'll drop some hints.'

He gestures to the seat beside him but I don't take it. Instead, I move closer, so I'm standing within the void created by his legs. 'I'll have another mojito.'

A frown flashes across his face but then he smiles, lifts a hand and orders our drinks. I don't know what his name is or why he's here in San Fran, in this bar talking to me, but before midnight I'm going to have my wicked way with him—Happy Birthday to me.

My best friends' half-sister is flirting with me. And my dick is growing harder by the second and I want to ignore the reason I'm here and take this in a totally different direction. I want to fuck her.

This I hadn't expected. I thought she'd be like the Harts. I thought she'd look like one of them, that something about her would remind me of them. I didn't expect to feel this zing of attraction, this aching need to possess her, yet it's running rampant through me, out of control, impossible to ignore.

But I do ignore it because Avery Maxwell is definitely off-limits. Isn't she?

'So you have a fancy title?' I murmur, leaning a little closer, pressing a hand to his shoulder. I'm kind of interested—the aristocracy is such a foreign concept to me—but at the same time this conversation is really just a means to an end. I know that in the morning I won't think of this guy again. I won't remember his name, his title, nor the colour of his eyes—even though they are a particularly striking shade of brown, as though someone's taken the top off a just poured espresso, that beautiful golden crema, and filled his irises up with that perfect pigment. They're surrounded by thick black lashes that give them the appearance of having been framed. Men always have the best eyelashes. Bastards.

'I do.'

'And it is?'

'I thought you were guessing?'

A smile lifts inside me. 'And what do I get if I guess it right?'

For a moment he hesitates, something flashes in his eyes that makes me wonder if I'm intimidating him. I'm used to that. I'm what men of a certain age would call 'forward'. How's that for a double standard? Do you have any idea how many men try to pick me up? And they're just 'men being men'. But a woman who knows what she wants and isn't afraid to go after it? Forward. A slut. Amoral. Take your pick, I've heard them all at one point or another.

'Earl of Castlewick?' I grin, lifting my mojito and savouring the flavour as it hits my mouth.

'Not even close.' His laugh is the last word in hot. Deep and rumbly, and somehow even that small sound has an English accent so my stomach twists. A familiar reassuring heat forms low in my abdomen, and I know exactly what to do with it.

I lean a little closer, catching a hint of the cologne he wears. It's woody and spiced and when I press a hand to his shoulder he's warm in a way that pulls me even closer.

'Give me a clue.'

He reaches for his Scotch, putting it between us as he lifts it to his lips, and again I have that feeling that he's trying to put the brakes on this—on me. And yet this isn't my first rodeo. I know desire when I see it and that's exactly what this man and I are feeling for one another.

Human, biological instinct. Desire, need, sex. I don't know why we as a society have overcomplicated this with all the emotional bullshit people try to layer over what is, essentially, a very animalistic act. Do you think any other animal bothers to dress sex up as something more than it is?

'Earl of McHotness?' Okay, that's totally sleazy but I don't care. It's worth it to see the instant flash of speculation that deepens his eyes from gold to burnt butter brown.

'I'll tell you mine if you tell me yours.'

I shake my head, enjoying myself despite the duality I sense in him. 'You don't want to even try to guess?'

He lifts a brow and shakes his head. 'I've never been any good at guessing games.'

I pout for a moment. 'What are you good at then?'

Another hint of resistance, like he's not saying the first thing he wants to. 'What do you think?'

'Hmm.' I move my hand from his shoulder to his arm, squeezing biceps that are well-shaped. 'You're fit. So you either work out a lot or have a job doing manual labour.' I move my gaze downwards, intending to look at his shoes, but instead my gaze lingers on his crotch. He's wearing a dark grey suit. If it were black or navy blue it might do a better job of hiding the fact his cock is either hard or getting that way but, as it is, I can see the evidence of his desire and it brings a smile to my face.

Emboldened, I move even closer, my hips brush against his inner thighs. If he were to shift forward on his seat—even a little—his dick would press against me, and you don't even want to know how badly I need to feel that.

'But, going by your suit and shoes, I'd say that's not it at all.'

'What's wrong with my suit and shoes?'

'They don't exactly scream carpenter.'

'No?'

'Not any carpenter I've ever met.'

'And you know a lot of carpenters?'

He's quick. We bounce off each other in a way that heightens my attraction to him. 'I've known a few.'

His eyes narrow infinitesimally, as though he's trying to pick me apart, piece by piece. Bless him. If only he knew what a waste of time that would be—not to mention energy. Why try to understand someone you're only going to know for a few hours?

'Sorry to disappoint you then, but I'm not a carpenter.'

'Oh, I don't think you'll be a disappointment.'

He's quiet, his eyes scanning my face, and then he shakes his head, a laugh I could best describe as rueful tipping from his lips. 'I'm flattered.'

'I have a place around the corner.' It's one of the reasons I come to this bar. Sure, it's 'the' spot to be right now, so it's also great for networking, but nothing trumps convenience. My work life is hectic enough—when it comes to my private life—what some might call 'social' life—I want ease of use.

Another laugh, this one a deep rumble. Now, almost as if against his will, he places a hand on the curve of my hip, his thumb sliding across my side so a shiver bolts down my spine.

It's such a small touch, but it feels amazing.

'Is there some kind of rush I'm not aware of?'

I consult the wristwatch I always wear—one of the few items of Mom's I still have. It's after ten.

'Haven't you heard? I lose my magic pumpkin carriage at midnight.'

'Ah. Leaving me with only a glass slipper to find you again?'

'I'm not that kind of Cinderella. There's no "finding me" afterwards.'

'So you disappear into thin air by midnight?'

'Pretty much.'

He considers this a moment then lifts a finger to my shoulder, watching its progress as he traces a line down my arm towards my wrist, then my hand. He laces his fingers through mine, frowning a little as he looks down at our interlocked hands.

'Let's talk a bit.'

I pull a face. 'Talk's overrated.'

Another laugh and I'm forced to consider why I'm still standing there. I thought he was watching me, I thought he wanted what I want. 'Look, Earl…'

'Barrett Byron-Moore,' he supplies, and I'm not disappointed. Frankly, that's every bit as British as I would have expected. 'Earl of Ashwyn.'

'Well, Barrett Byron-Moore, Earl of Ashwyn.'

My gut pulls as I say the double-barrelled name, liking the feel of it in my mouth. 'I must have read you wrong.'

'Oh?'

'Mmm.' I press a finger to the button at his throat, flicking it a little, my eyes not dropping from his face. 'I thought you were looking at me like you wanted a bit of…fun. But if you're one of those guys, then I won't waste either of our time.'

He squeezes my hand. 'What's "those" guys?'

'You know, the romance guy.'

'Romance?' Another laugh. They fall so easily from his mouth, beautiful rich sounds of natural amusement, and I briefly envy him that light-heartedness. 'Because I want to have a conversation with you? When did the bar for romance drop so low?'

'You know what I mean.' I shake my head impatiently.

'I'm afraid I don't.'

'Then let me spell it out for you.' I lean closer, so my mouth brushes his ear. 'I want to get laid. That's why I'm here. I don't really care who you are, or what you do for a living. I care that you're good in bed. Are you?'

He lifts his other hand to my chin, using his thumb and forefinger to push it upwards so our eyes lock and I'm trapped in the force of his inquisitive stare. I'm uncomfortable; I don't like it. I feel like he's seeing more than I ever share and I hate that. With great care, I push a bored expression into place and straighten, pulling away from him.

'It doesn't matter.' My smile is tightly dismissive. 'Thanks for the drink.'

I reach for it but, before I can leave, his hand has snaked out, grabbing me around the waist, pulling me back between his legs abruptly.

'Hold on a second.'

There's a frown on his face, a look in his eyes I don't comprehend.

'Why?' My heart rate has lifted a notch. I love men, but in a very limited use kind of way. I love their arms and their chins, that little divot I can dip my tongue into, right between the clavicles. I love strong legs and broad chests. I love men who are confident bordering on arrogant, because I am—with no apology—enough of a ball-buster in my work life that when it comes to sex I like a guy who knows what he wants—and how to give me exactly what I need.

Something about his strength as he pulls me towards him fills me with a rush of white-hot need. I swallow past a throat that is dry suddenly.

'Because I asked you to. Sit down. Talk to me.'

Disappointment bursts inside me.

'I just told you—'

'You don't do "talk",' he interrupts—another thing I'm not at all tolerant of in my business life but that, in this moment, with this man, I find strangely erotic. 'But I do.'

I tilt my head to one side, wondering a little more than I'd like about this man now. Even from a distance I could perceive his natural air of authority but up close, like this, I feel it wrapping around me and I have the strangest impulse to surrender to it.

'Will you make it worth my while?'

'And how would I do that…?'

He lets the question hang in the air searchingly, and so I supply my name almost on autopilot. 'Avery.'

'Avery.' Jesus. If I liked the taste of his name in my mouth then the sound of mine coated by his accent, on his lips, is like something out of an erotic fantasy. I close my eyes for a second, absorbing it, enjoying it, appreciating it as a connoisseur might a particularly fine wine.

'How about this?' There's a barstool behind me. I reach around and pull it closer, and then closer still, so that when I do as he's asked and sit down, my knees are brushing his inner thighs, our bodies as close as it's possible to be. Around us, the club hums and buzzes and that very busyness gives us a degree of privacy, as though we are in our own little bubble.

I reach for his hand and place it on my thigh, beneath the fabric of my dress.

'For every question I answer, you'll move your hand an inch or so higher.'

His Adam's apple throbs as he swallows.

'Deal?'

There's that duality again, like he wants this but he's also fighting it—fighting me.

'Deal.'

I relax, a smile curving my lips, lips that his eyes drop to and devour so heat spreads inside me, pooling between my legs.

'What do you want to talk about then?'

'What do you do, Avery?'

It's a boring—yet safe—first question. 'I'm CEO of my own company.'

'Impressive. What kind of company?'

I move my gaze pointedly to my legs.

A small laugh, but less robust this time. Almost shaky. He pushes his hand along my leg and a pulse of adrenaline kicks at my side. I want to cheat, to wriggle closer, but I don't. I know all about delayed gratification and that's exactly what I'm experiencing. The buzz of anticipation is its own reward.

'Ever heard of Moatsy?'

His eyes are guarded. 'Yeah.'

I'm not surprised. Everyone's heard of Moatsy. It's the fastest growing data protection company in the world. Not only do we track who's tracking you, we put safeguards on registered devices, making the sale of browsing information almost impossible. Corporations were my first clients but in the last couple of years the average Joe has become—quite rightly—concerned with the open slather collection of personal information for the purpose of commercial gain.

'That's me.'

'No shit. You're on my phone.'

His hand creeps higher. My pulse fires. 'I hope to be on a lot more than your phone before the night is done.'

No laugh this time. Just a look in his eyes that I can't analyse.

'How old are you?'

'Twenty-nine. You?'

'Do I have to answer the questions?' His hand nudges higher.

'I can make it worth your while.'

But before I can lift my hand to his cock he shakes his head. 'You'd better not do that.'

'No?'

'We wouldn't want the night to end prematurely.'

'Have you got something against telling me your age?'

For a moment a frown shifts on his face, and then he smiles, a lazy smile that's slow to spread. It sparks curiosity low in my gut. 'I got the feeling you didn't want to know anything about me.'

I tilt my head to the side, considering that. 'True. Still, a quid pro quo seems only fair.'

'Is that right?' His hand shifts slightly higher. I haven't technically answered a question but I don't point that out.

'I like to take as well as give,' I tease, moving closer so his hand brushes close to my sex.

His eyes narrow and I hear a faint hiss escape from between his teeth. 'I'm thirty-three.'

'And is there a Mrs Byron-Moore?'

'Mmm…' His noise of assent is a low rumble and I freeze. I might have very few standards when it comes to indiscriminate, passionate sex, but infidelity is a line I will never cross. I've got no interest in screwing another woman's husband—nor in getting off with the kind of man who'd cheat on his wife.

I reach down, curving my hand over his wrist, pulling it away. His expression doesn't change. He feels no guilt, evidently.

'And how would she feel to see you with your hand up my dress?'

'My mother has very little interest in my sex life.'

'Oh.' If I'd had any doubts as to how much I want him, the instant tsunami of relief would negate it. I am immeasurably glad he's not married, glad I don't have to walk away from the tension that's humming between us.

'Do you think I'd be here, doing this, if I was married?'

'It wouldn't surprise me.'

He looks…hurt. Fascinating.

'I'm not like that.'

I lift my shoulders. A lot of men think they wouldn't cheat, but in my experience that certainty's about as rock-solid as a block of ice on a summer's day.

'What brings you to the Bay?'

He hesitates a moment. 'I thought I was asking the questions.'

'Have I hit on something you don't want to talk

about?' He keeps his fingers where they are but shifts them from side to side, stroking the sensitive flesh of my inner thigh. I bite down on my lip to mute a groan.

'Not particularly.' A lift of his broad shoulders. My instincts tell me he's not being completely honest but I don't particularly care. Whatever this guy's business is, he has a right to keep it private. I've already said more to him than I have the last three guys I slept with combined.

'You're cryptic.'

He grins. 'I can be.'

'Do we know each other well enough yet?'

Another frown. Jesus. I don't usually have to push a guy into bed. This is a new experience for me. I contemplate walking away from him, but I feel both fascinated by and invested in him.

'For what, Avery?'

I roll my eyes. 'Come home with me.'

He leans closer, his hand stays where it is. 'You mean, come home and fuck you?'

I nod slowly. 'Unless you don't want to?'

His eyes hold mine and my breath hitches in my throat. I feel as though he's going to say no. Like he might stand up and end this. And I really, really don't want him to.

'Barrett?'

CHAPTER TWO

HER EYES ARE a dark shade of brown, almost black, and they're duelling with mine, challenging me, daring me to say yes, or perhaps to say no. I speak four languages fluently and I mentally use every curse word from each now, letting them fire through my brain as I wage an internal battle—between what I know I should do and what I want, more than anything.

I want to fuck her.

I felt like I was being slammed in the gut the moment I saw her, even before I had time to compute that it was, in fact, Avery Maxwell.

And if she were any other woman I'd have slid her G-string from her legs by now and given her at least one orgasm, right here against the bar of this nightclub.

But Avery Maxwell is my friends' sister. That makes her off-limits, doesn't it? I mean, the bro code still applies even when they've technically never met, right?

Or does it?

Isn't that some kind of patriarchal bullshit right there? To treat her with kid gloves because she happens to be a blood relative of some guys I really care about. What's my obligation here? They want to know everything they can about her, and it's pretty clear to me that I'm only going to find that out if I can contrive a way to spend more time with her. Sex ticks that box.

But it's more than that. I want her and she wants me. We're two consenting adults. I wouldn't be using that sexual attraction to find out what the Harts need to know, but it sure as hell won't hurt.

'Seriously?'

The look of confusion on her face tells me that she's probably never been rejected once in her life—and that's completely understandable. She's beautiful but it's more than that. She's alluring and whip-smart, and not afraid to show it. There's also a latent sensuality that makes me want to strip that dress from her body and claim her right here.

Fuck.

'Let me put it this way,' she murmurs, and she shifts on her stool so my hand, resting high on her inner thigh, is driven the rest of the distance. My fingertips brush against lacy underwear; she's warm and wet.

My cock jerks against my pants.

'I want to sleep with you.' Closer still and without my permission, my fingers begin to move, sliding aside the fine fabric of her underpants, parting her slick sex and pushing against her so her eyes lift heavenward and she expels a faint moan. 'I want you to come home and fuck me, and if it's good then I'll want you to fuck me again, and then I'll want you to get dressed and go away.'

Another litany of curses spreads through me. 'You don't pull any punches, huh?'

'I prefer to be completely honest about my expectations.'

'So I'm what? Like a gigolo?'

'Well, I won't pay you.' She grins. It's a sexy smile, intelligent and knowing, but I want to displace it. I drive a finger deeper inside her and she jerks, her eyes showing surprise and pleasure in equal measure.

'I'm glad to hear it.' I lean closer and she drops her head towards my shoulder. Her face is shielded; my frame is big enough to block her—mostly—from anyone else's view. I can't remember the last time I engaged in any kind of public sex act. Maybe as a teenager? In the UK I'm recognisable enough to warrant a degree of circumspection, but here in the States I'm just another guy.

I glide my thumb over her clit, her moans and sharp breaths driving me over the edge so a little cum spills from me. I haven't been this turned on in pretty much for ever.

So apparently I've dispensed with the morality of this, then.

She's my closest friends' sister.

And I'm about to fuck her until kingdom come.

And there's not a damned thing I can do to stop it.

Her hand lifts to my shirtfront and clutches it and her breathing gets faster. I thrust a finger inside her and she makes a low noise; her muscles squeeze around me, moist, warm, and her body trembles. Her orgasm is impossible to mistake.

Her responsiveness is one hell of a turn on.

She stays where she is, her head pressed to my shoulder, her body almost melded to mine, but against my shirt, in a voice that is hoarse and a little trembling, she says, 'If you don't agree to come back to my place I'm going to whip my dress off and beg you to fuck me right here.'

I have a chance to stop this. To take a moment and think—to work out if it's as stupid as I suspect I'm going to think it is in the morning.

'That's probably not the best idea,' I say in a voice that reminds me terrifyingly of my father's.

'You don't think?' She pulls back and winks, the gesture slow and hauntingly erotic. The last filament of control I have snaps.

'Then let's go.'

My place is two blocks away—it's not far—but each step beside this man is agony. I'm desperate to rip that suit from him, to see him naked, to taste every inch of him, to hold his erection in my hands, to pump him until he can barely breathe, until his knees are weak and he's afraid he's going to stumble to the floor. I want to take him deep in my mouth until I can taste him right at the back of my throat. I want to feel the weight of his body on mine, and I want to straddle him, taking him at my own pace, tormenting him with his need for me. I want to tie his hands to my bedhead and keep him like that for my pleasure.

The image practically sets me alight.

'Walk faster.'

He slants a grin in my direction. The problem is, walking faster makes it worse. Every step makes me more and more conscious of the heat between my legs, the moistness there, the pleasure he's already given me—a promise of what's to come.

'Want me to throw you over my shoulder and run the rest of the way?'

Jesus. That idea shouldn't appeal to me as much as it does but I can't shake the fantasy of how hot that would be. Like I said, I love a man who knows what he wants, a man who takes charge, because it's the polar opposite to how I ordinarily run my life. In the boardroom I'd never dream of letting anyone, let alone a man, try to take control.

'It's not far.' The words are breathless. 'Come on.'

We speed up by unspoken agreement until we reach my townhouse. Halfway down Twentieth Street, it's a testament to modern engineering, nestled amongst two of San Francisco's original terraced houses.

'Here…' I reach into my bag, fumbling my keys a little in my haste. I catch him eyeing off my home and feel a familiar burst of pride—I've worked hard to get where I am and this house is evidence of that. Of course it's only a fraction of my net worth. Most of what I earn goes to my charity, but this house—in a neighbourhood I fantasised about belonging to when I was a kid riding my bike out of Bayview—this is one indulgence I've allowed myself.

'Nice,' he says with a small nod. I don't bother replying.

There's no need.

This is an exchange, and not of information. I grab his hand and pull him after me, up the steps that lead to the huge glass door. I swipe my key fob and the two security pins click to unlock it. A moment later I shoulder through, holding the door open for him and sealing it shut as soon as he's inside. I reach for the light switch behind him and a second later I'm pushing up onto the tips of my toes, my lips seeking his, my body hungry to feel him all over again.

I kiss him hard, pushing him back against the wall, and he takes a second to respond, perhaps surprised by my urgency, but then his hands find my hips and he's holding me to him—as if I'd go anywhere—his fingers splayed over my dress so I want, more than anything, to be completely naked.

I'm driven by an ancient beating of a drum. I slide my hands under his shirt, connecting with the warmth of his chest, and groan because he's ridged with muscles and, oh, so warm. I grunt, needing more, withdrawing my hands purely so they can work the buttons. I move quickly, kissing him, then pulling away to see what I'm doing, then kissing him again, until finally the shirt is loose enough for me to push it down, over his shoulders, along with his suit jacket. I'm rough and fast; both drop to the wall behind him and, when he shifts, to the floor at his feet.

'Where's your bedroom?'

There's no time to climb the three flights of stairs though. I want him here, now.

'This way.' I kiss him again as I stumble backwards, his body seeking mine, mine needing his, our steps clumsy because we're moving as one. His fingers push at the straps of my dress and I pause only to let him slide it down my hips so I can step out of it completely.

Then he jerks his head back, his eyes pinning me to the spot as he looks at me for several seconds. I'm not wearing a bra and his eyes linger on the curves of my breasts and my nipples tingle and tighten beneath his intense scrutiny.

But I don't want to be looked at—even if it is with a level of admiration that's its own aphrodisiac.

'Fuck me,' I demand, reaching for him again, one hand sliding into my underpants and shoving them down my legs.

'Now.'

His laugh is throaty. 'We're still in a rush?'

'I am.'

But his eyes have the power to haunt me because

there's something in their depths I can't understand; for the briefest moment it gives me cause to wonder.

'What?'

'You're just—'

'What?'

'Really fucking hot.' He shakes his head, like he wasn't expecting that.

'Is that a problem?' I'm reaching for him again, this time at belt-height.

'No.' If I had any intention of knowing him beyond tonight I might have asked him what the hell was going on but I don't need to know in order to enjoy this.

'Fuck me,' I say again, pushing at his belt and zipper and lifting up to claim his lips once more. This time he lifts me up, wrapping my legs around his waist and striding straight ahead, right into the room I directed him to.

'This isn't a bedroom.'

'I know.' I fumble for the light switch, illuminating my kitchen.

'I thought we were—'

'Use your imagination, Earl of Ashwyn.' I nod towards the table on the other side of the room. Marble-topped and sturdy as anything, framed by a stunning view out over Noe Valley.

His grin is sheer sexy devil. 'As you wish, m'lady.'

I laugh but the moment he sets my ass on the edge of the table I'm not laughing, because his cock is right between my legs and I feel a sharp burst of anticipation, swiftly followed by a need that almost knocks me sideways.

His pants are loose on his hips. He reaches into his pocket and pulls out a wallet and—thank God—a condom, his eyes on mine as he simultaneously pushes out of his pants and rips open the foil square. Before he can do anything further I take it from his fingers, a smile playing about my lips.

'Allow me.'

His chest moves sharply with the intake of his breath. I grin, taking my time, letting my fingertips tease him, brushing his length lightly as I roll the condom in place, enjoying his obvious torment at the promise of what's to come. At his base, I wrap my fingers around his length, squeezing a little until I hear a curse escape his mouth.

He has a great body. The thought comes to me out of nowhere but faced with him like this I can't help but appreciate the form of his chest, the abdominal muscles, tanned, with a sparse covering of hair that arrows down his abdomen. His arms are muscled too, but lean and toned. I wonder again if he works out, or if he has a physically demanding job, then I shake my head a little because I don't want to wonder anything about him.

As if reading my mind, he drops his head and kisses me, his hands roaming my body, cupping my breasts, his fingers running over my nipples, his cock edging closer until he runs a hand down my side to my butt, scooping me forward on the table so I'm right on the edge.

'You're sure?'

A small laugh falls from my mouth, splashing between us. 'Do I look sure?'

His grin is lopsided. 'Hey, it never hurts to ask, right?'

I pull a face. 'I feel like I've made myself perfectly clear.'

'Yeah?' He moves closer, his breath brushing my forehead.

'Yeah.' I move my hands behind his back, my legs wide, needing him.

'You want me to fuck you,' he murmurs unnecessarily, and at my short nod he drives his length into me, hard and fast, no preamble, nothing, just a huge, hard dick that splinters my self-control and my sanity all at once.

'Oh, my God,' I groan, contorting a little, arching my back, feeling him so deep inside me, squeezing him hard, holding him where he is. But he's strong and it's easy for him to pull back, his almost complete withdrawal a form of torture. Then he's thrusting into me again and I'm crying out, his name dropping from my mouth without my knowledge. I lift a hand and run it through my hair, surrendering completely to the wildness of this, and of him.

His fingers brush over my clit—so gently I barely feel them at first beneath the heavenly assault of his cock's possession of my body—but then he moves them harder, faster, so a thousand sensations splinter through me and I'm incapable of a single thought. I feel as though I'm floating amid stars and space, far from this earth and all the pain she bears.

My orgasm catches me completely by surprise. It's fast. So fast and abrupt, coming upon me out of nowhere, so I jerk up and stare at him then close my eyes as heat spreads through me followed by blinding light and a sense of being out of my body. He's slowed down, letting me ride this out and feel every single burst of pleasure within my body.

But, just as my breathing slows, he pulls out of me completely, stepping out of pants I didn't realise he was still wearing.

'Hop down.' His voice is thick with his own desire—or is it his monumental control?

I do as he says because his authority is a complete turn on, and I blink up at him, waiting to see what he says now. In response, he spins a finger in the air, gesturing for me to turn around. My heart lifts up a notch, blood slamming through my veins, but I do it, turning so I'm facing the view beyond the windows, the table at my hips. His hands are there a second later, possessing my sides as though he was born to do just that, his fingertips gliding over my flesh.

'Bend forward.'

I swallow, my throat inexplicably thick-feeling, then fold forward at my hips, propping my elbows on the table.

'Good.'

Something shivers along my spine. I hold my breath without meaning to, and then he's nudging my legs apart with his, his hands moving back to my hips at first, holding me where I am. I'm so distracted by his touch, which alternates between feather-light and hard enough to be on the brink of causing pain, but the contrast of those tactile sensations imbues the simple contact with an eroticism that takes my breath away.

I'm so captivated by it that his thrust is unexpected, his cock driving into me from behind, taking me in a new and different way—like this I feel him differently and God, his hands—they run over my body, tormenting my breasts, plucking at my nipples in unison with his possession, so I'm stumbling over the edge of the earth, darkness and light blending together to make a cataclysmic rainbow of brightness.

Again his hands find my clit. I don't need it. His dick is more than enough. But, with his hand, I am powerless against this, my body completely at his command, my pleasure inevitable.

This time, as I explode with a loud cry, he follows, his body juddering against mine, his breath loud, and I feel every pump of his cock inside me, and that's a new kind of pleasure and torment. I stay perfectly still, enjoying every sensation as it travels through my body, the obliteration beautiful, the feeling so life-affirming that I smile to myself, my cheeks heated.

I don't know how long we stay like that, his hands resuming their lazy inquisition of my body, but I do know I'm tempted to stay right where I am, which in and of itself galvanises me into action.

I make a little noise before straightening, disentangling our bodies with true regret—but it's a regret I don't show a hint of in my face when I turn towards him, a smile on my lips.

I convey nothing of how tempted I am to ask him to stay the night. Truth be told, I think we could have a lot of fun if given a little more time, but time brings its own problems. Besides, I got what I wanted—what I needed.

Which means one thing.

'Thanks.' I lift up and press a kiss to his cheek. 'That was amazing.'

He arches a brow. 'I'm glad you think so.'

'Oh, I do.' I look around. His pants are just behind him. I bend down and catch them between my fingertips, pressing them towards him.

'There's a restroom just down the corridor.' I nod in that direction. His eyes narrow speculatively, and there's a pang of something inside me—a temptation to know what he's thinking. Except I don't care about that. So I clarify what I mean. 'If you want to freshen up before you leave.' I shoot a pointed look towards his dick, and the condom.

His laugh shows disbelief. 'Just like that?'

My heart shunts an extra beat of blood through me. 'Just like that.'

His gaze is heavy on me, demanding and speculative all at once. Heat prickles beneath my skin.

'I don't think so.'

CHAPTER THREE

I SHOULD GO. I know I should go but hell, her easy dismissal of me raises every damned hackle I have. Despite the fact she told me she'd want me to go away again, the reality of that is unpalatable. I shouldn't be here in the first place—a voice has been screaming inside my mind from the minute she started hitting on me in the bar, but I ignored it and I came here, and now that I've slept with this long-lost Hart I feel like the damage is already done. But the way she's trying to flick me away like a bug, because I've given her what she wanted, irks me.

It really, really irks me.

And it's petty and childish but I don't like that and I intend to show her just how much.

'Oh?' She crosses her arms over her chest. Huge mistake—it just reminds me of how freaking perfect her breasts are. 'Do you think you have any say in that?'

I grind my teeth together. Yeah, this is bullshit. 'I'm not done yet.'

Before she can get another smart question out,

I kneel in front of her, spreading her legs with my palms, my mouth pressing to her beautiful, wet sex. I feel her tremble in response, her exhalation of surprise, and I feel her surrender too, when her fingers start to drive through my hair. Good.

I flick her with my tongue, knowing where she likes it, knowing what drives her crazy, then I suck her sensitive flesh into my mouth, running my tongue over her seam until her breath is rushed and her hands are moving faster. Then I slow down, pulling back a gear, letting my tongue taste her inner thighs, drawing invisible circles there.

'Please,' she moans, so I bring my mouth back like the good little sex slave she apparently thinks I am. I drive her back to the brink of explosion. I can taste it, I can feel how close she is to coming, but then I slow down again, moving my mouth upwards this time, to her flat stomach, tracing a circle around her navel so she makes a noise of frustration and pushes at my head a little, trying to guide me down. I dip my head lower to hide my smile.

So much for wanting me to go.

'What's the magic word?' I murmur against her flesh, dragging my mouth sideways to her hips.

'Please.' She loads the word with resentment. I bite her hip and she makes a sound of surprise followed by a long, soft moan. 'Please.' No resentment this time. Just blind need.

'Since you asked so nicely.' I bring my mouth back to her sex and this time, when she's on the brink of an orgasm, I don't move my mouth to her thigh or her stomach, I don't slow down. I pull back completely and stand up, taking my pants from her hands.

Her eyes show complete shock. I ignore it and I have to stifle a need to laugh.

'This way, you said?' I gesture down the corridor.

Her expression shows fire and flame. She's pissed. Okay, she probably has a right to be but so do I!

'Yes.' She recovers quickly, too proud to show me how she's feeling.

She glares at me and I grin, mimicking her words. 'Thanks. That was great.'

I move away before I give into temptation and finish what I started, driving her over the edge once more using just my mouth. I discard the condom and dress quickly, splashing water on my face and staring at myself for a hard second in the mirror of her bathroom.

Jesus Christ. Guilt stares back at me. I don't even want to think about what I've just done.

You're like family. You're the only person we can trust with this, Barrett.

I sweep my eyes shut and see the three Hart brothers, men I've known since we were boys together, and feel like I've done something completely and utterly wrong.

What the hell just happened? I saw Avery Maxwell and it's like everything stopped making sense. I acted on instinct alone and, hell, I like to hook up with women—but not like this. I date them. I flirt.

I genuinely enjoy getting to know them, and after a few weeks it runs its course and I move on, or they do. But, with each and every woman, I'm open to the possibility that there might be something more there, something worth investigating.

Avery was—so utterly resistant to that. She wanted to be screwed, and as I button up my shirt I come to the realisation that if I hadn't come back here then any other guy in the bar would have done. She was determined to get laid tonight.

The thought fills me with a strange sense of impatience. She obviously does this a lot and it might be kind of old-fashioned of me but I feel a blade of fear for her—what if I were a complete sociopath? She invited me into her home knowing nothing about me. And her home is—I cast an eye about the bathroom and mentally draw back the details I observed. It's a townhouse in Noe Valley, beautiful and expansive. She's clearly financially well set up. Which could make her a target for any kind of bastard looking to use her then take whatever he could.

An irrational anger fills me at the risks she's taking. I have no business to feel that way—it's her life and she should live it how she wants but hell, she's also the half-sister of my friends and...and what? I've just come back here and had sex with her. Fantastic sex. Mind-blowingly addictive, I don't think I could ever get enough sex with this woman sex. But that doesn't give me any right to go all Big Brother on her.

Big Brother!

Crap. This is—way more complicated than it should be. What the hell have I done?

I stare back at myself from the mirror, accusation in my eyes—eyes that tell me I'm a dumbass for going to the bar instead of choosing a safe way to find out what I could about her. I could have made an appointment in a professional capacity, masqueraded as an investor or a potential client. But it wouldn't have changed a thing.

We would have ended up fucking on her desk instead of her dinner table, but the outcome would have still been the same. There was something about Avery and me that just demanded answering.

I've been with enough women to know when there's a different kind of spark. Not just desire or attraction but like a lightning bolt of 'must have' need, and we both felt that. Okay, maybe it was more just about getting laid for Avery. Maybe any other guy in the bar *would* have done, or maybe not.

I honestly think that our fucking would have been inevitable. *So what, jackass? Does that absolve you of all guilt?* I don't think so. For crying out loud. I'm here to find out what I can about this woman, to suss out if she knows anything about her impossibly wealthy family, not to get my rocks off.

I push my hands through my hair distractedly. Is there any way I can still achieve what I set out to do? Or has sleeping with her made it impossible?

And can I actually do that, anyway? Isn't it a massive betrayal to dig into her personal life after what we've just done?

It's not like it meant anything. She basically dismissed me while I was still inside her. If I was careful not to let it happen again? A wry grimace shifts on my face, because I think that could be almost impossible. If we're in the same room together I'm going to want her.

Besides which, Avery is clearly of the 'wham, bam, thanks for that' persuasion. She's probably not even going to want to see me again. Which means what? I stick around now, find out what I can and get out? Leave it to another one of their lawyers to explain all this to her?

I groan, shaking my head, because I've well and truly fucked up here, muddying the waters of what was already a delicate situation. 'Thanks a lot, asshole,' I say to my dick. 'Last time I let you call the shots.'

If only.

Okay. I'm not comfortable with what I've done. Clearly I've let down my friends and I've done something that borders on duplicitous with Avery, given what I know about who she is, and I'm pretty sure she has no clue about that. But I don't have a magical winding back time device. I did this—we did it. It was consensual, hot sex between two adults. But it was also a mistake, and it shouldn't have happened. Now that it has, though, I have to work out a way to achieve what I came here to do without letting

Avery feel used and hurt. Hurt? I almost laugh out loud. That woman has ice in her veins. I doubt hurt is something she's capable of experiencing. Still, I don't want to be an asshole to her. I have to tread carefully.

Managing difficult situations is a strength of mine and I have no intention of letting this one get the better of me. One way or another, I'll figure out how to fix this. And it all starts with talking to the Harts. Because sending me here to spy on her was wrong. They were blindsided by the revelation that their dad had a daughter none of them knew anything about, but that doesn't make it right to keep that from Avery. She deserves to know the truth. That certainty hits me like an anvil between the eyes—I wish I'd seen it sooner but, now that I have, there's only one way to handle this.

'A Mr Barrett Byron-Moore is here to see you, Avery.'

I jerk so hard in response I bang my knee into the underside of the desk. 'What?' I reach for my coffee on autopilot, taking a long drink and, unbidden, memories of that night career into me. It might have been four days ago but I can remember every look, every touch, every breath and sensation as though it were happening right now.

I remember his mouth against me, his tongue so damned skilled, I remember the pleasure building, then the frustration as he diverted to another part of my body, then the sheer, dizzying relief when he returned to my sex, bringing me right back to the brink of a huge orgasm.

Then stood up and calmly told me he'd get dressed.

Okay, maybe I deserved it. I'd been abrupt—even more so than usual—but that's what I do. Besides, men don't usually complain. I think it's kind of a relief to be told they can go. No hugging required. No *What's your number? We should do this again. Blah-blah-blah…bullshit-bullshit-bullshit* necessary. I'm a big girl, I can read the tea leaves just fine.

'He's here in Reception. Shall I send him in?'

Crap. Should she? I shake my head, but of course my assistant can't see that. 'Um…' *Um?* What am I, nine? 'Give me a moment.' I hang up the receiver as I stand, straightening my shirt. I tend to wear the same thing every day—a white blouse and faded denim jeans. Hey, if it's good enough for Zuckerberg and Jobs, then it's good enough for me. I hate the expectation that because I'm a woman I should dress a certain way or be obsessive about fashion. The thing is, I love nice clothes but, here at work, I don't want to think about what I'm wearing and I don't want to be seen as a clotheshorse. So I wear what I wore when I was a one-woman band, pulling Moatsy together, doing the coding, getting that first raft of investors. Every day I choose a different necklace though. Today, it's a chunky green beaded choker and I lift my fingers, toying with it so it jangles, an unusual indecision arresting me.

This is so completely not like me.

But, then again, this has never happened before. I don't think I've ever seen a guy again after he's left my place. Damn it! This is why I don't tell them who I am, nor what I do. I don't like to be tracked down. Leave no glass slippers, remember?

I grimace, shaking my head, wishing I felt purely annoyed instead of this burgeoning excitement snaking through my belly. Excitement? Why? What exactly do I want?

I quash the adrenaline and compress anything but annoyance from my expression. Because I didn't invite him here, I didn't give him the impression he'd be welcome and I have no idea why he's come but I clearly need to get rid of him again. And quickly.

I pull the door inwards and my nerves skitter at the sight of him. Gone is the suit. Today he's wearing a polo shirt and shorts, so I see more of his flesh than I was expecting. Even his feet—in flip-flops—are weirdly, unexpectedly erotic.

I grip hold of my annoyance. 'Come in.' The words are curt, as if to imply the exact opposite—*go away*.

But his grin is slow and relaxed, pricking me with renewed desire. Like I haven't been thinking about how freaking great he was in bed since he left my place the other night.

'Thanks.' His accent! How had I forgotten it? He grabs two Starbucks cups and, as he passes, holds one out to me. I contemplate not taking it, but where coffee's concerned I rarely say no.

Besides, it would be churlish and I'm not that. My anger is, despite my best intentions, receding, leaving me simply curious. Why is he here? What does he want?

'No preamble, huh?' he prompts, and I realise I've said the questions aloud. So I lift my shoulders, gesturing towards the sofa set in the corner of the room.

'I just can't imagine what brings you to my office in the middle of a work day.'

'I didn't have your number.' Like that explains everything.

'So?'

'How else would I contact you?'

'Why would you want to contact me?'

He sits down in one of the armchairs, his legs spread wide, his arms relaxed. He drinks his coffee, his eyes holding mine in a way that makes my body throb.

'I enjoyed the other night.'

'Oh?'

'Right up until you kicked me out.'

His honesty is fascinating. 'I told you what I wanted. What did you expect? Dinner afterwards?'

He laughs, shaking his head. 'How about lunch now?'

It floors me. 'Why?'

'Because it's noon and I presume you eat, right?'

I gesture towards my desk. 'I'm working.'

His eyes narrow and beneath the surface of his

charm I sense a hint of impatience. Annoyance, even. 'Take a break.'

My spine straightens. Hell, no. I was happy for him to take the lead during sex—I loved it, actually—but this is my office—my domain—and here I call the shots. 'I beg your pardon?'

I feel like he wants to roll his eyes. 'Half an hour. Is that going to kill you?'

In fact, I'm not that busy, but that's not the problem. 'You're missing the point.' I move across the room, sliding into the armchair opposite his. 'In case I wasn't clear enough the other night, I got what I wanted. Sex. I picked you up in a bar hoping you'd be a great lover, and you really were, but that's it. I never wanted to see you again. I'd apologise for leading you on in some way except I know that I didn't. So?'

His brows lift incrementally higher and then he laughs, a rumbling sound that unsettles me because I'm not used to being laughed at. 'Another time, I'd love to know just what the hell messed you up so badly, Avery.'

Hurt—unexpected and fierce—lances me. I know I'm messed up but no one ever calls me on that. No one really knows me well enough to see it—to see beyond the veneer of self-made tech success story that I project to the world.

'I think you should go.' Oh, great. My voice sounds quivery, all wounded and weak. That makes me angry enough to want to scratch something.

'Not yet.'

Why does a burst of relief flare in my belly, like I don't actually want him to leave? Because he's hot and the other night was the best sex I've ever had. Yeah, he was great, and I've been fantasising about him ever since, but that doesn't give him the right to come to my office, to sit there, refusing to leave.

'Look, Barrett, I know I didn't mislead you. Sex with you was great, but I don't do repeat performances.'

At that, something sparks in his eyes. Curiosity. It's unmistakable, like a beacon in the centre of his gaze, but there's something else too. Pity? Damn it, I want him to go. What is it about this guy that makes me feel like a vulnerable teenager all over again?

I'm twenty-nine and four days old and I've known too many men, too many shits of men, to let him or anyone get under my skin. Didn't I learn anything from my mother?

It hardens my resolve, and that's a very good thing.

'So if you're here because you want to date me, or even if you want to fuck me again, then you need to know that's not my jam.'

'Not your jam?' He leans forward a little, his eyes so speculative I feel their warmth across my skin. 'And what is your 'jam'?'

It's a question to which I have no answer. Outside of work, there's nothing particularly interesting about me that I can tell him. 'What are you doing here?'

I fix him with my best *get to the point* stare, which almost always works.

A line forms between his brows. 'I...wanted to see you again. To talk to you.'

'I don't do that.'

A quirk of his lips. 'You seem to be talking just fine to me. So tell me, is it only men you've slept with that you insist on ignoring?'

'Did I hurt your feelings, Earl?' I respond with the kind of voice you might use to a wounded four-year-old.

'No.' His retort is razor-sharp and, although it's the answer I was hoping for, something lashes me. Disappointment? What the hell is happening to me? I want him to go away again, and I want him to stop looking at me as though he's trying to peer into all the recesses of my soul, and I also want, more than words can express, to fuck him right now.

I close my eyes for a second, trying to quell that desire. Because I meant what I said—I don't do repeat performances. Second times lead to expectations and mess, and I don't want any part of that.

When I open my eyes he's standing up and that cements it. I really don't want him to go. Panic kicks inside me. What the hell?

'Have lunch with me.' He holds a hand out, expecting me to take it, and I stare at that hand with a lurch of frustration. What would it be like to be the kind of woman who could put hers in it, smile up at him and nod? To act as though lunch with this guy is just a simple, casual commitment?

'I said no.' I stand up then, bringing us toe to toe, and as soon as I've done it I realise my body is ignoring my 'no second times' rule. I press a hand to his chest, feeling his strength and warmth pass through my skin, certainty locking into place.

Once more won't hurt.

He stays still, watching me in that way he has, not moving away but not responding either, leaving it completely up to me.

'I don't want lunch.'

Finally, his voice husky, he murmurs, 'What *do* you want?'

'Isn't that obvious?'

His chest is moving faster, anticipation speeding up his breath. 'Avery, I came here because we need to talk.'

A small smile shifts over my face. 'I'm not interested in talking to you.'

CHAPTER FOUR

I'M TRYING TO hold onto sense and rational thought but her kiss shoots everything out of my mind, putting my body and my over-opinionated cock front and centre. I try to fight it, to resist desire, but then she lifts her hand to the back of my neck, pressing her breasts flat to my chest, and suddenly a thousand excuses fire into my brain.

We've already done this, so what's the harm in doing it again?

I'll talk to her afterwards.

We both want this.

But I need to remember my friends, the men to whom I am fiercely loyal, and the reason I came here. I need to stop this…

'Avery—' There's doubt in my voice.

She senses it, her eyes narrowing. 'What? You don't want this?' She leans forward a little so her breasts brush my chest. A groan thickens at the base of my throat.

I want her. I just know I can't have her.

'It's important.'

Her laugh is just a soft sound. 'I just met you. There's nothing more important between us than this.'

She's wrong. I need to tell her the truth. But then her fingers slip into my waistband and she's purring, 'Fuck me now and I'll think about talking—later.'

Is that the worst solution here? Is one more transgression a bad thing?

'You were such a bastard last time,' she grunts, pushing at my shorts impatiently, as though she can't wait to see me, touch me, feel me deep inside her. I'm harder than granite, my own needs fierce and uncontrollable.

'Yeah.' I was. I was angry—an emotion I rarely feel. But I don't apologise because I didn't expect the way her dismissal would make me feel. For the first time in my life a woman treated me like a disposable object. My self-esteem is assured enough that it didn't actually hurt, but it sure as hell pissed me off. 'I didn't appreciate being given my marching orders.'

Her hands still on the top of my boxers. 'That's who I am, Barrett, and it's what I do. I told you that.'

She did. I didn't take her literally. 'My mistake,' I say with a grin, showing her there are no lingering hurt feelings. 'Let me make it up to you?'

Her cheeks flush pink. 'I suppose so.'

I laugh croakily then kiss her. This kiss is different because I'm driving it, my tongue duelling with hers, my head bent to take advantage of her upturned face, my body pressing hers backwards, towards the two-seat sofa. It's nowhere near big enough but it will do for now.

Her fingers work quickly, undoing her own buttons so her creamy chest is exposed to me. I drop my mouth, chasing kisses across her décolletage, marvelling at the delicacy of her collarbone, the fluttering of her pulse there which tells me that even when she acts as though she doesn't give a shit, she really does. She feels just like anyone else; she just refuses to show it.

Why? What the hell happened to Avery to make her the way she is?

Wanting to know has nothing to do with the Harts. This is me wanting to understand her, wanting to get what's beneath her ice-cold veneer.

But her hands are around my cock, moving up and down my length so I can't think straight. Later. There'll be time to think, and to talk, later: after.

'If I was interested in justice, I'd pay you back right now.' She pulls away from my kiss and eyes my dick contemplatively.

'Oh, yeah?'

'I mean, I could take you deep in my mouth until you're this close to coming and then make you leave again.'

My cock jerks at the very idea. Not of being sent packing but of being inside her warm, wet mouth. As if she understands, she grins and moves forward, breathing over my tip so I shudder in an involuntary response, a hint of seed spilling out of me.

'Like this,' she murmurs and, before I can adequately prepare, her lips are on me, just the tip at first, her tongue flicking me, her mouth surrounding me, and then she opens wider, swallowing me in her mouth, pausing to adjust for my size before pushing forward until I press to the back of her throat. I have to brace myself on the sofa armrest. Her hands come around to my ass, holding me where I am, and then she moves up and down, along my length, her tongue devouring me, her mouth tightening until I feel pleasure starting in the base of my abdomen, spreading through me like an asteroid. I have to pull back now, to stop this. As if reading my mind, she opens her mouth and sits further back in the chair, leaving my dick glistening and so rock-hard between us.

'And if I asked you to leave now?' She arches a brow, reminding me of the way I left her high and dry the other night.

I grimace. 'Okay, it was a bullshit thing to do. As I said, I intend to make it up to you.'

'How?' Her eyes narrow, but I can barely string two words together. I'm this close to coming all over her and the idea of that adds fuel to the fire.

I need to get a freaking grip.

I look down at her, and the answer is simple. 'By finishing what I started.'

It takes me a second to pull her jeans and thong from her body, pushing them aside before kneeling between her legs, my eyes meeting hers. I want this so badly it hurts—I can still remember her taste, her sweetness and, hell, her responsiveness. As I bring my mouth to her seam and run my tongue over her sex, her little moans fill me with a burst of passion and familiarity.

Just like last time, her hands drive through my hair, pushing at it like that's the only way she can stay conscious. That idea is its own kind of heaven.

This time, when I feel her body tightening, when her breath gets rushed and her moans get softer and more urgent, I know I want to drive her over the edge. But not before I've had a little fun with her first. I move my mouth to her thigh, then down her leg to her knee, but my lips have barely grazed her flesh before she yanks on my hair, pulling my head up so our eyes meet.

'Don't you dare stop.'

I laugh, her passionate need my complete undoing. 'I won't. I'm only teasing.'

Her eyes widen for a second and a small frown shifts on her face before she shakes her head. 'Don't. That's not what you're here for.'

I bring my mouth back to her but her words chase themselves around my head, sparking my temper all over again. *Not what you're here for*. This woman commoditises sex in a way I've never quite seen before. As though I'm some kind of sexual food delivery she's dialled up for the afternoon.

Her hands drop to my shoulders, her nails digging into my flesh as she explodes, her orgasm soft but long, her moans flooding the room as she surrenders completely to the pleasure of this.

'Much better,' she says, when she can speak again.

'I'm glad to hear it.'

But before she's had too long to recover, I grab her legs and yank her down to the ground with me, surprising her so she laughs spontaneously. My gut twists at the sound. I like her laugh. More than that, I like her spontaneous reactions, when she's led by instinct rather than coolly contained.

'Condom?'

'In my wallet.'

She looks around desperately, sees my shorts and moves to them quickly. Her lithe grace and elegance are completely innate. She pulls a condom out and rips it open as she strolls back to me, then shifts between my legs.

I wait for her to spread it in place but, before she does, her head drops down over my dick and her eyes meet mine. 'Just a little bit more of this, I think.'

Who am I to complain? I prop myself on my arm so I can watch as her head moves, her dark hair a frustrating curtain because I want to see her mouth taking me deep inside.

It's like I've said those words out loud because a moment later her hands lift and she pulls her hair back, catching it over one shoulder so I have a clear view of what she's doing now. I feel her warmth and wetness surrounding me but, at the same time, I can see her soft red lips sliding over me and it is the hottest thing ever.

That tightness is back, the beginning of my orgasm. I reach down, putting a hand on her shoulder. 'Stop now.'

She pouts. 'Do I have to?'

'Mmm.' A guttural noise of agreement. 'You do if you want me to fuck you.'

She grins, an impish, sexy smile that shows me she knows exactly the power she's wielding right now.

'This time, I thought I'd fuck you.'

A second later the condom is on and she's straddling me, her beautiful legs spread across my hips, taking me inside her, deep, completely, her tightness making me groan slowly, my body utterly captivated by this experience, savouring every piece of it, every element.

I reach up and cup her breasts, feeling their strength, their weight in my hands, flicking her nipples so she bites down on her lower lip, tilting her head back. I want to see her; I want her to look at me. I push up onto my elbows, sitting up so I can drag a nipple into my mouth, distracted by the fact they're right there, and then lift my face higher, seeking her mouth first, my eyes searching hers. She closes them and speeds up, taking me deeper, her pleasure about to burst. I feel her muscles tightening around me and hear her frantic noises and right as she bursts with relief I let go of my self-control and chase after her, my orgasm ripping through me. She presses her face to my shoulder so I can't see her but I can feel every shudder as it tears through her body.

'Well,' her voice drawls through the room. She shifts a little, facing me. 'That wasn't on my agenda today.' She looks around her office as though this very localised hurricane has caught us both up in it and spat us out without our consent, landing us smack bang in the middle of her office.

'Nor mine.'

She lifts a brow, her hand toying with my hair as though she can't help it. 'Really?'

I frown. 'That's not why I came here.'

'Right. You wanted to *talk*.' She says the word with derision, shifting away from me at the same time, as though the idea is laughable, but I barely notice. Her body's separation from mine makes me want to grab hold of her and drag her back. I don't think I'm anywhere near done with Avery Maxwell yet.

But shit. She's right. I came here to talk, and about something that should have been more important than sex.

We trust you, Barrett—that's why we asked you to do this for us. If you think it's the right time to tell her, then do it. She's our sister. We'll leave it in your hands.

The conversation with Jagger is lodged inside my brain. They trust me, and this—sleeping with Avery—definitely shouldn't have happened again.

'Avery—' She's midway through pulling on her clothes. A lace thong and black bra, then her jeans. I watch her dress, finding it almost impossible to locate any words in my mind. 'I'm starving. Let's go eat something.'

Her hands still, midway through buttoning up her shirt.

'Stop trying to ask me out. I don't want to date you.'

That's not what I was trying to do but her intransigence, when a short while ago we were as close as any two humans can be, is infuriating. I stand up, crossing to her wastepaper basket and disposing of the condom before pulling my boxers on. My clothes are strewn all over the room. I eye them with a lash of frustration.

'But it's fine to fuck me?'

'Hey, you wanted it too.'

I shake my head. 'I'm not saying I didn't.' I move closer to her, but there's something so combative in her expression, so wary, that I still, keeping my distance.

She spins away from me. 'This doesn't *mean* anything, Barrett. It's just sex.'

'Sex always means something.'

Her laugh is a scoff.

'Even if it just means you desired that person. Sex is great. Wonderful. A way to connect with someone and be truly intimate. You use it like a drug—you're jonesing for a fix one minute and then you get your hit and it's out of your system. That's bullshit.'

Her spine stiffens and she turns to face me, ice in her eyes. 'It's my life.'

'Yeah, I know that, but Jesus, Avery, do you really want to live it like this?'

'Seriously? I've known you three seconds. You think having slept with me twice gives you any right to comment? Like you have some kind of hotline to my soul?'

What am I doing? This conversation is futile and definitely not why I'm here.

'Guys do this all the time and no one ever bats an eyelid. I bet you've had plenty of meaningless sex in your time.'

'I told you, sex always means something to me.'

'So you've never fucked some woman whose name you can't remember?'

'Never. I remember everyone I've been intimate with.'

That stuns her.

'I don't believe you.'

'I don't lie.'

I grimace because I'm kind of lying by omission right now, aren't I?

'Fine, you're the exception.'

'So you're what—using sex as a form of feminist protest?'

She glares at me. 'My point is, men have had a cavalier attitude to sex since time immemorial and yet you can't cope with the fact that I'm doing the same thing?'

'I can *cope* with whatever,' I dispute. 'You can sleep with whomever you want, whenever and wherever you want.'

'Geez, thanks, I'm so glad I have your approval.'

I shake my head. 'But you don't have to be so disrespectful with it.'

She's stunned. Her eyes flash with feelings and she shakes her head a little, as if wanting to contradict that. 'Did I hurt your feelings?' she says instead, that same condescending tone of voice she used earlier, like she's talking to a recalcitrant toddler.

'This isn't about my feelings.'

The phone on her desk buzzes.

We both stare at it, like it's somehow dragging us out of our own little world and into this one.

'Don't answer that.' She glares at me and does exactly the opposite of what I've said, storming to her desk and scooping up the receiver.

'Maxwell.' Her eyes shoot daggers at me as she waits for whoever's on the other end to speak.

Then a tight smile curves her lips. She casts a glance at her slim gold wristwatch before looking at me again. 'I can be there in twenty.' A pause. 'No, I don't have any lunch plans.'

She is *unbelievable.* Frustration fires inside me.

I watch as she replaces the receiver then calmly reaches into her handbag and lifts out a lipstick. She swipes it across her mouth and checks her appearance in a small compact mirror.

'If that's everything?'

Her cool dismissal of me—yet again—is like being scorched with acid. 'Fine. Dinner.'

Her laugh is laced with surprise. 'You don't give up, do you?'

'Avery, this is important.'

'How can it be important? I met you four nights ago. We've spent about two hours in each other's company. There is nothing you could have to say to me that could be deemed "important".'

I wanted to do this gently. To ease her into it, to get to know her a bit better to get a sense of how she'd react and what the kindest way to break the truth to her would be, but she's forcing my hand.

'I've got somewhere I have to be.'

'Wait.'

She pushes her clutch bag under her arm. I stare at her, something twisting inside me.

'What is it?'

'Your buttons are wrong.' My voice is deep, guttural. I cross towards her, my fingers hovering at the top one. 'May I?'

I've caught her off-guard. She didn't expect that. She compresses her lips and nods, looking over my shoulder. 'Thank you.'

Even the words are cold, like she resents this tiny, insignificant offer of help.

'Avery, it's not an accident that we met.'

That catches her attention. She drags her eyes back to mine, her expression carefully guarded. 'Isn't it?'

Shit. I've scared her. She's worth a small fortune.

She probably thinks I'm some kind of stalker or madman wanting to kidnap her and blackmail her. Hmm. Kidnapping Avery…throwing her over my shoulder, dragging her to some out-of-the-way cabin, tying her to my bed. *Stop it, dick.*

'I came here—to San Francisco—to find you.'

Her pulse is shifting for a whole other reason now. 'Why?'

'Because I need to speak to you.'

A furrow forms in her brow.

'It's about your mother.' A pause. 'And your father.'

His words come to me as if from another galaxy. My ears are screeching with the pounding of my blood, my feelings so completely off-kilter I can barely think straight, much less speak. I reach for my wristwatch on autopilot, feeling the fine metal there, running my fingers over it for strength.

I think of her often, even though I haven't seen her in so many years. I still hear her voice in my head when I make decisions, when I screw up. *Tomorrow's a new day, starlight. You can fix this.* My mother's a part of my soul.

And my father? I think of him often too. I wonder about him—who he is, where he is, why he didn't want me in his life. Why he left my mother to struggle the way she did.

I *don't* know who my father is, nor the story of his relationship with my mother, but this man obviously does—or he knows something at least.

It's been a long time since I've *felt* anything for a man I've slept with but right now I feel a sharp burst of fury. Betrayal, anger, disbelief, disgust.

'What the hell are you talking about?'

He's still so close, his hands on my shirt. I shove at his chest and it feels good, great in fact. I am enraged.

To have slept with a guy who had sought me out… to have slept with him *twice*!

'Do you have time to do this now?'

'Make it quick.'

'It's not a quick kind of conversation. Cancel your meeting.'

My heart rate accelerates. I should cancel it. I should pick up the phone and get my assistant to cancel it then I should lock my door and keep this son-of-a-bitch here until I understand everything he's trying to tell me.

But this business is everything to me. It's only with the business and its success that I'm able to fund my charity, and there's no way I'm going to let anything derail that.

Ever.

'No.' I reach for a pen on my desk and grab his hand—his warm hand, a hand that has pleasured me and somehow lied to me, all at once. I scribble an address on the back of it. 'Meet me there at six o'clock.'

I could invite him back to my place, but I don't want to do that. I don't want him in my house. How dare he lie to me? How dare he have known this right from the start—but that first night…he wanted to talk. He kept trying to chat and all I could think about was getting him into bed.

That doesn't matter! He should have tried harder.

'Avery—'

I shake my head, knowing there's nothing he can say that will make me less angry. Inexplicably, I feel a welling in the back of my throat, as though I'm going to cry.

'Just go, Barrett.'

'It's not—'

'Get out.' I snap the words at him, fury and hurt and confusion all mingling together. 'Please go.' Damn it, those words sounded wet with tears. Great.

Mortification comes to my rescue. I storm towards the door. 'Six o'clock.' He regards me for a moment and then nods.

As he passes me he pauses for a moment, his eyes boring into mine in a way I resent. 'I'm sorry.'

I jerk my gaze away from his in response, staring out of my window. I don't breathe again until I hear the elevator doors whoosh closed and know that he's gone.

CHAPTER FIVE

HE'S WAITING WHEN I arrive, a minute after six. My heart slams into my ribs, surprising me with its response. So too does the flush of desire that assails my central nervous system, as if my damn body didn't get the memo that Barrett Byron-Moore is a huge fat mistake I'm never going to make again.

I'm here for one reason and one reason only—to find out what the heck he knows about my mom. Then I'm going to tell him to get the hell out of my life.

'Miss Maxwell,' Erin, the manager, greets me. 'Some nice guy's waiting for you over there.'

'He's not that nice,' I mutter out of the side of my mouth, moving through the restaurant. He looks up as I approach, standing and gesturing to the chair opposite.

'Did you think I was going to sit in your lap?' I snap tartly, then regret it because, while I'm angry, there's no need for straight out incivility. I hold back an apology though, taking the seat instead, dipping my head forward a little.

The familiar sound of wine being poured into a glass catches my attention. I watch as he finishes, then reach for the stem, moving it towards me.

'How are you?'

'How do you think, Barrett?' I sip the wine. 'Just tell me whatever it is you came here to say. What is it you know about me? About my...parents.' The word is discordant because I've never thought of them in that way before. I had a mother and, yes, biologically, a father, but I never knew who he was, and he was certainly never a part of my life, except a gaping black hole.

'First, let me apologise.' He reaches across and puts a hand on mine. I resist the urge to flinch. Truth be told, the urge isn't anywhere near as strong as the one to turn my hand over and take hold of his. 'I had no intention of sleeping with you. That wasn't a part of this. But you were—'

'Persistent,' I offer, shaking my head, bitterly regretting that I fixated on Barrett as the man I wanted to use to soften my birthday night.

'Irresistible,' he supplies instead. 'Irrespective of the fact I came here looking for you, I wanted you. It wasn't about anything other than that—it was just you and me. But I should have known better, done better. I should have ignored that because this is too important to screw up.'

I don't say anything; I can't. Nervousness has me completely in its thrall and I'm not comfortable with that emotion so would prefer to be silent than show any hint of how I'm feeling.

'About a month ago, I found out about you.'

I swallow. 'You know who my father is?'

'Yes.' He takes a drink of his own wine. 'I knew him well.'

I close my eyes, sucking in a deep breath of air, a thousand and one questions flooding me. All my life I have wanted these answers, and now they're within reach I feel a dizzying sense of unreality. 'Knew him?'

'He passed away a few years ago.'

Anger and disbelief shred me to pieces. I don't know if I would have wanted to meet him but to be denied even that possibility seems like a new level of cruelty.

But why am I even thinking about that? The betrayal to my mom slams me in the chest. 'I know one thing about my father, Barrett. He ruined my mother's life. I hate him. I don't want to know anything about him,' I lie, drinking more wine.

I do. I want to know everything but it's too much. I look towards the door, contemplating my escape.

Perhaps reading my intent, he squeezes my hand. 'I understand that.'

I shake my head, and don't bother to fight the tears that sting my eyes now. Truth be told, I'm barely conscious of them.

'Avery, I've known your father since I was a child. My father and mother were close to him.'

I shrug my shoulders. 'So?'

'You should know that he had other children.'

My ears thrum with my blood, my pulse a tsunami inside me. 'What?' The word is louder than I meant. I swallow, drink some wine, slump back in my seat in total shock. Why has this literally never occurred to me? Did I think my mother was the only woman he'd lied to? Promised the world to and then ditched when it no longer suited him.

'Are you saying I have sisters and brothers?'

'Just brothers.' He pauses for a moment. 'Three of them. And three sisters-in-law.'

I dip my head forward, almost unable to compute this. 'You're saying I have blood relations I didn't know about.'

He leans forward so our knees brush beneath the table. 'They sent me here to meet you.' He pauses, his eyes scanning my face, and I'm too wired to care. 'To see if you'd like to meet them.'

My stomach squeezes. I look up at him, piercing him with eyes that feel and show far too much. 'You should have told me this way sooner.'

His guilt is obvious. 'I know. I wish, more than anything, that I had.'

I push that aside for now. I can deal with it later. In this moment, there are way more important things to focus on. I have brothers. Three of them!

'What are they like?'

His smile takes my breath away because it seems

to tunnel through time, transporting me to the first night we met, when I didn't know any of this.

'They're…a force of nature. Each of them, in their own way.' He pauses, his expression contemplative, and I don't mind the silence. I need a moment to re-group. I feel like the earth has stopped spinning. I throw back another gulp of wine, my head spinning. Brothers. Siblings. *Family.*

I have been alone for so long—over half my life now—I can't even imagine what it would be like to *not* be alone.

But I instinctively rail against that. Family is as family does. At twenty-nine, I'm not exactly going to leap into these relationships headfirst. They're not going to *feel* like family. Not after being raised completely apart, with no idea they even existed.

'The thing is, Avery—' God, I wish his voice say-ing my name didn't still have the power to pull my nerve endings taut, to make me intimately aware of everything about him. 'You've probably heard of them.'

Interesting. 'Why?' More wine. 'Are they some kind of famous? Rock stars? Actors?'

He laughs and my skin pricks with awareness. I don't bother to fight it any more. Sex is sex, and I love sex. Sex with Barrett is next level. But I don't want to think about it right now—even as I accept the inevitable likelihood that our bodies might seek one another out again. I can separate that from this—and from my anger with him for keeping the truth from me for even one minute. Sex is just a transaction and he's wrong—it can be delightfully meaningless, just as it has been with him and me.

'Not exactly. They're…in business.'

'Oh?' I run a finger over the rim of my glass. It's empty. After a slight pause Barrett lifts the bottle and refills my glass, sitting back in the chair and studying me with eyes that are rimmed with thick black lashes. 'Tech start-up?'

'They dabble in it.'

I frown. 'As investors?' My heart speeds up. Is that what this is about? Do they want to buy into Moatsy? Is that the reason I'm hearing from their proxy out of the blue like this?

'Yes.'

I feel like he's hesitating, so I lean forward a little. 'Barrett, just spit it out. Who are they?'

His grimace is self-deprecating. 'Jagger, Theo and Holden.' Their names are familiar, but it takes me a second to connect the right synapses. 'Hart,' he supplies, when I don't say anything.

And I can't.

I can't speak. I'm stupefied. And I'm enraged. I'm livid beyond description. I feel heat bursting through me, like it's going to eat me alive. The Hart name is a household one, synonymous with extreme wealth and commercial success. From casinos to hotels to airlines to textiles and manufacturing interests.

'Fuck.' I shake my head, drinking all the wine in one hit then shaking my head again, standing, my legs unsteady, my eyes seeing stars courtesy of the fury that's humming and buzzing inside me. 'I can't—'

'Avery?' He stands, his concern obvious. Anger is filling my eyes with hot tears.

'I can't do this.' I reach into my clutch and pull out some cash, throwing it onto the table. But he grabs it, pushes it back at me.

'I've got this.'

I'm too furious to respond. 'I have to go.'

I stumble a little then push out of the restaurant, the warm evening air not helping my temper nor the growing sense of nausea. I drank a glass and a half of wine far too quickly and as a result the world out here, on the streets, has taken on a kind of psychedelic feeling. Too loud, too bright, too swirly.

His arm in the small of my back doesn't surprise me but I jerk away from him anyway, wishing I hadn't when light pierces my eyes too harshly, sharp like a blade.

'I just need to—'

I dash at my cheeks. Angry tears are sliding down them. I gape for air and look around for a cab.

'Come with me.' He reaches for my hand, lacing our fingers together, and I don't fight it now. I go with him, until he pulls up beside a low-to-the-ground car with black-tinted windows. He opens the front passenger door. 'Hop in.'

I bite down on my lip and nod, too shell-shocked to say or do anything else. It's beige leather inside

with walnut grain. Everything about it screams sub-
dued wealth. Of *course* my brothers have that kind
of money. They sent this guy—a British earl—to
snoop on me! But the Harts? They're outrageously,
ridiculously, can't-even-imagine-it rich.

I shake my head, staring—in a state of shock—
out of the window as he takes the seat beside me,
clicking his seat belt in place. I feel his eyes on me,
the concern of his look even when I'm not facing
his direction, and then he starts the engine, pulling
onto the street without another moment's hesitation.

I barely notice the streetscape as we pass. Trees
blur, houses too, children playing, couples strolling,
an ice cream vendor. None of it sinks in. He takes a
turn and we're heading north on Van Ness.

The scenery changes a little, the closer we get to
the Bay, the history appreciable. I used to love this
area. We pass Ghirardelli Square, alive with night
markets, strung with fairy lights, and then he pulls
into the turning circle of one of the most exclusive
hotels in the area. Of course.

I don't even question what I'm doing here, with
him. I can't.

I turn in my seat, pieces sliding into place. 'So
you're saying my dad was their dad. My father was…
Ryan Hart?' The name comes to me after a small
delay, but of course I've heard of him. Who hasn't?
I close my eyes for a second, my stomach in knots.

'Yes.'

'And you knew him?'

'Yes.'

I shake my head, hating everything about this. I feel vulnerable and uncertain—two emotions I have fought all my adult life to avoid like the plague.

'Did he know about me?'

A muscle jerks in Barrett's jaw. My fingers itch to reach out and touch it. 'I don't know.'

I nod, closing my eyes.

'Come on.' His voice is deep, flooded with emotion, and a moment later he's out of the car, coming to my door and opening it.

I have been alone a very long time and if I don't exactly like it that way, I like the predictability of it. On my own, I know what to expect. But that's not to say I'm not irritatingly comforted by Barrett's presence as we move towards the hotel. Sliding glass doors and two suited bellhops greet us.

'Sir,' one of them says with a polite nod.

Barrett barely acknowledges him, but not out of rudeness so much as concern for me. I can see it all over his face. Well, what the hell did he expect? My legs feel unsteady, my palms are sticky with sweat and when the elevator whooshes us up into the hotel my tummy lurches but it doesn't stop, even when the doors ping open into a carpeted corridor. A large window at one end frames a view of the Bay, glistening in the evening light as the sun dips down. Barrett swipes a key card on a panel near the end of the corridor and a door springs open to reveal a large, beautifully decorated suite. High ceilings, plush carpet, shining timber furniture with a decidedly retro feel, sumptuous curtains and a modern kitchen.

'Have a seat.' He guides me towards a sofa and settles me into the cushions. I have been alone a very long time and yet I don't fight this—being cosseted and cared for—even though I know I will, soon. When I can. For the moment I feel so completely shell-shocked it's easier to surrender to this warmth than it is to fight it.

I hear the clinking of glasses, the pouring of liquid, and a moment later Barrett is by my side with a glass of Scotch. He hands it to me and takes the seat opposite, our knees brushing.

'It's good for shock,' he explains.

'Is that what I am? Shocked?' I lift my eyes to his and jerk my gaze away again almost immediately because of the worry there. I'm not used to that; I don't know what to do with it.

His jaw shifts, like he's grinding his teeth. 'You clearly didn't know?'

I shake my head. 'I had no idea who my father is. Was.'

He cradles his own Scotch without lifting it to his lips. 'Your mother didn't speak about him?'

'Not really.' I close my eyes and an enormous wave of sadness washes over me, thinking of my mother. 'I know he was married—or guessed as much. And I know he hurt her. A whole heap.'

'Ryan's gift,' Barrett offers with a terse shift of his head.

'Oh?'

'He was reasonably challenged when it came to personal relationships.' Another grimace. 'And that's putting it mildly. The man was…a disaster.'

I nod, his words a jumble in my mind. 'I just can't believe this.'

'That you're a Hart?'

I jerk my eyes to his. 'I'm not a Hart.' I take a huge gulp of Scotch, relishing the burning sensation as it assaults my oesophagus. 'But yeah, that he's my father.' I bite down on my lower lip, trying to make sense of this. 'I always wondered, when I was a kid. Most kids I knew had moms and dads. Grandparents.'

'But you didn't?'

'It was just Mom and me.' I swallow, my throat thick. 'I grew up in one of the poorest streets in San Fran. Life was tough. We were so broke, so hungry; Mom was always stressed. It was *hard*. And it was lonely. Mom worked three jobs when I was small. I was so different to everyone else. When the kids in my school were getting taken to Disneyland for summer holidays, I was home alone for days on end while Mom worked—we barely had enough money for food, rent; she was exhausted and stressed. And at night there were these drunks next door and they'd fight and shout.' I shake my head, the memories a huge part of the woman I've become, yet I don't like to dwell on them. That terror I had to grapple with on a nightly basis—that someone would burst through the flimsy door of our tiny flat at any point—is still so real, so easy to experience anew.

I push the memories aside, drink some more Scotch, my mind becoming increasingly numb as the alcohol I've consumed finally takes effect. 'I used to wonder about my dad and why he wasn't there. I used to hope that maybe he was powerful and rich, that he'd sweep in and rescue us, take us away from that awful place, take me to freaking Disneyland,' I say on a hollow laugh. 'Like Disneyland could fix everything. I used to dream of happy endings and all that bullshit. But he never came. We lived in that place until my mom died, and life never got easier, it never got better, and she never got over him.' Anger makes my words shake. 'I'm not a Hart.'

He puts a hand on my knee and I stare down at it, in the back of my mind wondering why I don't shove it—him—aside. This is something I need to process alone.

'You have three brothers,' he murmurs, his fingers moving over me gently, reassuringly. 'And they're great guys.'

I compress my lips. 'Well, yeah, sure. I mean, they grew up rich and without a care in the world. Why wouldn't they be great guys?' The strength of my bitterness surprises even me.

'You're not alone any more,' he tries again, and I laugh softly, a maniacal sort of noise, disbelief filling me.

'I'm no more or less alone than I was a week

ago. Some guy screwed my mom and I'm the result. That doesn't make him my father and it sure as hell doesn't make them my brothers.'

His frown pulls at something inside me, something I refuse to acknowledge.

'You're upset.'

I glare at him. 'I'm surprised.'

'That's understandable.'

'Gee, thanks.' And then, because I'm being unnecessarily rude to him, I shake my head. 'I'm sorry. It's just—'

But he lifts a finger to my lips, moving a little closer. 'Don't apologise. You can say and do whatever you want right now and it won't matter. I'm here for you. Grieve, shout, scream, cry—whatever you want.'

His words roll through me, his offer something I didn't know I needed. *I'm here for you.* I don't remember the last time anyone was 'there' for me. Except for shareholders, but that's largely self-interest, and limited purely to a professional capacity. The truth is, I work hard. Ridiculously long hours, which leaves very little time to let anyone close enough for them to be 'there' for me. And that's just the way I like it, I remind myself in the nick of time, right before I can let his statement make me feel gooey and warm.

I don't *do* warm and gooey. I don't do any of the things he's suggested. I process things—all things— in one way, and always have. Right back to the night of my fifteenth birthday when I sneaked out of my foster parents' home and went to a bar, found some guy to take my virginity and make me forget all about how damned alone I was.

'You want to be "here" for me?' I ask, taking another drink of whisky then leaning forward so I can put the glass on the coffee table in front of us. I turn to face him, my eyes scanning his features, dropping to his thick throat and the wisps of hair that appear above his shirt.

'Yeah.' A gravelly sound of agreement. I take his Scotch glass and partner it to mine then stand slowly, my hands reaching for my shirt in the same motion, fingers working the buttons until the fabric parts and I can shrug out of it.

'Then fuck me.'

His eyes probe my face, trying to read me. How I hate that! I hate it because it speaks of things I refuse to hear, and because I think he's probably really good at it, and I hate the idea of him understanding how vulnerable my past could—if I let it—make me.

I unhook my bra, then strip out of my jeans, my lace thong last of all. Naked, I straddle him, my eyes fierce when they meet his. 'All I want right now is this.' I roll my hips and feel his cock hardening between my legs.

'Avery...'

'Don't.' I shake my head, dropping my mouth, pulling his lower lip between my teeth. 'Don't ask me questions. Don't tell me things. Not now. Just... fuck me. Hard.'

* * *

The moon bounces off the bay, a streak of white light that is somehow ethereal and beautiful, despite the fact it happens every night. The moonlight dances from the bay to the hotel, brushing Avery's skin so she looks luminescent, glowing, like some kind of mermaid brought to live on land—no tail, but every ounce as magical and captivating. I lift a finger, running it over her shoulder.

Her eyes are heavy, her expression relaxed for the first time since I saw her at lunch time.

'I'll go soon,' she murmurs, the words heavy.

'Don't.' I move my hand lower, to the swell of her hip.

I feel her rejection of that, as though staying here the night will somehow *mean* something or commit her to something.

'Not yet,' I substitute, knowing—somehow—better than to appear to ask too much of her. 'You haven't eaten. Do you want dinner?'

Her eyes drift closed. 'I'm not hungry.' A moment later she's asleep. I watch her for longer than I realise, each gentle breath in and out, the undulation of her breasts, the moon against her skin, the parting of her lips.

She was exhausted and I'm the opposite. Wired, and wide awake. I push the sheet back gently and move from the room, flicking on the kettle I always travel with when I'm in the States, staring out at the bay while the water boils. It's after midnight, which means it's too late to call Theo, who's in Paris with Asha. Too early to call Holden and Cora in New York. But for Jagger, in Sydney, it's the middle of the day. I stare at my phone for a long time, recognising my hesitation and wondering at it.

Because I slept with their half-sister?

Yeah. I don't really want to go into that.

I should contact them though and tell them— something, an update of some kind. But what?

I make tea and carry it through the suite, onto the balcony. Then, before I can overthink it, I press Jagger's number.

He picks up on the second ring.

'Buddy! How's it going?'

'Good.' I frown. 'Okay.'

'Okay?' A pause. 'Have you met her?'

I close my eyes, and all I can see is beautiful, sensual, naked Avery. 'Yeah.' The word is gruff.

'And? What's she like? Does she look like us?'

I grimace. 'No.' Too quick. I soften it with a laugh. 'Lucky for her.'

Jagger's laugh shows me he hasn't picked up on my awkwardness. 'Seriously, dude. Curiosity is killing me. Tell me everything.'

I don't do that, obviously, but I give him the brief. Nothing about how hot she is, how I can't be in the same room as her without wanting to drag her to bed, nothing about the fact I find her compelling and fascinating. Just the details as they pertain to the Harts.

'She's…angry,' I say, though the word is a poor

catchall for the emotions I felt emanating from her the evening before. 'Finding out your dad could have been a part of her life all these years—' I shake my head.

'Christ, he was such a bastard.'

I nod, dragging a hand over my chin.

'Did you tell her he was like that with all of us? That she wasn't the only one who got the Ryan Hart treatment?'

A flash of protectiveness fires inside my chest. 'She's the only one he didn't acknowledge.'

'We don't know he knew about her.'

'I know that.'

'Does she know? Can you find out if she knows if her mom spoke to him?'

Unease spreads through me. Being an instrument of investigation no longer sits well with me. But I want to find these things out for my own interest, and to help Avery. I can decide afterwards what's appropriate to share or not. 'I'm pretty sure she didn't.' I hesitate, torn between loyalty to my friends and a need to do what's right for Avery. 'I'll talk to her about it,' I offer noncommittally.

'Does she want to meet us?'

I look over my shoulder, towards the window of the bedroom. I imagine her sleeping there, and my gut twists. The situation was complicated enough without us sleeping together thrown into the mix. Then again, it's not as if she's wanting anything other than this from me. On that first night she was abundantly clear about the kind of 'relationship' she prefers. She'll meet the Harts one day, and forget I ever existed.

'I think she needs time,' I say quietly, finally. 'It's a shock. She needs to process it, find out what she can about you. But yeah—' the word is a gruff acknowledgment '—I think she'll come around to that in time.'

'I want to meet her,' Jagger says, no hint of darkness in his tone. He's like a kid with a puppy on Christmas morning. 'Tell her that, okay?'

I almost laugh, imagining Avery's response if I describe Jagger's enthusiasm. She'd be terrified. 'I will.'

Jagger's voice, when next he speaks, is serious. 'Listen, buddy, I don't know if we thanked you properly for doing this.'

Guilt perforates my soul. 'Don't mention it.'

'Nah, I mean it. You put aside your own life to go and handle this for us. We owe you. You're a great friend.'

I stare out at the moonlight and see only Avery. 'I was happy to help.' I disconnect the call before guilt and self-disgust can eat me alive.

CHAPTER SIX

NOTHING MAKES SENSE. I look around the room—the beige walls, white bed, cream carpet, expensive furnishings—and flop back against the pillows, piecing the night together. I'm naked. Barrett. My stomach rolls. Desire punches me, hard. But there's something else. An ache low in my abdomen, a heaviness in the middle of my chest.

Pain. Hurt.

Mom.

I look around the room on instinct, making sure I'm alone—I am—and then squeeze my eyes shut to stop tears from forming. Mom. The man who got her pregnant and left her broke and alone was a billionaire. A freaking billionaire. Did she know who he was? Could she have contacted him, asked for help? Did she, and he refused?

I swallow hard and, despite the fact I'm scrunching my face up, a single tear leaks out of my eye, rolling towards the pillow.

I told Barrett a hint of what my life was like, but glossing over the details doesn't do the true misery of it any kind of justice. My upbringing was defined by loneliness, fear, sadness and poverty. I built fantasies up around my dad; I so badly wanted someone to come and help. I wanted someone to make my mom smile. As a kid, I instinctively knew I couldn't give that to her. I hoped he would come and every day that he didn't was like a fresh betrayal. This was the worst though. Knowing he was richer than Croesus, that he could have helped Mom financially, if in no other way. If he wasn't already dead I'd want to kill him.

This is such a mess. I've wanted to know about him for a long time but now that I do I wish I could put that monkey right back in the box.

And at the same time I don't. I want to know everything—that's my analytical, facts-based brain. I press my palms into my eyes, hard, to stem the tears and lie there for several beats of time, running through what I do know. And all roads lead back to Barrett.

He knew my father—he knew him well. And he's obviously tight with my father's other children. Any questions I have are best answered by him.

I shucked my clothes in the other room but when I step out of bed I see a pile of fabric folded neatly on the seat beside me. A quick investigation reveals a pair of pants and a shirt—both my size—as well as some underwear with the tags still attached. A quizzical frown crosses my brow but I scoop them up, moving to the bathroom where I shower and dress quickly, finger combing my hair over one shoulder as I walk out of the room. I take a second to steady my emotions. I learned a long time ago that indulging feelings is a weakness, and I'm not weak, ever. I fortify myself, calming my features, then step out, ready to face him and the reality of what he's just revealed to me.

I'm two steps into the enormous lounge area when I stop walking and stare. Barrett is sitting at the table with a laptop, a heap of papers, naked except for boxer shorts and a pair of glasses on the bridge of his nose. My body fires in a completely unexpected way.

Glasses?

He's hot without but with them he's every kind of fantasy brought to life. My mouth goes dry and I'm glad he hasn't noticed me yet, so I get a few more moments to soak in the sight of him like this.

Perhaps the rushing of my heart calls to him because a few seconds later he lifts his eyes, spearing me with his gaze, the question in his eyes one I don't know how to answer.

'You're busy?' I prompt, gesturing towards the table.

'Just catching up on some work.'

It's a statement that momentarily pushes my own issues from my mind. 'Work?' I pad closer. 'You mean you don't just get to be all feudal in your manor with your serfs and your gold?'

His grin cuts through me. 'Sadly, no.'

'Shame. What's this, then?' I move behind him, my eyes running over the documents. He takes advantage of my proximity to spin in the chair, one of his legs on either side of me.

'Treaties.'

'Treaties?'

'Mmm. I'm consulting for the EU at the moment.'

It's surprising on a lot of levels. 'What do you do, exactly?' I sway a little closer without meaning to.

'I'm a lawyer.'

'Working with the EU?'

'Right.'

'Wow.'

'Wow?'

'I mean, I thought you were just a hot piece of ass.'

He laughs and the sound is so welcome, so normal, that I feel that ridiculous lump threaten to form in my throat all over again.

'Thanks, I think.'

'It was a compliment, I think.' I shift a little, sitting sideways on his leg, not caring about the intimacy of this—the certainty it's temporary allows me to let some guards down. 'So what is this?'

'You really want to know?'

'I asked, didn't I?'

'It's part of a post-Brexit review into trade arrangements. The law—as it moves from territory to territory—can be difficult.'

'So you advise them on that?'

He nods.

'Why you?'

His eyes lift to mine, a frown on his features. 'What do you mean?'

'You're good at this?'

He laughs. 'I guess I must be.'

He's being modest or something, and I don't have time for that. 'How good?' I narrow my eyes, regarding him intently.

He lifts his shoulders. 'International law has always fascinated me. I've worked in it almost exclusively for a very long time.'

'Almost exclusively? What else have you got in your bag of tricks?'

I feel his demeanour shift, his mood alter almost imperceptibly. 'I handle a lot of the Harts' personal business. Trusts, wills, that kind of thing.'

His words are measured but they serve as a reminder to both of us of the dynamite that exploded last night.

'It's more of a favour than anything else. When I graduated, Ryan got me a job with the firm they use. I moved into international law pretty quickly but felt I owed it to Ryan—and the faith he showed in me—to keep working for him.'

Something grinds to a halt inside me. All my life I've felt like an outsider, I'm used to it, but I wasn't prepared for how it would feel to have this man speak about them—the Harts—with such obvious affection and familiarity.

'I see.' I go to shift off his lap but his hands grip me, holding me where I am.

'Ryan was a complicated man, Avery. Selfish, ruthless, intelligent, determined. There was no one in his life who wasn't, in some way, scarred by him. I'm sorry he hurt your mother.'

I bite down on my lip, wishing I'd asked Mom more, wishing she'd told me more.

'It sounds like that was his modus operandi.'

'You could say that.' He strokes my side. I turn to face him, not sure what I'd been meaning to say. I simply sigh, the small sound a surrender of sorts. I don't ever get close to people. I hate even the idea of that. And I'm not getting close to Barrett. But being here with him feels like the best way to process this weird turn of events. He's like airbags for this information car crash.

'Would you like some breakfast?'

I'm about to demur when my tummy rumbles audibly and a small smile creases my lips. 'I guess I would.'

Again, I go to move but he holds me where I am, reaching to his left for the hotel phone. He lifts it up, his hand straying to the elastic of my pants, sliding inside to my hip as he places a breakfast order. His touch is easy and familiar, and totally natural.

When he disconnects the call, his other hand lifts to my chin, holding my face steady. 'Let me tell you about your brothers.'

I bristle instinctively. I shake my head. 'Stop saying that. They're not my brothers.'

'They're Ryan's other children—'

'Yes. That's not the same thing.' I soften my re-action with a tight smile.

He nods thoughtfully, his eyes probing me. 'Let me tell you about them.'

It's dangerous though, like the opening of a door I don't know if I'll ever want to walk through.

'I'd rather talk about you,' I say honestly—sur-prising us both. 'I mean, just while we wait for break-fast,' I backpedal, shrugging, wishing I could draw the words back inside me.

'I'm not particularly interesting.'

'You're practically royalty.' I infuse my voice with lightness, reverting to the way I always behave when I'm flirting with a guy, because it's easier to keep someone at arm's length when you're being charm-ing. I shift away from him at the same time, and this time he doesn't stop me. I move into the kitchen. Several tea bags have been plonked in the sink. The image of them all squished flat in a line is strangely amusing. 'How long have you been awake?'

'A while.'

'Like—' I count. 'Seven teas a while?'

He laughs, a deep rumble. 'Apparently.'

'You want a coffee?'

He shakes his head. 'I don't drink the stuff.'

'You don't…drink coffee?' My look is one of complete non-comprehension. 'How is that even possible?'

He grins, a sexy grin that's slow and speculative and makes my breath heavy. 'I just don't like it.'

'But you brought coffee to my office the other day. Yesterday.' Was it really just yesterday? So much has happened since, I feel like a different person.

'Hot chocolate.'

I burst out laughing. 'What are you, five years old?'

He responds with a mock-wounded look. 'Hey, I know what I like, okay?'

I reach for a pod, inserting it into the machine then hit the button.

'Another tea then?'

A slight pause, as though he's surprised I can do anything as civilised as make tea and as polite as offer him one.

'Sure. Thanks.'

'Milk?'

He nods. 'No sugar.'

I make our drinks, wondering at this small act of normality—one could almost describe it as domesticity—and imagine what it would be like to be someone who yearns for this. People do, right? Lots of people spend their twenties convinced of the soulmate myth that there's some perfect 'other half' out there for them.

That if you just swipe right enough times you're going to get lucky and find the person you're destined to be with.

The person you could end up spending the rest of your life making cups of tea and pots of coffee for, sitting beside and, I don't know, arguing about *The Times* crossword with or whatever.

But that's never been my fantasy. It's never even been close to my field of expectation. I carry our drinks back to the table, placing his carefully in the midst of his paperwork before taking up the chair opposite, hooking my feet to the edge of the seat, my knees beneath my chin.

'So?'

'So?' He sips his tea then closes the screen of his laptop.

'Why are you a lawyer?'

I don't know if he's going to answer me. I hope he understands that I need time—I can't just rush headlong into talking about the Harts. I need to warm up to it, to feel comfortable and at ease. I'm not afraid of anything, but the more I learn about them the more real they'll become and I just can't say if I'm prepared for that yet.

He considers that for a moment, the sunlight glancing through the large windows catching his face in that golden light, and all I can think of, in that moment, is his effortless charm.

There is something compelling about him, something I noticed the night we met in a crowded bar, surrounded by handsome men who spent way too much time on their appearance. He stood out. He stands out now, and my stomach flips as though I've driven over the crest of a hill at speed.

'In many ways the law is simple.' I expel a breath

of relief. I feel that talking about this is akin to having dodged a bullet. 'It's black and white, reliable and fair. It's the backbone of society—something most people won't need to rely on in their lives but it's there if they do, a silent force of good, the ultimate protection.' His words have magic in them. It wraps around my soul. 'But it's also complex and in a constant state of flux, alive and reflective of society and its values, the balance between legislation and judicial law creating a humming, buzzing rhythm to the system. I find it…' he pauses and I hold my breath, entranced '…captivating.'

His eyes hold mine and the word seems to singe my skin, warm and mesmerising. My heart beats faster.

He seems to be waiting for me to speak but his words have temporarily robbed me of the ability to form my own.

'Have you always felt like that?' I over-compensate for how impressed I am by his answer, making my voice coolly inquisitive.

'No.' His grin is lopsided and—if it's possible—even more charming than before. 'I enrolled in law because I got great grades in school and was offered a place at Oxford. Initially, I studied it because I thought it prestigious and that it would make my parents proud.' He sips his tea, his long fingers curved around the cup. Until then, I would never have guessed that a man sipping tea could be so sexy and masculine.

'But that changed?'

'Mmm. I bombed out of the first semester. University was…lots of fun.' He lifts his shoulders and my heart skitters a little. I never went to college but I can imagine all the kinds of fun he means. 'I was more interested in that side of things.'

'Parties? Women?' I tease, sipping my coffee.

'Tick, tick.' His eyes pierce me.

'And you got over that?'

'My dad made me get over it,' he says with a small laugh. 'I went home for term break. He called me into his office—and that place scared the shit out of me back then, let me tell you.' He does an exaggerated shudder. 'My parents' home is really old. Stone, with marble floors and, while they modernised a wing for us to live in, dad's office is in the medieval heart of the place. Huge walls, dark wood panelling, cold like an ice-box, with deer heads mounted across one whole wall—and they watch you with their big glass eyes—'

I laugh at the image he's painting, but also curiosity pricks me because the kind of life he's describing is so foreign to me. He really is aristocratic—oh, so 'to the manner born'.

'He was mad at you?'

'Hell, yeah. He was livid. *"You might think all this gives you a right to skate through life but think again, son."*'

I try to imagine what that kind of parental input would be like. It's been a long time since I felt so aware of how much I lost when Mom died. 'He was strict?'

'He was right,' Barrett corrects. 'I wasn't taking life seriously. I got good grades in school without trying. I thought university would be the same but I was really only attending skeleton lectures by the end.' He shakes his head ruefully.

'So did he threaten you with disinheritance or something?' My voice is teasing.

'Worse. He pulled out the D word.'

I frown, not understanding.

'"*Your mother and I are very disappointed in you, Barrett.*"' He shakes his head. 'I'll never forget the way that felt. To know I was letting them down.' He runs his finger over the handle of his mug. 'I went back to university and got serious and it was like being shaken awake. I paid attention and saw what the law is, the vital importance of it, and fell completely in love.'

I reach for my coffee, cradling it between my chest and my knees, staring at the waft of steam coming from the top. His words are powerful and somehow frightening. His passion scares me—so too his honesty in discussing it, and his clarity of thought. I move away from his love of the law instinctively.

'They sound like good parents.'

'They are.'

'Do you see much of them?'

'A couple of times a month.'

'You don't still live in the grand old stone house though?'

'No. I have offices in London and Berne. I travel between the two and head home when I can. They're getting older so…you know.'

Inexplicably, sadness washes over me. I do know: parents die. My mom's death threw a grenade in my life and I've never been the same since.

I sip my coffee and lift my eyes to find him staring at me, his expression serious. 'What about you, Avery?'

I wait for him to continue with an impassive expression on my face but I feel the danger of what he's asking, the territory we're nudging closer to. 'Your mom passed away when you were fourteen?'

Such a gentle way to describe what happened to her. I look beyond him, unable to hold his inquisitive, intelligent gaze. 'Yes.' Then, after a pause, 'How did you know that?'

He doesn't blink. 'The guy that found you—a detective—had a small amount of information. It included that.'

My spine straightens. I'm not famous—not by any stretch of the imagination—but Moatsy's rapid ascent into the tech bubble has made me somewhat well-known. At least within certain groups. But, for God's sake, I pioneered software that could *protect data*. The idea of being spied on by someone makes my skin crawl.

'You hate that.'

'Yes.'

His laugh is soft, gentle, commiserating. 'Fair enough. That makes sense.'

I guess he probably does understand where I'm coming from. Someone like him would no doubt get a bit of press attention. I think about that—about googling him to check—and immediately cut that idea off at the knees. That's not what I do. That's not what this is. What happened to 'I don't want to know anything about the guys I fuck'?

Nonetheless, every minute spent with him sparks a raft of questions in my mind, and I'm natural answer-seeker.

'What happened, after she died?'

I swallow. 'That wasn't in the detective's notes?'

His expression shifts. '"Moved into foster care" doesn't seem like it really encompasses the truth of your experience.'

I grimace. 'No.'

'There wasn't anyone who could take you in? An aunt? Grandparent?'

'No. Mom was alone, except for me.'

'I'm sorry.'

I nod slowly.

'I had a lot of autonomy with Mom. I'd been alone a lot and grown up fast. She trusted me. I was, in hindsight, given an extraordinary amount of freedom for a kid my age. But I didn't take advantage of that. I was a good teenager.'

He doesn't say anything but his eyes silently will me to keep going.

'When she died, it was like—the world no longer made any kind of sense.'

I search for a better way to explain, but draw a blank.

'Was she sick?'

'No. She was broke and working just about around the clock to make ends meet.' I bite down on my lip, the awful truth of it all hitting me like a ton of bricks. 'I wanted to do a summer school in programming.' I clear my throat. 'I'd done some free lessons at the Y and the teacher had suggested it—I guess I had an aptitude. But there was no way we could have afforded it. I knew that but I still asked Mom if I could go, because I really wanted... I wanted to do it.' I close my eyes for a second, needing to catch my breath. 'After she died, I found the application forms. She'd taken on extra shifts at the bodega so she could get me there.'

His eyes are watchful; I can't quite meet them. The past is pulling at me, heavy and inescapable.

I sip my coffee; it's almost finished. 'She was working when two guys came in and tried to rob the store. She fought them. They stabbed her.' I close my eyes, sucking in a deep breath, trying to grab hold of my strength, to remember it happened a long time ago, but all I can think about as I sit across the table from Barrett Byron-Moore is that it was such a futile, pointless death.

'Avery, I can't—I'm so sorry.'

I blink, nod, don't look at him. I finish my coffee and stand up a little jerkily, moving to the kitchen, needing mental space and physical space too. I put a new pod in the machine and place my cup beneath the spout.

'I wanted to be legally emancipated. I'd been looking after myself for a long time—I didn't feel like it would be any different—but the social worker overseeing my case wouldn't hear of it. So I was sent to live with some family for a few years, until I turned eighteen.'

'You hear awful things about the foster system.'

'You hear good things too,' I say with a lift of my brows. 'I think people who volunteer to become foster carers are, on the whole, incredible.' I frown a moment. 'Even Jenny and Dave—' I never refer to them as my 'foster parents' '—were decent. They were just very, very different. They had no idea how to give me what I needed and I sure as hell wasn't what they were expecting.'

'Were you happy with them?'

'Was I happy? No. I was miserable AF. I literally hated every day. I'd lost my mom and everyone expected that grief to look a certain way and I didn't want to give that to them so I kept it wrapped tight to my chest and refused to let anyone see how devastated I was. I had nightmares for months about stabbing and blood. I used to close my eyes and see her and I just—' I shake my head, not because I want to push those memories away but because I don't make a habit of discussing things like this. 'They were happy to send me to the coding camp.' I imbue the words with amused cynicism even when my heart is still so heavy. 'I think they needed a break from me at that point.'

Sympathy is on his features. I work on lightening my voice even more, to squash that expression on his face. 'It was a light bulb moment. I loved it. And I was good at it—really good. I went back to Jenny and Dave's and they set me up with a computer in my room.'

'So why weren't you happy?'

I laugh. 'Because I wanted to be with Mom. Or on my own. Because they thought they could reform my soul. I hated that. I rebelled for the first time in my life. I'd sneak out in the middle of the night, go to the town bar, hook up with random guys, do whatever I could to piss them off. They were incredibly kind, good people doing their best to help me, but I couldn't see that at the time. I hated them and wanted to make their life hell.

'They never got cross with me. They never snapped. They were so patient.' I shake my head, old enough to be ashamed of the way I treated them, but not so different that I can really regret it. At fifteen I had already begun to understand that the thing that makes me happiest in life is not needing anyone—ever. Jenny and Dave were nice but I wasn't going to let myself care for them. 'Like I said, they're good people. I avoided them as much as possible, kept mostly to myself and moved out on the morning of my eighteenth birthday.'

'Did you have a job?'

'I was doing code checks for some app developers. It didn't pay much but it was enough to rent a small flat in the city. One of the apps was a data spying software, skimming user information from harmless-appearing sites. It scared the bejeezus out of me. Not the concept but how normalised that kind of behaviour has become. We almost expect it now. If we talk about a product, we'll get ads for it in our social media feed. We laugh about Big Brother, but it's not really a joke.'

'No.' His eyes roam my face.

'I wrote the Moatsy prototype in thirty-six hours. I didn't sleep, barely ate, hardly stopped. I was so determined to do something to improve online privacy.'

'And it took off?'

'Yeah. From the beginning. I think a lot of people are surprised by the extent of data monitoring when they really think about it. It was easy to explain the need for it. Companies were first—employees using workplace computers to trawl the web were unwittingly exposing corporate data to whoever wanted to see it. It was pretty easy to highlight the need for this protocol. Personal users followed. On the one hand I was surprised by the uptake, but also incredibly relieved and gratified.'

'Do you talk to your foster parents now?'

'Jenny and Dave,' I correct automatically. There's a knock at the door and I lift my coffee, moving towards it on autopilot.

'Right.'

I pull the door inwards. Room Service is here. The hotel staffer brings the trolley in but, before he can set the table, Barrett shakes his head. 'We'll be fine.' He stands up so I have a better view of his torso, his lithe figure, and my insides tighten with an unmistakable hunger.

At the kitchen bar he opens his wallet and pulls out a tip, thanking the waiter with a smile.

Alone again, I move back to the table.

'You were talking about your foster… Jenny and Dave.'

'I saw them a few years ago.' The memories fill me with guilt. 'Their daughter had cancer. It was hard for them. Hard for everyone. I spent some time with them, helped where I could. The last time I saw them was at her funeral about six months ago.'

He doesn't offer condolences now. His eyes hold mine for several seconds then he sits back at the table. 'You were screened to see if you were a match to donate bone marrow.'

Surprise shifts through me. 'Yes. How did you…?' I shake my head. 'Right. The detective.'

'It's how he found you. Your DNA flagged on a system he was watching.'

'That shouldn't have been possible!' I'm incensed. 'It was for private medical screening.'

He nods. 'Sounds like a violation of your patient rights.'

I eye the food on the table. I'm hungry but too wrapped up in our conversation to indulge that hunger. I return to my seat, watching him, a frown creasing my forehead.

'Sometimes hospital on-sell their data. For research. I guess if he had access to that database, somehow…'

'He's one of the best detectives you can get,' Barrett says gently. 'I don't think there'd be much he can't access.'

I nod, but the idea sits like a lump inside my chest. 'Fuck that.'

He laughs, and the sound pulls me out of my thoughts. 'I have no doubt you'll fix that too.'

'Yeah, just give me time.'

'Were you close to your foster sister?'

I fight an urge to tell him I don't get close to anyone, ever. 'She was only three when I moved out. I barely knew her.' But that line doesn't work in this setting. I would say that to a stranger but Barrett is no longer that. 'Cally was very sweet. Life's a bitch.'

It's hardly the most profound observation I could make but it's a good catch-all for my sentiments.

'Yeah. It can be.'

Hours later, back at my place, I can't shake the ghost of our conversation. I've showered, gone for a run, showered again, but still it haunts me, a hangover but of a grief-filled kind, so that there's an intrinsic sadness to me that I resent.

I go to the box without really meaning to, a glass of wine in one hand, my feet bare. I sit down on the floor in my bedroom and balance the wine carefully on the carpet before flicking the lid open. It's a small box, about the size of a shoebox but with only half the depth, and I've had it a long time. The things in there are random and disjointed—a concert ticket Mom kept stuck to her mirror with double-sided tape. I've never heard of the band but it obviously meant something to her. She kept the ticket for years so I've kept it too. There's her purse—I can never open it and look inside; it's too sad. The memories are so vivid there—her driver's licence, a meagre amount of cash, coupons carefully clipped from the papers, receipts in case she needed to return something for a refund, and a photo of me that was taken in the first grade.

Even without opening the purse a shiver of sadness moves through me as I move it aside. My fingers curl around the photo of her last. It's at the bottom, where I put it the last time I indulged this morbid streak. I lift it out and place it beside the wine glass, wriggling down onto my tummy so I'm at her eye height.

I love this photo.

It was taken a year after I was born and, even though life wasn't kind to Mom, she never really aged. Not in her eyes. I sip the wine—a delicate balancing act given my position—then smile at the picture.

'Why didn't you tell me, Mom?'

Her eyes smile back at me.

I sigh.

There are no answers here. Barrett has some answers—more than he's given me. Now I just need to decide if I really want them...

CHAPTER SEVEN

I PREFER CITY running to the gym but this city is sweltering hot and my English sensibilities mean I don't love the heat, so the hotel gymnasium it is. I increase the incline and speed, punishing myself more than usual.

Punishing myself? Yeah. That's what I'm doing.

I slept with their sister. The Harts. I've slept with her a lot and I have no intention of stopping. What's even worse—I love it. I love being with Avery, and I want to support her through this crap fest Ryan's left on her doorstep.

Why?

I barely know her, so why am I willing to risk my friendship with the Harts by prioritising Avery? I push my feet to the side of the treadmill for a second, bracing myself there and breathing fast. Would they be as furious as I think?

It's not that I've slept with her. I mean, that's bad, but what's worse is that sleeping with her could potentially put my reason for being here in jeopardy. They asked me to learn what I could about her, but

they also asked me to prepare her for meeting them.
What if being with her is clouding everything for
Avery? What if she refuses to meet them because I
mess up somehow?

I lift my feet back onto the still-spinning treadmill, picking the pace right up again. I can't let that
happen. Avery's been very clear about sex being just
sex for her. What we're doing doesn't need to have
any impact on how she decides to proceed with the
Harts. If anything, I can use our intimacy to my advantage—not in a sleazy way, just in that she's giving me more time. Time to sell her on the Harts and
the role they could have in her life... Maybe I don't
need to feel so guilty after all?

'Hey. It's me.'

It takes me a second to make sense of what he's
saying, and why. Barrett is downstairs from my
place? What's the time? I look at my mom's watch—
it's just after eight.

I grip the airphone tighter and open the flap
so I can see the video feed of my front door. Sure
enough, Barrett is there, and he's not empty-handed.
A large brown paper bag and a bottle of wine fill
his arms.

My stomach does a funny little loop the loop and
my pulse speeds up, but I keep my voice cool because
this I wasn't expecting. 'Why?'

I see him pull a face in the video feed. But I'm serious. I know I stayed over at his hotel last night and

that we got kind of intimate this morning—in terms of our conversation—but that doesn't explain why he's here now. I look towards the mantelpiece where I've temporarily moved the photo of my mom—it's weirdly sentimental for me but the discovery of a father and biological siblings makes me need to keep the memories of my mom closer than usual.

'Are you seriously going to make me beg from the front step?'

I consider that. 'I just…wasn't expecting you.'

'Avery. Open the damned door.'

My hackles rise but—given that there's no earthly reason not to—I press the buzzer then move towards the entranceway. He's shouldering it open right as I step out into the hall.

'I come bearing food.' He lifts his arms a little, showing the bag and wine.

'I see that. But why?'

He takes a step towards me, his expression bemused but something else too. Something darker, more analytical. 'Have you eaten?'

I shake my head. 'No, but—'

Closer still, until his body is pressed to mine, the food between us—I don't know what it is, but it smells delicious and my stomach rolls in unwanted reply.

'Nor have I.' Another movement and my back presses to the wall. His body, the smell of the food, his nearness and warmth—my senses are going into overdrive. A sensual drum begins to beat in my soul, stirring everything inside me, making me feel a thousand and one things all at once. Irritation, desire, lust, passion, annoyance, frustration. The cacophony of feelings is not one I welcome—I work in a black and white, linear fashion. My life is ordered and predictable, and I am always in charge of choosing who I spend time with, and when. His intrusion should be wholly unwelcome but it's not.

My heart skips a beat as our eyes clash—a true battle of the wills, except I'm not really battling Barrett so much as myself and my own inner wants.

'Barrett...' the word is both confrontation and surrender, contradictions surround me '... I'm not—'

I don't know how to finish the sentence. I'm not the kind of woman who wants to share takeout with a guy—no matter how hot he is. I'm not the kind of woman who shares her secrets with someone she's fucking. I'm not the kind of woman who sleeps with the same guy for more than one night. I conveniently ignore the fact I've already broken that last rule—multiple times.

'It's dinner,' he supplies when I stay quiet. 'There's nothing complicated about that, right? We'll eat. Talk. Drink some wine.'

He makes it sound so easy. More than that, he makes me feel stupid for resisting this. 'Like we're friends or something?'

He lifts his brow, shifts his body again, this time his hips brush against me so I feel his cock and my breath shifts through my lungs with a violent force. 'Or something.'

My heart skips another beat—how many times can that happen before it becomes a problem?

I'm glad at least that he doesn't try to imply we're friends. I like his honesty—I appreciate it and, more than that, it's unthreatening.

'What do you want to talk about?' I query because the eating and drinking I can handle. It's the heavy conversation that's left me feeling as though I've been through the wringer. I still haven't decided if I'm ready for more answers and yet I have a sinking suspicion he's a flame and I'm a moth.

He studies me and I keep my face bland with effort, concealing my thoughts with great care.

'I thought you might have questions about your brothers.'

I shoot him a look of frustration. He changes tack.

'I thought there'd be things you want to know about them.'

'I think maybe I know enough.'

He's still so close. It's hard to think like this, much less to keep hold of my anger, but I try anyway.

'I know they grew up in unparalleled wealth and luxury while my mom struggled to keep the lights on. I know they enjoyed Ryan Hart's money while my mom was killed trying to send me to a crummy holiday camp. I know they grew up together while I've been—' *All alone.* I don't say the words but I see it in his face that he understands. The air between us simmers with the strength of my feelings. I *like* being alone. I choose to live like this.

'You have every right to be resentful.'

I shift my gaze over his shoulder, my lips a mutinous line in my face.

'But you shouldn't let that resentment stop you from getting to know them. They're your family.'

I'm tempted to lash out at that, to deny it with everything I am, but I don't particularly want to reveal the strength of my emotions so I keep my voice light. 'The gospel according to Barrett?'

'Just some free legal advice,' he quips, his smile slow, lightening the tone of our conversation. 'If you don't want to talk about your brothers, we can talk about you instead.'

I balk at that. I told Barrett more about me this morning than I've shared with another soul, ever.

'I think I'm all talked out.'

'Fine. We'll eat in silence and then find something else to do.'

My heart hammers against my ribs. Desire forms within my veins, running rampant and hot through my body. This—Barrett—is unusual. Different. Threatening—because I can sense him trying to unpick me, to understand me and I don't want him to do that. I feel like I'm moving onto shaky ground. Every minute spent with him makes me uncertain and confused.

Except when we're in bed.

Sleeping with him is everything I'm used to—it's familiar and comforting and easy for me to control. It's an exchange I understand, one with a predictable outcome. Whereas I find it hard to quantify our conversation, or to predict what his replies to my statements will be. He surprises me constantly.

That makes me uneasy.

'It's just dinner.' He pulls away, straightening, but not before I catch the slight frown on his face. 'I presume you use your table for eating as well?'

And, just like that, I'm reminded of the first night he came here, when we'd been together on my dinner table, and the flash of need is so intense it almost hurts.

'From time to time.' I watch as he places the paper bag and wine onto the kitchen bench.

'Plates?'

I move towards him slowly, but with an unmistakable intention. My fingers find the edge of my shirt. I lift it up my sides, watching him as I do so. 'Over there.' I drop the shirt as I point away from him.

He doesn't look for the plates. He stays where he is, transfixed, watching me in a way that is a shot in the arm because it's rich with desire, and desire I get. It relaxes me to feel this, to know he feels it too, to be able to distil this all back to sex.

'Let's eat later.' *Let's talk never,* I silently add, making that mental commitment to myself. I'm done with deep and meaningful.

For a second—the smallest second—I sense his

hesitation and wonder at the root of it. He's a guy, right? Driven by biological imperatives.

Yes.

He is.

A second later he makes a gruff noise and pulls me to him, his mouth on mine instantly demanding and reassuring, his tongue in my mouth twisting me in knots. It is a kiss of combat and surrender. Ancient needs thunder in my soul.

'Fuck me,' I groan, pushing up to sit on the edge of the kitchen bench, bringing him between my legs, forcing at his jeans until the button opens and I can shove them down his legs.

He steps out of his pants, his hands lifting my butt, pulling me to him, and he carries me with ease, his mouth never once leaving mine. 'Bedroom?' The word is pushed deep inside me by his artful tongue. I swallow it, groaning, ripping my head away for a second.

'That way.' I shove my arm in the direction of the hallway. At the first door we pass, I push it inwards. It's a guest bedroom, not mine, and rarely used. I don't have houseguests. But it will serve a purpose right now.

As will Barrett—and then I'll get him to go away again. The certainty is reassuring. Once more, I feel like I've moved onto familiar ground and I like it here. I understand this.

Sex and go. A quickie. Why should anything else enter the equation between us?

'Fuck me,' I say again, but it's not enough to be fucked by him. I want to torment him, to take all that I can from his body, to pleasure him and be pleasured by him until he can't see straight.

He drops me onto the bed, his body chasing mine, his mouth seeking my nipples, dragging across me until I'm arching my back, each breast needing his attention simultaneously, making me wish there was another Barrett—or at least another of his mouths—nearby. His fingers, understanding, take over, plucking and rolling one nipple while his mouth enslaves the other, his tongue rolling and flicking, his teeth biting with just enough force to make my cries sharper. He kisses his way down my fevered body, pushing at my pants when he reaches my hips, his clever tongue teasing my sex so slowly that it's completely insufficient and I groan with need, begging him, pleading with him.

'You are so wet.' His words run over me like sun-warmed honey. I tilt my hips, needing him deeper, harder, needing all of him.

'Soon,' he promises, undressing me fully, his hands caressing every curve of my flesh—my calves, my ankles, the arches of my feet—revering me, worshipping me in a way that is dangerously close to that new ground I wanted to escape. Sex isn't about reverence and worship. It's about cataclysmic explosions of desire, mutual orgasms, satisfaction and enjoyment. Sex is fast and rough and loud.

Just when I'm about to tell him this he grips my

legs, parting them abruptly, and buries his mouth in me, his tongue intent now, his stubble stimulating every millimetre of my most sensitive flesh so I feel my wave of pleasure building, an orgasm inevitable, and I ride it hard, my fingers tangling in the bed linen, my body thrusting forward begging for more contact with his mouth, his mouth obliging until I'm tipping over the edge of sanity and awareness, until I'm purely sensation.

The relief is intense. Was it only this morning we did this? Before I left for my place, in the shower, wet and covered in foaming liquid soap? It feels like so much longer. I grip his shoulders as he moves up my body, returning to my breasts, my nipples almost painful now from the pleasure that's coursing through my body.

His mouth claims mine, pleasure passing from him to me, his kiss so demanding, so sexy that I lift my hips, silently inviting him to take me, needing him with all of myself.

His laugh is gruff and he shakes his head a little, but that only makes me more determined.

'Wait.' He pulls up, his eyes latched to mine in a way I find disconcerting—like he can see way more than I want him to when we're like this, all naked and tangled in the bed sheets.

'I don't want to.'

He laughs. 'Condom.' He kisses me again and lets the tip of his cock press to me, so the shock at what I almost forgot is obliterated by the promise of what's to come.

'I'm on the pill,' I say, surprising myself with the admission. Not just the admission but the invitation implied by it. *So we can do this without a condom.* God, where did that come from?

'I'm not.' He grins, teasing me, pulling away and standing. 'I'll be right back. Don't go anywhere.'

As soon as he leaves the room I'm gobsmacked. His retreat gives me a moment to regroup, to focus. He's dangerous. Sex with him is dangerous because it overtakes me completely, making it impossible to keep hold of who I am and what I want.

He walks in with a string of foil squares. My decision is immediate. I scramble off the bed, pointing to the space I'd just been occupying. 'Lie down.'

He lifts one of those thick dark brows, tosses the condoms towards the edge of the bed and—a little to my surprise—does what I asked. 'Like this?'

He gestures down the length of his body, his hands stopping just an inch away from his arousal.

'Yep.' I stare at him, the rigidity of his cock making my stomach twist, my knees weaken. 'Almost.'

He's watching me, his eyes trailing heat down my cheeks.

'Stay.'

He laughs, a sound that chases me all the way upstairs.

'I'm getting cold!' His voice hits me as I grab a

belt from my wardrobe, a smile tilting my lips as I move back down the stairs quickly.

He's right where I left him, staring at the ceiling, still hard, still hotter than hell. He turns to face me when I enter, his eyes dropping to the belt, sparking with something like enquiry.

'I don't think that's my size.'

'It's not for your waist.'

He pushes up onto his elbows. 'No?'

'Put your arms above your head.'

He doesn't.

'Come on.' I move closer, climbing onto the bed and straddling him, tracing my fingers down his chest. 'Trust me.'

His expression doesn't shift.

'You'll enjoy it.'

'Enjoy what?'

'Being my sex slave.'

'Oh, really?'

'What's the matter? Haven't you ever been tied up before?'

His laugh is deep and throaty. 'No.'

'Well, there's a first time for everything.'

His movement surprises me, his body bucking and flipping in one motion, toppling me backwards on the bed and, at the same time, reaching up and trapping my wrists. Arousal floods me but you know this about me already—I like being dominated in bed. But with Barrett I want to return that, I want to take from him, to drive him wild, to show him I'm still in control even when my body seems determined to give that up.

'But this could be much more fun.'

I bite down on my lip. 'Maybe you're right,' I murmur. But this is important to me. It's like I need to prove to myself that I'm still here, that my brain works even when my body is under the most intensely pleasurable assault I've ever known. 'But first let me do this.'

He stares at me, his eyes shifting over my face. 'Let you do this, huh?'

I nod slowly, his close proximity and the way his eyes are boring into me making something twist low in my gut.

He shifts then, moving to his back, dutifully lifting his arms above his head. Excitement begins to pound against me. Relief too. I weave the belt in and out of my bedframe, then do a figure of eight around his wrists, buckling it tight—not so tight as to hurt him but making any kind of escape impossible.

'There,' I murmur, sitting back a little to admire my handiwork. 'Now you're my prisoner.'

'It would appear that way.'

'Hmm. And what should I do with you?' I take great pleasure in eyeing his body, raking my gaze over him slowly, studying the ridges of his abdomen, the firmness of his thighs, the shape of his calves and ankles before letting my eyes devour his hard cock.

'Avery.' My name is a hiss from his lips.

I move closer, crouching between his legs, my eyes on his. 'Yes, Barrett?'

He drops back against the bed, pulls on his arms once as if out of habit, and then surrenders, right as I drop my mouth and take him deep inside me in one swoop, his cock against the back of my throat, so I feel him convulse and taste a hint of him there.

He groans, deep and low, moves his legs, but I keep going, taking him deep then letting him out, deep again, his strength only fanning the flames of my desire, his complete surrender an insanely powerful aphrodisiac.

Pleasure, pride and power burst through me.

'Avery...' My name comes from deep within him. I flick my gaze up the length of his body to find him watching me, his cheeks stained dark purple, his eyes fevered. 'You should stop.'

I grin against his cock, but don't pull away. I run my tongue down his length then over his tip, his sharply indrawn breath taunting me, thrilling me.

'I don't want to.'

He curses, drops back and stares at the ceiling. I feel his dick spasming, the promise of his release tangible. I pull away, watching him, knowing that if I don't stop this will be over—for a time—but not sure I care in that moment. I love this.

He swears again, pulls at his arms, then glares at me with a look that almost makes me sorry for him—because while I like to surrender control in a limited set of circumstances, Barrett clearly doesn't.

I can see his desire to take over, to grab my hips and drag me onto his dick, or to push at my head until it's over him again. He would do neither because he's not an asshole, but that need is there—a need to possess me, a need that I, right now, control.

'I could get used to having you here like this.' I reach for the line of condoms, ripping the top off the first one and hovering it over his cock. As the rubber touches him his body flinches, his hips bucking. I take my time rolling it in place, letting my fingers taunt him, their touch light and laced with promises, then I lift up on my haunches, holding myself above him so he jerks his hips, trying to bring himself towards me, driven by instincts with which I'm familiar.

'Patience, Earl of Ashwyn.'

He glares at me, no hint of a smile on his lips, a look of frustration in his eyes. I applaud him for going along with this. I know I need to put him out of his misery—and me out of mine. I drop forward, kissing his lips slowly. When he tries to deepen the kiss I pull away, peppering kisses down his body instead, back to his sheathed dick, rolling my tongue around the base of it then flicking his inner thighs.

'Not sure patience is my strong suit.'

He has been patient, though, all things considered. I lift over him once more and this time I give us both what we want—and need. My name, when he says it now, is not a curse and it's not a hiss; it's a caress and it breathes its way through my entire body, threatening—if I am not very careful—to alter my DNA on a fundamental level. I move faster, the fever to stop that driving through me, just as pleasure is a blade pressed to my side. Every time he tries to pull his hands free I smile to myself because there is power in pleasure and, right now, that power is all mine.

CHAPTER EIGHT

THIS ROOM HAS not a single personal detail. It's cream, white, with some gold details. There are no pictures, no clothes, no mobile phone chargers, nothing that indicates it has a resident.

'This isn't your bedroom, is it?'

She props up on one elbow, her body flushed, her cheeks pink and, despite the fact we've spent the last two hours exploring each other, I feel renewed sexual interest writhing through me. Her breasts are firm and rounded, her nipples dark. I reach forward and cup her breast, my fingers brushing over her nipples without hesitation. She bites down on her full lower lip, her teeth white.

'No.' She shifts her gaze, looking around as I did a moment ago.

'Where's your room?'

'Upstairs.'

I nod. We were impatient to get into bed. I don't think I could have waited much longer. But I know, on a cellular level, that it's so much more than that. There are parts of her she keeps boxed away from me, private, self-contained, completely to herself. I'd say there are enormous parts of her she holds that way, in fact.

'Anyway…' her voice is different—formal, stilted—and she shifts a little, moving away from me so my hand drops between us …thanks for coming over.'

I stare at her as the unspoken meaning of her words plays through my mind. *But it's time you were going now.*

It's more of the same bullshit. Keeping herself locked up, pushing me away. Is it because of my connection to the Harts? Because of how we hooked up that first night, and what I didn't tell her then?

Of course not. Even on that night she was explicit about what she wanted from me: no strings sex. She said it and she followed through, evicting me from her place once she'd got what she wanted.

And now?

Why do I feel like things have changed between us?

Frustration gnaws at me because I'm the last guy to be needy in a relationship but right now her constant pulling away is really getting under my skin.

'My pleasure.' I grin, as though I don't get the subtext.

'So…' she frowns a little '…thanks.'

I have to stifle a laugh. 'You hungry?'

Her frown deepens. 'Not really. You should probably just take dinner with you.'

Well, that's a little less subtext and a bit more 'get the hell out'.

'Avery?' I step out of bed, looking around for my boxers then pulling them on. 'You might not be hungry, but I'm starving. There's a bag of perfectly good, greasy takeaway in the kitchen and I intend to eat my bodyweight before I leave here.'

She stares at me, not quite sure what to say. I suspect no one's ever called her on her bullshit before. Then again, most men she brings back here to fuck are probably very happy with the deal. Get their rocks off and go? Perfect night out.

My chest constricts painfully. I turn away on the pretence of grabbing my shirt off the ground, pulling it over my head while that thought plays out in my mind. Just how often does she do this? And why does contemplating that make me feel like my ribs are being dismantled one by one?

'I just said I'm not hungry.'

I turn back to her, the surprise on her face almost making me feel like a bit of a dick, but I stay the course anyway. 'Yes, and what you meant is that you want me to go now we've fucked.' I cross back to the bed, putting a hand out to her. She stares at it like I've just told her I've got a resurgent diagnosis of the bubonic plague. 'I'm not into that. We can sleep together and eat together and laugh together and not have it mean anything more than we like doing those things together. It's not complicated. It's not dangerous.'

She stares at me, bewildered.

'I'm working on a report I have to deliver to the European Commission for Global Trade in two weeks. I'm not going to be able to stay in San Francisco indefinitely. So eat a meal with me tonight, and stop looking as though I'm asking you to marry me.'

That brings a small smile to her face. I'm not sure if it's the idea that I definitely have to leave the States or the absurd notion that I'd propose to her, but she's smiling and a second later she stands up, bringing her body towards mine.

'Well, that's a relief because my answer would be a resounding no.' She kisses me, hard and fast, then moves away. 'So what did you bring, anyway?'

'Chinese.'

'I love Chinese.'

I resist an urge to tease her by saying 'we're a match made in heaven' but I do grab her hand. 'What are we waiting for then?'

'Just let me grab my robe.'

I arch a brow. 'You'll fuck me on the table but won't sit naked across from me?'

'You're not naked.'

'Fair point.'

'I like you naked.'

I laugh. 'Right back at you.'

She whips my shirt off me, then snaps the waistband of my shorts. 'Bottoms only?'

I drop my gaze to her breasts, my gut kicking. 'Deal.' My voice is thick, heavy with pleasure and desire and satiation and all the things she did to me while my wrists were bound. Something I honestly would have said I would *never* be into, but with Avery it was intense in the most incredible way. The pleasure was blinding.

A minute later we head to the kitchen. It smells amazing, the takeaway having filled the air with an intoxicating combination of spices.

'You said the bowls are up here?' She nods, watching as I pull out a couple then grab some spoons. 'Wine glasses?'

She frowns, still watching me, then jolts, as if from a daydream. 'Over there.' I look where she's pointing and see glasses have been slid under a cabinet, like in a bar.

I pour a couple of glasses, slide one across to her.

'You seem very at home in the kitchen.'

I laugh. 'I'm literally pulling takeaway from a bag.'

'I know but you just seem—' She shakes her head. 'It doesn't matter.'

I don't really know where she was going with that and it doesn't seem important so I shrug and keep going, opening the container lids.

'Did you buy everything on the menu?'

I eye the mountain of food. Maybe I did go a little overboard. 'I wasn't sure what you'd like.'

'This could feed the homeless population of San Francisco for a week.'

Something about her words sparks a memory,

something I should probably have been more focused on this week than I have been. 'You run some kind of charity to do with that, don't you?'

She stiffens almost imperceptibly. She doesn't like the fact I know this stuff about her. I pass a bowl her way, keeping my voice measured. 'There were four things I knew about you before I came here, Avery. Your name, the fact your mother passed away when you were fourteen, that you run a successful tech start-up and that you founded a charity—though I can't remember the specifics of that right now. That's it—nothing more. No one has a detailed dossier on your life.'

She's quiet for a moment, moving towards the food, so I wonder if that's over. But as she moves along, putting a scoop of each dish into her bowl, she says with a calmness that feels a little like the eye of a storm, 'That's why you're here, though, right? To fill in the gaps?'

I'm momentarily quiet. She's right, but I don't know how to answer that in a way that doesn't make me sound like a contemptible person.

'I mean, they could have got their detective to keep digging. Or they could have come themselves. Instead they chose to send a middle man, someone who could find out what they want to know without them getting their hands dirty.'

So we're back to being combative, to pushing me away. 'Being a Hart is complicated,' I say slowly, thoughtfully. 'Protecting themselves is an instinct now. They didn't send me because they don't want to meet you.'

'They just want to know what they're dealing with first?'

I let out a sigh of frustration. 'Is that so wrong?'

'It's offensive,' she says, reaching the end of the food and pushing a fork into the bowl. 'It presupposes that *I* want to meet *them*—which I don't. I'm not some object to be evaluated and appraised, reported on at the next Billionaires' Bingo night or whatever you all do to pass the time.'

Despite the tenor of our conversation, I smile.

'We all felt it would be better this way.' She bristles and I hear it as she must—it sounds like I'm a part of their lives, that we're a team. It closes her out of that. I try again. 'It's not just about them knowing a bit more about you. I thought having time to get used to this, to ask whatever you want about them, and about Ryan, would give you a chance to adapt to all this before you're put in the same room together.'

'You continue to act as though it's a foregone conclusion that it's going to happen. I'm not interested.'

'They're family,' I say gently, moving around to her side of the bench, gesturing towards the table. She's not angry now, nor is she combative. She's… lost. Hurt. I see a glimpse of her vulnerabilities and I want to tear this house down and use every last bit of material to build a shield right here, just around Avery, just as she needs it.

'No.' The word is a swift rebuke, but it's under-scored by her pain. 'They're not. You keep say-ing that, as though there's some invisible bond that should mean something to me, but why? Because our dad happened to make all those women pregnant? Because he slept with my mom? That doesn't make him my father and it doesn't make them my broth-ers. It's just biology.'

I'm stunned by her reading of the situation. 'They're nice guys,' I say as she sits down. I take the seat beside her rather than opposite, not sure why, just knowing I want to be close to her for this con-versation. 'And, like it or not, they *are* your family now. You're a Hart.'

'Don't.' She shakes her head, reaches for her wine. 'I don't want that. I don't want anything to do with any of them, least of all their name.'

I put a hand on her thigh, drawing her gaze to me. When our eyes meet she softens a little, the tight-ness in her features relaxing as though she remem-bers who I am, what we've shared, and maybe even that she can trust me.

'Why not?'

Her lips compress. 'I just don't.'

'That's not an answer.'

'It's too late, that's why not,' she says, staring at me for a full three seconds before scooping some dinner onto her fork and eating it. I watch, waiting for her to continue. She finishes her mouthful then takes a drink of her wine.

She has another mouthful. She's not going to expand.

'It doesn't have to be.'

'I'm twenty-nine years old, Barrett. I've been alone a long time. I'm not interested in getting to know a merry band of long-lost brothers.'

'They only just found out about you too,' I say gently. 'It's not like they chose not to have you in their lives. In fact, knowing them the way I do, knowing what the bonds of family mean to them, I can say that they're not going to let this go. One way or another they're going to want to meet you, to get to know you for themselves.'

'And I have no say in that?'

'Of course you do,' I contradict, leaning a little closer. 'But I think you'll come around to wanting to know them too.'

'You don't get it.' She takes another gulp of her wine. 'My mom worked her fingers to the bone and my dad was one of the richest guys on the planet? I don't buy it that no one knew about me. There's no way she would have worked like a dog without asking him for some kind of financial support first. Which means that he knew about me and he refused to help her. Which means he lived his life not caring that my mom…my mom was…' She shakes her head, emotions heavy in her voice. She takes a breath, composing herself. I wish she wouldn't do that. I want her to be honest with me, even when that honesty involves tears and shouting.

'Ryan had a lot of faults but neglecting his parental responsibilities, with regard to financial support at least, wasn't one of them. I can tell you this without a shadow of a doubt: he didn't know about you.'

'You can't know that.'

I expel a soft sigh. 'Not for absolute certain, perhaps, but honestly, Avery, I think I can say it with confidence. I knew the man, and I know what lengths he went to in order to get custody of his sons.' I lift a hand, stroking her cheek. 'Let me suggest an alternative theory for you.'

She looks at me with eyes that are so huge, so awash with confusion that I want to kiss her back to happiness and pleasure, to force all of this from her mind and heart. But we've done that—a few times. It's important to cross these bridges now. I just want her to know that I'll cross them with her.

'Maybe your mother knew that about Ryan. Maybe she knew that if she told him she was pregnant, that she'd conceived his child, he'd fight her for custody. He was rich, he was mean, and he was all about his 'dynasty'. Maybe she knew that and decided she wanted, more than anything, to have you in her life. To raise you yourself. Maybe she didn't want to lose you, and she knew that if she told him she would.'

Avery makes an involuntary noise, a half sob, half muffled gasp, and stares down at her lap.

'That just makes me even angrier,' she says with a shake of her head. 'As if getting a woman pregnant should lead to a guy strong-arming her into giving up that baby to fill out his paternalistic bullshit about lineage or whatever.' Then, with a small glare at me, 'Then again, you're probably used to all that, given you're aristocracy.'

She's pushing me away again, this time by going on the attack. I don't buy into it.

'Did she ever tell you about him?'

The question surprises her. Avery bites down on her lower lip and reaches for her fork, toying with it in the bowl. 'Not really.'

'Did you ask about him?'

'I used to, when I was younger. She didn't say much. Every now and again she'd make a comment. Enough for me to glean how much he'd hurt her, and that she'd never got over that.'

I nod. 'Ryan was charming. He could convince just about anyone to do anything for him. It was quite terrifying to watch.'

'He sounds like a peach.'

I laugh. 'He was a one-off. But the guys—Jagger, Theo, Holden—they're some of the best men you could ever know. You can choose not to meet them—and maybe they'll even accept your wishes—but you'll be doing yourself a real disservice.'

'I don't need them.' The words are said like a battle cry. She issues it fiercely, her eyes meeting mine, so I wonder then what it would be like to be Avery— so determined to go through life alone, never relying on anyone, never letting them in.

'But does that mean you can't want them?'

She scoops some food into her mouth then swallows. 'You should eat. You were ravenous, remember?'

Conversation closed. Except I don't want it to be. 'I will.' To prove my point I take a large bite, drink some wine. 'Just because you've been alone a long time doesn't mean you have to keep living like this.'

A pause. I watch emotions I don't understand pass across her face. 'How I live my life is none of your business.'

She's right. Frustration builds in my gut.

'Why don't you let me tell you about them? Maybe if you knew what they were like you'd change your mind.'

'Unlikely.'

'Then let me tell you about Felicity.'

'Who's Felicity? Wait, don't tell me. I have a long-lost sister now too.'

'Felicity is your niece.'

That surprises her. She turns to me quickly, her lips forming a perfect 'O', as though it hadn't occurred to her that having brothers would lead to having sisters-in-law and nieces and nephews too.

'She's only a baby, a year or so old. She's cute and funny and incredibly opinionated. Do you want to see a photo of her?'

'No.' A sharp denial. 'You have photos of her with you?'

I roll my eyes affectionately. 'Try to stop Jagger

from sending them. Seriously, I must get six WhatsApp messages a day, all with photos of Felicity and updates of what she's doing now.'

This slice of the Harts is having an impact on her. She's starting to think of them as real people, not an abstract concept, not just strangers who've hurt her with their absence—even when that absence was completely out of their control.

'I didn't see that coming. After their childhood— they were all pretty messed up by Ryan, you know— I thought none of them would ever have kids, settle down. Now they're all married and I'm the last man standing.'

That captures her attention. I've inadvertently led her away from the Harts and back to me, and she sees the opportunity to wriggle out of this conversation. 'And you're quite the ladies' man?' she prompts, smiling slowly, relief obvious in her expression.

'Not really.'

'Liar.' She grins. 'I'll bet you have a different girl in every city.'

Her assumption is exasperating. 'No. I'm not like that.'

'There's nothing wrong with being like that.'

I sigh. 'That's not what I meant. Sure, I like women, I like dating, I like sex, I like fun, but I'm not like the Harts. My parents have as close to a perfect marriage as you could get. They're happy, respectful, committed, content. I always thought I'd have that one day too.'

'But?'

'But what?'

'Well, you're what? Thirty?'

'Thirty-three'

'Right. And single. So? You never met anyone you wanted to turn into the next lady of the manor?'

'Countess,' I correct automatically. 'And nope.'

'Why not?'

I frown. 'I don't know. I've dated a heap of great women.' She spoons some food into her mouth, nodding, waiting for me to continue. 'But I suppose my parents have set me up with some unrealistic expectations. I want a relationship that's perfect.'

'No relationship is perfect.'

'No,' I agree. 'But close to. I'm always open to where something might go, but I am usually disappointed.' I lift my shoulders. 'One day I'll meet someone and I figure I'll just know.'

'Like in the movies?' she teases.

'Yeah, just like that.' I grin, something sparking in the centre of my chest cavity.

'Being alone is really not so bad, you know.' She drinks her wine. 'You get used to it.'

'What about you?' I push past her statement. 'Do you do this often?'

She lifts her brows. 'I can honestly say I've never done this in my life.'

'Eaten takeaway with a guy?'

'Slept with a guy multiple times over the course of a week and shared meals with him too. This is the closest thing to dating I've ever done. And, just in case you're reading into that—it doesn't mean anything to me except that you're crazy persistent and really good in bed.'

I feel a dozen and one things at that. Annoyance, irritation, amusement and, unmistakably, the hot blade of jealousy thrusting through me. 'So you pick up random men, what? Every night? Every second night?'

'Does it matter?'

'I'm just curious.'

'No judgement, right?' She rolls her eyes and I gather she gets judged a lot.

'No judgement.' I put my hand over hers, drawing her gaze so she can see honesty in my eyes.

'I like sex too,' she says simply. It's on the tip of my tongue to make some kind of smart retort like, *Tell me something I don't know*, but I don't because it would be stupid and exactly the kind of judgemental ass comment she's warned me against making.

'The truth?'

I brace myself. 'Sure.'

'I don't do this often at all.' She eats a little more dinner and I'm ashamed of the unmitigated pleasure that's leaping through me. 'Maybe a few times a year, when I get an itch that needs scratching and I can't quite reach it myself.' She winks and great. Now I have an image of Avery getting herself off and my cock is growing hard in my very insufficient boxers, the cotton shifting perceptibly.

'The night we met was my birthday. It's kind of a tradition I have.'

More feelings assault me. Sorrow and sympathy, that she chose to spend her birthday in that way.

'Oh? Since when?' I cover those feelings carefully, keeping my voice bland, almost bordering on disinterested. I have her measure now—she scares easily if she thinks my questions are getting too intense. Gently, gently.

'Since I turned fifteen.' She lifts her shoulders. 'It was a few weeks after Mom died. I'd just been placed with Jenny and Dave. I was pretty fucking miserable.' Her laugh is hollow. 'They were really kind, in hindsight, throwing me a birthday party with their family, getting me a cake, balloons, a phone. I was furious. I felt like they were trying to become my parents, to replace my mom—' Her voice cracks; she covers it by clearing her throat. 'I sneaked out, went to a bar.'

'And lost your virginity to…?'

'Some random.' She smiles but it doesn't reach her eyes. There's sadness and defiance in her features now. 'In the toilet stalls. It was not the stuff of romance novels but, at the same time, it was just what I needed.' She tilts her chin, daring me to disagree.

I don't. I understand the healing power of sex, the ability it has to confer a sense of intimacy when we need it most. I lean forward, pressing our foreheads together.

'I'm glad we could celebrate your birthday together this year.'

She blinks, surprised that's my only comment on this. And then she kisses me, a kiss that is soft and slow and that grips something inside me and doesn't let go.

'I don't want you to be alone, Avery.'

She pulls back. 'I'm not interested in dating you, Barrett. I'm not what you're looking for.'

I ignore the strange feeling inside me and shake my head. 'You have family out there—family who desperately want to meet you—and I can't help but think how much you'll regret it if you pass that opportunity up.'

'I really won't.' She's putting more space between us now, straightening and reaching for her fork once more.

'You say that, but you don't know.'

'And you do?'

My laugh is hollow. 'Oh, Avery. Yeah, I know. I'd give just about anything I possess to have another day with my sister. You don't get it, but you've been given a gift. To have three brothers out there—great guys you will absolutely love—and to choose to turn your back on that?'

'You had a sister?'

'Yes. I know what I'm talking about here. Family is precious. You shouldn't dismiss that so quickly.'

She swallows, her expression shifting. 'What happened to her?'

I don't talk about Caroline often, but when I do people usually tiptoe around the subject. I appreciate Avery's directness.

'She got sick.' Apparently, I'm not able to be quite as direct. 'And died.' My lips shift into an awkward-feeling shape. I think it's an approximation of a smile.

'When?'

'Seventeen years ago.'

'So she was still young?'

'She was seventeen.'

'And you were sixteen. Close in age and close in general?'

'Yes.' I eat something even when my stomach is too tight to contemplate digestion. 'We grew up in the countryside. There wasn't a lot to do. Our parents abhorred technology, television—all that American pop culture that was infiltrating our lives—so we spent a lot of time together, growing up. We used to put on talent shows for our poor mother and father.' Now my smile is a little more natural. 'Losing her was the hardest thing I've ever been through and not a day goes by that I don't think of her, that I don't wish I could have done something to save her.'

'I know what that's like.' Avery leans closer, and I don't think she's even aware she's doing it; it's just like a compulsion to be near me, to share this together.

I don't deny what she's said, even when it's not quite accurate. Losing someone you love is a unique grief, but where her mother's death was one of those awful random events that could never have been prevented by Avery, my parents and I will always feel a degree of culpability for my sister's death.

'What kind of sickness was it?'

I stiffen a little, my reticence now surprising me. 'Do you mind if we don't talk about it?'

She blinks. 'I...of course.' She furrows her brow, looks towards her Chinese and takes a bite.

Silence hangs between us, heavy and full of sadness and serious thoughts. What we need is a circuit-breaker on all this. 'What if we make a deal?'

She looks at me and my breath catches somewhere in the region of my throat. She's so beautiful, and never more so than like this—hair tousled, expression curious, eyes genuine and softened, completely open to me, not pushing at me, holding me at a distance.

'Let me take you out tomorrow night.'

'A date?' The words are a little shrill.

'No more so than this.' I gesture to the food. 'Does it matter what we call it? It will still be you and me and all our hang-ups and reasons for not wanting more than this, just two people hanging out, having sex, eating some food, having some fun.'

'And what do I get in exchange?'

I laugh. 'Two people hanging out, having sex, eating some food, having some fun?'

She lifts a brow. 'I thought you said a "deal". That just sounds like an invitation.'

'Fine. What do you want in exchange?'

She considers that for a moment. 'That's easy.'

'Yeah?'

She pushes her bowl away and stands, holding a hand out to me. 'I want multiple orgasms and twenty-four hours without hearing the word Hart.'

Give us an update, man. You're killing us.

I read the text from Holden with a scowl and a sinking feeling in the pit of my stomach. The line I'm walking feels fraught on both sides. There's Avery, who I want to make happy, and who I want to get to know better. There's Avery, who I'm addicted to and driven to want to help through this. And then there's these guys who I've known all my life, who I love like brothers. I jam my phone into my pocket, the sense that I'm being a terrible friend sitting heavily on my shoulders.

Except I'm not. I'm working hard to get Avery to open up to them—that must count for something, right?

CHAPTER NINE

THIS IS A DATE.

I don't care what I said to Avery to get her to agree to this, it's a straight-up date and I'm straight-up nervous. Me! Barrett Byron-Moore. I don't think I've ever felt nervous before a date in my life. I love women, and that includes getting to know them. Most dates are the same—or similar enough—to know what to expect.

But Avery is different. I don't want to do what I ordinarily would—dinner, drinks, dancing. The idea of anything so commonplace with someone like Avery almost makes me laugh.

No, I need to pull out the big guns—more than that, I want to. I want to surprise her, and I want to take her breath away. Multiple times.

I almost cancel on him. My fingers hover over the keyboard of my phone frequently. A couple of times I actually tap out a short message.

Something's come up. I can't make it.

But each time I delete the message, sending the words back into the ether and wondering why I ever agreed to this—and why I'm going along with it still.

What is it about Barrett that makes me put all my usual rules aside? They're not even rules—they're instincts—finely honed and always right. But with Barrett I ignore them, each and every time. He's persuasive and he's sexy but it's more than that.

I like spending time with him, and I like the way I feel when I'm with him. I like the way he looks at me, the way he is with me. What the hell does that even mean?

I've been alone since Mom died and, realistically, a lot longer than that—Mom loved me to bits but she was never around. I don't think I've ever really got comfortable with someone—to talk to them about me, my life, my losses. So why do I find myself opening up to Barrett?

Do you mind if we don't talk about it?

When I asked about his sister and he shut the conversation down I was…hurt. And then surprised I cared so much. When had that even happened? And then curiosity took over, a curiosity I resented because when I wasn't lifting my phone to cancel our plans I was tempted to load up an internet browser and search him—and his whole family.

The doorbell buzzes. Right on time.

My throat is thick with nerves, my heart racing. I take one last look at myself in the mirror, hating that I even care what I look like, hating that I spent so long choosing what to wear. What a freaking stereotype! In the end, I went for a summer maxi dress. It's still stinking hot out there and in this dress I feel like me. I pulled my hair up into a loose bun on top of my head and applied some make-up—enhancing my lips and eyes.

At the front door I hesitate, and then make a noise of frustration. 'Let's just get this over with!'

I wrench the door inwards and my breath bursts through me, driving all thoughts of me and what I look like from my mind, leaving only room for Barrett—to appreciate him, to admire him. He is overwhelming to all my senses. Dressed in faded jeans and a polo shirt, his hair pushed back from his brow, aviator sunglasses in place—that he pulls off as I step out.

'Hey.' His deep, gravelly voice is so hot I want to tell him to cancel whatever restaurant he's booked us into and to get his butt into my place. But he holds a hand out and his smile is so full of something like anticipation that I miss my opportunity. 'You ready?'

'I think so.' I pull the door shut behind me, then put my hand in his. *It's not too late to get out of this.* 'Yeah. Let's go.'

Everything is a surprise. From the car that collects us—a black SUV with darkly tinted windows and a driver behind the wheel—to the champagne he pops as we pull away from the kerb, pouring expertly and handing me a glass, to the conversation he makes as we drive away from my home, away from the city.

True to our agreement, it's light, and there's not a single mention of the Harts. Thank God.

It's only a twenty-minute drive—enough time for a glass of champagne and to spark my curiosity. I don't recognise where we are until the car pulls to a stop—Barrett has occupied all of my attention for the entire drive.

'The airport?' I murmur as the driver opens my door. But not any part of the airport I've been to before.

'A private airstrip?'

My eyes skim the surroundings and land on a huge jet. 'Hart Brothers' is emblazoned down one side in big gold lettering.

I freeze, panic flooding me.

'Barrett?' He steps out behind me, putting a hand around my waist, his fingers stroking my hip.

'Relax.' He breathes the word against my temple. 'It's just a means of transportation. They're not on board.'

'I don't want—'

'It's just a jet.'

'A private jet owned by them.' My eyes slam over 'Hart Brothers' and I feel an ache deep down, a pain, and I'm sure it shows in my eyes because he draws me closer, dropping his face nearer to mine, understanding in his features, a look of complete sympathy.

'This isn't going away, Avery. One way or another, you're going to have to face up to the fact of who you are.' I suck in a tortured breath. 'But not now. To-night, this is just a means to an end.' He pauses, his eyes roaming my face gently. 'Trust me?'

I bite down on my lip, eyeing the jet once more. I *do* trust him. Which scares the bejeezus out of me. I don't trust *anyone, ever*. It's like a rule I have, one I didn't ever consciously make but that I've been living by for a really long time. Trusting people is dangerous. Happiness comes from independence—not reliance.

'Fine.' And then, unable to shake a frown from my face, 'Where are we going?'

'You'll see.' He drops his arms, catching one of my hands in his, lacing our fingers together and drawing me towards the jet. My heart thumps as we get closer—this obvious wealth, a sign of the dispar-ity between them and me—hits me hard. There's a sense of disbelief and anger but also awe, because this plane is like something out of a fantasy. It is the last word in luxe—and it's not like that's a foreign concept to me.

'So you don't have your own plane then?' I tease, choosing a seat from the many available. There are armchairs and sofas, each with a seat belt buried in the cushions.

'I don't travel enough to warrant it.' He lifts his shoulders.

It naturally leads to me wanting to ask about the owners of the jet, but I don't. I'm already breaking a shedload of my own rules.

'No? I would have thought with your job you'd be in the air a bit?'

'Once a fortnight.' He lifts his shoulders. 'Sometimes more. Not like these guys.' He thumbs towards the back of the plane, indicating the ghosts of the Hart brothers. 'Sometimes they fly daily. They have businesses all over the world and like to be on hand.'

Perhaps he senses my reticence to be drawn into that subject because he leans towards me conspiratorially, 'Plus, between you and me, I don't think there's anything wrong with flying commercial.'

'But not tonight?'

'This was easier.'

'Where are we going?'

'You've already asked that.'

'You didn't answer.'

'And you think I will now?'

'I have ways of making you talk,' I tease, putting a hand on his thigh, creeping it higher slowly until a throat clearing indicates that we're not alone.

'Miss Maxwell, Mr Byron-Hughes, welcome aboard.'

'Thanks, Edward.' Barrett doesn't flinch. 'All set?'

'Yes, sir. We'll have you on the ground in a little over an hour.'

I mentally calculate where we could get to in an hour. It's too close for Napa, but maybe there's another wine district within an easy flying distance.

'Great. Let's go.' There's a repressed enthusiasm

in Barrett's response that has me turning to face him again. The evening sun glints in off the windows and hits his skin so he appears—for a moment—to shimmer gold. He's *excited*. What the heck has he organised?

Once we're in the air Edward brings us some more champagne and a platter of food. Cheese, deli meats, seafood; it's delicious. 'I didn't even realise I was hungry.'

He grins. 'Cheese will do that to you, in my experience.'

'I do like cheese.'

He angles a little in his seat, looking at me better. 'You didn't finish telling me about your charity.'

'I didn't *start* telling you about my charity,' I say after a beat. 'And it's not "mine". I founded it but there's a board now.' And I still donate a heap of money each year, I add silently.

'Right. What is it?'

'We work with homeless people—particularly women and children.'

'Not men?'

'We have a sister charity we partner with, but no. Our focus is on women and children because they tend to be the most vulnerable out on the streets.'

'What made you start it?'

'The neighbourhood I grew up in,' I answer easily. 'I couldn't get from school to our apartment without passing at least two dozen people sleeping rough.' I shake my head. 'I used to look at them and wish

I could do something to help—I think, when I was young, I didn't realise that we were really only one missed pay check away from joining them.'

'And there weren't sufficient charities already in operation?'

'Oh, there's loads,' she says with a nod. 'But we're different. I started off focusing on sanitary items— an essential that's often overlooked—but now it's expanded. We offer re-education and training. We have dedicated offices for people to go to and up-skill—whether that's administrative or clerical, re-tail, we offer vocational training that will make it easier to get a job—and keep it. We collaborate with rehab clinics to get people clean, sponsoring atten-dance and incentivising maintenance. It takes a co-ordinated effort. But, most importantly, we counsel people to look to their potential and remember their dreams—dreams that are so easy to lose in the day-to-day struggle of staying alive.'

He's staring at me like I've just cracked the atom.

I lift my shoulders, a little self-conscious but also so passionately captivated by my beliefs in this that I keep going. 'What if the person who could cure can-cer is sleeping under the bridge, you know? Isn't it our human responsibility to capture the potential of our society as a whole?'

'I'm full of admiration for that,' he says, and I hear it in his voice.

'I guess I know what I could have become, what might have happened to me, if I hadn't found the one thing I'm good at. I was lucky. I want to take that luck out of it. We have aptitude screening, and our counsellors really get to know the clients. We have a pretty good job success rating—over sixty per cent of our candidates have gone on to find and keep jobs in the last twelve months. Obviously I'd like to get that closer to a hundred per cent but there are always other factors at play. It's not perfect, but it's important.'

'Yeah.' He nods, then grimaces. 'And now I feel like I've wasted the last ten years of my life.' He laughs self-deprecatingly, my heart juddering a little at the sight of him like that.

'Why? You don't like what you do?'

'I love it, but it's hardly the noblest pursuit. Not compared to your one-woman crusade to save the world.'

'Ah.' I grin. 'It's hardly a one-woman effort. I'm barely involved now.'

'You finance it?'

My cheeks flush pink. 'Like I said, I make a donation each year.'

'A considerable one, I'd bet.'

Last year seventy per cent of my income went to the charity. I shrug. 'It's important.'

'I think…' He pauses, frowning, shakes his head.

'What?'

He drives a hand through his hair. 'This might sound incredibly condescending, but I think your mom would be so proud of you, Avery.'

* * *

His words are still floating through my mind, making me buzz and glow, when the plane touches down. Unlike a commercial flight, there have been no announcements as to our location, the flight crew obviously clued in on the fact Barrett is surprising me.

Before we disembark he reaches into his pocket and pulls out a silky black piece of fabric.

'May I?' He holds it up towards my face.

My pulse hums, the idea of being blindfolded by Barrett sparking a thousand and one thoughts and not one of them is PG. 'Uh-huh.'

He turns me around, lifting the fabric over my eyes and tying it behind my head, so I can't see a thing.

He has to guide me down the stairs, and then ease me into a waiting car. It begins to move. With my eyes blindfolded like this, I'm hyper-aware of everything. The gentle thrum of the engine, the rustle of Barrett's clothing as he moves, the feeling of my dress against my body, my nipples against the fabric—I didn't wear a bra—his masculine scent, then the sound of something—a soft buzzing noise. I frown, lifting my hands to the blindfold, instinctively wanting to remove it to investigate that latest noise.

But Barrett's hand on mine stops me. 'Leave it.' It's a gruff command.

My heart turns over in my chest.

A minute later, the unclicking of a seat belt. His, not mine. His body moving, and moving easily, which makes me think we're in some kind of limousine, with enough space in the back for a man of Barrett's size to move freely.

His hands on my ankles make my breath snag. Anticipation begins to hum inside me, desire a raging torrent.

'You said multiple orgasms, right?' His hands move slowly up the insides of my legs, his fingers tracing invisible lines, and I nod, mumbling something that might have been a, 'Yeah, I did.'

I lift my butt off the seat as his fingers connect with the silk of my thong, making it easier for him to slide it down my legs. My dress is cotton. He bunches it up my legs, higher and higher, the feeling of it rubbing against me almost enough to make me weep and come, all at once.

His hands are firm as they grip my knees, pushing them apart, exposing me to him completely, and for a moment there's nothing. Just me in the back of a limo—I presume—with this unbearably sexy Brit crouched between my legs. But then his lips press against me, his tongue pushing into me, his mouth sucking my clit; my sex, his mouth, we're so wet, I'm so turned on, heat flashes in my belly. I move my legs but his hands are firm, refusing to let me shift, keeping me just as he wants me, his dominance fierce and flaming. I arch my back and push further forward on the seat, giving him better access—not that he needs it. He is so good at this. It reminds me of the first night we were together, of the way he effortlessly brought me to the edge of climax again and again and then withdrew, but this isn't like that. There's no withdrawing tonight, there's no taunting, no point-scoring.

This is Barrett at his best.

I'm on the edge of an orgasm and he must know that because his hands curve around to my ass, pulling me even closer, pressing me hard against his mouth so I feel his tongue and his lips and the stubble on his jaw and the sensual overload is impossible to cope with.

I crumble in his hands, against his mouth, moaning words that make no sense, words that have their own cadence and etymology. I am in freefall and I have no idea if Barrett would ever be able to catch me but I don't care. The fall feels too good to give a shit about the landing.

'Are you ready?' Thirty minutes later, my body is floating. Barrett clearly took my objectives seriously. The car trip here—to wherever we are—has been an invasion of all my senses and I am practically in the clouds now.

'To sleep for a year?' I joke back, smiling in the direction of his voice.

And, despite what we've just shared, his hand over mine feels intimate and warm, his fingers curling through mine like they were designed for that.

What the hell is happening to me? Since when do I think soppy crap like that?

'No sleep right now, princess.'

Princess? I pull a face but a second later, when he lifts the blindfold from my face and I see where he's brought me, everything makes sense. Barrett has just gone and made all eight-year-old Avery's dreams come true. I stare at the sign with disbelief, then look back at him.

'You…brought me to Disneyland?'

'You said you've never been.' He shrugs, like this is nothing, like this gesture isn't the beginning and end. In all these years I've never told another soul about that, and I've never even really thought about it, to be honest. If I'd wanted to, I could have come here at any point in the last ten years. But the fact Barrett listened and organised this, that *this* is how he wants to spend this night…

'We said we'd have fun,' he murmurs, but there's something in the words, like he's uncertain, worried he's messed up, going out on this Disney-shaped limb.

'Oh, we will,' I reassure him, lifting up and brushing my lips to his impulsively, spontaneously. 'But don't think I won't be wearing mouse ears in three seconds flat.'

The joy on her face is like a beacon. I watch as Avery buys a stick of candyfloss bigger than her head. 'You're going to have to help me with this.' She laughs as she walks back towards me. The sun has long since disappeared but the night is still warm and balmy. Fireworks burst overhead, bright sparkling shots of light flaring through the night sky, illuminating that signature castle in the centre of the park. I push all thoughts of the Harts from my mind—trying to ignore the sense of guilt that has been dogging me for the last few days. All I want to focus on right now is Avery and that smile of hers.

'I'll help you.' I grin, dropping my head and sucking some of the ridiculously sweet candy in before pulling back. 'That's kind of gross.'

'It's not gross,' she responds with mock offence. 'Are you kidding? It's the best thing ever.'

I loop an arm around her waist, walking side by side through the theme park. It's a busy summer night but we weave through the throngs of tourists with ease, moving almost as though we were one person.

'I can't believe you organised this.' She laughs, a soft sound, then lifts her face to mine.

'Why not?'

'It's just so thoughtful.'

'I can't be the first guy who's ever done something thoughtful for you?'

Her expression shifts a little. Consternation, worry. I read her like a book—which should, in fact, worry me, but doesn't.

'Actually, you are.' But her smile is bright, falsely so. My heart hurts for her—for how hard she works to push people away. For the fact she's spent the last ten years working her butt off, building her business and her charity but reserving herself for no one, indulging in sex when she gets a physical yearning but otherwise completely alone.

I want to ask her about that. I want to ask her what she sees for her future, where she sees her life going. I want to ask her what kind of guy could induce her to settle down but, before I can form any of those questions and certainly before I can wonder why I crave the answers, she uses the candyfloss as a pointer and exclaims, 'Space Mountain! Let's do it!'

Who am I to say no to that kind of excitement?

CHAPTER TEN

AS THE PLANE descends back over San Francisco I can't help but just watch her. She's fast asleep, the candyfloss rush having finally worn off but the mouse ears still perched atop her head. If I thought Avery Maxwell would be too cool to get into the spirit of Disneyland, boy, was I wrong. I'm wearing a souvenir T-shirt she bought for me while I was grabbing us some fries, for Christ's sake. She shifts a little in the seat and the mouse ears move, almost losing their grip. I reach across, straightening them, then my hand drops to her cheek, skimming across her soft flesh there. She stirs and I withdraw, not wanting to wake her.

When the plane touches down she moves but stays asleep, so I lift her up, cradling her to my chest as I stride off the plane, breathing her in, holding her tight.

The car's waiting. As I ease her into it she wakes, looking up at me, her eyes full of sleep and dreams. 'I had a really great time tonight.'

My chest feels like it's about to split wide open. I smile. 'I'm glad.'

And I am. But I also feel like I've cheated. Taking this night, spending it with Avery, pretending this situation isn't hell kind of complicated, was great, but I know this is coming to a head. I owe the Harts more than this; I owe them my allegiance.

Allegiance? Like I have to make a choice? They're not two warring countries. There's no reason this can't be made to work. Avery's upset and hurt but she doesn't know Jagger, Theo and Holden like I do. She's judging them for the sins of their father. If everyone did that, the Hart brothers would never even speak, let alone be as close-knit as they are.

But what's the long-term plan here? Once Avery meets the Harts, do I just drop out of her life? Become her friend, like I'm friends with them? Or do I push for us to keep doing this? The idea takes hold, slipping inside me, jolting me at first with the impossibility of that and then with the necessity of it. Because I don't want her to become a stranger to me and I don't want her to become just a friend.

So what do I want?

'Are you coming in?' She lifts her eyes to me as we slow down outside her place.

I nod, not even considering going back to the hotel. 'If that's okay?'

She hesitates a moment and I barely breathe, then she nods. 'Sure. Come on.' This time she takes my hand and I follow behind her.

* * *

Having slept most of the flight home, I'm wide awake now. I make him a tea, and me a coffee—I long ago passed the point where coffee after a certain time has the power to keep me awake—and carry them onto the deck. It's an hour past midnight but the heat hasn't dissipated. This summer has broken all the records, and it feels like it's never going to end.

I pause just over the threshold of the deck, my eyes dropping to his chest, the shirt he wears. I bought it as a joke. No way did I expect him to take it from my hands, find a restroom and swap into it. It's gaudy and tacky and cute and so not Barrett, and yet he wore it all night and, I have to say, he looks the bomb in it. Of course.

A smile lifts my lips as I cross to him, handing him the tea.

'Thanks.'

I stand beside him, sipping my coffee, trying not to overthink this. Last night he told me he has to leave the States in less than two weeks. This guy's not going to be around for ever—there's no harm in enjoying this for now, knowing it won't last much longer.

I can relax. Enjoy it, and him, to the fullest and then go back to normal. I'm not breaking any rules—not badly, anyway.

'I almost googled you today,' I surprise myself by admitting.

'Yeah?' His gaze falls to mine, enquiry clear on his features. 'Why?'

I take another sip of my coffee then rest my elbows on the railing, looking out over the twinkling city. 'To find out whatever I could.'

'You're curious about me?'

I resist that. 'I'm curious about everything.'

He smirks a little, like he knows it's more specific to him.

'You don't need to search for information about me on the internet. You can ask me anything.'

'Except about your sister?'

I feel him stiffen beside me. He's quiet for a long time and then he shifts, turning his back on the view, bracing his elbows on the railing, his face angled in my direction. 'What do you want to know?'

My brow furrows. 'I don't want to make you talk about it. I just meant I was curious.' My expression is almost apologetic. 'I don't like unanswered questions.'

'Nor do I.' His eyes sweep my face.

'Forget I asked.' I wish I could eat the words back up. He has every right to keep his secrets—especially about something like this. 'Honestly, I have no business even thinking I have a right to know.'

That brings darkness to his face, a look in his eyes I can't interpret. 'Of course you do. This isn't about me wanting to keep it from you specifically; it's just something I always struggle with. It happened seventeen years ago but time hasn't made it any easier.'

The last time I tried to console him by drawing a parallel between our grief he reacted awkwardly so I don't do that again, even when my personal experience has me understanding what he means—it hasn't got easier for me either.

'Caroline was a happy kid, you know? We were pretty sheltered, how we grew up. Our parents controlled our social circle; we had a small, close group of friends.'

Including the Harts, I add inwardly, knowing I can't let myself forget this man's link to my past, the reason he's come to San Francisco, and that if I were smart I'd hold onto the fact he lied to me that first night—even if it was a lie by omission. But none of that is at the forefront of my mind any more.

'We left our small local school to attend different high schools, ones with better reputations academically. They were bigger, with more resources, huge campuses, and while I thrived on that, Caroline just wasn't cut out for it. She found the social pressure unbearable.'

He closes his eyes for a moment and I wait for what's coming next, wondering how his thread of conversation could link to her potentially getting sick.

'She started to lose weight one year. None of us really noticed—or I sure as hell didn't.' He lifts his shoulders. 'But after a few months it was impossible to miss it. Her bones began to stick out; she got so thin, Avery, she was like—' He shakes his head.

'My parents thought it was a phase, that it would pass, but years went by and she never got better. I'll never forget her eyes, how hollowed out they became.' He shakes his head sadly. 'Caroline starved herself to death.'

I draw in a sharp breath, lifting a hand to his shoulder, pressing it there, lost for words. 'I had no idea. My God, Barrett, that must have been so hard to watch.'

'Hard to watch? Hell, it was—' His hands tighten and his eyes lift towards the sky. 'I honestly feel like I can do anything, half the time. But standing on the sidelines as she wasted away, unable to help, unable to fix it… I will never forget how that felt. The powerlessness of my parents, seeing them swallowed by grief. Even now, my mother isn't the same—she lost—we all lost—so much. Caroline died in front of us and none of us could save her.'

'Did she go into hospital?'

'Oh, clinic after clinic after therapist after clinic. She'd put on a little weight while she was there and then come out worse than ever. Nothing worked.' His voice is bleak. There is a pang of something in the region of my heart for him.

'We all saw therapists, to help us help her, and to help us get through it. It didn't work.'

I move to stand in front of him, not knowing what to say but knowing my body can offer comfort. Closeness. Touch.

He puts a hand on my hip, keeping me where I

am, making space for me so I fit right there, in the voids created by his shape.

'It's not about vanity. I think that's the biggest misconception people have about eating disorders. It goes so much deeper than that. She changed schools and everything that was familiar and comforting in her life evaporated. Uncertain and feeling out of control, she did what she could to take that control back.' I feel his ragged intake of breath. 'Until *that* was out of control and she didn't realise it.'

I don't know what to say. I stand close to him, inhaling his masculine scent, my breaths in unison with his, and I hope he feels all the words I'm not offering. I hope he understands how much sympathy I feel for him, how much I wish I could fix that somehow.

'Grief is hard, guilt too. My parents were broken by her death. Our lives had this gaping emptiness. For years we were just… It was impossible to be together and be normal. Her absence was everywhere and in everything. But, over time, we've found a rhythm with it. We talk about her, remember her, mark her birthday, laugh, cry.' I lift my face to his, and something jerks inside me. There's an intensity of emotion that almost bowls me over and, more than that, I'm hyper conscious of what a uniquely special man he is.

'How is it possible you're not married with three kids?'

The question—so out of left field—obviously

catches him unawares. Despite having asked it, it does the same to me.

'Why do you ask?'

'You're just unusual. You're so...' I search for a word, draw a blank '...nice.'

It's like saying today was hot. Blatant understatement. He immediately reacts, his eyebrows shooting upwards, his lips quirking into a small smile.

'Nice?'

'And hot.'

His laugh is soft, from low in his belly, and I'm immeasurably glad to hear it after the sadness that was so heavy in his voice a moment ago.

But he sobers almost instantly, lifts his hands to my face and cups my cheeks, holding me steady. 'I didn't feel very nice, the night we met. I should never have slept with you, knowing what I did.'

I was furious with him, but somehow, over the last few days, that anger has dissipated so completely that I can barely even remember feeling it. I don't feel anger for Barrett now. Instead I feel...nothing I want to analyse, but things that worry me enough to have me pulling away, blinking up at him like I'm waking up from a dream. My heart is beating faster, my body flushing with something like adrenaline.

What am I doing?

What the hell have I let happen?

Why am I standing on my terrace with this guy, hugging him, listening to him bare his soul, holding him close? I feel a frown shift on my lips and try to suppress it but the air around us has changed. Gone is the relaxed sense of confiding from a moment ago. I'm tense now. Worried about what we're doing. Not right now, but in a week's time...a month? He's leaving, sure, but what if he leaves and I actually *miss* him. Isn't that the risk I'm running by spending all this time with him and getting to know him like this?

Since when did I get more interested in *him* than his body and what he can do with it?

Within the space of a few seconds I understand what I'm feeling and why and I know with unswerving clarity what I have to do.

I reach for the straps of my dress, pushing them down my arms slowly, watching him so I see the moment his expression shifts from his own guilt to one of curiosity, then bemusement and finally sensual surrender. I toss my dress away from me and stand before him wearing only a silk thong, my eyes holding a silent challenge.

'Want to go for a swim?'

A muscle throbs at the base of his jaw, his eyes shifting from my body to—briefly—the pool behind us.

'Right now?'

I step forward, pressing my near-naked body to his. 'Yeah, right now.'

I pull his clothes from his body, my fingers tracing his flesh as I remove each item of clothing until he stands in just his underwear. I curve my hands inside the elastic, grabbing hold of his ass, bringing him closer to my body, desire weaving through me like magic and silk.

He grins, but it's a smile that doesn't quite make it to his eyes. I don't care. With every moment that passes I feel more certain that I have to end this with him. I don't know why I've let it get this far, but it was stupid and wrong. Not just because I don't do this kind of thing but because of his connection to the Harts. Why didn't I just slam the door in his face, refuse point-blank to have anything to do with him and them and keep going on with my life?

Why indeed?

That's a question for another time. Right now I want to fill myself with Barrett and all the pleasure I know he'll bring me.

'Fuck me.' It feels good to issue that directive, good to remind him that, first and foremost, this is a physical thing. Tonight was sweet, but I don't want sweet. I just want to be alone. Me, my business, the charity, my life. Predictable, ordered, familiar, mine.

His smile is slow to unfurl. 'I thought we were swimming.'

'I mean, we can swim if you want…'

He reaches for me, lifting me easily, in a way that drives me wild, pulling me to his waist, wrapping my legs around his back and then he's kissing me, his mouth claiming mine with a hunger that can't be faked. His desire is as red-hot as mine. He carries me across the pool deck and I lose myself in that kiss—so much so that the first indication I have that he's moved towards the pool is when we splash right into it. He laughs as we hit the water, breaking our kiss to look at me, to see my reaction. Shock, confusion, amusement.

'Hey!' I punch his arm. 'That's not what I meant.'

He catches me, brings me back to his body and deepens the kiss, his body beneath the water warm and strong. I groan, needing his kiss and him, pleasure radiating through me.

Beneath the water's surface, I push his boxers away then curl my hands around his cock, letting my fingers run the length of it, enjoying the sensation of its strength and hardness, wanting him so badly. Condoms are nowhere nearby so I have to be patient—not really my strong suit—but I make do, kissing him, pressing my body to his until we are both panting and ragged from needs that can't be met right now.

I'm almost at breaking point when finally he draws me from the water, disappearing for the briefest moment possible to grab protection. He comes back, his eyes on mine as he sheathes himself, so I look away because there's something so powerful in his gaze, something unspoken and fierce and demanding and I can't—won't—answer it.

He brings himself over me, and I reach for him at the same time, still not looking at his face. Instead I concentrate on how this feels, on every flicker of sensation his body's contact sparks within me. I close my eyes, feeling him, committing parts of this to memory. He spreads my legs, his touch so familiar and perfect, and drives himself inside me so I writhe and arch my back, pleasure infiltrating my soul completely.

'Barrett…' His name spills from my lips again and again, a plea in its syllables. But a plea for what? Release, yes. The release pleasure can bring and the release of knowing this is over. I can't do this. I need to put an end to it. And I will—later.

As his cock takes possession of me his hands run over my breasts, my nipples, then one returns to my clit, stroking it, his fingers moving over me until I'm driven to the point of insanity. He takes a nipple in his mouth, rolling it with his tongue. His stubble, his warmth, my body wet from the pool, the night warm, the air thick; every sense is heightened by this. I twist beneath him, my body craving greater contact with his.

'Fuck, Avery, I'm—'

He doesn't finish the sentence. His orgasm explodes between us right as my own crests through my body, so our cries mingle, our breathing frantic, our hands digging into each other's backs, bodies, as though we can control this. He buries his head in my shoulder, his body weight on mine divine, his breath rough in the hollow of my neck, and he stays there for a long time, so long that pleasure has seeped from me, leaving me with a hollowness in my chest.

His laugh is a little unsteady. 'Well, that was…'

'Great.' I press my hands to his chest, barely

able to breathe now, needing him to go. What the hell have I been doing? The question keeps circling through my brain. Why did I let him take me out today? Why do I keep doing this?

'Quick.' He says the word with a hint of apology. Holy crap. Barrett can't seriously be thinking there was *anything* even remotely defective in what just happened between us? I have never been with a guy who can get me off so fast, so thoroughly, so reliably.

'Fast isn't a bad thing in my book.'

He tries to catch my eyes but I don't look at him. 'No?'

'I'm a computer programmer. I value efficiency.'

'Avery?' His voice is low, deep, and it brushes against me, sparking all the sensations I just experienced all over again. I look at him now, because I feel like it would be churlish and rude not to.

'Are you okay?'

I swallow, his concern almost unpicking the resolve I've made. 'I'm fine.' I push at his chest once more, a little harder this time. 'But I have a huge day tomorrow. I'm going to have to call it a night.'

I stand up, grabbing my clothes from the deck and moving towards the glass doors. Panic is inside me, quickening my step, but there's coldness too, a commitment to my decision that's reassuring. 'Thanks again for tonight,' I call over my shoulder, placing my dress inside the laundry door then moving back to the lounge in time to see him walk in from the deck, pants on, shirt being pulled over his head as I watch.

When he looks at me I see concern on his face. I hate that. 'I'm fine,' I say again, smiling. 'Just tired.'

'And you want me to go?' He says the words in a way that's measured and calm, but I know he's feeling a thousand things. Annoyance, impatience, anger, confusion.

'Yes.' I tilt my chin towards him, daring him to argue.

He tries to pin me with his gaze, to read me through my eyes, but I blink away, looking towards the door. 'Thanks again for tonight. I had fun.'

Nothing. Silence. I wait, and I wait, and a few seconds later there's the sound of him moving. Towards me, not the door. I brace myself, desperately needing him to go, needing to fathom what the hell is happening, and to be more like myself again.

'I had a good time too.' He cups my cheek—he does that often. When I don't say anything and barely look at him, I feel the whisper of his sigh against my cheek. 'Goodnight, Avery.'

'I have to be in LA anyway. It's no drama to come to San Francisco after.' Theo's voice thunders down the line. I grip the phone, staring out of my window, a frown on my face that's been there for the two days since I left Avery's.

I haven't seen her since. I texted twice and got brusque replies. That, coupled with the way she dismissed me after Disneyland, has left me in a shit of a mood. And now this?

Despite my uncertainties with Avery—and my annoyance with her too—Theo's suggestion sends a sharp spear of panic through me. 'I don't think that's a good idea.'

'Come on, man. We're dying to meet her. What the hell is she like?'

My laugh is involuntary. 'How long have you got?'

Silence greets this. I drag a hand through my hair wearily and search for a sanitised way to describe Avery.

'She's...fierce.'

'Fierce?' Theo digests this, then there's the scuffling of something. His hand over his phone. 'He says she's fierce.'

'What the hell does that mean?' I hear Holden's voice and, despite my mood, smile.

'It means she's intelligent and confident and self-assured and basically a girl version of you guys.' And as I say it I realise how true it is, right down to her fucked-up attitude to relationships. Funny, I always presumed that was a hangover from their father's influence but maybe it's just genetics. Maybe they're all biologically pre-programmed to have an element of fuckery when it comes to love.

Love? Jesus. I drop my head forward, pressing it to the glass, concentrating on my breathing for a second.

'Great. Then she'll see the sense in meeting us.'

'Hang on.' That pulls me out of the web of my

thoughts. 'Just don't do anything yet. She still needs time.'

'Time? What the hell, man? What's time going to do?'

'You've had longer than she has to get used to this.'

'Not by much.'

I consider that. 'No, but you knew what Ryan was like,' I add. 'This is more out of the blue for her. A family—a father—wasn't even on her radar. She gave up on that a long time ago.'

My chest feels a little like it's being weighted with cement. I imagine Avery growing up, as a teenager, after her mother died, and I wish I could wipe away that pain, I wish I could help her past it.

'You're going to need to do this slowly,' I say after a moment. 'Don't all show up here *en masse* and expect her to welcome you with open arms. Just one of you should come first. God, I don't know.' I shake my head, imagining that, and all I can sense is how ambushed Avery will feel. 'Leave it with me a bit longer, okay? I'll see what I can do.'

'Thanks, man. Just…tell her we're here. Tell her we're family.'

I close my eyes, a sense of something constricting my abdomen. They are family. Theo, Jagger, Holden and Avery. I'm not. 'Yeah, I will.'

I disconnect the call and stare out at nothing in particular, wondering at the mess I've managed to get myself into—and how the hell I'm going to get out of it.

One thing's for sure—Avery is in way over her head. The panic in her eyes the other night was unmistakable. She couldn't have got rid of me any faster if she'd tried. Whatever boundaries she insists on keeping between us aren't going anywhere—at least, not quickly.

And who am I to expect her to give up the habits of a lifetime for me? There are so many reasons I need to let this go. Her relationship to the Harts, my job in Europe, her own hang-ups about relationships—we might have a hell of a good time together when she lets down her guard but that's rare and I can't see Avery changing any time soon.

I have to let all of this go and focus on the reason I came here—this is for the Harts.

CHAPTER ELEVEN

FOUR DAYS AFTER I last saw Barrett and I realise why I can't stop thinking about him. The answer has been in front of me all along and I've been ignoring it, stubbornly refusing to acknowledge a key part of my personality.

I don't like having questions unanswered.

I have three brothers out there and I know pretty much nothing about them, except what's in the financial papers. I don't mean what I could find out on the internet, anyway; I mean the *real* them. I don't really want to know them, but they're a part of me in a weird kind of way. Our biology is connected, and pretending that's not the case is going against the grain for me.

I have questions about them and, until they're answered, Barrett will occupy too much space in my head. Once I've got the answers I need I can box this whole thing away—him included—and never think of him again.

That's it—easy. Simple. I don't know why I didn't see it sooner. Sex is beside the point. Sure, he's an amazing lover but I've had great sex before and I'll have it in the future. There's no point muddying the waters of what we are by getting intimate with him again.

I just need him to clarify a few things then he can go back to England or wherever he's presenting his report, and I'll get on with my life. Alone, just as I like it. Once I've got these answers I'll be able to start forgetting him, and how he made me feel.

And how's that, Avery? A voice—my mother's—makes the demand of me.

I ignore her, pick up my phone and write a text.

Hey. Are you free later?

I put the phone down and focus on my work. An hour later I realise I'm checking my screen almost obsessively and get up, pacing across to the windows of my office. It doesn't help to distract me. In order to reach the windows I have to walk past the armchairs and sofa, and those are now full of Barrett memories—memories I find impossible to blank. Closing my eyes, I inhale deeply, surprised to realise how much he's got under my skin. Not just him, but this whole damned situation.

I have hated my father all my life—without knowing anything about him except that he wasn't there for my mom. But what if Barrett's right? What if he never knew about me? What if she was scared he'd take me away so she never told him? My heart squeezes painfully, because surely there were times when she considered that. It would have been so much easier for her without me. And did she ever think it would be better for me? My heart squeezes again, harder this time, and a thread of disloyalty turns my blood to ice. Would I have chosen a life of wealth and luxury?

No.

That wouldn't have been enough to turn my back on my mom. But family? My stomach rolls. Brothers? A sound escapes me without my consent, a sort of anguished sob, and my eyes burst open, landing on my phone. Yes, for brothers, for family, for noise and company, for anything to combat that pervasive sense of loneliness, I might well have wished my father had been a part of my life.

Another sob. I stalk across the room and swipe my phone off the desk right as it buzzes.

Hi Avery. Sure—where and when?

My stomach loops. His message is distant. Cool. I don't want anything from him, but the idea that he's annoyed at me, frustrated by me, impatient with me, threatens to split me in two. I tap 'reply' and stare at the screen for several seconds.

There's a place in South Beach—The Lighthouse. Do you know it?

I can Google.

Of course he can. I swallow past a strange heaviness in my throat.

Great. Four o'clock?

Sure. See you then.

I ache to write something else, but what? What else can I say? There's nothing. I have no promises, no apologies, no explanations. This is who I am, and I owe him nothing. I just wish he'd go away so I can start forgetting about him, and stop feeling like this.

But I'm nothing if not disciplined. I have a few hours before I need to leave. I settle down at my desk and force myself to work with a singular determination.

It's a converted warehouse that was, at one time, used as a fish market. The ceilings are impossibly high, the window spanning from floor to ceiling, the view of a South Beach street charming and rustic, the high rises of the financial district just visible. I scan the café but there's no sign of Barrett. My pulse accelerates as I contemplate, briefly, that he might not arrive. But of course he will—he's a good guy. Good guys don't say they'll do something then fail to follow through.

I order some sparkling water and peruse the menu, even though I don't feel like eating. Ten minutes later, on a whim, I look up just as he strides through the door. My heart stutters to a stop in my chest. He is impossibly beautiful.

The word is not what I'd usually choose to describe a man I've slept with, but it's the only word I can find in that moment. Tall, confident, handsome, sure, but it's so much more than that. He says something to a pretty waitress in torn jeans, a black shirt and a grey apron. Her hair is shaved on one side and braided on the other. His smile sparks an answering one in her. A spark shifts through me.

Jealousy?

Not likely.

Curiosity, more like. Barrett would have no problem meeting women. I think about that for barely a second before forcing my brain not to go there. The waitress gestures in my direction. He turns. Our eyes meet. My heart stops.

I force a smile to my face, stand up a little awkwardly as he walks over. In my peripheral vision I'm aware of people turning to look at him. He's not famous. While he might be well known in England, here in America he's nobody, but Barrett could never really be a 'nobody'. His charisma and charm is a clearly discernible force.

A second later he's at the table, his hair ruffled, his skin tanned, smelling like sunshine and an alpine forest and something else so addictively good I want to groan.

'Hey.' My voice is hoarse. I lean forward, intending to brush a kiss against his cheek, but he stiffens so I make it the quickest kiss in history, barely touching him before pulling back. 'Thanks for coming.' I gesture to the seat opposite.

He slides into it, nodding as he does so. 'Of course.'

The waiter appears then, her eyes drifting to Barrett so often that I get the drift. She's interested. She thinks he's hot.

'What can I get y'all?' Her accent is from the Deep South, her smile twinkling.

'Double espresso,' I say without missing a beat.

She nods, turns back to Barrett. 'And for you, Barrett?'

Great. They're on a first-name basis. The smile he gives makes my stomach loop. It's not like it's a special smile; he's not trying to impress her. It's a reflexive shift of his lips, but it's so full of genuine courtesy and kindness that I feel hollowed out inside. 'I'll grab a beer. Thanks.'

'Courtney,' she reminds him with a flirtatious laugh, leaving without another glance at me.

'Well, you've certainly made an impression,' I drawl, the words unmistakably catty.

He doesn't rise to the bait. 'What can I do for you, Avery?'

Straight down to business, then. I swallow, reaching for the mineral water to buy time. 'I don't want to meet them.' I drop my eyes to the table top. 'I'm not ready.'

Silence.

'But I want to know a bit more about them, and I thought you could tell me some stuff.'

A pause. I wait, and then risk a glance at his face. He's watching me in a way I can't interpret, his eyes impossible to read. 'Of course.' The words are gravelly. 'What would you like to know?'

I spend the next hour telling her all the little things I can think of about Jagger, Theo and Holden. I tell her about the time Jagger broke his arm climbing a tree to the top. I tell her about their college life, I tell her about their birthdays and their heartbreaks and their successes; I tell her all the things only I know. But I save the biggest one for last.

I tell her finally about Holden Hart, and the shocking discovery a little while ago that he wasn't, in fact, Ryan Hart's biological child. I tell her how it took him a good year or so to come to terms with that. How he pushed everyone away and made life generally hell for his loved ones until the tipping point about a year ago.

'What happened?' She's on her second double espresso. I wonder how she's not jittery as hell.

'He realised family is about more than biology. It's a choice—who do you want to be in your life, how do you want to live it? He was fighting to be alone, but his brothers wouldn't let him. They wouldn't let him go.'

I see her mouth contort, her eyes hovering on the table top so I want to reach across and grab her chin, levelling her face to mine, but I don't. I don't want to touch her because I'm terrified I won't be able to stop and more and more I'm coming to realise that she doesn't want me to comfort her; she doesn't want anyone's pity, comfort—nothing. She wants to go it alone.

'I can't see them letting you go either, Avery.'

This startles her. She finally looks at me and I feel what she feels—terror. I understand it and I want to fight it with her. I want to stand by her side while she deals with that, but that too is the last thing she wants.

'Why?' It's a strange question.

'Isn't that obvious?'

'Not to me.'

'You're their sister.'

'I'm just…'

'Don't say it.' Damn it, I can't help myself. I reach across, putting my hand over hers. Her eyes fly to the gesture, staring at our hands. 'Don't say you're just the daughter of a woman their dad slept with. It's not true; that's not how it works.' I slide my thumb across hers. 'You have three brothers and they want you in their lives. They want you to be a part of their family. I don't understand why you'd deny yourself that.'

'That's because you can't possibly imagine what my life was like.'

'You're wrong. I don't have to have lived it to see what you went through and to understand why you resent Ryan. And maybe even your mom, a bit, for the choices she made. But Jagger, Theo and Holden haven't done anything wrong here. As soon as they found out about you—'

'They dispatched a friend to snoop around.'

I expel an impatient breath. 'As a precaution and a precursor to meeting you for themselves, yes. They want you in their family but they're not stupid. They're three of the wealthiest men in the world, and they're used to managing the public's perception of their lives, the media intrusion, and they're used to people wanting things from them.'

'So they thought I'd what? Show up on their doorsteps and demand a seat at the boardroom table? That I'd want a controlling stake of Hart Brothers Industries?' She makes a guffawing noise. 'I wouldn't touch it with a bargepole.'

'They wanted to do some research so they could work out how to move forward. So far as I know, there's been no talk of denying you anything that's your birthright.'

Her face drains of colour. 'I don't want it.' The words are bitter, laced with hatred and rage. 'I don't need money. I don't need them.'

'Avery—'

'I had a family too, Barrett! I had a mom, and she died. I'm not choosing to be alone—I *am* alone, and that's okay. I'm not going to betray her by getting all buddy-buddy with people who mean absolutely nothing to me.'

I understand every single thing she feels but that doesn't stop me from wanting to argue with her, to throw common sense in her face.

'Listen to me,' I say quietly. 'You're upset and you need time to come to terms with this—which is what I told them. They—'

'When did you tell them that?' Her question is rapier-sharp, cutting through me.

'What?'

'When did you have this conversation—about me—with the Harts?'

'The other day. Does it matter?'

She presses her lips together and stares past me. 'No.' But it does. Something about that has unsettled her.

'You know that's why I came here.'

'Sure. To spy on me. I'd just forgotten for a moment.'

I open my mouth to reject that but she keeps going. 'How convenient for you that I fell into your bed. That must have made it so much easier.'

'That's incredibly unreasonable.' I keep my voice quiet and low, calm even when a sense of outrage is bursting to life in my belly.

'Is it? Within an hour of meeting me you knew more about me than you ever would have if you'd chosen to approach me any other way.'

'I didn't go to that bar intending to hit on you.' I force myself to calm down. 'You were the one who asked me to come home with you, remember?'

'I didn't know who you were,' she reminds me. 'But you did.'

'Yes. And I felt bad for that. I didn't intend to sleep with you, which is why I told you the truth.'

'After you'd slept with me again.'

She glares at me and I feel as though I'm losing my grip on this, and her. 'Listen, Avery, I don't want to argue with you. Us sleeping together is a separate issue to the Harts. They're your brothers and they want to meet you. I've explained that you need time, but they're not particularly patient. I think you should prepare for that.'

'I don't want to meet them.' She stands up then, her eyes hitting mine, a fierce, angry warning in them. 'Thank you for coming to see me today.' She throws a twenty onto the table and spins away, stalking through the restaurant.

No fucking way. I scrape my chair back and follow her, barely noticing when the waitress tries to get my attention. On the pavement I catch Avery, grabbing hold of her arm. 'Hang on a second.'

She stops walking and I drop hold of her, but stay right where I am, so close I can smell her shampoo—like honey and lavender. Chasing her out of restaurants feels like something I'm getting good at.

'Stop running out on me.' The words are laced with the strength of my feelings. 'Just stop running away.'

'I'm not.' Her eyes are suspiciously moist and I

know she hates that because she blinks a thousand times.

'Yes, you are. You're running from yourself, your family. And from me.' I say the last word on a groan, dropping my face to hers, brushing her lips with mine, wanting her, needing her.

She kisses me back, hard, angrily, and I taste her tears and they break my heart. But a second later she's pushing at my chest, putting distance between us. I stand there, stunned. Her breathing is rushed, her face pale.

'This is my life—I can do whatever the hell I want.'

'And what do you want?'

She stares at me for several long seconds and I wait, my breath held captive by my lungs. 'Oh, go to hell.'

When she stalks away this time I let her go, but I watch her all the way to the corner, where she turns and fades from view.

Fuck it, I'm completely screwed.

I've had three vodkas, no dinner, and I feel like I can finally put Barrett and the damned Harts out of my mind. So why am I here, staring at Barrett's hotel room door, contemplating pressing the buzzer?

Because I want to be with him one last time. I didn't know, last time, that it would be the end for us, or I might have slowed it down, remembered more about it. I don't do seconds, I'm usually happy with a brief encounter, but Barrett's been more than that—I'm not dumb enough to pretend otherwise—and I don't feel like we've had the closure I need.

Or maybe it's just that I've had three vodkas, no dinner, and he looked pretty fucking great at the café today.

I knock before I can change my mind and as soon as he pulls it open I launch myself at him, not giving him a second to question this, not giving him a second to question me. I kiss him hard, just like outside the café earlier. I kiss him and I swallow any questions he might have, any conversation he may want to make.

I'm done talking.

My hands push at his shirt, lifting it up his body, over his head; we have to break our kiss but as soon as the shirt's gone I'm back, scrambling up his frame right as he lifts me, holding me to him so I feel the hardness of his chest, his cock, all of him, and I move my hips, trying to get closer to him, needing him, wanting him so badly it hurts.

'What the fuck?' He doesn't stop kissing me though. Instead, his hands push at my own shirt, freeing it from my body, his mouth dropping to my breasts, pulling at a nipple through the bra so I arch my back and lift my arms, needing so much more. He understands, carrying me through the hotel suite towards his bedroom, his mouth on mine the whole time.

Relief splinters inside me as he drops me back against the mattress—the certainty that the oblivion of pleasure is at hand all that I need.

One last time and then I'll leave, and this time it will be for good. I promise.

CHAPTER TWELVE

It's NOT UNTIL she's naked against the crisp white hotel sheets that I force myself to wake up from this fantasy. What the hell is Avery doing here, like this? And why am I going along with it? *That's easy, dumbass.*

'Please…' She moves on the sheets, her body shimmying as she reaches for me. Her nipples are taut, her pupils huge, her lips swollen from the force of our kissing, her chest red from my stubble. I stare at her and something inside me snaps. I reach for a condom and pull it on with a sense of grim focus. I want her, but not just like this. Not just now.

My body comes over hers and she parts her legs quickly, wrapping them around me, drawing me closer. I pause at her entrance, look at her face. Her eyes are scrunched closed, and whatever broke inside me a moment ago snaps again.

'Look at me.'

She doesn't. On a groan, I thrust into her, holding my cock deep inside Avery, and then I lift a hand, cupping her face, drawing it towards mine. 'Look at me.' The words are gravelly now, hoarse and filled with something a lot like pain.

She does, blinking towards me then looking away.

'Don't. Don't look over there. Look into my eyes, Avery.'

'Why?' She writhes beneath me, trying to get me to move like she needs, to give her what she wants. I have no doubt she'll go away again after that. Panic makes me desperate.

'Because this isn't just sex. We're making love and that includes looking at each other.'

I pull out of her and then thrust forward, and she groans, closing her eyes.

'Look at me.'

She does, glaring at me and, despite the fact her body is rampant with desire, I can't miss her emotions—her anger, her frustration.

'Let yourself feel this,' I say, moving gently now, slowly, while my eyes stay locked to hers, daring her to look away. She doesn't and, as I move, pleasure drives anger from her face, but whenever she looks away from me I draw her gaze back to mine, so that when we come, our bodies moving to that climax in unison, our eyes are meeting, sharing, communicating.

I drop my face, burying it in her neck, breathing her in, my heart thumping hard against my ribs. She shifts beneath me after only a minute, pulling away from me, pushing my arm off her, getting off the bed. When I look at her she's shaking a little, and her gestures are fast, rapid.

'Thanks for that.'

'This again?'

She looks around but only her pants are in here—her shirt is out in the lounge.

'What?'

'You've got what you want so now you leave? Until the next time you want this itch scratched?'

'No. There won't be a next time.'

I contemplate that, something sharp at my side. I want to shout and scream but at the same time I don't want to hurt her, I don't want to upset her. Fuck, this woman is in my head and I can't get her out.

I compress my lips, the finality of her statement unnerving me and pissing me off in equal measure. 'So that's it? You walk out of here and go back to your life?'

'As opposed to?'

'Staying and facing the music.'

'And what music would that be?'

I can't help it. I stand up, moving closer to her so our bodies connect and our faces are just inches apart.

'This. You and me. The future.'

She pales even further. 'What do you mean?'

'I mean that we've been sleeping together and at the same time falling in love, and you might think you can just click your fingers and bring an end to that, but you can't. I love you and that's not something you can just put back in a box. This is real, Avery. You and me, the way we make each other feel—all my life I've been waiting to meet someone like you. I've met enough women to know how different you are—how different this is.'

'I'm a challenge,' she snaps, shaking her head and stepping away from me. 'And you're deluded if you think any part of this is love.'

'Every part of it is love,' I correct, following her into the living room. She scoops up her shirt and drags it on without a bra. 'Avery, have you ever felt like this?'

She opens her mouth then abruptly shuts it again. A minute later she speaks. 'This is a weird situation. The Harts, the reason you're here—'

'Is completely irrelevant to this.'

I swoop forward, catching her hands and lifting them between us. 'I'm not talking about them. I'm talking about you and me, the way we make each other feel. I'm talking about your strength and your fire and your soul and your heart. I am completely in love with you, Avery.'

She frowns, like I'm speaking a foreign language.

I exhale, speaking calmly. 'You're used to being on your own. That's become something you pride yourself on and I'm asking you to turn your back on that. I'm asking you to open yourself up to a relationship with me—not just sex, love, real, lasting love. I'm asking you to trust in something you've never seen with your own eyes—a happy ending. I'm asking you to trust *me* that we can have that, together. I'm asking you to let me put my heart in yours and keep it there for the rest of our lives.'

Jesus. So much for going slowly. She looks like she's about to pass out. She wrenches her hands away from mine as though I'm spreading acid over her flesh.

'No, God, Barrett, what the actual hell? Don't talk like this, please.'

'Like what?' I ask gently, even when I feel like I'm being split in two. 'Don't be honest with you? Don't point out the obvious?'

'I don't love you.' The words tumble out of her mouth like a fast-flowing waterfall. 'I will never love you. I'm not interested in you for that.'

'You're scared of loving anyone,' I correct quietly.

'Don't do that. Don't psychoanalyse and don't treat me like I don't know my own mind.' She draws herself up to her full height. 'All my adult life I've copped this kind of shit from men who can't understand how a *woman* can have sex and walk away again. Like that makes me deficient in some way or a traitor to my gender when men have been doing this for ever.'

'This isn't about other people and how they choose to live their lives and it's not about how you lived your life before we met. It's not about that,' I correct.

'It's *always* about that. Women are judged by every double standard in the book if they dare admit to enjoying sex.'

'I think women loving sex is just about the hottest thing in the world.'

She glares at me, waiting for the other shoe to drop. So I let it.

'But you don't do this because you enjoy it.'

'Oh?' A beat passes. 'Don't I? Then tell me, Barrett—what do you know about me that I don't about myself?'

'You use sex as a form of control. Control of yourself, of men. Sex is one of the best ways to get close to a person, to feel connected and at one, but you use it to prove to yourself that you can get off and keep a complete, cold distance. Sex is a power play to you.'

Her mouth drops and her breath rushes from her, hitting me in the throat.

'Fuck you.'

'I'm sorry if you don't like that, but it's the truth, as I see it. The second we've had sex you need to put an end to it; you have to kick me out, push me away, show me that you hold all the cards.'

'That's because I use sex as a means to an end and once I'm done, I'm done. What the hell is wrong with that?'

'Nothing, if that's truly what you're doing, but it's not. You do it to show yourself that you're still happy being alone. You can sleep with a guy and walk away. You don't need anything else.'

'What would you know?'

'More than you think.' I grind my teeth together.

'When Caroline was dying, and I saw that shrink, he explained how eating disorders work—how it's not about vanity but about control. And the same could be said of you. You don't hook up with guys because you enjoy it and you want to have fun and get naked. That's what *I* do with the women I sleep with, but newsflash, Avery, I still treat them with respect and civility. I still get to know them, enjoy speaking to them, laughing with them. Because I don't fear closeness like you do. You fear it and you use every opportunity at your disposal to show yourself that you're not going there.'

'Fuck you,' she says again, louder this time.

'You're pushing me away, but just—don't. How about you just stop for a second? Let the wheels stop spinning, let everything stop. Don't think. Just feel. What do you feel in *here*?' I point to her chest, waiting, staring at her. She stares back, and hope lifts me because I know I'm not alone here. I know she feels what I do.

'I feel nothing,' she says, contradicting my certainty. 'No—' she shakes her head '—I feel angry! I feel furious. How dare you come into my life under false pretences then pull it apart, bit by bit? You have no right.' She dashes her hand through the air and looks around until her eyes land on her clutch purse by the door. 'You have no right.' The words are quieter, shaking.

'I love you.'

'Bullshit.' She glares at me. 'You're some kind of

masochist or something, going after the first woman who's *not* jumping up and down to become Countess whatever. That's all this is. You can't handle the fact that I'm not interested in you.'

'If I can't handle anything it's the fact you're actually going to push me away now, despite how great this is.'

'This doesn't feel great, Barrett. It feels like hell on earth.' She wrenches the door open. 'No sex, even the best, is worth this. Don't ever call me again.' She sucks in a deep breath, like she's waiting for me to say something. I rack my brain but draw a blank. 'And tell the Harts to go to hell.'

'Wait.' It's the best I can do in that moment. 'Just—don't go yet.'

'Why? Why should I stay?'

The earth is shifting beneath me. I love her, and I honestly think she loves me, but maybe I'm wrong? Maybe I've read this whole thing wrong. Maybe I don't know her like I think.

'You have ignored me at every opportunity.' She stands tall, her back ramrod-straight. 'You have ridden roughshod over everything I've said and asked of you. But not this time; I won't allow it. I'm not what you think, and I don't want what you're offering.'

The pain is strangely dull. An ache inside me, slow-spreading but undeniable.

'I never want to see you again. I want you out of my life and out of my head.'

'I'm in your head because I'm in your heart.'

A harsh laugh. 'You are unbelievable. How many times and in how many ways can I tell you that I don't love you?' She glares at me, her words like arrows darting through my bloodstream. 'And, what's more, I honestly think I hate you right now.'

I compress my lips, wanting to fight but also knowing maybe she's right. I have been ignoring her this whole time, ignoring what she's said because I've had faith in how I think we both feel.

'You don't mean anything to me. In a week's time I won't even remember your name.' Her chin tilts defiantly and she holds my gaze for several seconds before stalking away from me. I watch her go, my gut twisting, and the worst of it is, I don't doubt her words any more. When Avery decides to do something she's unstoppable and right now she's decided to erase me from her life.

She's been trying to push me away from the beginning and, finally, I have to let her, even when that hurts like hell.

I have no idea if he passed my message along to the Harts. Maybe he did and they're just really bad at taking no for an answer as well because, six weeks after I left Barrett's hotel room, it's become impossible to ignore them.

It started slowly. An email from Jagger, which I ignored. Then an email from Theo, and finally from Holden. A second email from Jagger mentioned Barrett and my heart almost froze in my chest.

Barrett's explained that we need to take it slowly. We just want to meet you—to get to know you, little by little.

Barrett explaining anything about me fills me with a strange ache low in my chest.

Six weeks since I last saw him and I have barely stopped thinking about him. After two weeks I forced myself to accept that it's more than sexual infatuation. If that were the case, I could go to a bar and hook up with some other guy, just like I used to. But I don't want that. My body craves Barrett.

And it's so much more. Tears fill my eyes when I think of the time we spent together. Every conversation is scored like lines in my heart. Worst of all is that last one.

I don't love you. I will never love you. I'm not interested in you for that.

I will never forget the way his face moved in response to those words. The look in his eyes—hurt and sadness—and all because of me.

You don't mean anything to me. In a week's time I won't even remember your name.

If only he knew that I have remembered his name and everything about him every single minute since that night. If only he knew? I shake my head because if he knew that it would mean—something terrifying. Something real.

I don't fear closeness like you do.

Maybe he was right. Maybe that's why I've been

alone for so long—maybe this is less about independence and more about fear? Maybe the reason I have been point-blank refusing to have the Harts in my life is because I'm afraid that if I let them in we'll grow close and then they'll hurt me or leave me.

My stomach twists and my breath burns.

I've been through this time and time again over the last six weeks, until my brain feels like it's mushy and my head about to explode. I suppose I've agreed to meet them to prove him wrong, in a way. To show him—and myself—that I'm not afraid of this.

But honestly, I am. I'm terrified. I stand outside the hotel—despite having a hotel and casino in San Francisco they've chosen a neutral location, perhaps out of deference to me. It's thoughtful but it hasn't ultimately helped my nerves.

I am freaking out.

At least in meeting them today I can get them off my back. They're not going to let this go, so by coming here, letting them see me, ask me whatever they want to know, I can go away again and put them out of my mind.

I stare at the sign, knowing they're waiting for me—I should have been inside fifteen minutes ago. But my knees are weak and all I want, in this moment, is Barrett. I wish he were here. I wish he were standing beside me, holding my hand, walking in with me. I would feel so much better if I were doing this with him.

The thought fires something in my belly. Frustration, because since when did I become dependent on anyone? Let alone him. I can do this.

I use that thought to propel me forward, inside the glass doors and across the foyer. A receptionist smiles up at me.

'Good evening, ma'am. Can I help you?'

'Thanks. I was told I'd need a key to access the elevators—I'm going to the penthouse.'

'Yes. Do you have some ID, Miss Maxwell?'

I flash my driver's licence and the receptionist studies it for a moment then smiles and hands me a key card. 'Elevators are to the left.'

'Thank you.'

I cross the tiled foyer and press a button. An elevator swooshes open almost immediately. Before I can doubt what the heck I'm doing, I swipe the card. A light blinks on for the penthouse.

This is it, then.

'Maybe she's changed her mind?'

My chest hurts. I haven't felt normal all day, knowing what this means. Knowing I'm about to see Avery again is a huge part of that, but this isn't about me. I'm not here because I want to see her more than anything else on God's good earth. I'm here because I know what this must be costing her, and I know how she must be feeling, and I want her to have at least one familiar face in the room. Just in case she needs me.

No sex, even the best, is worth this. Don't ever call me again.

I have heard those words a thousand times since she spoke them. They have filled my sleeping head to form nightmares I want to fight against; they have become a part of my living breath—because the temptation to pick up my phone and call her has almost overwhelmed me at times.

A need to hear her voice—but not as it was on that night, full of anger and recrimination—is a compulsion inside me.

But that's not why I'm here. I told Avery how I felt and what I wanted and she made it abundantly clear she didn't feel the same way. Looking back, every bit of time we spent together was characterised by her pushing me away, drawing boundaries, trying to keep what we were in one little box of her life. I was the one who pushed it forward, who tried to turn it into something else.

Maybe she was right. Women generally tend to throw themselves at me. Meeting someone like Avery was fascinating; perhaps it was the novelty factor that made me…but no. I dismiss the thought almost instantly. It was more than that. It was just Avery and me, the way we were together.

I loved everything about her.

'She would have emailed,' Jagger responds to Grace's quiet remark. The air is thick with anxiety.

'She'll be here,' I say firmly.

'How do you know?' It's Theo now, watching me with those intelligent eyes. I keep my expression carefully blank of any emotion.

'If she said she's coming, then she's coming.' I can't explain my certainty more than that. I can't explain that I just *know* Avery.

'But what if she—?'

The buzzing of the doorbell interrupts whatever Asha was going to say. I stand up, looking at the assembled Harts. Six adults, one baby sleeping in a room of this penthouse, and me, some love-sick fool who feels as though his heart is about to slam out of his chest at the prospect of seeing Avery again.

'That must be her.' Cora stands up too, her smile a little tight—she more than anyone understands this, having seen what Holden has been through because of Ryan's irresponsible behaviour.

'Yeah.' I look towards the door for a second before galvanising myself into action. 'I'll get it.'

CHAPTER THIRTEEN

I DON'T KNOW what I'm expecting. One of the brothers. Maybe a hotel maid. Not Barrett, even though I'd been wishing for him with all my heart a second ago.

He pulls the door open and smiles at me, a smile that is familiar and understanding and so filled with kindness despite the awful things I said to him that my knees almost fail to support me. Six weeks compress into nothing in the blink of an eye. I stare at him, feeling every moment we shared like they're happening all over again, and feeling every single moment we've been apart like each one is a kind of eternity.

'Barrett? What are you doing here?'

'I thought you might need a friendly face.' He looks over his shoulder, moves a little closer to me. 'Is that okay?'

As though I might not want him here. I can't blame him for feeling doubt on that score, after what I said. I hate that we argued like that. I hate what I said to him. I hate that I hurt him. I hate that he left. More than anything I hate that I want to apologise to him, but this isn't the time because I can't pull him outside and be alone with him when there's a host of Harts waiting to see me.

'Yeah.' My voice is hoarse. 'I'm...glad you're here.' It doesn't come close to saying what I really feel. I am beyond glad. His presence is everything to me in that moment. 'Thank you.'

He drops his head in a silent nod. 'Of course.' It's businesslike, almost as though he's simply discharging an obligation. 'You ready?'

I'm more ready now, with Barrett here, than I was a moment ago. 'I just want to get it over with.'

He opens the door a little wider and, deep inside the penthouse, in a beautiful living room framed by windows that showcase the water like a sparkling backdrop, are the notorious Harts.

'Oh, God.' My stomach loops. He reaches down and squeezes my hand reassuringly—at least I presume that was his intention but it's not reassuring because it sets off a cacophony of feelings inside me, like being buzzed with a live wire.

My eyes jerk to his and it's even worse. Electricity sparks between us. I pull my hand away then smile awkwardly, apologetically. Fuck, I'm a mess. How could he have *ever* thought he was in love with me? He is such a great guy. So nice and kind and mature—Exhibit A, him putting aside that night, that fight, and coming here today just to support me. Who does that?

Barrett, that's who. The same Barrett who listened to a throwaway comment about Disneyland and understood that it was a dream of my heart and so made it happen for me.

At the entrance to the lounge my nerves become almost deafening. The room is full of people. I look from one to the other, trying to see familiarities in them, things about myself that I can recognise, but there's nothing really.

They stand up. My stomach loops. Barrett's hand in the small of my back propels me forward.

'Avery, this is Jagger.' He starts by introducing one of the brothers. He has blond hair, cropped close to his head, and eyes that are thoughtful. 'And Grace.' He indicates the woman at Jagger's side. She's pregnant, about six months along, I'd guess.

'Hi.' Her smile is loaded with warmth. Jagger is just staring at me, like he's seen a ghost.

'Hi.' Anxious. High-pitched. I swallow.

'Theo and Asha.' He draws me to another couple. They're holding hands, and I feel Theo's anxiety. Somehow, it's relaxing to me, that they might be nervous about this too.

'Pleased to meet you.' Again, it's Asha who speaks, not the Hart.

I nod jerkily, not quite able to return the sentiment.

'And Holden and Cora.' Cora's smile lights up her face. Holden regards me with the same sense of hesitation I'm feeling. That relaxes me even further.

'Some family reunion, huh?'

A couple of them laugh.

I feel Barrett's breathing beside me. I feel his heart beating, somehow. I feel everything.

'Have a seat.' Jagger gestures to one of the armchairs. I choose the sofa instead, hoping Barrett will sit beside me.

'Would you like a coffee?' Barrett offers, his eyes warming me to the tips of my toes.

I bite down on my lip, so close to tears at his perennial kindness, and even more so because I honestly don't deserve it.

'Or something stronger,' Theo offers over Barrett's shoulder.

I'd love a coffee—just to have something to do with my hands—but I don't want Barrett to leave the room. I shake my head jerkily.

'No, thanks.'

His eyes narrow almost imperceptibly and then perhaps he understands, because he takes the seat beside me, not close enough to touch but he's there, a wall of strength at my side.

'This must have come as quite a shock,' Grace says after a few quiet, awkward moments.

I look at her gratefully. 'You could say that.'

'We didn't know about you.' It's Holden. His voice is gruff, his bearing defensive. I warm to him. I get the feeling we're kindred spirits, and not just because of the surprises we've borne. It's strange, given that he's the one I don't actually have a biological connection to.

I nod. 'Barrett told me.'

'It was an accident we even found you.' Theo now. I nod once more.

'The thing is—' Jagger takes over '—our father was a bastard. He never saw a beautiful woman he didn't want to take to bed.'

Grace lifts her hand and runs it over Jagger's back, soothing him, her smile sympathetic.

'He was selfish and pretty much didn't give a shit who he hurt. We saw that time and time again,' Jagger continues.

'Our home was pretty much a warzone,' Theo explains further. 'It gave a new meaning to the term "honeymoon period", because for a brief time, after he'd first married a new wife, or moved some woman in, there'd be peace and happiness. But it never lasted. He'd cheat. A lot. Some women turned a blind eye to that, others made him pay non-stop.'

Sympathy shifts inside me. Honestly, I've been so focused on my own fallout from this that I didn't really stop to think about these men, and the boys they were, and the way they were raised.

'He knew he wasn't my father,' Holden cuts in, his eyes boring directly into me. The woman at his side, Cora, moves a little closer to him, and something strikes me about these six people. They're a family—and their love is so completely apparent. Their love as couples, the way they're supporting each other, helping each other through this, and the way the brothers finish each other's sentences.

It makes me feel completely empty and alone—

and not in a good way. Not in the way I've spent the last ten years boasting about, like being alone is a sign of independence. Maybe independence is about strength, and strength comes from relying on some people, sometimes.

'But he never thought to tell me that,' Holden continues. 'He didn't leave a note, he didn't give Barrett a heads-up, even knowing Barrett would keep it confidential until after Ryan's death.' Holden shakes his head in frustration. 'I have no idea who I am because the man who raised me never thought about it. He was careless and that carelessness has left a path of destruction in its wake.'

'We've all hated him on and off for years.' Jagger's smile is laced with grief. 'Though we've loved him too.' He sighs. 'But we understand why you'd hate him.'

I look to Barrett without meaning to. His eyes meet mine and it's a literal shot in the arm. I smile— just a very small lift of my lips. He smiles back. My heart stutters.

'I hate what he did to my mother,' I say softly. 'But, from what Barrett's told me, I don't think it's likely he knew anything about me.'

'We've come to the same conclusion.' Theo nods. 'He would have insisted on raising you.'

I swallow, sweeping my eyes across the men in the room, thinking how different that would have felt, growing up with them, not with my mom. Tears bring a taste of salt to my mouth; I swallow it away.

'That's what Barrett said.'

'Barrett knew Ryan as well as we did.' Holden stands, moving to the bar. 'You sure you don't want something?' he offers, grabbing out a sparkling mineral water for himself.

'A water would be great, thanks.' He grabs another bottle for me, walks across and places it in my hand. I stare down at the label, overwhelming emotions filling me.

'The thing is, Avery…' Jagger again. 'We've already paid for the sins of our father. A lot. And we don't want to keep doing that. You're our *sister*, and we want you to be in our lives.'

Barrett clears his throat softly, warningly.

'I don't mean right away,' Jagger hastens to add.

'We don't want to scare you,' Theo corrects.

I laugh, despite the seriousness of this. 'You guys, I'm not—there's no rule book for this. We're all flying completely blind. I'm way outside my comfort zone, as I'm sure Barrett's told you.' They all look at each other a little quizzically.

'Actually, he's given us frustratingly little information about you,' Holden throws in. 'Probably why we kept harassing you for this meeting.'

My heart turns over in my chest. I don't risk looking at Barrett again.

'The whole Hart thing is a bit overwhelming,' Cora says gently, and I wonder then about these women and their paths to love with some of the highest profile billionaires in the world. 'But you get used to it.'

'The planes and private islands kind of make it worthwhile,' Grace interjects, with a grin that shows me she's joking.

'It's not—' I shake my head. 'I understand how you feel. You're curious. Blindsided, right? But I'm not—' What? In the market for a family? I look at all of their hopeful faces and feel something shift inside me. Something hard and sharp, something that I've carried for a long time gives way, leaving me with a sense of confusion and uncertainty, a worrying niggle that I've been very wrong for a long time. I sigh. 'I'm not sure what we should do next.'

'I am.' It's Theo.

We all look at him expectantly.

'Avery, will you join us for dinner?'

I thought dinner might mean eating out but, instead, they cooked and I watched in awe as the Hart family became like something out of a telemovie, the kind I used to watch an inch from the set as a kid, unable to believe the quick conversation, the affectionate ribbing, the sentences not finished because it wasn't necessary—they understood what they were saying without voicing all the words. I watched while they cooked and we ate together, and the whole evening was surreal and wonderful but also it existed in a kind of dream state because Barrett was there and I found my eyes tracking him constantly, watching him and how well he fit in with this family—if I didn't know differently, I would have thought he was one of them, but he's not; he's an outsider like me.

Except neither of us is an outsider really. He grew up with them, and knows them intimately. And I'm their sister. My heart begins to pound as that explodes through me—no longer just an abstract concept I can weigh in my hands and decide if I want to grab hold of it. I *am* their sister—fact, reality, my existence. My pulse rushes. Trying to deny this was the stupidest thing I've ever done. Did I really think I could pretend this wasn't happening?

My eyes dart to Barrett. He's talking to Asha—Theo's wife—and she's laughing at something he said, leaning close conspiratorially. I watch with curiosity. It would be stupid to be jealous—she's married to Theo and clearly adores him. But I'm reminded of Barrett's universal appeal, his charisma and charm, of how completely he stood out that night in the bar.

My gaze lingers on them for a moment, my pulse a deafening tone in my ears, but not because I'm jealous. No, it's because I'm seeing everything so much more clearly, like accepting the reality of this—that I have a family, whether I want them or not, makes it impossible to keep pretending certain other things aren't a part of who I am.

I've been trying to control every aspect of my life, including my feelings, but that doesn't make them any less real. Not wanting to get hurt doesn't make me any less likely to love—it just makes me a coward for not acting on it. What was it my mom used to say? *Only fools don't feel fear. Only fools let that fear control them.*

Was that what I was doing?

He lifts his gaze to me and for a moment there is just him and me in this gorgeous penthouse, our eyes locked, our breathing in unison. And then I look away because I'm terrified of the strength of my feelings—and I have no idea if I'm going to let that keep controlling me or not.

'I'll walk you down.' It's Jagger, his smile kind, his wife Grace busy tending to their baby Felicity, who's just woken with a bad dream.

'Oh, you don't have to—'

'It's fine.'

I look past him to Barrett, who's sitting watching me, his expression guarded as though he's waiting for me to say something, but I have no idea what. My stomach loops.

I want Barrett to come with me—to walk me down so we can talk. But I don't know how to manoeuvre that and he's not offering. Uncertainty rushes through me. He said goodbye to me with the others—just a general goodbye, nothing special, nothing to indicate he feels anything at all for me now, except for kindness—the same kindness he'd feel for anyone.

Someone says something to Barrett but he keeps looking at me for a couple of seconds, offering a small smile that is laced with resignation and fare-well, and then turns towards Theo and Asha.

My gut swoops to my toes.

'So we'll see you tomorrow?'

It takes me a couple of seconds to catch what Jagger's said, let alone what he means. Then I remember—we're having dinner again.

My heart speeds up. Barrett.

'Yeah, sounds good. Let me know what I can bring.'

'We've got it covered.'

The elevator doors ping open; we step inside. I mull over this, looking at him a little uncertainly then focusing on the shiny metallic doors.

'How long did you say you're in town for?'

'Just a week.'

I nod. 'All of you?'

'Holden and Theo might stay a few days longer—we've got to get back to Sydney for Grace's dad's birthday.'

Despite the knots in my tummy, I smile at that—at the picture of happy domesticity and normality it paints, the idea that, even after a childhood marred by the mistakes of Ryan Hart, Jagger has found his way to a happiness that is real and genuine, to an extended family that is full of love.

But the knots in my tummy don't dissipate; if anything, the fast movement of the elevator makes them worse, so when the elevator lands on the ground floor and the doors ping open to the lobby, I rush the question, 'And Barrett?'

If Jagger thinks it's odd, he doesn't show that at all. 'He flies out tomorrow morning.'

My chest feels as though it's being split wide open. 'Oh? So soon?'

'He's got a meeting in Amsterdam.'

I nod, trying so hard not to show how I'm feeling, even when I'm sure it must be written all over my face. 'Right.' A bright smile. 'Of course.' I step into the foyer.

'Thanks for coming tonight, Avery. We know how hard it was for you.'

'It was a lot easier than I thought it would be, actually.' I can barely smile. I'm numb at the idea of Barrett going away again so soon. 'See you tomorrow.'

I turn and leave before I can do something really stupid like cry, or ask Jagger for advice on how to fix everything with Barrett.

An hour and a half after leaving the penthouse, I'm starting to think waiting for Barrett was a really stupid idea. Three cups of coffee and I'm restless and uncertain and wondering if maybe he's going to stay in the penthouse rather than leave it—or perhaps he's got another room in this hotel? I was banking on the fact I thought he'd follow me out, but ninety minutes have passed and there's still no sign of him.

Which leaves me with what? What are my options? I lift my phone from my bag and open our messages. But when I scan up through the history and see the last ones we sent each other, my heart feels like it's going to break.

There's a place in South Beach—The Lighthouse.
Do you know it?

I can Google.

Great. Four o'clock?

Sure. See you then.

That's what we became in the end. I hurt him on
the Disneyland night. I did everything he accused me
of—pushed him away, because he'd broken through
so many barriers by then I was terrified of never
being able to put them back in place.

Now my biggest fear isn't that I'll get hurt or be
left alone, it's that I'm incapable of being in a relationship with someone and not hurting them. And the
idea of hurting Barrett like I already have, of doing
that again and again and again because of who I am
is enough to turn my blood to ice.

I love him. I really do, but when I think about
it I realise loving him means walking away from
him—for his sake. Barrett Byron-Moore is one of
the kindest, sweetest guys in the world and he deserves a woman who will bring him only happiness.

That's not me.

'Oh, crap.' Tears sting my eyes. I stare at the coffee cups for a second and feel like a total fool. Pulling a twenty from my purse I slide it under one of
the saucers and stand up, blinking my eyes furiously.
Out of habit I scan the foyer, right as the elevator

pings open and Barrett strides out, his head bent, his eyes fixed on the ground before him. I stay where I am, staring at him, my body paralysed into inaction, watching him walk across the lobby.

This is it—the moment to let him go, to do what I know I should. Am I really strong enough though? At the doors he lifts his head, looking towards me without intending to find me, with no idea that I'm still there. I can see that on his face—the genuine shock in his features. He stops walking, turns to face me, stares for several long seconds so I have no idea what he's going to do, and then, finally, he walks in my direction.

My heart leaps and leaps. My stomach crunches.

'Avery?'

I nod. Then feel like an idiot. He wasn't actually asking my name—it was shorthand for 'why are you still sitting here?'

'You left hours ago?'

'An hour and a half,' I clarify defensively, then grimace because it's not a substantive fact to dither over.

'Right. Did you—?' He frowns. 'Were you wanting to see them again? To go back up?'

I shake my head, words failing me.

Crap. Don't cry. Just—hold it together.

'No, I—'

Make something up! Tell him you had an urgent work call! Anything other than admit the truth.

'Didn't feel like going home yet.'

He nods, like this makes perfect sense even when it's quite absurd.

'And now?'

'I—' He's going to call me a cab. He's going to help me get home, because that's what Barrett does. He helps, he's kind, he's awesome. Suddenly, the fact he once loved me makes me want to weep because the gift of his love is just about the best thing in the world and I threw it in his face as though it were worthless.

'Want me to walk you?'

Something snaps in the region of my heart. 'To walk me…to my place?'

'Sure. Why not?'

I frown. It's only a mile or so from here. 'Where are you staying?'

His lips compress in a line and for a second I see something like sadness shroud his expression. 'I'm not asking to spend the night with you, Avery. I'll grab a cab from yours.'

'I didn't mean that.' *Exactly. You can't even open your mouth without saying the wrong thing to him.* I close my eyes for a second, regrouping. When I look at him, I hope he sees genuine apology in my face. 'I'd like it if you'd walk me home.'

He nods, but there's tension between us now, and I hate it. My chest hurts. 'How did your presentation go?' I ask as we step out of the sliding glass doors onto the street. It's late, but there are still a few people around, cars humming past.

'It went well, thanks.'

'I'm glad.' Silence. Awkward, heavy, accusatory silence. 'Jagger says you have a meeting in Amsterdam.'

'Day after next.' He nods, pausing beside me at a set of lights.

I consider this. 'So you—?'

'Yes?' He looks down towards me, our eyes meeting, my heart pounding.

'You came just for this?'

Something shifts in his expression, something he tries to suppress. 'Sure.' He jams his hands in his pockets.

'I—'

'How did you—?'

We speak at the same time. He lifts his brows, urging me to continue.

'No, you go.'

'I was going to ask what you thought of them.' We cross the road side by side, a careful distance apart, not touching. The coldness of that, the difference to how we've been in the past, fills me with a deep ache.

I bite down on my lip. 'I think they're…nice.'

'Nice?' His brows shoot up.

'Normal. Just a family, and a happy family. I think I was fighting this whole situation without really thinking about what I was doing.'

I want to expand on that, to tell him I did the same with him, but I'm so freaking nervous I can barely string two words together. I've never done this before and it's not like six weeks ago—it's not like the night he told me he loved me. I have no idea how he feels about me now—I only know that I reacted to him in a way that most people would struggle to forgive.

'I'm glad you feel that way. They're good people, Avery. And they care about you; they want you to be a part of their family.'

'I know.' I smile at him, the smile costing me because my heart is breaking apart.

'I—'

'They—'

He laughs now, a soft sound that makes my insides squeeze. So familiar, so different.

'Your turn.'

My nerves increase exponentially. We keep walking and with every step I hope some form of clarity will come to me.

'I was glad to see you tonight.'

Silence. We walk side by side for a while, and then his voice emerges, gravelly and deep. 'I wasn't sure you would be.'

'Really?'

'Sure. We didn't exactly part on friendly terms.'

My chest squeezes.

'So why did you come?'

'Because I knew how huge this was for you.' He shrugs. 'I thought a familiar face might make it easier, and I figured if you didn't want me there you could just tell me to go away.'

'Right, like I did last time.'

'Technically, you just told me not to call you, but yeah, more or less.'

I stop walking and close my eyes, wanting to blot the memories out and bring air into my lungs. I feel as though I'm drowning on dry land, right here in the middle of Noe Valley.

'Barrett—' When I open my eyes he's watching me. That doesn't help. 'I'm sorry about that night.' The stars twinkle overhead. He doesn't move; it's almost as though he's not breathing. I search for what else I want to say, but then he gives a half-smile and turns, beginning to walk again.

'It's fine.' His words come from over his shoulder. I move quickly to keep up. 'I mean, you were pretty clear all along. I don't know why I thought things had changed between us.'

He's still ahead of me. I reach out, grabbing his wrist so he stops walking and turns to face me. 'Because they had, Barrett. Everything had changed and I fought that so hard.'

His expression tightens. There's wariness there, a look of confusion. 'It doesn't matter, right?'

Right. Because he doesn't love me any more. I missed my opportunity. Except—he's here. To support me. He didn't say he came to make this easier for the Harts. He came for me. Why would he do that if he didn't still care? And isn't love supposed to be more robust than that? Barrett's never met a woman that he fell in love with. Do I seriously think it would have evaporated at the first hurdle? Or is that just my attempt to throw excuses in my way so I don't have to be brave and tell him that I love him too? Because maybe he doesn't love me, but I think he still does, and unless I'm brave he's not going to do anything about it.

This is all down to me.

'I messed up.' Jeez, it feels so good to say those words. 'I mean, I really messed up.'

He stops walking again, and I see from his back that he's drawing in a deep breath before turning to face me. 'Yeah?'

Still there's that wariness. Man, I need to get him to trust me. I need to— 'I've never known anyone like you. Even from that very first night you were so different, and fascinating, and you challenged me in every way. I have no idea what love is meant to look like. I'm not like you. I didn't grow up with parents hugging on the sofa or whatever. I have no experience of this. I just know that seeing you became an obsession with me. I thought about you constantly—I *think* about you constantly—and the more entrenched you became in my DNA the more I wanted to send you away and get back to my "real" life because needing someone like I needed you is the antithesis of what I think of as safe.'

My words settle between us, sharp and urgent. He stares back at me, his mouth opening as his mind works to process the things I've said.

'I wasn't ready to admit that to myself, and I sure as hell didn't know how to put it into words. That

night, when you told me you loved me, I freaked out.
I panicked and I did the one thing I know how to do
really well—I pushed you away, just like you said.
But if you don't think I've spent every single minute
of the last month and a half missing you like wildfire
then you're crazy. I love you, Barrett. I think I started
falling in love with you the minute we met and I know
I'll never stop. I'm sorry I didn't understand that, and
I'm sorry I hurt you. Most of all I'm sorry that maybe
you won't want to trust me again, but if you'll give me
another chance I promise I won't mess this up again.'

He continues to stare at me. Panic and pain writhe
inside me. 'I get why you'd—'

His finger presses to my lips, silencing me for a
moment. I stand there, looking up at him, my eyes
filled with all the hope I carry in my heart.

'I love you,' I say, muffled against his finger.

He keeps staring at me, and then he drops his
hand, putting it on my shoulder.

'These last six weeks have been the worst of my
life and I have no idea why I haven't called you but,
seeing you tonight, everything slammed into me and
I don't want you to leave here without knowing how
I feel.' A frown pulls on my lips. 'I don't know how
that works. You're in London and I'm here but I want
to make this work, somehow. If you want to.'

He makes a noise—a laugh? A groan? And then
he's kissing me, his lips crushing mine, his arms
wrapping around me. Thoughts become impossible
to hold onto. I surrender to this—the physicality of

our togetherness, feeling everything, loving it, loving him, needing this. I know it's complicated but I don't care. We'll work out complicated.

I pull away, just so I can look at him to make sure this isn't a dream, and he smiles at me, a dazed kind of smile, like he didn't see this coming.

'You have no idea how much I wanted to hear those words,' he says gently, running his thumb over my lower lip. 'I didn't come here with any agenda, and I sure as hell didn't hold out any hope, but I wanted, with every fibre of my being, for it not to be the end for us.'

He weaves his fingers through mine, so we start walking towards my place once more. My heart is about a thousand times lighter now, though.

'I couldn't tell how you felt about me,' I admit. 'I didn't know if you still loved me, or if you were angry at me—'

'Angry at you? Are you kidding me? When I opened the door and you were on the other side it took all my willpower not to barrel you back into the elevator and whisk you away somewhere.'

'I didn't pick up on that.'

He shakes his head ruefully. 'I felt it, Avery.' He angles his face towards mine. 'Why did you think I was there?'

'Because you're a great guy—kind and sweet and thoughtful—and you wanted to do the right thing by me?'

'That's true.' He laughs. 'The bit about me wanting to do right by you. I would always have come today, to try to support you, but every word you said was like sandpaper against my flesh because I wanted you to talk just to me! I wanted to be the only one in the room, hearing all your words and thoughts. I desperately wanted to be alone with you.'

'You barely spoke to me at all.'

'Yeah.' He squeezes my hand. 'I was afraid if I started I wouldn't be able to stop. And I didn't want to monopolise you. This night wasn't about me.'

My heart spins inside me. 'You really are a great guy.'

'You're not so bad yourself, Avery.'

But that sobers me. 'The thing is, I'm not like you. I'm worried—'

'What is it?'

'Part of what scares me is that I might hurt you. That you…'

'Go on.'

'That you deserve someone better.'

He smiles, a dazzling smile, and begins to walk. We turn a corner and I see my home, just a block away.

'Well, that's an easy one to answer.'

'Yeah?'

'There is no one better. Not for me.' He pulls me back into his arms. 'You are my other half, Avery Maxwell, and I'm really hoping you'll agree to be that for the rest of our lives.'

My jaw drops. 'Are you—?' *Is he proposing?*

He grins. 'Not yet. I mean, unless you want me to.'

I'm silent—surprised by how much I do want that.

'I'm saying you are everything I've ever wanted in life, and that one very long lifetime with you won't ever feel like enough. We can work out where we live and how we make this work, but not making it work isn't an option. I'm saying you've made me the happiest man on earth right now and I want to think of an appropriate way to thank you.'

My heart turns over in my chest. Tears fill my eyes. 'I can definitely think of one way.'

'Yeah?'

'Come home with me?'

He grins, pulling me closer to him. 'Really? You don't want me to catch a cab back to my hotel after all?'

I punch his chest playfully. 'I never did! That was all you.'

He drops his head so our brows are touching. 'Well, if it's okay with you then Avery, do you mind if I spend the night?'

'And every night for the rest of your life,' I agree, lifting up so my lips can brush his. 'I promise I won't ever send you away again, Barrett.' And I'm earnest and honest, meaning everything I say. He carries me the rest of the way home and I honestly doubt my feet will ever touch the ground again.

EPILOGUE

'WELL, WHAT DO you think?'

'Besides how loud it is?' I blink up at Barrett, my smile showing that I'm not serious. It's true, though. The noise has become almost deafening. But it is the very best kind of noise—that born of happiness and love, of sheer giddy joy. It is the noise born of a rich tapestry of family and friends.

We are surrounded by those we love most in the world. Strange how admitting I loved Barrett was like opening the floodgates to love in general. It was easy to love my brothers, easier still to love their wives, and Felicity and the other children? They hugged their way into my heart in no time flat. As for Barrett's parents?

I shift my gaze across the crowded gazebo, spotting them easily. They are on the edge of the dance floor, he in a tuxedo and she in a stunning mauve dress, all frothy and elegant. Their eyes hold and they move in perfect unison. They are, as Barrett told me over a year ago, the epitome of love and connection.

'I think it's perfect,' I correct a moment later.

One of our little flower girls—still wide awake despite the lateness of the hour—toddles towards us and Barrett sweeps her up. Eleanor—Felicity's younger sister—grins shyly then nuzzles into his chest. A moment later, Grace appears.

'She keeps running off.' She laughs, holding her hands out to her. Jagger is right behind her, Felicity cradled over his shoulder, fast asleep. Their satin dresses are cream in colour, their tights an opaque white. Somewhere along the line, Felicity has lost one of the shiny ballet slippers she was wearing earlier and one of her stockinged feet has become wet and muddy, courtesy no doubt of the flower-dotted field where the wedding party is taking place.

'How's it going, bro?' Jagger grins, the fact that Barrett is now officially 'part of the family' something all my brothers are pretty pleased about.

'Couldn't be better.' With his spare arm he wraps me close, and my heart skips a beat at the near perfection of this. Near because, even in this moment, when I have almost everything I could ever want in life, I am conscious of my mother's absence. It's not a heavy sadness though—not like it used to be. Loving Barrett has meant talking to him about my mother, sharing things, bringing her back to life in a way that I never comprehended to be within my power. It's just like he explained about Caroline— I needed to find a way to honour Mom, and I have. Talking about her makes her more a part of my life and I'm grateful for that.

Theo arrives, followed by a waitress carrying a tray of champagne. 'Too many empty hands.' He grins, gesturing for us to each take a drink. I do, cradling it between my fingertips, breathing in its sweet fragrance.

Behind him, I see Asha with her phone pressed to her ear, and baby Pierre asleep in her arms. Pierre is the spitting image of Theo—the family likeness is striking. I even see a little of myself in him, something in his eyes when he's watching you, and for someone who thought they were completely alone most of their lives, you can imagine how surreal that is.

The song comes to a gentle close and Holden and Cora join us next. She's stifling a yawn. At nearly nine months pregnant, I have no idea how she's still awake, let alone smiling beautifully and walking on wedge heels.

'Sorry.' Asha moves to stand beside Theo, her phone tucked back in her clutch purse.

I shake my head in response to her apology. 'Work?'

'Always.' But her smile shifts to Theo.

'Well?'

'We did it.'

We all wait, and then she encompasses us in her look. 'Angel Pie just won Brand of the Year.' She refers to the teen cosmetic line she developed and launched a few years ago. 'It's huge recognition—we were going up against some heavy hitters, including Fleurs Sauvages.' She names her parent company, which was founded by her grandfather. Her eyes drift to their son, fast asleep in her arms, and then shift to Grace and Jagger's daughters. 'It just felt so important, for this generation to have access to cleaner cosmetics. But I never expected it would achieve all this.'

'I did.' Theo kisses her cheek. 'I'm so proud of you.'

My heart turns over in my chest. The love that surrounds us is palpable.

'Has everyone got a drink?' Jagger addresses us.

'Hang on a second.' Holden retrieves a glass of juice from a passing waiter. I eye it a little enviously as he passes it to Cora. 'Okay, now we're good.'

'A toast.' He lifts his glass and we all follow suit. 'To the happy couple. A man who has been, for as long as I can remember, a brother to us, and a woman we are so lucky to have now as a sister.'

'To the happy couple.' They chink in unison. I swallow past a lump of emotion in my throat.

'To the Harts,' I respond, eyeing them slowly. 'I thought I was complete.' I look up at Barrett, my heart almost hurting with how full it feels. 'It's because of you that I met Barrett and because of Barrett that I remembered it's okay to love.' I'm sure my smile is unbearably romantic. I don't care. If a woman can't be soppy on her wedding day, then when can she be?

'To family,' Cora adds. 'And all the ways it completes us.'

'To family.'

* * *

Much later, when all the guests have gone, Barrett and I stand in the middle of the dance floor, surrounded by twinkling fairy lights, enormous flower arrangements and a quiet army of staff, clearing away the evidence of the wedding. Despite the lack of music, we sway in one another's arms, needing nothing but the beat made by our hearts.

'This place is pretty special.' I shift my gaze away from him, to look towards Ashwyn Hall. It is like he described, but so much more homely than I'd imagined as well. I've been here three times. Once to meet his parents and then, a little over two months ago, for my thirtieth birthday—his parents insisted on organising dinner and a cake. That was the night we got engaged—not far from here, beneath an enormous, ancient oak tree. Somehow, in the intervening months, they pulled this beautiful country wedding together. It was everything I could have hoped for—but, to be honest, so long as I was marrying Barrett I wouldn't have cared where or when.

'It's home—' he grins '—away from.'

For the moment, home is New York. It's a compromise—easy for me to get to the West Coast and for him to fly to Europe, and it has the added advantage of being near two of the three Harts. Jagger, Grace and the girls come over a couple of times a year and we head to Australia at the drop of a hat. Our honeymoon is taking us to the golf course and resort Jagger bought a few years ago, near the Great Barrier Reef.

'I never thought I'd be into all this tradition and stuff.' I turn back to him, my blood rushing through my body.

'But now?'

Something like apprehension moves inside me. What if he's not happy about this? But then, it's Barrett. Barrett, who is kind and good and perfect.

'Now? I can't wait to bring our child here and tell them the tapestry of history they've been born into.'

He grins at me, nodding. 'I like the idea of that.'

He doesn't realise what I've said. 'You do?'

'Yeah. Children. Our children.'

My heart stutters. 'Well, that's a relief.'

He slows, stops dancing altogether. 'It is?'

'Yeah. I mean, I think it's too late to change your mind now.'

'What do you—?'

I curve a hand over my still-flat abdomen. 'Remember the night we got engaged?'

His eyes stray towards the oak tree beneath which, on a carpet of grass and a sky full of stars, we made love for hours. 'Vividly.'

Then, as the penny finally drops, 'You're pregnant?'

'Yep.'

'Avery—' My name is an exhalation on his lips. 'I can't believe it.'

'I'm serious.'

He grins. 'I just mean… I had no idea. How did I not know this?'

'I was waiting until the perfect moment to tell you.' And then, because we're always completely honest with each other, 'And I was a little worried I was tempting fate. Like life was too perfect somehow.'

That sobers him. He drops his forehead to mine. 'Haven't I told you that you deserve everything good in this life?'

I bite down on my lower lip. 'I really feel like I have that.' I lift up and kiss him softly.

'And you always will, my darling.'

*   *   *   *   *

BAD MISTAKE

JC HARROWAY

MILLS & BOON

To G, my very own Big Guy. xx

CHAPTER ONE

Nick

MY MISTAKE-MAKING DAYS are in the past. That's what I repeat as the lift ascends and I brace myself for the vision that I'm certain awaits me on the other side of the doors. Even for a guy who likes to watch, four months is a long time to ignore the ultimate in female temptation. Especially a woman who's paid to showcase her astounding body. But I'm here to protect my client for the next five days while ignoring all the parts of her that make this assignment torture.

I release a sigh, calling on the last line of defence—my hard-won control—in order to face the many challenges I'm up against. The most infuriating is my client's inability to follow the simplest of safety instructions: *wait in your room.*

The lift doors part, the humid, chlorine-scented air rushing in like fog. Of course she chose to hang out at the hotel's pool—a move probably designed to taunt me to the max. Because the pool most likely means a bikini. A bikini means I'll have to avoid looking at her long legs and womanly hips, her sensational arse and pert breasts. All that topped off with the face of an angel wearing a playful smile that could charm the birds from the trees...

I deserve a fucking medal.

I exit the lift and enter the indoor pool-complex, trepidation a tight ball in my gut. My eyes latch onto the object of both my drool and my dread.

Lady Brooke Madden. Model, socialite, businesswoman. The only thing currently in my life that I *can't* control.

Adrenaline smacks me in the head. As predicted, she's bikini-clad. The sight of her relaxed and being herself, not the polished, bubbly, untouchable version the public see, is like walking into a lamppost. Every damned time.

Her name and title scream breeding, class and elegance—and there she doesn't disappoint. But her being everything I'm not, and the opposite of my usual type of woman, is not what causes my sleepless nights and vivid dreams, nor what wakes me rock-hard and dreading another day at the 'office'.

It's the less obvious parts of her I'm drawn to. That almost childlike concentration—as she stoops over her knitting, which makes her seem younger than almost thirty. Her sexy, world-famous body is sprawled over a pool-side lounger, shapely legs casually bent at coltish angles. And her signature white-blonde pixie cut frames a face of doe-eyed sweetness that's too girl-next-door for the savvy businesswoman and brand ambassador who's here in Milan to walk Europe's most prestigious runways.

I shove aside the irrelevant attraction and search my bottomless supply of patience. I've been staring for at least a minute. She hasn't once looked up.

I clench my teeth, chasing the calm I've honed to perfection over the years since I last gave free rein to bursts of emotion. Why couldn't she simply wait for me as instructed while I made a sweep of tonight's fashion-show venue? Despite employing me for her safety, she seems to think the only dangers out there are people toting cameras equipped with tele-photo lenses, sniffing out a story worth selling.

I ignore the pulse thumping in my head as I skirt the otherwise deserted pool. It won't do to show any sign of exasperation. One thing I've learned about Brooke Madden in the four months since she first contracted me for her security—she loves to push boundaries, especially mine.

My fingers curl into fists as I formulate the verbal bollocking I'm obliged to deliver. This twenty-four-seven detail is new territory for us, but my rules are the same. There will be no international scandal—not on my watch. After all, I too have a business to run.

I wait next to her lounger, my rigid body fighting frustration. Does she have no regard for her personal safety? I'm six-foot-four and I keep the physique of a heavyweight boxer, my body the tool of my trade. I'm standing a foot away but she still hasn't noticed my presence. She's clearly deafened by the music coming through her ear buds and too focussed on her damned knitting.

Next time she requests my services I vow that I'll be *busy*. She's just too much trouble. And too much temptation.

Give me strength...

My temperature spikes, beads of sweat forming on my brow. In my line of work, I often meet Brooke Madden's type. Privileged, wealthy women who possess endless power but are naïve to the dangers in the world outside their own sphere. But *I* know those dangers. I've been a part of that darkness. The daily battle for order, control and emotional distance is the price I pay for carrying a piece of it inside me.

I glance down. Whatever it is she's knitting looks fit for the bin. I've never wielded a knitting needle, but even I can see the many holes studding the pale blue knitted rectangle.

'Bloody hell,' she mutters, withdrawing one needle from the stitch she's just worked with frustration and pulling off half a row of stitches in the process. Her shoulders slump. She stares at her handiwork as if the dropped loops of wool will miraculously jump back into place of their own accord.

I'm half-tempted to learn to knit myself, just so I can fix her knitting disasters along with her security and travel logistics. Yeah, right...

No, my role here is simple: protect her and ignore all...*this*.

'What is it meant to be?' I ask, tired of waiting for her to notice my not insignificant—some would say intimidating—presence.

She gasps, one hand flying to the valley between her perky breasts. 'Oh, you made me jump… Hi.'

A tiny frown forms between her perfectly arched brows as she tugs the ear buds from her ears. Her cheeks darken, the colour sliding down that elegant neck of hers, and probably further, to the tops of her incredible breasts. Not that I look. Indulging my stare by dipping that far is strictly off-limits.

I'm so practised at curbing my desires that I've committed every tiny intricacy of her bright blue eyes to memory. I linger there now as I fight the irritation simmering in my blood that she ignored my express instructions.

She holds up the knitting, waving it in my direction as if I'll miraculously be able to decipher its final destiny. 'It's a cardigan, for my baby nephew. Clearly it's a work in progress.' She observes the disaster of holes and tangled wool, her full mouth a little down-turned.

I swallow my rush of amused affection, press my lips together and fight the indulgent smile that has no place in my relationship with this woman.

'Why don't you just buy something?' I don't arse-kiss my famous clients. But she's a conundrum. And, the more I get to know her, the greater the temptation. She has an international modelling career. She's an obscenely successful businesswoman. A household name. She could buy a cashmere version of whatever tiny, delicate garment she's knitting a million times over, but clearly she's determined to master the skill and spread the home-made love to all her friends and family.

She nods, a grin of delight dancing on her lips. 'I should. You know, I like that about you, Nick. You don't fawn like most people. You give it to me straight.' She fidgets with the knitting, wrapping the loose wool around the needles and stuffing it inside her knitting bag, which is emblazoned with the caption *Knitting is my Superpower*.

'So, what's up, Big Guy?' Her wide-eyed innocence is a little act she puts on every time we have a conversation like the one about to go down.

It's almost as if she deliberately tests me with her nicknames, her teasing and her playful personality. Hoping to rile me up enough that I'll flirt back. But my riled-up days are long gone. I'm no longer the reckless young man who once used his intimidating size to earn the respect I mistakenly thought mattered.

'Oh dear, not *that* face...' She smiles, resting back against the pillow and stretching out those endless million-pound legs.

'What face?'

She likes to believe she knows what I'm thinking, but if she could read my mind she'd probably fire my depraved arse.

'The one you do when you're trying to be formidable. I'm immune to it, by the way, but I know it works on other people.'

'So why do you keep hiring me?' I'm not her only security, and it's been hard enough up until now doing the local, one off events. I've started to dread the phone ringing because, aside from being a logistical challenge, she's an enticement I just don't need. But like and idiot, I agreed to this business trip.

A small smile shapes her lush mouth. 'I did my homework. Asked around. Everyone recommends you, Nick.' She tilts her head provocatively, as if I'm a prize cow and she's deciding which cut of meat is the juiciest. 'Although they warned me not to expect idle chit-chat.'

'I talk when there's something worth saying, which is why I need to remind you of the safety recommendations I outlined back in London.'

She uncurls her body, rising from the lounger as if she's being paid to model that bikini—elegant, confident and with some nefarious intent glinting in her eyes.

'I know you said to stay in my room, but it's so peaceful up here in the afternoons. That's why I stay here when I'm in Milan. And I had all this pent-up energy.' She laughs, a tinkling sound that, despite my rigidity, flutters down my spine. 'I wanted to get in a swim before the show tonight.'

'Lady Madden, I can't do my job if you refuse to take my suggestions for your safety seriously.'

She huffs, her hand ruffling her short hair in frustration. 'I've told you a thousand times, Mr Rivers—just call me Brooke.'

She grins more widely, a taunt I'm only too happy to ignore along with the rest of her sensational body. 'Look, I checked that the pool was deserted before I came up here,' she says, donning a hotel robe and scooping up her belongings.

I look down. Despite her statuesque height, I tower over her. 'You didn't hear me approach. I could have been anyone.' I point out the obvious perils of her ignoring my instructions, for which she pays me handsomely. Because I'm the best—personal protection, handler and driver all rolled into one. And while my business, Rivers Security, employs plenty of competent staff that could run this relatively straightforward and low-risk gig, Brooke Madden is the type of woman to demand the personal touch.

Another reason, if I needed it, that she's way too rich for my blood.

She shrugs with nonchalance, although her eyes flick to the roof-top views of Milan. Then she takes a pointed look around the pool. 'We're the only people here. You need a pass key to even access this level.'

She shoves her feet into flip-flops. 'Come on, Nick, I just fancied a swim, and then when I saw I still had the place to myself I stayed to relax a little. I was perfectly safe.'

I clench my jaw. 'Safety is a relative term. The world is a lot less safe than most people realise. And there's no point me being here if you're just going to run roughshod over my professional recommendations.'

No one is always perfectly safe, a lesson I learned in prison. And the person she's most at risk from is me and my fantasies. On the short walk from the lift to her lounger, I envisioned taking her on every available surface this room has to offer. Seeing those crystal-blue eyes wild with arousal, hearing that sweet voice of hers beg for my cock, watching her sultry mouth take my length...

Yeah, safe as houses...

I knew she'd test my detachment and restraint. She always does. Fortunately—or unfortunately, depending on your viewpoint—these days I have discipline to spare. And, as this afternoon's stunt proves, I need it in spades for this client. As her employee, there's a power differential that just doesn't work for me.

Yep, a nice big stack of reasons to keep my dick in my trousers...

Bored of my lecture, she huffs and moves past me. 'Don't be so paranoid.'

'A little bit of paranoia is why I'm good at my job. Why you employ me,' I say, following her towards the lift, my stare determinedly avoiding the way her arse moves under the robe.

'You have other charms,' she tosses over her shoulder with a provocative look. 'There aren't many people I trust enough to have around me twenty-four-seven.' She presses the call button and gazes up at me from under her long lashes in her most flirtatious look yet.

A ripple of unease grips me, tensing muscles. Brooke is a level-headed, practical woman. I have to hope she doesn't imagine we can share more than our turbulent working relationship.

Never going to happen. Not with a woman like her.

A woman who makes me feel a little out of control every time she looks at me, as if trying to figure me out. A woman who'd no doubt run if she knew all the depraved things I want to do to her until I've worked her from my system. A woman I want to drag into the darkness with me…

'You're due at the Palazzo Giorno in an hour,' I remind her, bringing us back to business—a charity fashion-event at a sixteenth-century mansion a few blocks away in central Milan. She's the star of the show, a favourite of the biggest fashion houses in the world.

Brooke nods. 'Thank you for taking care of me so thoroughly.' Her voice is smoke and sin and seduction, despite the rest of her being sunshine. But, just like my body and mind, my ears too can be disciplined.

'I'll jump in the shower and meet you in the lobby in thirty minutes. Will that restore your good humour and banish that scary look from your face?'

I bite my tongue. I rarely display good humour.

And she should be scared. If she had any idea how I want to take care of her—not her welfare or her time management, but her flippant mouth and her sinful body and her sexual pleasure... But I'm not here for that. I've stepped out of my lane once before with a woman like Brooke—easy to fall for but out of my league. The safest risk is no risk at all.

'Text me when you're ready and I'll escort you downstairs,' I say in my usual bland tone. There's no point torturing myself with the room next to hers to simply meet her in the lobby. I need to stay close to her for work. No other reason. Protecting Brooke Madden might present my toughest challenge to date, but I've survived worse. I'm up to the task.

She invades my space now so I'm hit with the scent of her warm skin—a hint of chlorine and the enticing undertones of pure, fuckable woman. Not that fucking her is an option. Not only is she a renowned socialite, the daughter of nobility and one of the UK's most successful exports, she's a client for the next five days. My usual 'one fuck and run' won't work. And in recent years I've developed tastes—ones that help me stave off the worst of my darkness and harness control—that would no doubt shock Lady Brooke Madden to her well-bred core.

'Such a gentleman,' she purrs, her enticing eyes tracing my face.

My body feels so rigid, I might snap with the effort of keeping still. Every impulse I possess clamours for just one touch, just one kiss of that mouth that loves to tease and taunt.

'I'm no such thing. I'm just here to protect you.' Nothing more, nothing less.

And ignore you in order to protect myself.

Because I've spent most of my adult life defying my own base instincts. Bad instincts. One fateful decision, one hot-headed moment of weakness as a youth, changed my life. Better to avoid Brooke's kind of temptation altogether so there's no way I'll repeat the same mistake.

'Of course. But all work and no play makes for a very dull Brooke, so please try to lighten up,' she says, wrapping the robe across her sublime body and tying the belt. 'You've worked for me long enough to know that all I do is work. I love it, of course. But the down side is that I'm always hiding too. Sometimes I just want the freedom to do something normal, like swim in a hotel pool.' She sighs. 'Even that's complicated.'

The lift closes, trapping us in a confessional cocoon. I'm not made of stone, as much as I'd like to be. She's endlessly intriguing. The least dull person I've ever met. Playful, full of boundless energy, charming, funny and kind.

'Lighten up?' I say. There's no lightness left in me, only darkness. And she's the opposite. Another reason I shouldn't have taken this job. But she's persistent. Persuasive. Pushy.

Tell me about yourself, Nick.

What do you do for fun, Nick?
It's okay to relax a little, Nick.

Even if I wanted to lighten up, which I don't, I wouldn't do it with her. Our professional relationship works just fine for me, despite the attraction. We're from different worlds. Ever since my young life imploded at my own reckless hands at the age of eighteen, I've avoided women like Brooke Madden. She's too much like my ex-girlfriend—influential, privileged, used to doors opening without resistance. Even though I brought the helpless and defeated feeling upon myself, I never want to be victim to it again.

Now the life I've engineered for myself is disciplined, predictable and as safe as I can make it. And, aside from taking this job and the temporary temptation of this woman, there's no room for error.

Her lips twitch in a nervous snigger. 'I know you haven't done an overnighter for me before, and I'm here to work, but I also deserve a little down time.'

I bite my tongue. It's not my place to curtail my client's activities.

But...

'In order to protect you I need notice of any unscheduled movements. Anything not on the itinerary forwarded by your assistant requires my prior approval.' Damn, her plans have been set for weeks. Typical Brooke to throw in some impromptu 'fun', whatever the fuck that means. Perhaps a knitting circle...

'Of course,' she says, eyeing me with a curiosity that makes me want to don my dark glasses. 'I appreciate everything you do to keep my name and pictures off the Internet, but surely together we can come up with safe ways and places for me to let my hair down?'

She laughs, then strokes the closely shorn hair at the nape of her neck. 'Not literally, of course.'

'Can we?' I think of all the ways I want to show her a good time, ways miss Goody Knitting Needles would probably quail over. Most involve her naked and following my directions. I'm certain that's not what she has in mind, although I'm not blind to the fact that she finds me attractive. But, despite the flirting, she's too radiant to drag into my darkness, even for a short while. And too risky.

She nods nervously. 'Yes. I don't employ you to babysit me. I have a public profile, but I'm not a nun.'

More's the pity...

'Let's improvise,' she says with a sexy smile. 'That's why I've tagged on a couple of days in Saint Moritz once my work in Milan is complete—a little winter break away from it all. I'm due a holiday and, since I no longer date, you're it to keep me company, I'm afraid.'

I say nothing, my brain still filtering images of Brooke at one of the clubs I frequent, and bombarded with curiosity as to why she no longer dates... My mouth dries at the idea of entertaining her exactly the way I want...

Why is she pushing this agenda? She's usually

astute enough to take the hint that I'm not one for small talk or sharing stories. I'm going to be the worst company she's ever had.

The Brooke Madden too busy doing her thing to see me is hard enough to ignore. This inquisitive, engaging version showing me glimpses of the real woman behind the public persona, and the prodding at my defences is hellish.

The lift reaches our floor and relief drains through me like a cold shower on a hot day.

At her room she hands me her knitting bag while she rummages in her robe pocket for her key card. 'I'm usually pretty energised after a show so, in the spirit of full disclosure, I'd like you to take me for a nightcap later tonight. Somewhere quiet and classy.'

She pushes into her room and turns to face me. 'Okay?'

I want to say no. To confess I prefer it when she's safely tucked up in bed, *her* bed, and I can retreat to my own room from some much-needed breathing space. Not only from the physical temptation, but also because wanting her with the ferocity I do reminds me of my biggest failure, the series of events that decimated my life and the lives of the only two women I've ever loved.

Instead I suck it up, lock down any emotion unrelated to doing my job and nod.

Five nights, four more days.

Protect her. Protect yourself. And never work for her again.

CHAPTER TWO

Brooke

KNOWING NICK IS here somewhere, watching me, floods my body with arousal. His closeness always leaves me fizzing with sexual frustration, but the fact that for the first time I have him captive for five long nights makes this trip ripe with possibilities. Not that he'd allow himself to notice if I walked around naked and painted high-vis orange.

Now there's an idea...

The odds he'd act on our obvious mutual attraction are zero. He's so controlled. So disciplined. But that's why flirtation and seduction were created.

I wait in the wings for my cue for the final walk of the show, my adrenaline spiking to dizzying heights. I recall the way Nick looked at me by the pool—with predatory intent, as if he'd wanted to devour me. Is he looking at me now with the same hunger? Oh, he's usually very good at concealing those urges, and even better at ignoring our chemistry. Or perhaps, while reeling and then recovering from my last disastrous relationship a year ago, I've only now given myself permission to open my eyes where Nick is concerned. Perhaps Neve and Grace, my best friends, are right—it's time to make something happen.

Warm, syrupy heat settles in my pelvis.

If I'm honest, the thought of getting physical with my big, brooding bodyguard—the perfect fling candidate for a woman with my trust issues—was why I suggested the 'get laid' pact with Grace and Neve over cocktails one night. Those two embracing their own holiday flings—Grace in Fiji and Neve in the Maldives—means there's no way I can chicken out. But, despite those heated looks and Nick's clear interest, my side of the bargain—seducing Nick—seems less likely than ever.

At the signal from the show director, I emerge onto the runway, which stretches the entire length of the stunning baroque ballroom. The walls and high-vaulted ceilings are decorated with intricate gilded frescoes, and I strut in time to the haunting classical music. The full, hooped, couture gown I'm wearing as part of this Winter Fantasy charity fashion show sways with my swinging hips in time to the beat. I feel hundreds of eyes on me, but I'd settle for just one pair. Conker-brown and haunted…

It's electric as usual, a buzz I love. But, instead of focussing on walking in skyscraper heels, I'm thinking about my own winter fantasy—Nick Rivers shaking off his detachment and touching me, kissing me, fucking me…

At the end of the stage I strike a pose for the audience, lapping up the applause, which is normally all the thrill I need. But tonight it's dampened, as if finally acknowledging the undercurrent of chemistry between Nick and I has highlighted the gaping holes in my complicated, lonely life—the biggest being sex.

I lock my smile in place, trying not to think about my struggles with trust or relive the horrible feelings of vulnerability and betrayal. Since my ex Dave went public after our split with intimate details of my life, even selling nude pictures to the tabloids, I've had no stomach for dating. Being Brooke Madden is not like having a regular job. I'm the sole owner-operator, CEO and public spokeswoman rolled into one. A position that requires me always to be stage-ready and, consequently, always hiding parts of the real me.

That's why a fling with the insanely sexy Nick is just the boost I need. He's discreet, barely speaks and I won't have to worry that he'd kiss and tell.

I lead the line of predominantly Italian models backstage to rapturous applause, probing why the euphoria I usually feel is absent tonight. I've spent my entire life on display in one way or another. First as the daughter of Earl Piers Madden and Lori Colt— my prominent politician father and my actress and fashion-icon mother—and then later as my own career took off. I'm used to the constant attention.

But sometimes I wish I was an ordinary person.

Maybe then I could simply invite Nick for a drink, walk into any bar unrecognised and just see where it leads.

But my public prominence complicates everything. Dating isn't straightforward when there are people out there who'll pay for exclusive secrets or candid photos. The down side to a life that on the surface seems to be all glamorous parties and international travel is zero privacy to be yourself. And, worse, never knowing if someone wants you, the real you, or simply their five minutes with your public persona.

Of course, I also have the enormous privilege of being able to make a difference. It's a delicate balance, one I've grown up watching my parents try to navigate.

Fear shudders through me. I've also watched scandals all but ruin their marriage, and occasional death threats rule their lives and those of my sister and I. Is locking down who I really am, keeping my private life separate really such a high price to pay to keep myself and my family safe?

Nick would protect me from a slight breeze, which is probably why I feel so comfortable around him—physically and emotionally. I know from the background check I did on Rivers Security that he's ex-armed forces. When he first began working for me, he hinted at a turbulent youth. But who doesn't make mistakes? I have. I've trusted the wrong people. Naively given over too much power in relationships. Made strangers' opinions of me responsible for my self-esteem.

Considering how many times he's worked for me in the past few months, I know depressingly little about him. But I don't need his life story to know he's unlikely to sell my underwear on the dark web.

He's too self-contained. Too straight. Too focussed on his job.

Which is why I'll likely fail with my grand seduction plan. Dejected, I kick off the punishing heels torturing my feet and scoop them up as I head for the changing rooms. The object of my lust is wound so tightly by his rules and control and silent watchfulness that it seems he'd never surrender to anything as frivolous and irrelevant as sexual attraction. But I know he feels it.

'No, your days are numbered, Nick,' I mutter as weave my way past the other models in various stages of undress, bidding farewell to a few who I've met before.

If I don't succeed in seducing him I'll have to suffer through the rest of the week pretending I can't feel the heat radiating from him any time he's close. Or that I'm blind to his muscles bulging through the black jeans and T-shirts he habitually wears like a uniform. Or immune to the seemingly impenetrable wall of indifference and his blank gaze.

I sigh, removing the heavy chandelier earrings as a dresser helps me with the buttons at the back of the couture gown. I reach for some make-up-remover wipes and begin cleaning my face.

When I first met Nick four months ago, when he accompanied me to an industry awards show, he'd worn a tuxedo in order to blend in. I'd all but drooled down my own chin. When some fans had jostled a little too closely, and he'd slotted his hard body between them and me and discreetly asked me if I was okay, I'd felt myself blossoming back to life after the long and lonely months of betrayal post-Dave.

I told myself it was a response to his kindness and that my infatuation would fade. But, here we are, months later and no end in sight.

He wants me too, so why is he putting up such a fight? And how can I resist such a thrilling challenge—hot, fast and furious sex with a man who's probably…how did Neve put it…*packing a trouser-leg full of knitting antidote.*

I smile to myself, my heart thumping at the thought of having him captive for a few days—plenty of time to penetrate his rigid control and reap the benefits.

With the row of buttons undone, I slide the exquisite designer ball-gown down my arms and step out of the creation with care respectful of its price tag. I sling on a robe and head for the showers, still thinking about Nick.

When I finally emerge, clean and relaxed. the backstage area is quiet and devoid of the post-show hustle and bustle. I dress slowly, the glide of denim and cotton sensitive against my skin. Spending twenty-four-seven with Nick has amplified my arousal to an urgent degree. How will I sit next to him in the car in this worked-up state? How will I say goodnight without pouncing on him and kissing those full lips I've never seen smile? How will I sleep, knowing his big, masculine body—built for power and strength—is likely naked in the room next to mine, controlled, coiled and ready to pounce for my protection?

If only he'd pounce for our mutual pleasure…

I tousle my damp hair, finger-combing the short strands into the signature style I can't shake, then glide some moisturiser on my scrubbed-clean face and head out in search of Nick, and probably another missed opportunity. I'm dejectedly working my way through the narrow corridors and deserted rooms behind the scenes when I hear feminine laughter. One of the darkened rooms has open French windows that lead to a small walled garden.

I step just inside the room, guided by the low outdoor lights and the unmistakable smell of cigarette smoke. A few of my fellow models must be lingering to socialise after the show. I contemplate joining them. It will delay the torture of Nick's company. It might be fun, and I can practise my halting Italian which never seems to improve, no matter how much time I spend here.

I recognise the two women as fellow models who'd walked the runway with me tonight. Although I've never met either of them before, one of them, a dark-eyed brunette, is exactly my type. She reminds me of Freya, the girlfriend I had at uni.

But the two women aren't socialising over a cigarette.

They're kissing.

I freeze in the dark, my heart lurching into my throat. I'm openly bisexual, but being brought up by public figures and then dealing with the blow of Dave's betrayal has made me fiercely protective of my private life.

As a little girl I would watch my mother prepare for an appearance or a red-carpet event, dabbing my tiny fingers into her make-up palettes and smearing my mouth with her lipstick.

'We're putting on our faces, aren't we, Brookie?' she'd say. With her bright, camera-ready smile she became a different person—no longer just my mum. As if her career was one big game of dress-up.

I too learned to paste on a smile and become Brooke Madden, while drawing a line in the sand about subjects I wouldn't discuss, like who I date.

And then Dave dropped his sensationalist bombshell.

I make to back up and leave the room in search of Nick, but I can't look away from the arresting sight of the couple, perhaps because of the crushing pressure of my loneliness. Their kiss seems tentative, as if it's their first together.

In my Nick-induced state of arousal, I grow hot. I'm envious of their lack of inhibition and conflicted by the illicit shame of watching. The blonde, the more confident of the two, grips the brunette's face and slides her lips over the brunette's. A hint of tongue. A self-conscious giggle.

I close my eyes and fantasise about the taste of Nick's kiss.

Oh, to be so free to embrace a moment of fierce attraction. To forget the possibility that someone might see. To just be yourself—a regular woman with wants, needs and the desire for honest connection without the threat of betrayal.

I need to find Nick.

My eyes flutter open and I back up a few paces towards the door I entered through, desperate to stay silent and leave the couple to their moment of intimacy. I'm intruding, no better than the paps that sometimes hound my every move, sniffing out a social *faux pas* or a scandal or just a bad hair day.

Soft, feminine moans trickle in from the garden. I take another peek. Their kisses have grown deeper, more passionate. The blonde slides one hand to the breast of the brunette—who I can see isn't wearing a bra—her thumb locating the peaked nipple.

I gasp, low and hushed. My core clenches, my pulse throbbing in my clit. I press my thighs together, grateful for the seam of my jeans, but it's not enough. Because it's Nick's hand I feel on *my* aching breast. Nick's thumb I feel circling *my* taut nipple. Nick's grunts of pleasure and encouragement I hear ringing in my ears…

I close my eyes again, leaning up against the doorframe as I indulge in my Nick fantasy for a few decadent moments. Soon I'll have to face him and pretend once more, just like he pretends. I see his leashed passion in the clench of his jaw whenever I stray too close. His restraint, his indifference, a mask. I feel his invisible barriers go up when he shuts down any hint of a personal conversation. But I also know from the crackle of awareness arcing between our bodies like static that we'd be so good together.

I press my fingers between my legs to ease the relentless throb that has been there since I made the call to Rivers Security a few weeks ago, requesting his personal overnight service for my trip to Italy.

Having him to myself for five days feels so decadent. I know his every mannerism—the texture of his dark hair, the flat, expressionless slant of his delicious mouth, the evasive flicker of heat lurking in his conker-brown eyes when his guard slips. Despite looking like the bog-standard tough guy, he's a complex man. Flawed. Compelling.

I sway on my feet, oblivious to everything but the images of Nick in my head and the fierce longing infecting my blood.

The sound of a familiar voice jolts me back to the present.

'You know, voyeurism is considered a crime.'

CHAPTER THREE

Brooke

I GASP, MY eyes slamming open and my hand dropping from between my legs. I spin towards the hushed deep and familiar voice. Nick lounges against the wall in the darkened corridor, his face cast in shadow. His posture is casual, his hands slung in his pockets, one booted foot crossed in front of the other. But his dark eyes burn into mine with shocking new intensity.

My body floods with desire and determination.

And a scalding bolt of shame.

I'm standing here, apparently getting off on watching two people being intimate when I'm usually so practised at presenting a careful image to the world.

But it's his fault. I was overcome by the arousal I always feel in his presence. I roll my shoulders back and jut out my chin. 'They're just kissing,' I whisper. 'In public, I might add.'

I should have known he'd come searching for me.

How long has he been there, silently watching with his brooding stare? Fear trickles through my blood. Just like Dave who, as it transpired, had no integrity or sense of decency, Nick could expose how he caught me watching another couple if he wanted. Sell a sordid story to the gossip mongers. Offer me up to social media trolls who think they know me because my body is used to sell clothes.

I'm aware that I tend to overreact when it comes to keeping my private life out of the tabloids. But growing up, everything my sister and I did reflected on our politician father, although my sister's inconspicuous adult life as a mother and librarian gives her layers of protective anonymity.

And after the Dave scandal, the last thing I want is for my parents to learn along with the rest of the world that their daughter has a wild side and enjoys watching.

But Nick is nothing like my ex. Instinct tells me he'd never sell me out.

I turn to face him, keeping my voice hushed. 'I'm pretty sure the crime of voyeurism involves nakedness and sexual acts.' Having his eyes on me laces my blood with the fizz of excitement.

Perhaps subconsciously I knew he'd find me. Perhaps I wanted to make something happen beyond our designated roles of client and protector. Perhaps he'll see my sexy side. See that I'm more than a cardboard cut-out plastered on a billboard. Of course, he doesn't know that I was fantasising about *him* instead of watching the kissing, but maybe now he'll be forced to see me as more than the public Brooke Madden.

He's looking at me as if I'm a fascinating stranger. Watching me with that intense look, so familiar but also cloaked in newness. Is Nick enthralled by my little act of rebellious voyeurism?

My body sags with relief. At last something more from him than detachment and indifference. It makes me want to continue where I left off when he interrupted. Perform just for him so that I can hold onto that elusive thread of his rapt and penetrating attention. Tie myself up in it until he's forced to admit he feels the same pull. Until he's forced to act on the desire he hides so well behind those dark, unreadable stares.

'How long have you been there?' I ask, my throat so tight with longing that talking is painful. Should I tell him that it was him I saw behind my closed eyes? His kiss that I imagined? His touch that I craved?

'Long enough,' he replies, tightness in his square jaw.

I appraise his lazy slouch against the wall, searching for that rigid indifference he wears as well as those dark jeans that hug his thick thighs and toned backside. But it's not there. He's trying to look unaffected, but his broad chest moves with rapid, shallow breaths. He's excited. Intrigued.

Finally…

'Don't you think that this behaviour is reckless for someone in your position?' he asks. 'Even for someone who likes to push the boundaries as you do, it's surely a step too far? For the second time today I've crept up on you. I could be anyone walking in here to see you turned on, snooping. I saw you touch yourself.'

Despite his cautionary reprimand, his voice is thick, heat banked in his dark eyes. And he's still across the corridor. Watching me.

This is my chance to bring the sexual undercurrents between us to the surface. 'I only watched them for a few seconds—I had my eyes closed when you interrupted. I was thinking about…something else. But I'm not ashamed of my desires. And no one saw me… Except you.'

'Except me,' he iterates, calm and controlled, where I feel like I'm about to combust because, despite his lecture, this tense moment is the most intimate one we've shared.

Why is that? Why is a man of the world, as Nick most certainly is, fighting so fiercely? It's way beyond professional ethics. The look he gave me at the pool this afternoon burned my bikini to ash—the same look he's shooting me now. I swallow hard and press my thighs together to ease the ferocious throb of arousal.

'What were you thinking about?' he probes, voicing the curiosity to which he's previously seemed immune.

My heart kicks at my ribs in a rush. His personal question frees me to be completely honest. To take that leap I promised myself when I made that stupid pact with my friends.

'You.' My confession echoes across the space between us.

He makes no move or reaction. But his stare probes mine, each second slamming through me with deafening force. This is my opportunity to test his resolve. To finally lay my desires out there so he can no longer pretend he's ignorant of my interest.

'Not the two women outside?' he asks.

I shake my head. 'I'm bisexual, and they're beautiful. I couldn't help but watch them for a few seconds.' I shrug.

Spoken aloud, my admission that I felt fascinated by the couple's abandon jolts through me, leaving me exposed and vulnerable. But I feel safe with Nick. I want to allow him into my private world and be myself.

I drag in a bolstering breath. For me this conversation is cathartic. Heady. Liberating. And, just as I'm revealing the real me, I see the real Nick. See a man hiding from his own demons. And I know all about that defence mechanism.

'I trust you to be discreet about this,' I say. 'And, in answer to your earlier question, no, it didn't feel reckless. It felt freeing.'

I turn my back on him. The women have progressed from kissing to heavy petting. Time to get out of here and leave them to their privacy.

'We should go,' I whisper, because a sixth sense

alerts me that he's moved closer. I feel him in the dis-turbed currents of air raising the hairs on my arms.

'Why would you open yourself up to a virtual stranger if discretion is so important to you?' he asks at my back.

I close my eyes and search the private part of my-self, the one tired of hiding the real me behind my public image. Tired of being wary and not knowing who I can trust.

'Because I sense you don't care,' I reply. 'Because always protecting my private life is exhausting. Be-cause I'm safe with you…aren't I?'

The last is a whisper. My breath shudders out, tainted with fear. What if I'm wrong? What if I've made another colossal error of judgement—trusted someone unworthy the way I mistakenly trusted Dave?

Nick now has the power to expose me to public criticism and opinion.

My mother's wisdom rings in my ears. *Don't give them any ammunition to fire at you, Brookie. Be the good girl. Be who they want you to be.*

'Yes, you're safe,' Nick says on a reluctant sigh, as if he doesn't want my confidence.

Anticipation hijacks my pulse. Because he's still here. Still skirting the edge of my personal space as if he's scared to step over the line but can't walk away. Can he feel, as I do, how this moment, this conver-sation, bonds us beyond our professional working relationship? Almost as if we're becoming friends.

But there's too much heat and spark between us for us ever to be friends.

Yet, where I welcome a closer connection with this complex man who makes me feel that I can be myself, Nick, with his distance and denial, probably feels the opposite. Trapped, maybe. I've just confessed I've had sexual thoughts about him, after all, and he's said nothing.

'I apologise if my confessions have overstepped our professional boundaries.' I feel his warm breath on the back of my neck. Sense his solid and imposing presence closer than ever before. The hairs at my hairline prickle to attention and my stomach performs cartwheels.

'Tell me,' he whispers. 'Do you want to be one of those women?' His masculine, all-Nick scent and intoxicating question spin my head. I struggle to breathe through this sexually charged moment that shunts us firmly into new territory.

I shake my head, glance at him over my shoulder, my pulse throbbing between my legs. 'No. I want to be right here.'

We've never had such an intimate conversation. I've never been this close to him, so close I could lean back into his touch. It's overwhelming, as if we're strapped into the same parachute about to dive from a plane.

His stare bores into mine and I forget the women outside. Forget what we're talking about. All but forget my own name.

'Do you want to leave? Go back to the hotel?' His heat radiates along my back, the air between his body and mine magnetically charged. Why does it feel as if he's asking something more than his bland question? I don't want to move a muscle because I don't want to break this spell. I want him to touch me with his big, strong, capable hands. I want him to spin me round and kiss me. Back me up into the room and against the tables stacked in the corner and not be able to stop himself from losing control and fucking me right here, the way those uninhibited women are helpless to resist their attraction.

Because I'm helpless to resist the urges I have for Nick. I'm done doubting and second-guessing.

'No. I want to kiss you.' I bite down on my lip as the shock of what I've said registers. Adrenaline buzzes through me until I want to run from the words I've just confessed to a man in my employment. But then follows a flood of relief in my veins. The truth is out at last.

Silence beats in time with a countdown roaring through my head. I hover, desperate to know what the expressionless mask on his face means, to know if he's ready to acknowledge our relentless chemistry. Instead I close my eyes once more, suspended in the delicious possibility of this moment of honesty. If this one charged encounter is all we ever share, I'll take it.

Then my heart stops altogether. Nick's warm fingers encircle my right wrist. A gasp escapes my throat and I immediately want to re-absorb the tell-tale sound. It's the first time he's touched me beyond professional handshakes. Just as with the gasp, I'm helpless in the face of the tendrils of delight that zap through my body, which sways drunkenly at the euphoric contact. I want to rest back against his broad chest and firm muscles.

But I don't want this momentous moment to end. I sense that Nick wants to keep hold of his control, because he's *always* controlled. Why would this be any different? But, oh, how I'd love to see inside his head…

I try to relax under his touch but his loose grip feels like a welcome shackle—alien but loaded with possibility.

Nick firmly directs my pliant and willing hand back between my own legs. I gasp at the contact of my own fingers on my heated, swollen flesh through my jeans.

'Open your eyes, Lady Madden' His breath tickles my neck, a strand of his hair brushing my cheek. 'You're missing the good bit.'

I obey his thrilling command and blink my vision into focus. The women are still there, only now the blonde's hand is under the brunette's skirt. Both women look our way. I hold my breath, shock and shame paralysing me. Nick's grip intensifies on my wrist. But then they're kissing again, lost in themselves, seemingly uncaring of our presence.

My heart re-starts and I collapse against the wall

of Nick at my back. I'd fall without his solid sureness guiding me to be this reckless. To trust him and my own instincts. To snatch this illicit moment.

'How long have they known we're here?' I ask.

I feel his shrug. 'They don't seem to care that we're watching. Maybe they even want us to watch.' His seductive words are whispered against my neck, his breath hot. I want his lips there, tasting my skin, but given the way I feel—like a wire strung taut to snapping point—I'm not sure I'd survive the fulfilment of all my Nick fantasies.

I bite my lip to hold in a moan at his participation in this decidedly erotic sexual encounter. I twist my head so I can see his face.

'Rub yourself,' he instructs, looking down at me with all the lust I wanted to see ablaze in his dark eyes. Like his puppet, I comply. 'That's it,' he says, his free hand coming round to pop the button on my jeans and slide down the zip. I sway, my head light with longing for his touch.

I've never done anything like this before, but now I'm wondering if Nick has.

Silently, he urges my own hand inside my underwear. It's hotter than if he were touching me directly, although that greedy part of me still craves his abandonment and loss of restraint. A slither of awareness, disappointment, splits the heady cloud of arousal in which I'm suspended. Even now, when we share this unexpected and erotic interlude, he's withdrawn and controlled.

But he can't hide the heat his body generates or the rapid thud of his heart against my back. It's not indifference, but something else that keeps him in check. And, now I sense his passion, feel it coiled in him like leashed power, I intend to learn all there is to know about Nick Rivers.

But for now I'm too weak with need to stop. Too desperate to take any scrap of himself he's willing to give. I glide my fingers between my legs, my head spinning with triumph when Nick continues to hold my wrist, still part of this but also maintaining a degree of that distance and detachment he's perfected.

My backside is nestled against his steely thighs and the thick rod of his erection prods the small of my back. I'm so turned on that I'm slick and swollen.

'Watch them,' he says, his voice rough. I glance sideways. Nick's stare follows the movements of my hand inside my underwear, his breath ragged, his body pressed to mine. He's with me, turned on, trapped in this carnal moment, the most liberating and honest of my life.

This isn't about the couple outside; it's about us.

I nod, although I'm more aroused by him watching me, by the knowledge that, despite his previous denial and fight, we're in this together.

My arousal spikes, hot and insistent. My orgasm builds even before I've had a chance to find any sort of rhythm.

'Don't stop,' he says, his command soft but with the power of a bellow, because I'm lost, alive, soaring. Bound to his whim by my own freeing abandon, the craving for him that I've spent months ignoring and the sinful little secret we're sharing.

The brunette comes seconds before me, but I'm too engrossed in Nick and my own pleasure to spare more than a cursory glance at the women. He surrounds me with his powerful, solid aura, his gruff, commanding voice and rough breaths and his low grunt of triumphant encouragement as I stifle my own climax-induced cries against the back of my hand.

It's so hot. I'm melting in an inferno. Stunned. Speechless.

But it's over as abruptly as it began. The last spasm barely dissipates before Nick wordlessly removes his hand from my wrist. He steadies me, his hands on my hips, and then steps away.

My body sways, searching the heat of his once more, but I'm reeling alone.

'What's the matter?' I spin on him, confusion a hot ball in my chest. Every muscle in my body has been stripped of the lovely languid sensation of seconds ago. I convulse, shivering. 'Are we done?'

I try to pull myself back together after such an abrupt withdrawal, but rejection is ice in my veins.

'I'll wait for you in the car,' he says, his gruff voice clawing its way back to professional. Distant. And full of denial.

CHAPTER FOUR

Nick

THE IMPRINT OF her sublime body, weakened and uninhibited, is a brand on my skin. My dick hates me
for the venomous, unfulfilled ache. The atmosphere
in the car is tense with the unspoken. I force my stare
to the road and away from Brooke beside me in the
passenger seat. I can't bear to see her confusion. Her
hurt. Or the questions I'm sure fill her unguarded
eyes. That doesn't mean I don't feel those questions
like blows to the side of my head.

And I deserve every one.

I grip the steering wheel as I manoeuvre the narrow cobbled streets behind the Palazzo Giorno. A
litany of warnings pounds through my head, first
and foremost my single professional rule: no fucking the clients.

What the hell possessed me to touch her? I curse
my weakness. My indulgence.

But I couldn't stop. She looked so ethereal and…
lonely standing there in that darkened room, her de-

sire to watch so honest. Something about her earlier confession of how she can't date and the hesitant way she hid in the shadows drew me into the scene. She ceased being an untouchable and remote caricature and became a hot-blooded woman.

Delicious and dangerous.

When she embraced a spot of voyeurism, it forced to the front of my mind everything I've tried to ignore since my first assignment for her. The way she owned her pleasure... Her honest vulnerability... Her bravery in confronting this rampant chemistry, there since our very first meeting. It shifted something inside me, rattled one of my self-imposed shackles.

Need roared through me, shattering the zen-like calm I've spent years perfecting and which I wear as armour against my former life. Years spent locking down the reckless part of me that allowed emotion, raging hormones and some twisted sense of maleness make my decisions.

In one moment of perfect candour, with one privileged glimpse of her inner desires—a part of her no one else gets to see—Brooke managed to shake the rock-solid foundations of everything I thought I knew about her. Superficial, fabricated things I used to restrain my feral attraction to her. But now, with the scent of her arousal still lingering in my nostrils, my previously tried and tested convictions snap. The snarling beast in me rips at the chains that I've worn for so long, I've grown accustomed to their weight. But I'll never again allow emotion to dictate my actions like I did seventeen years ago. The fallout is too damaging. The consequences too painful. Lust is just another emotion to be tamed and managed, and I've had years of practice.

And I never asked for Brooke's trust. She just handed it to me. The last time I allowed someone close enough to earn their trust, I destroyed it. Destroyed her. Destroyed myself. I clench my jaw in frustration, ignoring the physical discomfort in my groin while I patch my control back together. Just because I participated back there, nothing's changed.

I've still got this. I'm still in command of myself.

Right. That's why you want to pull over in the nearest pitch-black alleyway and bury yourself inside her...

Guilt laces every painful breath I take. I cast a sideways glance at Brooke. She's staring out of the window. Her famous profile reflects the glow of the passing streetlights, so I can see her angelic face is blank. But she's just a woman. A beautiful, complex, normal woman. Sometimes triumphant and sometimes lonely.

Real.

That's what made me cross the line with her tonight.

Brooke shifts, dragging me from my thoughts. 'So, where are you taking me? I still want that nightcap,' she says, glancing at the GPS display on the dashboard.

'You have a five a.m. start tomorrow.' I grip the wheel, battling the thick clouds of sexual tension filling the car. The memories of those throaty little whimpers she made as she came against her own fingers will likely stay with me until I die.

Fuck, I need to get it the hell together. Just because the fascinating and addictive Lady Brooke Madden has a dark and daring side…just because she was turned on by watching and seems more real, more riveting…doesn't mean she's still not dangerous and out of my league. She still reminds me of Julia, the ex-girlfriend I abandoned and betrayed years ago in the worst way.

Brooke's still a mistake waiting to happen.

That single touch of her wrist, her scent—feminine, seductive and expensive—and her soft body leaning on me as she touched herself was enough to confirm I'm in deep trouble.

But I haven't cracked yet.

Her stare is hot on the side of my face. 'I'm not sure what happened back there, but I need to process it—preferably with a Scotch in my hand.'

'Can't you just forget it?' I snap, wishing I could erase the memory of her body undulating against mine while I tried to hold myself rigid and detached.

I sense her outrage. 'It's not something forgettable. At least, not for me.'

Nor for me, but I'll die trying. I have to.

'We'll need to talk about it, Nick,' she says. 'Tonight.'

Instead of commenting, I change direction with an internal groan of acceptance, heading for a bar housed in another of Milan's classiest hotels. I'm certain Brooke would like to drink in the grandeur of a five-star establishment, and their security will likely be up to my standards.

I keep my breaths slow and steady—I've got this. So I tempted her over to the dark side... She should have known better than to mess with a man like me. I have my own secrets. Surely she can tell just by looking at me that I'm definitely no angel?

And yet she surrendered herself to my twisted nature.

But my lust for this woman changes nothing. I won't allow one raunchy little rich girl to decimate my hard-won discipline, something I've definitely mastered in the years since I believed I had a heart and foolishly thought myself safely in love. I've learned to curtail my own base instincts, denying my needs, controlling them, so I can live with myself after my mistake.

But Julia's returned affection was tested, shaken and eventually broken at my own hands. Yes, her loyalty was rocked by the whisperings of parents who, quite rightly, thought me beneath their daughter. Influential, powerful people just like those in Brooke's sphere.

But they'd been right. I proved that I wasn't good enough.

Shoving those shameful memories aside is like scraping up broken glass with my bare hands, so I'm a little raw when I park and accompany Brooke into the hotel. Eager for a reason to take her back to her hotel and say goodnight, I scan the place for dirt bags who might recognise her or paps who happen to be in the right place at the right time. The last thing I want to do is talk about my momentary lapse of judgement, professional ethics and human decency, but this is my job.

She's my job.

With a resigned sigh, I settle my focus on work. Brooke selects a booth and I slide in beside her on the leather seat. She orders a Scotch from our waiter and turns to me, her eyebrows raised in a question.

'Water, please,' I say to the man, who nods and moves away.

'Water?' she asks. 'What's it going to take for you to relax, Big Guy?'

'I'm working,' I say, ignoring her nickname. It's not too late to reclaim our former professional boundaries after what happened backstage. If she thinks we can just fool around during work hours, she's mistaken. I'm not a hired plaything.

'You're paying me to be on the clock twenty-four-seven.' A hellish assignment I'm now regretting. Because I wanted to unleash my desires. I wanted to peel the skin-tight denim from her legs, lay her down, sling her long, toned thighs over my arms and put my mouth on her until we were both incoherent with this ferocious chemistry I battle.

She narrows her eyes. 'If I said you were off the

clock now, if we left the car here and walked back to our hotel, would you have a drink? Loosen up a bit?'

'I don't drink.'

'You don't drink?' Her eyes round as she takes sip of her speedily delivered Scotch. 'That explains a lot.'

Her insight would make me cringe if I wasn't so mean and downright stubborn. 'The occasional beer, perhaps.' I shrug. 'What does it explain?'

She regards me for a few minutes. 'Well, I assume it's a control thing.'

I rest back against the seat, sensing that she's done pussyfooting around with polite enquiries and intends to go for the jugular. But I can handle one little case of inconvenient and misguided sexual attraction until the job's done.

'Alcohol lowers inhibitions and delays reaction times. I could hardly do my job if I was rolling around pissed.' I harden my stare and hold her breathless attention captive. 'Protecting *you* is my job.'

Breath shudders out of her in an excited whoosh, perhaps at the idea of being my sole focus. Then she leans back, triumph glowing in her startling eyes. 'So what happened backstage… Was *that* part of your job?'

Oh, so we're going there. 'That was…an aberration. A temporary moment of indulgence.'

I should have fled the minute I found her in that darkened doorway, the air thick with her arousal, but I'd been too turned on by her voyeuristic streak to think straight, let alone act normally.

'It won't happen again.'

My blunder becomes apparent when she says, 'What if I want it to happen again?'

'What you want has no bearing on me. I work for you. I don't cross that boundary.'

Rather than looking dejected, she seems enthralled. 'Yes, you do an excellent job, which is why I keep hiring you for my security needs. But tonight you *did* cross that boundary. You participated. Your body wasn't withdrawn and evasive and work-focussed——even though you're trying to return to that place now, presumably out of fear.'

I grin, forcing that same body to relax despite her piercing intuitiveness.

'What my body wants is immaterial.' My jaw aches with the force of my clenched teeth because it's growing harder and harder to deny myself one little taste of that delicious taunting mouth. Harder to deny her the concession she wants. Because she's shown she can handle me calling the shots. She handed me control the way she handed over her trust.

The dissatisfied ache in my balls returns, twice as fierce as when she shattered in my arms.

'Just because I find you physically attractive doesn't mean I intend on acting on that. *I'm* the one in charge, not my dick.'

And I have specific tastes. Would Lady Madden be interested if she knew how very similar we are?

'What makes you think you're my type?' I ask, remembering how besotted I'd been with Julia. A woman from a world that I didn't understand. Another woman in possession of all the power in our relationship. Yes, I'd been the one to ruin what Julia and I had, but I'd also fallen victim to that power when her love had come tumbling down. I'd been shut out at my lowest ebb and I can't even blame her. But I won't be that helpless again, no matter how tempting the inducement.

And temptations don't come more potent than the real Brooke.

'I've seen the way you look at me.' Her sensual voice chips at my resolve. 'I felt your excitement. Neither of us can hide this attraction, Nick. You're just putting up more of a fight. It's got me wondering why...?'

Of course she'd ask the million-dollar question. But, now I've seen that she's not as angelic as she looks, perhaps I could have one little taste... But not like this. I'm not her gigolo.

'Well, it wouldn't do to ogle my wealthy, influential clients, now, would it? I'm a businessman with staff to pay. And this conversation could constitute sexual harassment.'

Her chin juts in outrage. 'That might be true if you hadn't touched me first, hadn't held me against your chest while I made myself come under *your* direction.' She knocks back the rest of her drink in a single swallow and slaps the empty glass on the table in challenge. 'So you're in charge of this thing between us—great, but be honest about it. I was.'

New respect for her floods through me, each wave stronger than the last. I need to get a handle on my attraction before my control frays and I do something stupid. But maybe that's the answer—screw her and walk. I'm a one-time guy. I ensure that the one time is as safe as it can be and avoid emotional entanglement. That's how I control the impulsive streak inside me and prevent history repeating itself.

Maximum protection against feeling.

'Look, this situation doesn't work for me.' I should have shut down this conversation at the start. 'As my client, you inherently hold all the power. And, while that works in a professional capacity, I don't roll that way when it comes to fucking.'

She gawps, delighted that I'm opening up this way. 'I… I agree—there is an imbalance in our working relationship—although I'm at risk too. I've stopped dating because I've had lovers betray me, sell little titbits to the highest bidder. But I feel safe with you.' She leans her elbow on the table and lowers her voice. 'I don't want all the power. It's just sex.'

I barely hold in my snort of disbelief. *Just sex…?* One of the most powerful and, if not carefully managed, destructive forces in the world. Strong enough to create life. To tear the heart right out of a person's chest. To bring a grown man to his knees if he's unable to handle the emotional fallout.

My twisted arse controls sex more fiercely than all other areas of my life combined. But she's right— there is a way to redress the power imbalance. A way to have her on my terms. Her little show earlier proved she's open to a little sexual exploration. So why not…?

I take in every facet of her exquisite face—her crystal-blue eyes bright with excitement, her parted pouty lips plump and inviting, the slope of her neck exposed by her tilted head.

'You really want to play, Lady Madden?'

Her nod is instant. Eager.

Ah, baby... So much to learn.

'Sure you can handle me?' If she wants a little tour of the wild side, to play by my rules, who am I to deny her?

Heat flares in her eyes, turning her from beautiful to incandescent. 'I think I'm up to the task, as long as you can let go of a little of your control and blur the line…'

'If you want anything beyond my professional services, there'll be a whole lot more control, not less. Still think this is what you want?'

She nods, her determined chin lifting.

'Well, you can start by doing something for me.' Now that I've seen how open she is to exploring her kinky, voyeuristic side, I can risk exposing a fraction of my own darkness.

For the right incentive. 'Fine.' Her voice carries that breathy quality I heard just before she came on her own fingers earlier, fingers I wanted to lick so I could taste all that sweetness I've imagined between her thighs. 'What do you want?'

I sit back. Grin. Such an open-ended invitation… But I'm not going to sell her secrets like those creeps of her past she just mentioned. I'm bound by more than our professional contract, presumably the reason she feels safe enough to flirt with this chemistry despite her past betrayals.

'I want you to start taking your own protection seriously. If I say wait for me, you wait for me. No going anywhere alone. Not even the hotel pool.'

Her eyes narrow with momentary irritation. I think she's going to call the whole thing off. My chest thumps with a mix of relief and unexpected hollowness.

'Okay. You say jump and I'll ask how high.' She props her elbow on the table and rests her chin in her hand. 'Anything else?'

Oh, she's playing with fire.

'That's a dangerous offer for a man like me… I like the sound of it. So since you asked so nicely— you want my touch, it comes with conditions. And it happens after hours, outside of our working relationship. Because, where sex between us is concerned, I want all the power, understand?'

She lifts her chin. 'Why? What will I get?'

Good question. I fucking love that she challenges me. That she's determined to get hers.

'Pleasure,' I say, my dick stirring at the glazed look already transforming her eyes.

'Okay. I agree. No more unaccompanied movements.' Her voice is breathy, making my blood pump harder. 'After hours, you're in charge. And in return…' I practically hear her mind whirring with possibilities now she thinks she's getting what she wants. 'I want the kiss that you denied me backstage.'

I laugh, a mean sound devoid of humour. 'This isn't going to go the way you want. I'm not some expensive pedigree lap dog you can make jump to your bidding.'

She huffs, batting away my objection. 'Good. I want a sexual partner who isn't going to run to the media with tales of my private life, not a pet.'

'If and when I touch you, I'll absolutely be off the clock. I'll be the one calling the shots.' I let my comments settle for a beat. 'And, seeing as you were honest about your desires, I'll be honest too.'

I lean closer, catch the scent of her warm skin, a tickle of her arousal. She'll either love or hate what she's about to hear. Either agree to my rules or fire my perverted arse.

'Just like you did tonight, I like to watch. Up for a little game of exhibitionism?'

CHAPTER FIVE

Brooke

THE AIR IN the hotel lift seems to pulse with phero-
mones, every beat jolting my body. I ache between
my legs, so turned on by the promise in his sexy
voice and the slightly tortured look on his face when
he said the words, *I like to watch.*

The thrill of victory buzzes through my nervous system, but now it's clear that this won't be
the straightforward and frenzied coupling I've fantasised about.

Still, good things come to those who wait…

The questions in my head deafen me to the thundering of my own heart. Why does he like to watch?
Will he touch me? Is his kink a cause or an effect of
that control he needs?

I shudder out a sigh. I'm out of my depth but also
sick with longing. In a public life where I make all
the decisions and calculate all the risks, I welcome
that rush of freedom I felt earlier with Nick. There's
something so liberating about conceding a little con-

trol in this one area of my life—sex. An area sorely neglected thanks to the betrayal and humiliation I felt after Dave and the sex scandal, which killed my last hopes that I could have any sort of *normal* dating life. I hadn't even known he'd taken the nudes of me he'd sold along with his tawdry little kiss-and-tell exposé. My legal team were on it in a heartbeat, but the pictures are still out there. Nothing is ever gone forever on the Internet.

For a solid month my home had been besieged by media. Pictures of my serious, conservative father—who'd been considering a controversial and well-publicised bill in the House——had filled the front pages next to my blurred-out nudes. My mother had just finished a critically acclaimed West End play and had been about to start her breast cancer chemotherapy, but people had only wanted to cover my juicy gossip.

Prickles of dread race over me like acupuncture needles. What if I'm wrong about Nick? I've been wrong before. Shamed, attacked and professionally renounced, thanks to the intimate photos Dave made public. Not only had I had to face my friends and family, I'd lost lucrative and prestigious endorsement deals, despite my publicity team's best efforts to quash the scandal. My mistake had cost me my trust and dignity, and had damaged my brand.

Growing up, I'd watched my parents have no private life. I've had caution, discretion and secrecy drummed into me until it's the first thing I consider before any action or decision—public or private. Mum in particular cites her own mistakes—trusting the wrong agents, being too candid in interviews, her initial naivety with regard to nudity—as examples of how *not* to do it. And I respect her advice. She's my role model to emulate, both as a parent and a professional.

My parents understand the impact of fame and notoriety and have always tried to protect me and my sister from the worst elements.

That's why the shock of Dave's betrayal hit me so hard.

I let myself down, but I let my parents down harder.

Panic sinks in its claws. I turn to Nick, urgency in my voice. 'You won't photograph me, will you? I don't want that.' I flush at not having already asked this vital question. I trust him, but I need to be certain. I'm not free to take those kinds of risks when it affects my loved ones.

Nick's jaw clenches, the fiery flicker of anger in his dark stare. 'No. I'd never do that. What kind of man do you think I am?'

His frown is formidable. I've never seen him upset. Mildly irritated, perhaps, as he'd been at the pool.

'Sorry. I didn't mean to insult you. I've just experienced that kind of man, sadly. It's made me cautious.' His outrage and confusion tells me that, unlike the rest of the world, he probably didn't see the love-rat sex scandal that dominated the head-lines for a while.

He steps closer so I'm forced to crane my head back to keep his blistering eye contact. 'I'm sorry that you've been betrayed. But I'd never do anything without your consent. Understand?'

I nod, overwhelmed by his powerful, competent and sincere bearing. He's the calmest, straightest man I've ever met. What you see is exactly what you get with Nick.

My doubts evaporate.

'Thank you.' The private part of me that I pro-tect, the part I hide whenever I'm in the public eye, craves freedom from constantly projecting Brooke-Madden.com. Feeling liberated by ceding control of our chemistry to this man should be paradoxi-cal. But I believe that Nick is focussed on my plea-sure. He's already proved that with his seriously impressive restraint. Not many men I know could walk away from a sexual scenario unfulfilled as he had earlier.

The lift doors slide open, ending what felt like the longest assent in the history of lift journeys. I practically glide to my room, my head full of the possible scenarios. I'm desperate to feel his mouth on mine—those generous lips, usually pulled into a straight line, the scrape of his dark facial hair, per-haps his strong hands holding my face or speared through my hair…

I'm working myself up into a sexual frenzy. Perhaps that's Nick's clever plan——to build anticipation so much that I'll expire if he doesn't touch me soon.

At my door, I fumble with my key card, strung out on adrenaline. On the third attempt, I succeed. I pause with the door barely ajar.

Nick's body heat warms my back. His breath tickles the nape of my neck.

'Good night, Lady Madden.' His tone is neutral, as always, but now I can't hear his voice without thinking of sex. 'Remember to lock the doors, including the one adjoining your suite and mine.'

I shudder at the hidden meaning of his instructions. The adjoining door between our rooms hasn't once been *un*locked. There's only one reason he'd remind me to lock it and that's if he's suggesting I do the opposite.

'Call me Brooke,' I say for the umpteenth time, my stomach tumbling. I look up. He's cast in shadow from the dim corridor lighting, his expression unreadable on the surface. But challenge and the hint of promise glow in his dark eyes, kicking up my pulse and the flutters in my pelvis. I can't wait to get inside. I can't wait to do his bidding and earn my reward.

Him.

'Goodnight, Nick.'

Without another word, we enter our separate rooms.

The closing click of my door jars me into action. I flick on the lights, slip off my shoes and dump my bag. Blood rushes so fast through my head, I feel dizzy with longing and excitement. I pour myself a glass of Scotch from the crystal decanter on the bar to steady my nerves then pad into the bedroom.

Now that it means so much, the innocuous-looking adjoining door looms from the corner of the room. I barely noticed it before. I press my ear against the wood, my heart trying to break free of my chest. There's nothing but stillness and the thud of my pulse.

Is he there, silently waiting on the other side?

I turn the lock and rest my hand on the brass door knob while my core tightens with need. I crank open the door a notch and peek through the gap. Another closed door, the one on Nick's side.

I leave my door ajar and toss back the rest of my Scotch.

Anticipation laces my blood with wild energising endorphins. I'm high waiting for him to accept my invitation and just walk through that open door. High at the thought of him watching me. High on the promise of his kiss.

I shed my clothes, leaving a trial on the floor for him to follow as I head for the bathroom. I turn on the shower and with a gasp step under the hot spray. My skin is so sensitive, my nipples already hard peaks under the force of the water. It's my third shower of the evening, but I feel as if I'll turn to ash if I don't somehow quench this fire Nick has lit inside me.

I wash myself all over, the glide of my own hands enough of an aphrodisiac. Nick's little game of show-and-tell has me so riled up, I'm teetering on the edge of bliss.

I know from the outline of his burly body that he's one hundred per cent ripped, hard male. His cock at my back earlier felt long and thick. And this little role-play thing we have going on... Just the memory of his gruff voice transformed by desire is enough to clamp the walls of my sex in delicious waves.

I open eyes I hadn't realised I'd closed and peer through the fogged-up glass in search of him as I turn off the water. But I'm in no way disheartened to discover that I'm alone. Perhaps he watched me shower. Perhaps he's there now, witnessing the glide of cotton as I towel-dry every part of my turned-on body.

Time to prolong the show. If he likes to watch, what better way to nudge at his restraint than with some good old-fashioned temptation?

I stride into the bedroom naked. The adjoining door is just the way I left it—open an inch or two, no more, no less. My stomach drops a fraction, nerves and uncertainty getting the better of me. There's no noise beyond the whoosh of my own pulse. No sound of his breathing or tell-tale scrape of his zip.

But what if he is there? What if he's watching as he promised?

I turn back the sheets and dim the lights. I retrieve my trusty, indispensable dildo from my bag and settle against the cool, white bed linens, my back to a mountain of feather pillows and my legs spread.

He likes to watch…he wanted a show… Well, he'll get one.

I slide my hand down and stroke myself. I gasp at the first delicious touch, quickly spreading my thighs and locating my clit.

I hear a creak of old floorboards, or I might have imagined it, because he doesn't appear, nor do I see any movement in the crack of the door.

But the thought of him watching spurs me on. I slide the dildo inside, finding a rhythm that soon has me panting and writhing against my own hand, my stare boldly fixed on the doorway. A challenge and a seduction.

I want him to appear. To join me, put his mouth on my taut nipples and my hungry clit. But also I don't. I want him frozen, transfixed, helpless. I want him frustrated enough to touch himself while he watches.

This is the hottest sexual experience of my life and he's not even in the room. For all I know he could be asleep or engrossed in some dubbed Italian movie. Or he might be there right now, watching me get myself off for the second time tonight.

I close my eyes and lose myself in this fantasy, this role, my body aflame. It doesn't matter where he is; I made something happen. He knows that I want him and that I'll take him on his terms.

He has all the power and it's a heady feeling.

My orgasm builds. I hold my trembling legs open

as I plunge the toy inside myself, imagining I'm filled with Nick's cock, his body braced above me, driving into me and driving me insane. As the climax crests, sucking the air from my lungs, I open my eyes and stare at the door, cries of ecstasy ripping from my throat.

When I'm spent, I toss the toy aside and collapse back onto the bed while air barrels into my chest. Wow… That was one powerful orgasm.

But…

Hollowness quickly replaces the elation. Quite literally, anti-climax grips me. I want to see him. To touch him, taste him and test the control of the man occupying all my thoughts and fuelling my shocking fantasies.

Was it all for nothing?

I close my burning eyes, swamped by the familiar loneliness I've battled since Dave taught me how foolish it was to trust a lover.

I'd hoped for something brief, intense and safe with Nick. I can be myself with him, not the puppet created for public acceptance. I see fire and shadow and dangerous passion caged in him and I want to burn in the darkness until I feel reborn. But has he leashed all those things inside the voyeur in him for reasons I don't yet understand?

Then I hear a sound and freeze. Keep my closed eyelids still for fear I'll spook him or discover the noise was just a figment of my wishful thinking.

I lie paralysed for endless breathless seconds. My

limbs twitch with the pressure of inertia. My mind screams in the darkness behind my eyes at not knowing if he's really out there, at arm's reach.

Irrational fear spikes. It could be anyone there beyond my closed eyelids. But I catch his scent—manly musk, pure Nick. I feel warm breath on my parted lips, my own chest bursting for release.

Euphoria washes over me anew.

Then his kiss lands. Feather-soft at first. It's barely a swipe of his mouth against mine. I curl my desperate fingers into the sheets, instinctively knowing the minute I open my eyes, the minute I acknowledge his presence beyond responding to his kiss, he'll withdraw behind his control and distance himself.

This is his fantasy. He's in charge. And, now I'm finally getting what I want, I'll do anything to comply. Including nothing.

His lips glide over mine, demanding, building in pressure. I catch the quietest of grunts from his throat. I smile. That small noise brings a surge of triumph. I'm now certain that he *was* there. He *did* watch, and that grunt tells me he was as affected by my display as I was performing for him.

So he likes to hold back, delaying gratification. But our chemistry, our attraction, can't be denied for ever, as this incredible kiss proves. I melt into the mattress as his tongue pushes into my mouth, seeking entrance. His hand curls around the back of my neck, raising my head from the pillow. I open up for him, meeting his tongue with mine thrust for thrust. I moan under his kiss, which is every bit as dominant and decadent as I imagined. And somehow more so for the anticipation he's just put my weakened body through.

Then it stops. Cool air bathes my lips. His hand leaves my neck.

My eyes flutter open in protest.

Nick is fully clothed, braced above me on locked arms. I catch a brief look of tortured confusion in his dark, smouldering eyes. He can't control the windows to his innermost feelings the way he controls the rest of his body.

A tiny frown forms between his thick brows, before his neutral mask slips back into place. 'Good night, Brooke.' His voice struggles for his beloved control but cracks as, at last, he speaks just my name.

The small triumph pounds my heart. But before I can reply he spins on his heel and withdraws back to his room. The quiet but final click of the adjoining door jabs at my euphoria like a pin popping a balloon.

CHAPTER SIX

Nick

EVERY MUSCLE IN my body fights the urge to interrupt Brooke's high-fashion photo shoot in the Piazza del Duomo, Milan's grandest square. This early on a clear November morning it's way too cold for the wispy strapless gown she's wearing. No wonder she's shivering. If only I could bundle her away...

Of course, I do no such thing. She's a professional. Uncomplaining. And, from the way she looks at me, confused and haunted, her huge eyes made even bigger by make-up artistry. I'm probably the last person that she wants to be around. And every second that Milan's imposing gothic cathedral and biggest tourist attraction is cordoned off for this shoot costs Brooke's client money.

I grit my teeth. No doubt they can fix her blue lips with make-up and clever editing. But every shiver that judders through her small frame rips me open. And, after last night, I'm as raw and exposed as I care to be.

Because she was... I'm too scared to use the term *perfect*. She handed me the reins of the chemistry that I'd stupidly tried to deny, becoming the epitome of strong femininity.

Irresistible.

When the shoot director calls a break, someone rushes over to Brooke with a padded jacket. I follow her inside the makeshift tent that was erected in the square to keep the worst of the elements from the crew and the digital editing equipment. I find Brooke huddled in a corner near the heater.

I hand her a coffee.

'Thanks,' she says, her eyes full of grateful adoration as she removes the lid from the cup to blow onto the steaming surface.

'Do you want my hat?' I ask, pulling it from my pocket. I don't give a shit about the hair and make-up they spent the two hours before dawn creating.

'No thanks.' She looks away, her expression pinched, as if she has plenty to say but is biding her time.

I get it. She probably expected more than a single kiss last night. But I warned her this would be on my terms. I never promised to be her knight in shining armour, because I don't make promises. I can usually avoid others' expectations by keeping my distance.

I'm selfish. Twisted. And rigid. I learned the hard way that anything else makes me weak and I'll never be that again.

Kissing Brooke has reminded me what's at stake.

I clench my hand inside my pocket as I'm hurled against the wall of memories. I knew I wasn't good enough for Julia the day we met at a house party. She was smart and beautiful and strong, just like Brooke. She had her life all figured out, even at eighteen. But, despite the divide, we both fell hard and fast. Until my weakness ruined us. I let her down. Left her alone when she needed me most through a single act of recklessness and loss of control. I confused what it is to be a man and became a cliché.

But I also lost more than I knew it was possible to lose. I not only disappointed those who loved me, needed me, but also ripped my own life apart with no hope of repairing the damage that I'd inflicted.

The sickening shame I've spent my entire adult life battling rises up, threatening to choke me. This is why I fought my attraction to Brooke. Why it still needs to be managed. Because she makes me feel that I could be back in that desperate place in a heartbeat. She makes me crave something that's dangerous.

Last night she gave me everything. And it would have been so easy to take it all. To let go of my restrictions and gorge myself on the real Brooke. But, even if I could survive that, I have nothing to give her in return. I'm emotionally barren, as she now knows.

I glance down at Brooke's delicate frame where she's engrossed in her knitting project. She carries the knitting bag everywhere. At least the shivering has subsided somewhat, chasing off some of my protective urges. I should never have kissed her, because her trust and her confidences remind me of another woman who wrongly assumed that I'd never let her down.

And Brooke's already been betrayed big-time by some arsehole. I knew of her before she became a client, but I never really kept track of her personal life. Even after I started protecting her, I focussed my research on known stalkers or death threats rather than gossip. But last night I had to stop myself from searching the Internet for tell-all stories or perhaps a sex-tape scandal.

What kind of lowlifes has she dated—spineless, opportunistic dickheads…? Of course, I'm no better.

I swallow hard, new respect for her blooming in me like fucking sunshine. Even cautious and uncertain she'd made herself vulnerable to me. For me. So I can keep hold of my precious control.

Because, without it, I remember. Without it I feel eighteen again—devastated and with only myself to hold to account. Control and discipline and withdrawal is how I rebuilt my life after my big mistake, so now I'm not even sure that I exist in isolation from those bonds.

And now I've been sent the ultimate test—Brooke Madden.

Until I stood behind that unlocked adjoining door last night, I believed I could walk away from her brand of temptation. But some primal part of me, a part I thought I'd mastered years ago, drove me to creep into her room and watch her shower. I already knew her body is perfection. I've spent months working for her, watching. And I filled in the blanks with my excellent imagination.

But seeing her naked—pert breasts, a gorgeous rounded arse and a completely bare pussy—I had to loosen my fly at the sight of her flushed, trusting and turned on by the idea of performing for my eyes only. She didn't know I was there. Anyone who's spent time in prison, or the army for that matter, learns stealth and silence—and I've spent time in both.

But performing for me excited her.

I couldn't stop watching the sensual glide of her hands against her skin.

Her show—bold and erotic—just about brought me to my knees. It took all my spare energy and focus to stay silent while she pleasured herself with that dildo. When she came, her eyes unknowingly on mine, I followed her, silently spilling over the front of my jeans like a fucking teenager.

That's what she reduced me to. Me. A man who can fuck for hours and stave off a climax. A man who practises self-denial as the ultimate form of discipline, the way I train my body for maximum fitness and peak performance. A man determined to control this at all costs.

But I couldn't control the kiss. Because she tasted like summer, cookies and sex all rolled into one delicious experience. Despite coming hard only moments earlier, I struggled to pull my lips away from hers. Like a starving man, I wanted to slide my mouth over every part of her soft, pliant body. To turn her moans into screams. To lose it so badly that I filled her tight pussy with my bare cock and made her come over and over and over until this madness stopped.

All that shocking, ferocious need unleashed from a single kiss...

I look down at the delicate slope of her exposed neck. My fingers itch to touch her skin. But that's exactly the reason I won't. I can't allow myself to feel, which is where indulging those powerful urges with abandon will lead.

Just as I stopped the kiss, a feat akin to ripping out my own guts with my bare hands, I'll deny myself now. That's what I've done since Julia—kept control over my body. Control over what I am. A man so easily led to recklessness by emotions that it's safer to fight their very existence.

Brooke abandons her knitting and stands, swishing the full skirt of her dress out of the way. 'I'd like to go and greet some fans.' She indicates the crowd of onlookers behind the cordon across the square.

I glance at the shoot director who is still clicking through the shots with the photographer, wishing they would bloody hurry and wrap this up. Protective urges re-tighten my gut. Not the security-based ones for the Brooke of yesterday, but deeper urges for a woman I know a little better now. Exposed, raw, confusing.

She's worming her way under my guard. Can I still be objective? Would I have been as concerned that she's cold yesterday, before the kiss? Or is my judgement already dangerously clouded?

I eye the fans clamouring for her, waving banners and yelling. She's a big deal, especially in Milan, fashion capital of the world, but then she's a household name. Everywhere she goes, fans follow, their unpredictable tendencies and mobile phones pointing her way a security headache.

I check my watch. 'You need to change.' Part two of the shoot is on the Duomo's roof terrace. 'And a meet-and-greet is not on today's schedule.' I'm being a dick; the crowd looks innocent enough—tourists, families, children. And it's my job to facilitate whatever she needs.

'We had a deal,' I remind her, because I can't forget what she did last night. I can't shake the taste of her kiss or the sound of her moans. And she owes me some client compliance after that monumental wobble in my personal convictions.

'And I'm keeping my side of it.' Her stare flashes with defiance. 'All I want to do is greet some fans with my bodyguard in tow. I could have just walked over there without you.'

I snort. 'I'd like to see you try.' I'm good at my job and she knows it.

'I don't know if you've noticed, but it's freezing,' she says, squaring up to me with a tilted chin. She's tall for a woman, five-ten, but I'm taller. And, now

I've discovered that she's a greater risk to my emotional armour than I imagined, I'm less inclined to be conciliatory.

'Some of those people have been waiting for hours.' She drains the last of her coffee and places the cup in the rubbish bin. 'I'm not going rogue, I'm just asking you to do your job while I say hello and pose for some photos.'

Her reminder that I'm here to guard her, not fuck her, settles the worst of my over-cautious gut reaction. My job is easy—protect her, full-stop. Walking away from her last night while she was naked and vulnerable…with the taste of her kiss in my mouth… was the real test.

Because, as I feared, I need to shield her from myself. Not only my worst tendencies. I'm a risk to her image. Her image is her livelihood. If the media sensed any whiff of a physical relationship between us, they'd dig into my past for their stories. She wouldn't like what they'd find.

At my reluctant nod we cross the square to the cordoned-off crowd, where Brooke turns on her Lady Madden charm for those assembled. She signs autographs and positions herself into fan selfies while I loiter close, stiff with guilt.

I'm selfish. She's a world-famous icon and I'm an ex-lowlife. I'm bad news for a woman of her profile but, if I can keep a lid on the sex, control that, I can keep the rest of her at arm's length. Because it's too late for total denial. Now that I've tasted both her surrender and her kiss, I want more.

I watch her interact with her fans. If I indulged in jealousy, another pointless emotion, I'd feel it now. Her beautiful smile sells. Every part of her sells. It's the reason we're standing out in the open on a freezing morning shooting some high-end ad campaign for God only knows what. But, unlike me, these people haven't seen the hundred other versions of that smile. The playful one when she teases me, or the hesitant one when she laughs at herself, or the triumphant one I witnessed last night as I reluctantly abandoned her lips.

Fuck… If not for the past seventeen years of discipline and calling the shots in my brief sexual relationships, I'd be buggered. I smother a sigh and practise my apparent detachment.

When she slips into stilted Italian in order to converse with the locals, new respect for her slashes through everything I've just told my smug brain. She could easily hire an interpreter, but she's learning a second language instead, something I'd failed at badly as a kid. The young woman she's talking to can't be more than sixteen or seventeen and whatever Brooke says to her makes the girl well up with delighted tears.

I can no longer ignore that Brooke is humble, and real, and likes to laugh. That she's brave and wants to use her fame to make a difference—the breast cancer charity work scheduled tomorrow is only one of the many causes she champions.

What am I doing with such an ethereal creature? I should abandon our physical relationship, not lure her into some filthy bargain where I get everything I want and something I don't want—her trust—and she gets the scraps I give in return.

'Can I have your hat after all, please?' she asks, bringing me back to the moment. I take it from my pocket without hesitation and hand it over, checking my watch as I do so she knows it's time to wrap this up.

Instead of putting the hat on herself, she hands the black woollen beanie to the girl in the crowd, who hugs her with rounded eyes still brimming with tears.

I conceal a frown. It's not that I'm possessive about my hat. I wanted to give it to Brooke back in the tent. But she's dragging me into her altruism, into her light, showing me more glimpses of the real Brooke Madden than I care to witness. All I need is to focus on the sex on my terms.

'What was that all about?' I ask as we make our way across the square towards the cathedral.

'She's a fan, a fashion student here in Milan. She's been waiting since five this morning. Her cheeks were like ice.' Brooke shrugs and ducks through a heavy oak side entrance, away from the queue of tourists waiting to enter the iconic building. 'I'll replace your hat—thank you, by the way.'

For the first time today the wariness leaves her

eyes when she looks at me with gratitude. My heart thumps—I hadn't realised how much I hold out for that smile of hers to be directed my way. Why does this woman, a woman I now know is sensual and adventurous and rocks her own sexuality like a voyeuristic goddess, make me feel like a fucking clueless teenager with a runaway dick?

When she emerges from the makeshift changing room—a screened-off corner of a cavernous attic space above the cathedral—wearing yet another revealing gown, she fries my brain with renewed lust. She sits in the relocated make-up chair for a touchup. I scroll through some work emails as a distraction from the temptation to drag her back behind the screens so I can lave every inch of her body with my greedy tongue.

'So, let's talk about what happened last night,' she says, her eyes closed for the make-up artist's brush.

I ignore her. I can't think about that kiss without getting hard, and we have an audience…

Brooke must sense one of the reasons for my hesitation because she addresses the Italian make-up artist fixing her face. *'Parli un po' d'inglese?'*

'Niente.' The woman shakes her head and glances my way with curiosity.

'Scusa,' Brooke says, smiling at the woman before flicking me a look. 'We're good. Rosa doesn't speak any English.'

I sigh and pocket my phone. Better to get this over with. The sooner Brooke adjusts her expectations, the better. And I really need to confess my criminal conviction so she knows exactly who she's playing this risky game with.

'Why? Are you disappointed?'

I know what it's like to disappoint someone—it's the reason I haven't seen my mother in months. On the surface she acts proud of her only son, despite the way I behaved as a young man—knocking up Julia, brawling, going to prison and then losing everything I loved in one hit. But I see the truth in my mother's eyes when she thinks I'm not paying attention. And I can't blame her. I'm nothing to be proud of.

Rosa begins applying some sort of powder to Brooke's face, neck and bare shoulders with a giant brush, lighting her skin up with shimmers like glitter.

Fuck, she's luminous enough in her natural state...

'I'm not disappointed,' says Brooke, keeping her tone mild. 'I'm frustrated.' Her eyes meet mine in the mirror and I try to ignore their vulnerability. 'Why did you stop?'

'Because I could.' I don't want to play games with her, not mind games anyway. But nor can I risk becoming sucked in too deeply by her irresistible, down-to-earth charm. By my own possessiveness. By this physical need for her. Keeping a safe distance is how I stay emotionally disciplined. And, despite her every-day qualities, she comes from another world. A world of power and influence to which I, and the fans outside, don't belong.

She smiles at a Rosa, who says something in Italian and then moves away, her work complete. 'Well, when a woman is naked and laid out before you ready and willing, most men would do more than kiss.'

I cross my arms over my chest. 'I'm not most men.'

Her stare traces my torso in a way that heats my blood before she looks back up, completely unperturbed by my evasiveness. 'That's very obvious. So, do you always just watch? Don't you ever touch? It must take a lot of self-restraint.'

Talking about my sexual preferences when my head is full of the things I'd like to do with her wakes my inner beast. I'd like nothing better than to show her exactly how I like my sex, office hours be damned. The table in front of her holding the make-up paraphernalia looks sturdy enough... The mirrors are perfectly angled so I'd get a wraparound view while we fucked... If the crew wasn't here, I could burrow underneath that voluminous skirt and give her exactly what she's hinting at...

'We're really discussing this here?' I ask, more turned on than I should be by her dogged persistence.

'Yes, I don't see why not.'

'I thought I made it clear. I touch, but on my terms.' Why am I telling this darling socialite from the British aristocracy about my depraved world? Just because she's into a spot of kink. Can I really expose her to my dark side, when the risk for both of us is so high? For her, because she has to project Brooke Madden the brand, and for me because she tests my denial to the limit. I've already allowed her to make a mockery of my rules. Ones there to ensure I don't hurt anyone else the way I hurt my ex, my mother, myself…

'I don't mind the terms.' She swivels her chair away from the mirror so she's facing me, her eyes bright with challenge. 'Last night was fun, but I want more than dribs and drabs.'

My stare follows as the tip of her tongue wipes her lower lip. Perhaps she could handle me and my twisted baggage after all.

'Sex is the only thing on offer,' I remind her. If she imagines some sort of fairy tale—the ex-con and the princess… Never going to happen.

'That's all I want.' She tilts up her chin, exposing her slender neck.

I snort, wondering if there's time to go down on her before the next part of the shoot. 'The word *fun* isn't working for me, though.' My blood boils at the hunger in her eyes and the answering pulsing in my groin.

'Call it whatever you like.' Her eyes narrow with determination I've come to both love and dread. 'But it's going to happen, Nick.'

CHAPTER SEVEN

Nick

DAMNED RIGHT IT'S *going to happen—but my way.*

I press my lips together, braced for what feels like a fall from the Duomo's roof to the cobbles below. Because, even after one kiss, I know being physical with Brooke will test every inch of my restraint.

'You know, for a man who loves control, isn't it better to orchestrate the sex rather than allow it to sneak up on us both?' Those delicious lips twitch. For the first time in years I wish I could shrug off the self-imposed shackles of my discipline. Wish I were free to simply drag her to the nearest flat surface and lose myself.

It's been so long since I acted on instinct.

At eighteen I arrogantly thought I had life all figured out. Then Julia got pregnant. After the initial shock we made plans for our future—not the one either of us would have chosen so young, but one we vowed to make work. Then my reckless streak turned my best intentions, my dreams and Julia's, to ash.

I pulled back after that. Locked down any chance of that happening again. Made control an art form.

And, now I've worn these shackles of self-denial for so long, what if I let go and then can't claw back that control? Pain slices through my lungs, seizing my breath. The last time I lost it, I also lost everything, including a part of my own soul that I'll never get back.

No, I'd rather dictate my own punishments than suffer more painful ones. A little sexual frustration is a small price to pay to avoid devastating consequences. But I can't divulge any of that without sharing the details—something I never talk about. The pain is still too vicious and raw and shameful.

Taking my silence for hesitation, Brooke sighs. 'Look, my last break-up a year ago all but destroyed me and my reputation—I lost endorsement deals because of those nude pictures my ex sold. Some would argue that I was the victim, but I blame myself. I was too trusting. Naïve. And the worst part was that it hurt my family.' She looks down, the confidence draining from her expression and posture, so she looks almost like a little girl playing dress-up with her mother's clothes and make-up, not the international supermodel she is.

But her eyes, when she raises them to mine, conceal her very grown-up pain.

'I can't just hook up with some random person I meet. Most people just want me for all this.' She waves her hand, indicating the fantasy of her current appearance. 'They don't want the real me—the klutzy knitting version…' She smiles with the self-deprecating humour I love.

She's so strong. She struggles with trust but still manages to speak and live from the heart. I fight my own smile, thinking of her hole-riddled knitting, my chest thumping hard. She's doing it again—enticing her way under my skin so I know I have no hope of sleep tonight, just as it eluded me last night after that kiss.

'There are things you should know about me beyond the fact that I can't be responsible for your emotional happiness,' I say.

Her defiance flashes. 'I'm responsible for my own happiness. I'm not talking about emotions. Just sex.'

'I'm only interested in the kind of sex *I* like.' My eyes burn into hers as if drawn there by unseen forces out of my control.

'What kind of sex is that? Because I liked what we did last night.'

I shrug, avoiding looking at those lush lips, which are parted in fascinated astonishment. 'Intense… some would say deviant. Unforgettable. But not usually described as "fun".' I repeat her descriptor back to her, as if it's distasteful, because I have all sorts of visions of those lips I tasted last night, the same ones painted red now, parted around my cock. Nope, *fun* is way too frivolous a word for that kind of pleasure.

'I usually find partners who complement my tastes, so everyone knows what they're entering into. No expectations and no disappointments.' I stare into her expressive eyes, the ones I'll likely see staring back at me from some billboard back in London when this gig is over. Everything about her is expensive, classy, seemingly untouchable. But I've seen the same eyes glazed with arousal. Seen them riddled with doubts. And narrowed in frustration when she's bent over her disastrous knitting.

Yes this woman is nothing like she seems from a distance.

'I think I've proved, twice, that I'm willing to complement your tastes, so why don't you show me what you mean? I might surprise you.' Her voice turns husky with repressed desire. I know this because I've heard her come twice now. Heard the moans and cries she makes, the stuttered breathing.

'Is that right?' I *know* she'll surprise me because nothing about her is what I expected when I agreed to this extended job. In small doses, during daylight hours, she was easier to resist. But now, when there's no quick escape…when she's saying all the right things and I've already had one little taste…

'There are easier, safer, options for you to have a little fun than with me.' I'm running out of excuses save for the juiciest one—my police record. There's still fight in me, although it comes with a vile taste in the mouth, suspicious of jealousy.

'Perhaps.' I catch sight of her fingers curling into the arms of the chair. 'But I told you—trust is a big thing for me. I know you're not going to steal and sell my underwear.'

'No, selling it would be a waste… I'm sure.'

She laughs. She gets my sense of humour, although I'm only half joking, the animal in me dying to get a closer look, smell and taste of all she has to offer. But I know my tendencies—a little of the delectable Brooke goes a long way. I need to keep my exposure to this intense chemistry leashed. Dole out the dribs and drabs the way an addict hopes to limit their consumption.

'I don't want to sound like a spoiled little celebrity, but can you imagine how exhausting it is having to hide the real you all the time? Second-guessing the motives of everyone you meet? Promoting Brooke Madden the brand, without a toe out of line?' She blinks, the vulnerability in her eyes slashing through what's left of my defences. 'Last night was…freeing for me, Nick. I didn't have to do anything or be anyone. Just myself.'

My blood roars, demanding that I show her more. Show her everything. I brace my hands on the back of her chair and swivel her to face the mirror. Our eyes meet there—me standing at her back. My palms burn to touch her bare shoulders. To stroke her shimmering skin. To feel if it's as silky as I imagine. My breath traps in my chest as I treat myself to a miniscule concession—a brief, almost accidental swipe of my right thumb against her upper arm.

The contact blooms through my body from that single point. One touch is not enough. I want to feel her under me and over me and wrapped around me.

'You know by now I'm a voyeur,' I say, watching the flare of heat rush over her skin. 'Not the sleazy, illegal Peeping Tom variety, but the consensual kind.'

'Why?' she asks, lightning-quick.

'What…? Not vanilla enough for you, Lady?' I dodge the question, not sure yet how much I want to reveal about my kinky-arsed ways.

She narrows those trademark eyes of hers a fraction. 'I'm open to other flavours, Nick.'

'It's a control thing. I need the distance.' Admitting this feels as foreign as my stilted attempts at *Buongiorno*. She's drawing me out even while I try to stay tightly coiled. 'I touch on *my* terms. And then I walk.'

Her eyes go wide. 'Always? Have you never had a relationship?'

I shrug, back-pedalling from the lure of her infectious openness. 'One. A long time ago.'

Memories assault me anew. I loved Julia. Loved our baby. One mistake, one momentary lapse in judgement, snatched them both away. Disempowered, and left alone with the consequences, only regret and devastation remained. A cold, dark and lonely place.

I can never go back there…

'I'm not interested in relationships. Only this.' I shrug. I've been as honest as I can.

'I've heard there are clubs for that kind of thing.' She blinks rapidly, the effect accentuated by the false eyelashes she's wearing. 'Is that where you go to find these like-minded partners?'

I grow hard just at the idea of taking Brooke to a club. 'Sometimes. There's one here in Milan, in fact.'

Her eyes spark with excitement and challenge. 'So why don't you take me to this club? Show me what you like?'

'We'll see.' I move away from her temptation and glance at my thumb, which is stained with glitter from my moment of indulgence.

'Think about it, Nick, because last night I wanted to explore all this…' she points from my head to my feet and back '…but I never had the chance.'

Think about it… There are so many Brooke fantasies crammed into my head, I feel as if it might explode. Willing and eager to embrace my desires and concede control, she's a danger. But the idea of her hands on me…her mouth on me…makes me hard enough to decimate what little self-preservation I can muster.

At that moment I'm saved by the shoot director. 'We're ready for you, Brooke.'

I breathe a sigh of relief as she stands and heads out onto the roof terraces of the Duomo. I watch her pose against the backdrop of the cathedral's gothic, gargoyle clad spires and imagine her at Club Vivace, posed in my sexual fantasies.

A very bad idea.

Resisting Brooke Madden is becoming its own trial by fire.

CHAPTER EIGHT

Brooke

I RUFFLE MY shower-damp hair and glide on some lip balm using the sun visor mirror from the passenger seat. 'Well, if you won't take me to this club of yours until this evening,' I say, waggling my eyebrows suggestively because it messes with his head when I flirt, 'Let's go sightseeing.' If Nick is intent on applying the brakes so he can keep this under his strict, kinky control, we can spend the afternoon getting to know each other as consolation.

He looks like a man counting to ten for patience. I hold in a small smile as conflicted torment rolls from his big body like an invisible shield. But did he expect I would allow him to dictate this at a snail's pace? Yes, he can call the shots, but he left me high and dry last night. Well, not exactly, but I want more than a single kiss and some cryptic and evasive answers. Now I've cracked his outer shell, I want everything he's willing to give. But I'll need to tread carefully—opening Nick up is like prying open a stubborn oyster.

Although, I can't deny that his brand of slow-burn seduction is both torture and the most excitement I've ever had.

'I know it's not on the schedule, but I promise to comply with all your safety requests.' I paste on a goofy smile. 'Pretty please?'

His lips twitch before he presses them into submission. 'I thought we agreed—no more unscheduled visits.'

'Come on, Nick. I'm starving. There's a market in the Navilgi district and some nice restaurants. I've been to Milan so many times, I like to simply absorb the atmosphere over a yummy lunch and a glass of wine.'

He flicks me *that* look. The same one he issued when he told me to lock the door adjoining our rooms—desire warring with restraint.

I shudder with delicious anticipation. 'I'm pretty sure that lunch is on the schedule.' Although lust is quickly dislodging my appetite.

I want to push him, to learn all there is to know about this man who guards himself with the same ferocity he applies to keeping me safe from the bad guys.

'You'll be recognised.' His lips form a stubborn flat line that I want to kiss away.

I pull a hand-knitted bobble hat from my bag and tug it on, presenting my disguise to him with my best winning smile. 'I'll wear a hat.'

He glances at me sideways, his intractable stare

softening with amusement. A gentle sigh leaves his body less tense, and I taste victory.

Settling back against the leather seat, I watch him drive for a few minutes. I love the sexy way he handles the wheel, confident and unruffled as he negotiates the rather terrifying Italian traffic, which is all horn-honking and impatient hand gestures.

The memory of last night's kiss comes to me once more as it has all morning. Soft and exploratory at first, and then bold and demanding, as I'd imagined. And then nothing. It felt as if he'd set a timer and thirty seconds was all he'd allowed.

Is that a voyeur thing? Or a Nick thing? Part of the control he needs?

Intrigue settles over me like the glide of silk against my skin. Why does he restrict himself? Why so disciplined? What is it that's left him so restrained and withdrawn that he's resorted to controlling everything—including sex, which by nature is pretty wild and spontaneous? Or should be.

'Can I ask you a question?' he asks, shocking me from my imaginings of what tonight will bring and if it will be as intense and liberating as last night.

'Oh, I love this game.' I'm so excited by his unexpected request that I turn to face him as he drives. 'Of course—ask me anything.'

'Do you actually enjoy knitting?'

I deflate a little, chewing my lip. I love to knit. I'm just crap at it. 'Yes. But I think I like the idea more than the execution.' I pull the hat from my head and run my finger over one of the holes from my many dropped stitches. 'I'm not very good at it, but I find it relaxing. I like creating something with my bare hands. And it's something just for me—no expectations attached. Does that make sense?'

He looks my way but says nothing, only watches me with that blank expression. But, as with every time I confess something to this man, I sense my admission is in safe hands. That he understands me, perhaps more than he wants to admit.

Yes, we're both hiding from something, aren't we, Nick?

As he's clearly in a conversational mood, I plough on.

'My mother recently had breast cancer. I'm sure you heard, as the story was leaked to the papers. Anyway, I attended all her chemo appointments with her and we'd just sit there while she had her treatment, chatting and knitting together. We both find it calming, although unlike me my mum does actually have some skills. My sister has just had a baby—my first nephew—so Mum and I are furiously knitting booties and hats, and I'm struggling my way through a cardigan.'

He frowns. 'I'm sorry to hear about your mother's diagnosis. Is she in the clear now?'

I shrug, because I don't want to think about my mother's mortality. 'Yes, I think so.'

'So you're close, then? You and your mother?'

I nod. 'She's sometimes frustrated with my choice

of career, because she understands the pressures of public life and wanted something different for her daughters. My sister wisely avoided the limelight, so now I bear the brunt of her concern. But most of the time we bumble along well enough. What about you and your mother?' He's never talked about family before. He's never talked about much of anything before.

He stiffens and I immediately have my answer.

'My mother is a good person,' he says. 'Hard working. Kind. I guess I'm just not a very good son.'

I can't help the snort of disbelief that escapes. 'I very much doubt that. But I only know you through work. Tell me, what do you do when you're not working? I'm certain it's not knitting.' I smile, trying to lighten the conversation and encourage him to open up.

He presses his lips together. I assume he won't answer, but then he says, 'I train. I take mixed martial arts classes and I teach self-defence.'

'You do? I'd love you to teach me a few basic moves if you have time. It's something I've wanted to learn for ever, but somehow haven't made a priority. Do you teach women?'

He shakes his head, focussed on driving. 'No. I teach youngsters. Boys mainly.'

He must sense my surprise, because he elaborates without any prompting. 'You should make it a priority. The best form of defence is to remove yourself from a threatening situation. I focus on showing kids how to do that as quickly and effectively as possible. The safest way to defend yourself is to avoid trouble in the first place. Self-defence is about creating a window of opportunity in which to run. It's never about fighting.'

He's passionate about this, perhaps the reason he's spontaneously being frank, where normally I have to drag out every word. Curiosity buzzes in my head. 'That makes sense. You sound like you've had personal experience...' Perhaps in that troubled youth he uncharacteristically once mentioned.

He grips the wheel more tightly, tension moving through his powerful frame. 'Young men in particular often don't know their own strength. A single moment of anger, lashing out with emotion, can have long-reaching, often devastating consequences.'

My pulse leaps. I wish I could see the expression in his eyes, something I've learned are Nick's windows to his true feelings.

'I teach lads to harness their strength and use it to make good choices. I wish I'd had someone to teach me that as a teenager.' He swallows and I can hardly breathe. Besides revealing the voyeurism thing, this is the closest he's come to confessing something personal.

The car grows stifling with the unspoken.

I press my lips together, holding inside all my questions. I look at him with a deeper intent, look beyond his rugged good looks and solid calm presence, sensing deep inner struggle and regret. And perhaps pain.

My throat grows tight, aching for Nick and his secrets. I know what it's like to feel as if there's no one trustworthy to tell. But he's proof that there's always someone safe to confide in.

'I'm sorry that you didn't have that,' I say, wishing he'd trust me to be his sounding board. 'Teenage years are tumultuous for most people. For me it was when I first acknowledged my sexuality and the confusion and shame attached. I've come to terms with those feelings now and my family were great. But I'm hesitant to be publicly open about my dating life. There's more at risk than just public opinion directed my way.'

'You're worried about your parents?'

I nod.

'Their lives have always been so public, so transparent. I hate burdening them with my tabloid privacy breaches too. That's why I'm so protective about my private life. Any negative press I generate gives unscrupulous people another reason to pry into their lives. It's not fair.

'I had a girlfriend, at uni. I was already signed to my modelling agency at that time, and I started to become well-known in my own right. She struggled with my lack of willingness to talk to the press about our relationship. She couldn't understand that I didn't want to talk about my sex life, only my work. She thought I was ashamed. She could be jealous, too.

It eventually caused our break-up. Since then I've made it clear to people I date that I want to keep my relationships off-limits in any media I do.'

'That must be hard. The media can be relentless.'

I shrug, because there are worse crosses to bear. 'I'm lucky that I have people in my life who support and understand me. And I'm glad that your students have you to emulate. It certainly sounds like a hobby that beats knitting—way more rewarding.'

He stiffens. 'I'm no hero.' The set of his jaw is tense once more. 'I made a mistake once. It ruined my life. The lives of others. If I can stop that happening to someone else through teaching self-defence, it helps me to sleep at night.'

I swallow my shock. I'm too scared to probe deeper, in case he once more shuts me out, but I want to help. To understand what motivates him to be so withdrawn when he clearly has so much wisdom and understanding to impart. 'Is that why you think you're a bad son?'

His lips are tight as he pulls out of the traffic and parks up, avoiding my question. 'We're here.'

But now I'm desperately curious. I know how devastating mistakes can feel. How we punish ourselves and carry guilt. I can relate to this side of Nick. I watched every mistake my parents made, big and small, torture and haunt them over the years, amplified by the often negative publicity that followed. I felt the sting of my own naivety—my dating mistakes devastating not only me and my broken and betrayed heart, but my loved ones too. Because my heartbreaks become public property. Picked over by strangers.

I settle on a quaint *trattoria* next to Naviglio Grande, Milan's Grand Canal for lunch. Forgoing the pretty outdoor tables lining the canal, we duck inside out of the cold. Maybe Nick will be more talkative with some food in his stomach.

'I apologise if I said something to upset you,' I begin when we're seated at a cosy table in the window with a red gingham tablecloth and when the waiter has taken our order. 'You never talk about yourself, so I became over-enthusiastic with the snippet of information.' I swallow back how much knowing him means to me—the warmth of a deeper connection with someone I've grown to care about beyond our professional relationship. We're similar in many ways, and refreshingly different in others.

'I *was* serious about you teaching me some self-defence moves, though. I'd really appreciate it, if you have the time.'

Nick rubs a hand over his face—a rare move for the usually unflappable man. 'Sure. I can do that. So, tell me about this dirt-bag who stole your underwear.' When he's serious, his body becomes menacingly still.

I hide my shame behind a sip of my wine, a glass of Lombardy red, while I frame my answer. I've been gullible. Too open and trusting. Hardly attractive qualities.

'I was joking about the underwear, although I've had other personal things stolen—mail, jewellery, clothing. My parents once had a cleaner who stole my father's toothbrush. He became paranoid that she was going to sell his DNA for cloning or something... People will steal anything if they think they can make a quid or two.'

Just then our food arrives. I'm so hungry, I ordered an *antipasto* platter that could have fed four— delicious local cheeses, olives and cured meats. I tuck in while Nick observes me from across the table.

'Aren't you hungry?' I ask, my mouth watering between bites.

Nick shrugs. 'I'm still processing what you've just told me. You definitely need to learn some self-defence.'

My next swallow is painful. I hate thinking of myself as vulnerable, but he's right.

'My ex, Dave, was worse than the thieves, though. He's the one who leaked the nude pictures that the entire world saw.' Humiliation momentarily robs my appetite. But I want him to know that I too have regrets. 'Some mistakes are harder to shake than others, especially if you're in the public eye and those mistakes make for entertainment. Trusting the wrong person is my biggest regret. Because it also hurt my family.'

He shakes his head. Looks as if he's about to share after all. But then he says, 'I didn't see them. I don't read celebrity gossip.'

'Well, you must be the only person in the world to have not seen me naked—' I break off, my face burning, because of course he *has* seen me naked. Last night when I performed for him...

'Dave was a bit controlling.' I twirl my wineglass. 'When I realised that was his game and broke things off, he didn't take the rejection well.'

Now Nick knows how stupid I behaved in the past—naively thinking I was safe to be myself with a man I clearly didn't really know.

He regards me with a frown so harsh, I wouldn't want to be in Dave's shoes if they were ever to cross paths.

'The worst part was that he knew just how to hurt me in return,' I say. 'He knew my struggles to keep parts of my life private. He'd met my family many times, and because he's in the music industry he claimed that he understood the pressures. He knew my mother was getting her cancer treatment and he went public with his photos anyway. Knowing it would hurt my mother, knowing it would embarrass my father. All just to get at me.'

I toy with my bread, breaking off chunks. Nick hasn't eaten a thing.

'And yet you trust me... Sounds like the last thing you need is a connection with someone like me.' His stare is intense.

'Why?' I ask, the hairs lifting on the back of my neck.

He sits forward, resting his forearms on the table.

'I have a criminal record and sexual proclivities that some would find distasteful. I'm exactly the kind of man you pay me to protect you against.' His dark eyes glitter, daring me to take umbrage at or react to this new information.

My heart kicks at my ribs, part excitement, part burning eagerness. But he's right. On paper I shouldn't want anything more with him than to have a working relationship.

'Well, we all have our secrets. I didn't know about the record, but it's no else's business who I employ.'

Is it rude to ask what he did?

'But we're not talking about just my professional services. You want more than that.' He tilts his head in that way of his, an unapologetic half-shrug. 'Why don't you ask me what I did?'

I focus on his eyes, trepidation creeping over my skin. 'Did you go to prison?' I ask, wanting the details, but also certain they won't change the way I feel about him.

He smiles, that glittering glint of challenge in his stare. But now I see vulnerability too, the same emotion I see when he talks about needing control. It's more than a sexual kink. It's a way of life…

'Yes. A long time ago,' he says. 'I was eighteen. I served my sentence. I'm rehabilitated and reformed in the eyes of society.'

I can tell there's a part of him that doesn't completely believe those words. I'm struck speechless. Not because I'm appalled, but because he's letting me in at last. This is the mistake he regrets. A part of the real Nick—the one he keeps locked down with his rules and his control and his restraint.

Why does it feel as if he's still punishing himself? As if he genuinely believes I'd change my mind about us because he made a mistake half a lifetime ago?

'What did you do?' I ask. I'd be stupid not to know. It can't be that serious, otherwise it would have surfaced in the background check I'd had performed before I hired him.

His grin is cold and doesn't reach his eyes. 'I was a stupid young man. I had no real male role model, so I made up my own version of what it is to be a man.'

I wait, my stomach tight with nerves. I can't believe Nick, the man I've known all this time—professional, dedicated and patient—is capable of a heinous act. But I don't really know him despite the hours of one-on-one time we've spent together. 'Taciturn' is an understatement. Still, I've always known him to act with honesty and integrity.

He must see my confusion.

'Don't worry—you're right to feel physically safe with me,' he reassures me. 'I'd never hurt you or anyone else.' He takes a sip of water and I feel what this costs him. I'm about to tell him that it doesn't matter, that he doesn't have to talk about it, when he speaks again.

'I got provoked into a fight. I threw *one* punch. That's all it took for the other guy to be hospitalised.'

'Did you start it?' My voice is barely more than

a whisper. Is this why he loves control? To protect himself from making another mistake? Understandable, but surely a little excessive, given the passage of so many years? Years in which he's paid his debt to society, served his country and built a successful business protecting others and inspiring young men to avoid the same fate.

He shakes his head. 'I was protecting the girlfriend I had back then—Julia. Some guy picked a quarrel in a bar. I thought the only way to defend her was to be a tough guy.'

'Well, that's understandable.' Part of the reason I feel so safe with him is his dominating physical size. If I needed someone on my team, I'd want Nick. But it's hard to imagine him losing his head. I've never seen him even close to angry.

He shrugs away my comment. 'Now I'm smart enough to do things the easy way. I should have walked away. Saved myself a lot of grief.'

'How long were you in prison?' I ask, feeling unsettled despite my rationale that he's a reformed character. But he's right—the press would have field day if they caught any whiff of a relationship between us. My father would pop something—violent crime is always a political hot potato.

Actions cost votes, girls. Make good choices. Even now I can hear my father's caution, from every time my sister and I left the house growing up. We couldn't attend parties in case there was under-age drinking or drugs. We had to vet the school friends we brought home. We even had to sit through hours of coaching on what *not* to say if asked.

But now I have Nick talking, finally opening up, I want to know him even more.

'Four months.' He looks away as if reminded of painful memories beyond a brief period of incarceration.

I'm lost for words. I live a privileged life. Always have. I have no idea what prison is like. But Nick's still very much haunted by his past.

'When I got out, I joined the army,' he says, a faraway look in his eyes. 'Learned discipline and self-respect. Grew up.'

My chest aches for his pain. There's more to the story. I want to push but I respect his privacy, and I feel the return of his emotional distance like an electric fence. 'Well, like you said, you served your time. You turned your life around. And now you mentor youngsters and run a business protecting others. And here we are.'

'Yes, here we are, Lady. With nothing in common and a million reasons why going to that club tonight is a bad idea.'

But, rather than turn me off, his story makes me respect him more. He's more real now. Flawed. A good man who made one mistake. My attraction hasn't dampened in the slightest, if that was his plan.

'I disagree. We both have secrets. Both made mistakes. I think we have lots in common—chemistry for sure. I assure you, my eyes are wide open. I know what I want, Nick.'

And what I want seems to change, become less clear and more complex, with every hour I spend in his company. Taking one last leap of faith, I speak the most burning need.

'I want you to know that you can talk to me, if you need to. That you can trust me.'

'I don't need to trust you,' he says, those dark eyes of his back to being intense and penetrating. 'I just have to protect you.'

Of course he would retreat after confiding something so personal. And he's still on the clock. But tonight…after hours…is a different story.

'Well, protecting me means staying close and keeping your eyes open, right?' I say in a playful tone. Things need lightening up. A reminder that his confession hasn't deterred me. 'I'd say we're a perfect match in that regard. You being such a kinky bastard.'

A blast of genuine laughter erupts from him, dousing me in its brilliance until I catch my breath. I don't think I've witnessed it up until now. His unrestrained smile is a thing of breath-taking beauty, changing his entire face and revealing deep grooves around his mouth. I want to know this Nick with twice the ferocity, his multiple facets as compelling as they are complex.

'Kinky bastard…?' he asks, traces of playfulness lingering around his lips. He selects an olive and tosses it into the air before catching it between his teeth.

I nod, the atmosphere around us now charged with sexy flirtation and possibility. I wish I could just lean across the table and kiss him. Instead, I finish my wine. 'So, is there dancing at this club of yours?'

'Dancing isn't on the schedule.' He tucks into the food with gusto.

'No, it isn't.' We reach for the same slice of salami at the same moment and our fingers brush, sending jolts of delight to all my erogenous zones. 'But the schedule doesn't count after hours.'

He mutters the F-bomb under his breath, conceding defeat with a slump back into the chair. 'Fine. You dance. I'll watch.'

I wink, already planning my outfit. 'Sounds perfect.'

CHAPTER NINE

Brooke

RATHER THAN BEING hidden down some dingy back alley, the venue Nick suggests is housed in the Palazzo Pietro, a neoclassical building more in keeping with a library or museum than a sex club. But, for all its grandeur, Nick assures me that Club Vivace is prohibitively discreet.

As an extra precaution Nick insists we forgo the main entrance for the service access. At the reception, I tremble with leashed energy and anticipation, my skin sensitive against the fabric of the slinky little black dress that I chose for the occasion. I'm too far out of my comfort zone to pay much attention to Nick's conversation with the receptionist as we check our mobile phones and sign the paperwork required for admittance. Nerves that I'll be recognised battle with the excitement clenching my stomach, but I take full responsibility for being here. Nick is finally gifting me a glimpse of his private self.

The heavy thump of dance music vibrates the

walls and floor under my feet as I walk behind Nick down darkened womb-like corridors. My legs tremble with every step, but exhilaration dances low in my belly too. I've always wanted to come to a club like this. I never dared risk it back in London, so close to home. I'm too well-known and most days have paps camped out on my street. Just because Nick knows the owner and smuggled me in through the back door is no guarantee that I won't wake up tomorrow to discover my face and those of my parents plastered all over the Internet. And, with every negative story that's written about me, there's a risk that my sex scandal will be resurrected.

Despite the privacy measures taken for members' peace of mind here at the club, exposure of my private life resulting in harm to my parents is my deepest fear. Personal attacks sting worse than professional criticism. My mother was reproached for seeking cancer treatment at a private hospital, something that created added heartache at a stressful and terrifying time. No doubt if she'd chosen the National Health Service she'd have faced scorn for taking someone else's spot when she can afford to pay.

Sometimes you're damned if you do and damned if you don't.

Icy chills of dread rush over my skin. I swallow hard, wishing I could I hold Nick's hand for comfort. This risk is worth it, because he's brought me somewhere important to him, and I feel closer to him than ever. But I very much doubt that he's the hand-holding type. Nick's touch is carefully doled out—on my wrist, that single astonishing kiss and the almost reverent brush of my arm this morning that he thought I hadn't felt. And, because of its rarity, he's ramped up my yearning and anticipation so I'm crazed for his touch.

We arrive at the very heart of the nightclub. My eyes dart round for hints of what to expect, but it's just like a regular club—crowded bar, dancing bodies distorted under the frantic strobe lighting, deafening dance music. It's also full of dark and intimate nooks and corners.

Nick guides me to one of these near the bar. I order a couple of shots, knocking them back for Dutch courage while Nick sips a beer. Then, with the taste of vodka in my mouth, I cast Nick a final seductive look and head onto the dance floor.

Operation 'Seduce Nick Out of His Trousers' is on.

Let the fun begin.

I've always loved the abandon of dancing. The energy at Club Vivace is contagious. Everyone else seems lost to the sultry beat. I close my eyes and dance. I forget that I might be recognised. Forget who my parents are. Forget that I'm Brooke Madden.

Knowing Nick is probably watching me, planning whatever is in his dirty mind, sends flutters of anticipation deep into my pelvis and makes my nipples tingle against the fabric of my dress. The heady feeling of liberation returns, stronger than before. I'm dancing alone in a Milan sex club, lost in myself, and I've never felt more alive. By bringing me here, Nick has provided a safe haven so I can be myself. And he can be himself. He likes to watch, and I'm addicted to performing for him.

I raise my arms over my head, sensually swaying my hips from side to side, slowly enough to seduce. I feel the weight of his stare from across the room. It touches every inch of my body, sparking electricity as surely as if it's his touch. It feels like my very first major runway walk in the euphoria stakes— dazzling and exhilarating.

I open my eyes and our stares collide, his dark and dangerous. I freeze, so taken aback by the look of sheer unadulterated need on his face. For a split second he doesn't look like Nick. He's a tortured stranger. One with pain and doubt, desire and urgency, in his eyes.

The rest of the club fades away.

Heat and passion and understanding pulse between us like an invisible force field. I catch my breath, fire pooling between my legs. I move in his direction, no longer interested in this game of cat and mouse. I want him close. I want his touch. I want to connect with that broken part of him that speaks to me.

Now that he's shown me that he too is hiding his vulnerabilities, his pain, my need is almost unbearably vicious. Almost overwhelming. Yes, I still want to test his restraint, the control he wears like a straitjacket, but now that I know it's a shield protecting him from his past mistakes I also want to catch him when he lets go.

There are no guarantees in this life when it comes to what really matters. No fail-safe protection. Not wealth or status or power.

All we have is today and the hope of tomorrow.

Nick's eyes narrow at my approach, as if he sees my intent. Where I've lost my trust in others, Nick seems to have lost his trust in himself. He's stuck. Trapped behind barriers he's constructed in order to keep me, and probably everyone else, at arm's length.

I want to give him what he's given me—a safe space to be himself. Acceptance. That's why I needed him to bring me to a place where he feels in control. To show him that he's as safe with me as I am with him.

I reach him, hunger and desire pounding through my blood with every beat of my jacked-up heart. 'Dance with me,' I say, trying to convey my desperation in my eyes. I want his lips, his touch, the brilliant passion I see him struggle to contain.

'Not here.'

I nod, my body on fire for him to show me everything that he is—the good and the ugly. My soul's yearning to connect on a primal level. Just a man and a woman.

'Okay. Show me where,' I whisper, anticipation building like a roaring blaze.

He places his beer on the bar and takes my arm.

I'm instantly weak with ecstasy at the possessive and gentle curl of his fingers around my bicep. My legs wobble. Only his hand—big, sure and warm—grounds me and keeps me upright. When we exit the nightclub area, his hand slides the length of my forearm until we're holding hands. I grasp his fingers, my insides flipping cartwheels when he grips mine in return. It's every bit as comforting as I imagined. He may need control, but inch by inch he's allowing me closer.

He glances my way, questions in his eyes. I smile. I'm being led into the unknown and I want him to see that I go with him willingly—no, eagerly.

No doubts.

Beyond the main nightclub lies a warren of dark corridors and rooms, most concealing their secrets behind closed doors. I hurry after Nick's longer strides, arriving at another dark corridor, this one lined on one side with windows set into alcoves.

My breath dries up, nerves strangling me as we pause at the corridor's entrance. Nick faces me, stepping up close and keeping hold of my hand.

'You sure you want to be here, Lady?' His searching stare moves over my face as if he can read the tumult inside.

'Yes.' I crave the reassurance of his beautiful smile. But it's a luxury and, like all the best things, more breath-taking when it does make an appearance. 'Call me Brooke tonight, please.'

There's no room for teasing nicknames or going

back to our former professional distance. Even if it means employing someone else for my future security needs, I want to be more to him than a famous woman whom it's his job to protect. I want him to know me as I truly am. To be real to him, just as I want to see him undone. Unrestrained. Exposed.

He gives a single decisive nod of surrender. Then he grips my face with both hands. I think he's going to kiss me and my knees almost buckle. But, where his stare carries a new intensity, it's still shuttered.

'Everyone using these rooms enjoys being watched, understand?' His eyes trace my mouth as he speaks, as if he's recalling our first kiss, as I am. As if craving a repeat. How can he hold himself back…? I know he feels the same burning desires I do.

I nod, excitement throbbing in my throat and robbing me of speech.

'They can't see us, but they know when someone is watching—there's a sensor. A light comes on.' His low, steady voice boosts my confidence. 'We can stop wherever you like, or just walk on. It's *your* decision.'

I nod. My blood pounds so hard I feel faint. 'I trust you,' I assure him, reaching up to peel his palm from my cheek so I can once more hold his hand. Perched on the precipice of something new with him, I've never felt more alive. More free. Despite stating that he needs to be in charge of this, he's giving me all the control of the situation, all the choice. Any nerves or lingering reservations flee.

We move down the darkened corridor. I grip

Nick's hand more tightly, my steps small, hesitant, as I enter the first windowed alcove.

My stomach plummets. The room beyond the glass is dimly lit but empty. In the low lighting I make out a luxurious bedroom with a four-poster bed and black satin sheets.

I move on, aware of Nick's ragged breathing beside me, his body close, his hand gripping mine as if he too is nervous. My body hums with arousal—new and dizzying levels. I understand now why this feeds his self-control because, while the anticipation is a thunderous roar in my head, I feel empowered. Strong. Invincible in a way nothing or no one in my life has ever made me feel.

Until Nick.

At the second window I suck in an involuntary gasp. This room is occupied. My first conditioned reflex is to step back. My back makes contact with Nick's solid chest. I sag into him behind me with relief at the thundering of his heart. His arm comes around my waist, and I grip his hand once more, entwining my fingers with his, grateful I'm not alone in this exhilaration.

A man and woman occupy the room. Both are naked. The woman sits on the edge of the massive bed, braced on her straight arms while the man kneels on the floor between her thighs, performing oral sex.

The display is so carnal that our mere presence here on the other side of the one-way glass feels somehow taboo even though, intellectually, I know they enjoy being watched. But I can't move. I can't look away.

Through the roar of blood in my ears I grow aware of the sound of my own rapid and harsh breathing. I feel Nick's heat at my back, his breath a warm tease on my neck, stimulating my nerve endings. I'm enveloped by the manly scent of him. He's everywhere.

I look up over my shoulder. Just as backstage after the fashion show, he's watching me, watching my reaction to the couple rather than the action itself.

And his eyes are ablaze with lust.

I drop my head back onto his hard shoulder, feeling his scruff against my cheek. His arm is a steel band around my waist, his erection obvious in the small of my back. The intimacy of this blasts through me like an explosion. It's not about the strangers. It's about us. Nick and I, sharing this moment of complete and utter trust and abandonment. He's showing me this side of himself. It's more profound than any prior sexual experience.

It's addictive.

Nick dips his head, his whisper warm against my ear. 'Do you want to hear them?'

I nod, aroused but also conflicted. My upbringing and society's norms compound the feeling that this is somehow wrong. But we're all consenting adults. No one is being coerced or exploited, a fact that's confirmed when the man on his knees glances our way with a small smile on his face—he knows we're here on the other side of the glass.

Nick presses a button on the wall, flooding us with the sound of the woman's cries of pleasure and the man's grunts of satisfaction. He pauses, says something to her in Italian that I don't quite hear and then lifts one of her legs, draping it over his shoulder before delving back in. She grips his head, watching him but also glancing at the window, at us, from time to time.

'Why do you like this?' I whisper, trembling with need. I lift my arm overhead to tangle in Nick's dark, silky hair and hold him closer. I crave deeper understanding of his past and his pain. I burn to know all there is to know about this man who seems to have infected my consciousness and made me probe my own deep desires like no previous lover.

His cheek grazes mine, his breath hot, jolting my nerve endings. 'Because I can enjoy it without being a part of it.' His voice is low and resonant with arousal. His lips brush my skin. Not a kiss, but from him it's somehow more than a kiss. Because every move he makes is measured and meaningful. I sag deeper into him—he's practically holding me upright, I'm so boneless.

'I'm detached. In control,' he says. 'I can stay or walk away at any time.'

My heart judders with fear behind my ribs. Am I right about Nick? Is he too broken by his past for true intimacy? I can empathise with his regrets without knowing the details, but whatever has caused him to be this way has cut soul-deep.

'But I don't want you to be detached with me,' I whisper, my throat a hot ache of need.

My words settle in the fraught air. His fingertips press into my waist with a fraction more pressure, as if he can't help himself that tiny indulgence. I spin away from the window and look up at him for a beat, needing to see on his face that he feels as wild and unrestrained as I feel even if, for his own reasons, he's still fighting the complete loss of inhibitions.

It's written all over the harsh, handsome planes of his face, which is taut with everything he's trying to hold inside. His eyes are anguished and I can no longer hold back.

I hurl myself against his chest, my lips colliding with his, too desperate to connect with him and drag him towards pleasure to wait a second longer. The force of my body slamming against his dislodges his finger from the button on the wall that allows us to hear what is happening in the room and we fall into silence. Silence that quickly fills with the sound of my own pulse and the needy whimpers I can't contain as I kiss Nick Rivers the way I've wanted to for months.

CHAPTER TEN

Brooke

IT'S NOT A controlled kiss held to ransom. Instead it contains my every desire, every demand, every searing need. I push my tongue into his mouth, feel his counter thrust and revel in it. Nick hauls me from my feet with one strong arm around my waist. He stumbles back against the wall of the alcove we're occupying and scoops me up. I straddle his waist to feast on his glorious kisses—his firm, insistent lips and the powerful, sensual surge of his tongue, his unrestrained abandon which matches mine.

It's everything I dreamed.

It's as if he's flicked a switch. As if he's done fighting his own boundaries. As if he's finally unleashed himself to take what he wants. He spins us around, reversing our positions so I'm pressed against the wall and he's holding me there with his hips between my legs. His erection is right where I need the friction. Spikes of pleasure blank my mind.

I'm just sensation. Euphoria. Release. Out of

control, as if we're trapped in the centre of a hurricane.

Then Nick pulls back, his eyes almost black with desire. Searching. Serious. Soul-destroying in their beauty and depth and vulnerability.

'What are you doing to me?' he pants out.

It's rhetorical, another kiss swallowing my answer. He cups my face, pinning my mouth under his plundering tongue and voracious lips.

'Where can we go?' I ask, my hips rocking desperately against his hard length.

He sobers a little, his eyes clearing of the lust-drunk glaze. He lowers my feet to the floor and then takes my hand, this time with wonderful urgency.

I rush after his ground-eating strides, barely cognisant of him keying in a code at another closed door on the opposite side of the corridor from the windowed rooms. We fall into a darkened bedroom almost identical to the one we've just peered into to watch another couple have sex.

The music from the nightclub is piped here from hidden speakers but at half the volume. The rhythmic and hypnotic beat of the dance track gives the room a sense of sensual privacy. A club just for two.

But, now that I'm bereft of Nick's intoxicating kisses and the blur of arousal, caution creeps over my skin. I scan the room for a window or large mirror. My stomach twists with uncertainty. I trust him to protect me, but I'm also aware of my location. *Socialite Heiress Frequents Milanese Sex Club* is not a headline I want my parents to wake up to tomorrow morning.

He sees my furtive checking and tugs me close. His stare pins me with his trademark intensity. 'This room is different. Private, understand? We didn't sign up to be watched, and I'd never do anything without your consent.'

I nod in relief and sway towards him, desperate to lose myself in the passion he showered upon our kissing only moments ago. But, apart from the inferno of heat in his eyes, he's back in control. I shiver as he slowly strips off his black leather jacket, heels off his boots and loses his socks.

Saliva fills my slack mouth. I could watch him strip every day for the rest of my life and be blissfully happy. He's so masculine. So sure of himself. So mind-numbingly sexy.

'But you like to watch,' I say, loving the further flare of excitement in his eyes.

He smiles. Genuine. Seductive. That wondrous sight that is so rare, I feel humbled, awed and desperate to make him smile over and over...

'I'll watch *you*.' He removes his T-shirt and pops the top two buttons on his jeans, where his erection is an impressive bulge.

I wet lips that are still sensitive from his kisses and aching for more. My eyes rake over his bare chest for the first time. I'm a kid in a sweetshop—Nick's sculpted body decorated with intricate tattoos and a smattering of dark hair is a divine feast. He's like a fallen angel, his eyes dark, dangerous and a little wild. He's looking at me with similar hunger, and I want to burn in the heat and passion I see coiled inside him.

My heart lurches in an insane and poorly timed moment of doubt. 'Does it always need to be strangers that you watch?' I say, tentative about asking the wrong thing, but also needing to know that I'm enough for him.

'No.' He shakes his head slowly, a sexy smile playing around his mouth. 'I could watch you for hours. Days.' He cups my cheek and rubs the pad of his thumb over my parted lips. 'Your display last night almost killed me. I came in my own fist at how sexy you are. How uninhibited and spontaneous.' He closes his eyes and drags breath through his flared nostrils. When he reopens his eyes, I want to swim in the perfect pools of his expressive irises.

'There are lots of ways to watch—mirrors, through a camera, finding some sexy, raunchy goddess who likes to perform for you when she knows you're watching.' His smile is a ghost of the rare, full-blown variety but, knowing its scarcity, my breath snags with yearning.

'I wasn't sure if you were there,' I whisper.

His eyes narrow, sparks flying. 'Oh, I saw everything. The shower. The dildo. The look on your face when you came for me.' He presses his mouth to mine—fast and fierce. 'You wanted to dance,' he goes on, his voice tight with that same lust I witnessed in the corridor. 'So dance. Just for me.'

He steps back and lowers himself into a wing-

back armchair, spreading his thighs in a comfortable, lazy sprawl.

The excitement flying through my system makes
me shudder. I kick off my shoes and glance around
the room, locating a remote control on the bedside
table. I turn up the volume of the music and start to
dance—slow, seductive, sensual moves which carry
me in Nick's direction.

I stop just out of arm's reach. Nick likes to deny
himself. Delayed gratification is part of what turns
him on. Rushing in all eager and grabby won't help
me to achieve my goal—Nick helpless, letting go of
that restraint. And devouring me with all that sup-
pressed craving.

I lock eyes with his, deliberately shimmying the
straps of my dress over my shoulders to expose the
tops of my breasts. I'm not wearing a bra so my nipples strain hard and obvious against the silky material. His stare darts there, his nostrils flaring as if
he can't get enough air.

I'm light-headed myself—this tease, the anticipation, is working its magic. I turn my back to him and
gyrate my hips until the dress slips to the top of my
butt, hopefully exposing my lacy thong for his eyes.

I smile to myself. Nick's harsh breathing is loud
enough to compete with the dance track. Over my
shoulder I watch the flare of his pupils as I slide the
dress over my hips. I bend to scoop the fabric from
the floor, purposefully taking my time so Nick can
feast his eyes on my scrap of underwear and what
it fails to conceal.

When I turn back to face him, his grip on the arms of the chair seems to be the only thing keeping him seated. His thick thighs are spread wide. His erection strains at the fly of his jeans and his chest gusts out choppy breaths.

'Don't stop,' he orders.

I raise my arms over my head and shimmy my hips, aware my breasts are thrust in his direction, nipples proud and begging. Oh, I want to beg. But I want to perform, too, until he can't take any more.

His stare rises from my breasts. 'Can I touch you?' His voice is so raspy, he sounds like a stranger. And he's asking me for permission...? When for months I've craved his touch like a starving woman? When I've teased and tortured and seduced, doing everything in my power to have him where he is in this moment?

My stomach muscles clench with longing. I want his hands on me more that I want him buried inside me, but I also want more of Nick than his carefully doled out measures. I'm determined to play him at his own game. To draw out the anticipation until his control is a frayed and ragged thing. Until burning arousal consumes us both in the flames.

With effort I shake my head, denying his request. Excitement and hunger shift over his features. His cock flexes against his fly.

Triumph sings through me.

My embracing the game, prolonging the moment of surrender, excites him. I sway closer, positioning myself between his thighs, not quite touching.

Every tilt of my hips inches me between his spread legs. The body heat he's generating sears my skin. His leashed desperation is like electricity crackling in the air before a storm.

I brace my hands on the chair arms where his fingers flex, his knuckles bloodless-white. My breasts are level with his face, which is taut with repressed lust.

'Kiss me,' I say, dipping my head so my mouth is one swoop away from contact. I can't hold out any longer.

He lifts his head from the back of the chair and finds my mouth, his tongue surging forward to meet mine. It's our only point of contact, heightened for the fact. Every nerve-ending screams for more.

I'm about to collapse into his lap when he breaks away, his eyes blazing with need. 'Can I touch you?' This time his question is gruff, full of bite and the desperation I've longed to hear.

I stand, the kiss having rendered me helpless to my own needs. The insides of my thighs are slick with arousal. I want him too much for role-playing or games.

'Yes. Oh, please, yes.'

My lips have barely stopped moving before Nick surges from the chair, scoops his arms around my waist and in two strides hauls me onto the bed.

I'm deposited against the cool sheets, and then he's on top of me, his mouth ravaging mine while I moan and claw at his thick muscular arms and bare chest. His body suffocates me, all scalding heat against my breasts and corked power crushing me in his arms. My hands can't stay still, hell bent on exploring every slab of sculpted chest and back, every muscle, every inch of fevered skin.

I want to kiss him all over, to marvel at the intricate designs of his tattoos—some script, some geometric patterns—and the taste and scent of his skin. But that would involve losing his mouth, and I'm too high on his thorough kisses to stop. Too high on triumph that I'm finally getting what I wanted—Nick unleashed.

He breaks free and I whimper. His sensual lips are swollen and reddened. 'Fuck, you've tortured me for months.' For a split second he looks shocked by his own admission. Then he dives for one breast, his mouth swallowing the distended and needy peak. I cry out at the thrill of pleasure, digging my nails into his biceps to hold on to my sanity.

'Yes, Nick. Don't stop…please.' Now he's finally mine, I never want to leave this room.

Nick lavishes, licks and sucks one nipple, and then rips his mouth away to repeat the divine torment on the other.

'Oh…my…' I gurgle some inarticulate sounds. I'm making an embarrassing amount of noise, gasping and wailing, but it's too good. I couldn't stay silent if I tried. I just hope these rooms are soundproof.

'I need you inside me,' I say, cradling his head, my fingers flexing against his scalp and languishing in his thick dark hair.

He releases my nipple with a long protracted suck and rears back on braced arms. 'And I need to taste this gorgeous pussy.' He slides his hand over my mound and cups my sex, his beautiful features taut with desire.

'Yes!' I hiss.

He spreads my thighs without ceremony and presses a kiss right over my clit through the fabric of my underwear. My hips buck off the bed and my head arches back. That's when I notice the mirrors on the ceiling.

I gasp and Nick chuckles.

They capture the entire scene. Me spread-eagled wearing only a nude lace thong. My pale skin ethereal against the black sheets. Nick's large frame hunched over me, his back muscles bunching and his dark head buried between my thighs. I whimper at the carnal sight.

Nick smiles at my reaction. 'Enjoy the view.' He slips the fabric of my thong aside and the cool air and his warm breath hit my exposed lips. I gasp.

'If only you knew how much I've wanted you. How hard it's been to ignore all this.' I look down. Nick's staring, stroking one thick finger through my arousal and over my folds. Nothing Nick does is impulsive or rushed and now I'm torn between greedily hastening this along and languishing in every decadent second of his coveted attention.

'I want you too,' I say, anticipation a sharp metallic taste in my mouth. But when I look back up to the mirrors, watch the scene as if from outside my own body, I shake with the eroticism of the moment he's created for us.

Then he licks me. His flattened tongue swipes over my flesh and then focuses on my clit. I cry out, the pleasure streaking along my nerve endings like bolts of lightning.

'Nick... Nick...' I chant his name, gripping his head as he sucks and tongues me higher and higher.

He spears one and then two fingers inside me and that's when I notice he's watching us too, from a mirror on the wall. I turn my head to the side, catching his gaze in the reflection. It's as if we're watching another couple, only better. Because it's us.

He holds my stare in the mirror, his mouth and fingers still working me like a man starved. I suck in a breath at the look of triumph, need and raw hunger in his eyes. His abandon is better than I'd dreamed because he's not only let me in physically, he's cranked open his emotional fortress.

The room blacks out as I'm tossed into an orgasm so powerful, all my other senses shut down for long agonising seconds. When I resurface, open my eyes, Nick is naked, his erection straining up as he sheaths himself in a condom.

Wordlessly, he climbs over me on the bed. He traces my face with one palm. He leans over me, kissing me with that leashed passion I've now grown to expect as he encourages me to turn onto my stomach and rise up onto all fours.

I comply, eager for his penetration at long last.

I'm facing the mirror.

Our eyes connect there. He grips my hips, his fingers flexing into my skin as he looks at our reflections. I see in his eyes that he's losing what's left of his control.

In case he's waiting for my permission, I urge, 'Do it, Nick. Fuck me.' Because I'll die if I don't feel him inside me soon.

His stare holds. He clenches his jaw and pushes inside me so slowly I want to weep. But his hand on my hip, his gritted teeth and flexed jaw, stops me slamming backwards and impaling myself. He's still controlling the pace, where I'm desperate to race to the finish line so we can start all over again.

He's big, thick. I force myself to relax as he works his way inside me. The look of intense pleasure and agony on his face freezes every part of me, including my heartbeat. When he's fully seated he drops his chin to his chest, his long, agonised exhale the only sound he makes.

How can he do that? I want to scream my pleasure to the skies. Even now, buried as deeply inside me as he can go, he's contained. Fighting for control. But his emotions are clearly displayed in his dark eyes. He's struggling every bit as I am to contain this intense pleasure.

But it's his show. That doesn't mean I can't play dirty, of course. I clench my pelvic floor muscles around him, satisfaction tugging a smile from me as I hear his low groan. His eyes slam to mine in the mirror.

'Playing with fire, Brooke?' He presses his chest to my back, reaches around and tugs on one nipple with his thumb and forefinger. This time the clench of my internal muscles is involuntary, but no less delightful.

'Yes. But you make me burn. Please move…' I'm begging now, but I'm past caring.

He positions my body exactly the way he wants it—a shift of one thigh here and a tilt of my hips there, so I'm spread wider to his penetration, and presumably for maximum view in the mirrors.

Gripping my hips in his tight grasp, Nick starts to thrust into me, holding me close to him so I feel every scrape of his length inside, and I'm stretched almost beyond pleasure.

'Can you come again?' he asks, his stare burning into mine with such ferocity I want to look away. Because after everything we've shared today—kinks, confessions, this club—his eye contact is the most intimate. How didn't I notice before how much emotion he displays in the depths of his eyes? And why, oh why, did he fight this so hard?

I nod, because amazingly I'm close, and I want to perform for him until I collapse from exhaustion.

I take my weight on one hand and slide the other between my legs, caressing his balls before finding my clit, which is greedy for some more attention. His eyes flare with heat and he watches the reflection of my hand moving between my thighs in time to his thrusts.

It's the wild, frenzied coupling of two people who've waited too long. It's everything I wanted, and I love every second of its perfection.

'Come for me, Brooke,' he says huskily. With a

few swipes over my engorged clit and with Nick's continued thrusts I come, screaming out my orgasm as I try to keep my stare locked with Nick's in the mirror.

He slams into me over and over, his jaw clamped, nostrils flared as he fights his own mounting climax to ride out mine to the last soul-destroying spasm.

I watch in wonder. Thrilled to be finally getting everything I've craved for so long. Nick Rivers undone. For me.

But at the last minute, when I'm finally spent, he pulls out, scoops his arm around my waist like a steel band and hauls me into a kneeling position, my back pressed to his chest. I feel his cock pulsing between our bodies in the small of my back. He buries his face against the side of my neck as he comes without a single sound.

I stay still as he bucks against me, crushing my body to mould against his until he's wrung dry and collapses us both back onto the bed.

The euphoria and triumph I felt at the best sex of my life dies out, leaving me close to inexplicable and ridiculous tears, and with one depressing thought.

Nick is broken. Punishing himself. And I need to know why.

CHAPTER ELEVEN

Nick

I FEEL HER questions build as I lie still under her, the painful thud of my heart mocking the calm, controlled exterior I'm trying to project. But she cut my restraint to shreds. I close my eyes, flashbacks going off behind my eyelids. Brooke embracing this club when I knew it was her first experience. Dancing for me, her beautiful stare displaying her every feeling. Her sexy striptease and how she instinctively heightened my desperation for her through a hint of denial…

She gave me everything I said I needed and it still wasn't enough to keep me in control. Because she's perfect. Too perfect. Still as dangerous as a steel blade to my throat.

Panic rolls through my stomach. I don't need her to be any more of a temptation. I can't allow this connection to get away from me. And yet in less than three days she's managed to bewitch me so thoroughly, I'm already hard again. Desperate to touch her again and again and again…

But good sex is an emotional experience. That doesn't mean I can allow this woman to undo the barriers I've spent years constructing. Barriers that make me the man I am. The man I want to be.

I don't want to hurt her but, from her pensive silence and the wounded expression I caught on her face as I pulled her down to the mattress, I guess I already have with my messed-up need to stay detached.

Yeah...real detached, dickhead.

I wanted her so damned much that I almost lost my mind. Almost lost complete control. With every ragged breath I try to claw it back. But the sick sense of dread tells me it might be too late.

'Why didn't you come inside me?' she asks, her question jabbing between my ribs.

I bide my time, my fingers toying with her short silky hair, which smells like sunshine and sin. I could lie. Construct some excuse that won't expose the very heart of me and how I'm too twisted and ruined for any woman, let alone a woman like Brooke. But she's smart, and after everything she's given me tonight she deserves more than the scraps I've given her up to now.

Her gentle reassurance earlier over lunch all but slayed me. *I want you to know that you can talk to me, if you need to. That you can trust me.*

But no amount of talk will change what I did, or return what I lost. This post-coital emotion is as pointless as my regret. It changes nothing.

She must feel the defeated exhale that recoils my chest under her head.

'I don't have any infections and I'm on birth control, if that's what you're worried about.' She looks up, a pinch of confusion settled between her brows and a glimmer of hurt lingering in her eyes. 'And you were wearing a condom so...you know...double protection.'

I've hurt her. Hurt and insulted her.

Fuck.

I rest my hands on her back, stroking her warm skin so I can find the strength to formulate the right words. 'It's not that. It's not you.' Shit, that's the best I can come up with...?

Bile reaches the back of my throat and I swallow the shame down hard, feeling small and stupid. Of course my weird withdrawal is partly a safety thing. Habit I've formed over seventeen years because I made that mistake with Julia. But how can I tell this incredible woman all my shameful secrets? How I was once young and reckless enough to act without thought for the consequences? How I got Julia pregnant and naively, arrogantly, believed everything would work out? How I'd then landed myself in prison and she'd lost our baby. How Julia herself almost died.

Pain shoots through me as if my terrible cascade of mistakes happened yesterday.

All that I am, all that I do, prevents me from feeling like I'm freewheeling back towards those bleak days. That dark place of grief and impotence and utter self-inflicted aloneness.

Brooke stares, peeling away layers of me with the questions banked behind her emotive eyes. 'Didn't you enjoy yourself?' She nibbles at her lip, and I tug it free with my thumb and kiss the exact same spot.

'Of course I did.' I roll onto my side to face her, keeping my hands on her, keeping her close.

She frowns, calling bullshit. 'It's just that you were so…quiet.' She offers a hesitant smile. 'I'm seriously impressed—I'd need to be gagged to stay that silent at the height of pleasure.'

I slide my hands from her hips to grip her backside, pressing her against my semi-hard dick. 'Well, that could be arranged…'

She laughs a sexy, throaty chuckle and rolls her eyes. I take a deep, shuddering breath. She was amazing—embracing something new, giving me her trust and her passion and a safe space where I might release my own.

But I can't. I don't let go completely. I gave her my standard moves. The contained version. No feelings. No risk.

The spasm in my throat chokes me. I'm an arsehole and I don't want to be responsible for damaging this amazing woman's self-esteem. She did absolutely everything right and stayed true to herself. It's me who's the coward. Emotionally crippled.

I cup her face, tilting her delicate chin up so our eyes connect. 'Can you imagine how little privacy there is in prison, or in a barrack room full of soldiers, for that matter?' I ask. 'You learn to be quiet. I guess it's just become habit…' It's a half-truth that slashes fresh shame through me.

'Oh. I didn't think of that.' Her finger traces some of the ink on my chest, her eyes darting. 'So what about…you know…the pulling out? Have you had a bad experience or something? Because the way we did it, there's zero chance of unwanted pregnancy.'

'I know.' I wince. I want to talk about this as much as I want to take up knitting to keep her company. I don't really owe her any explanations. She had a good time. I could hide my weird behaviour behind the kinkiness she already knows about.

But…

Every second we stare in silence—something I usually embrace because I'm not one for meaningless chatter—my heart thuds faster until I fear I'll pass out. Now I've crossed the line with this woman, when she's embraced my kind of sex, I should give her something in return, even if it's just peace of mind that my reservations and rules are about me and in no way a reflection on her.

This is why it's easier to walk away at this stage.

I hold her close, stroke my hand up and down her back. 'Everything about tonight was amazing. You're perfect. Delicious.' I press a kiss to her unsmiling lips. She won't be satisfied with platitudes, no matter how true or heartfelt. And they are.

Brooke is like rich, dark chocolate… Addictive and decadent.

This time my sigh is loud. 'I don't normally talk about this…' But I care about Brooke. She's confessed her own issues about her relationships, her fame and her past betrayals. I don't want her to regret what happened tonight.

'I was careless once, as a youth,' I tell her. 'My girlfriend, Julia—the one I told you about—got pregnant, but she lost the baby while I was in prison.' I rip out the words as quickly as possible to limit the damage, but they still shred my throat like the slash of razor blades, their power as potent as the day I heard the devastating news.

Brooke gasps. Shock transforms her stunning face. 'Oh, Nick.' She grips my waist more tightly. 'I'm so sorry.' She buries her face against my chest. It's both comforting and claustrophobic, because it exposes the memories.

My mother visited me in prison. I'll never forget her expression of pain and disappointment, which as it turned out was to be only a fraction of mine. I can never forgive myself for what I did, because Julia, my mother and my innocent child all paid the price for my immature recklessness. For my mistake.

'It was a long time ago.' I swallow my resurfaced shame, shoving the memories and the feelings of helplessness back down my throat like a jagged pill. But how easy it is to relive the scalding self-disgust and remorse.

If only I'd been there for Julia, perhaps it wouldn't have happened. We had everything—we loved each other. We were going to be parents. Discovering I was going to be a father, albeit a young one, had given my life a purpose for which I'd been searching. I got a job and started saving for our own place. And then in one rash second I turned that bright future to ash.

My incarceration added untold stress to Julia's pregnancy. She visited me, stood by me, but I know she faced questions from her parents, who thought she deserved better. Losing the baby was my punishment. A punishment Julia didn't deserve because it was *my* fault.

And that's the end of this well-travelled path. It's always the same. The buck stops with me.

'Let's shower and get out of here,' I say, jumping into action as a distraction technique. I disengage from her, stride to the bathroom and flip on the shower, hoping the hot water will block out the brutal home truths in my head.

This is what happens when I don't keep my guard up. I remember. I relive. But I can never atone. All I can do with my control is keep myself safe from feeling again. Keep those in my sphere safe with distance from me and try to close the lid on the past.

Brooke joins me under the shower, silently watchful as we soap up and regard each other for long, uncomfortable moments. I might as well be washing in acid for the effect of her quiet scrutiny, even though she's likely only deciding how best to respond to my revelation.

'You're still punishing yourself, aren't you?' Her expression is one of concern and understanding.

But I don't want her compassion. I want her desire, her playfulness—even her fucking trust is better than this torture. Because she's forcing me to look internally. And I know exactly what lies at the centre of my cold, black soul. Shame and guilt and blame.

I close my eyes for a second and duck my head under the spray. This was the risk of allowing her too close. The very thing I feared. She's intuitive, perceptive, emotionally intelligent. She sees what I'd rather hide, just as she's honest and open about her own need to protect something of herself from the public.

She slides her hand around my waist, her fingers flexing against my skin. It's torture that I crave. 'You don't blame yourself for…losing your child, do you?' she whispers.

'Wouldn't you?' I flick the water out of my eyes and stare.

I do blame myself. It was my fault. I behaved like a hot-headed thug and landed myself in jail. I left my girlfriend alone to deal with the fallout of a difficult pregnancy and the demands of her disapproving parents, who by then understandably hated my no-good guts. I don't blame them for trying to break us apart. They were protecting her, as I'd failed to do. I can never move past the feeling that if I'd been by her side, instead of abandoning her and putting her in an impossible position, we might not have lost our baby.

'I don't know how I'd feel, Nick. I wouldn't presume to understand that kind of heart-breaking grief. But I know blaming yourself changes nothing. For you, I wish it would, because I understand now that you've spent half of your life trying to make amends. That's sentence enough, surely?'

I stare, too raw from her words to do or say anything. Warm water sluices us. I can't move, because all I want to do is…

What? Fall to my knees and hold her until this pain and regret dissolves? It won't work. The threads of it are woven through me at a cellular level. There's no washing away that degree of blackness.

'Did you and your girlfriend stay together… after?' Brooke asks, her voice low, as if coaxing a scared animal. And she's right. I'm caged by my past mistake. And now I'm trapped by my weakness for Brooke.

I shake my head. 'No. But I don't blame her for anything. A criminal who knocked her up and then wasn't there at the worst moment of her life is hardly worthy of regret.'

The frown is back between her brows. I'm not hiding a god damned thing from this woman. 'But you said you fought protecting her. It must have been a terrible time for you, too.'

I reach for the shampoo to stop myself from touching her again, the need like nettle stings on the palms of my hands. I lather up my hair and pass the bottle to Brooke, who's looking at me with caution and puzzlement, as if there's a way to fix this. Fix me.

'I could have walked away from the fight,' I say, hating the weakness I'm forced to admit. 'Protected her that way. I made the wrong decision that day and I have to live with the consequences.'

I wanted to be there for Julia, for my child. But I'd rendered myself powerless by landing in jail. When she lost the baby and I was eventually released, I knew from the look on her face that I'd killed her love, and she could never forgive me, and that made two of us.

And now that powerless feeling threatens again, because this woman sees through me. She sees my pain and regrets, probing close to a place I fight hard to protect with everything I have. Because, if I don't protect that place, there's a risk I could become that man again.

Brooke's stare fills with compassion I don't deserve. 'You made a mistake, Nick. One. There's not one person on this planet who hasn't done that.'

I swallow hard, fighting to get the words past my tight throat. 'One is all it takes.' Then I wish I hadn't spoken at all. Because I feel myself opening up with this woman like a damned flower in the sun. She *is* the sun. I need to resist, because I'll burn to ash if I allow her to lead me to look too closely at myself.

Brooke looks down with a nod and then peers up

at me from under her lashes, as if testing my reaction
to her candour and how far she can push. 'I understand that, and I don't want to cause you more pain,
but I hurt for you.' She rests her small fist over her
breastbone, as if she too is heart-sore. 'I think you
are punishing yourself. And I wish you wouldn't.
You both lost so much. It must have been a devastating time for you, too.'

I shrug. 'I'm a big tough guy, can't you tell?' I
never gave myself time to think about my own feelings, too consumed by the pain I'd put everyone
through. As soon as I left prison—as soon as I'd re-
connected with Julia and discovered that it was less
painful for her just to move on, that my consolation
was too late and unwanted—I knew I was alone. No
baby. No girlfriend. No prospects.

My mother tried to be there for me, but I pushed
her away too. I couldn't stand the disappointed look
on her face that told me I'd also let her down. So I
learned detachment, a habit I've never quite shaken. I
don't blame my mother. She lost the son she thought
I was and a grandchild in quick succession.

Brooke says nothing. Her eyes are so full of understanding, I can't bear to look at her. She makes
sense, but all it does is remind me of the reasons I
would normally be headed out the door by now, out
of her life for good. No explanations necessary.

Because who the hell would want this emotional
closeness when it's laced with the pain of a million
shards of glass?

Water pounds us. Rivulets of suds pour over her pert breasts and stomach, between her legs in a caress I ache to mimic, if only to shut out the recrimination in my head. Frustration and helplessness rip through me. I lash out before I can stop myself.

'We fuck one time and now we need to share our feelings?' I say, my tone icy as I trace the line of suds over her collarbone and the curve of her breast with my fingertip, stopping at her hard nipple.

I want to lick them off. To lose myself in pleasure. Now I've had one taste of the woman who's burrowed so far inside me, I may never get enough. But I'll find the discipline I need to control this. I always do. It's a fight for life.

Disappointment wars with arousal in her eyes. 'I get it. It must be very hard to talk about this.' She tilts her chin. 'But even big tough guys like you feel things strongly. Someone in your line of work needs to keep everything together, to be in control. I understand that, and I reap the benefits. But you need to let go every once in a while. We all do.'

She steps close so her nipples brush my chest and my cock grazes her mound. 'What happened between us in there——' she tilts her head towards the bedroom '——that was you holding back physically because you think it will protect you emotionally.' Her eyes meet mine, new resolve glittering. 'Does it work?'

I want to laugh in her face. To say, *yes, yes it does*. It always has in the past. But not with her. She's different. I can no more lie to her that I can fight the urge to crush her lips under mine and block out the truth. I do just that, drawing her face up to mine so she has to cling to my waist for balance while I kiss her quiet.

My tongue delves inside her mouth and the sensation of falling spins my head, just as it did when I finally pushed my cock inside her tight warmth and I thought I'd never survive.

She grips my wrists and tears her mouth from mine, panting. Her eyes flash with pain and challenge and anger. 'I'm safe, Nick. Next time, I want you to come inside me,' she says, declaring in her determination that there'll be a next time.

'I never fuck without a condom,' I throw back, my tone flat. 'Not going to happen.'

'Neither do I. That's how I know it's okay for you to let go with me.'

'Why would I do that?'

'Because you're safe with me, just like I'm safe with you.' She looks down and I follow the path of her stare, watching her hand wrap around my hard dick.

I stifle a groan. How can I want her again so soon and after literally tearing out my heart for her? I can't leave this time as I normally would. I tell myself it's because she's a client. That I'm still on the clock. But it's a lie. She's dangerous. Addictive. All the more reason to resist her pull. And I'm an expert at keeping people at an arm's length.

I slide on what feels like a smirk, when everything inside me wants to fight the inclination.

'If you really want me to come inside you—' I slide my fingers around her slender neck, drawing her mouth up to mine once more so there'll be no more talking '—you can always get down on your knees.'

Her pupils flare. Instead of walking away as I half-expected, she smiles, still fisting my cock. 'With pleasure, but I want it all this time.' She drops to her knees without hesitation, looking up at me through those endless lashes as she angles my cock towards that full, pouty mouth of hers. Her tongue flicks over the head, a tease. But there's no humour in her eyes, only steely determination and terrifying perceptiveness.

'You like to watch.' She laves the head of my cock with laps of her tongue. 'But you don't want to be seen yourself.' Her gentle caresses to my balls taunt me. Make me crazy both to deny her and give her my all, as she wants.

Before I can speak, she takes me inside the blissful haven of her mouth and I have to bite my tongue to stop the groans of satisfaction that want to rip free. I brace my hands on the walls of the shower cubicle and curse under my breath as I watch her swallow me, her stare all but stripping the skin from my body.

Then she pulls back. I free a grunt of protest.

'But I see you, Nick.' She pumps my length and

my hands curl into fists. 'I see you and I want you just as you are. So give me everything.'

And then she's on me again, moaning while she sucks. Taunting me with her own pleasure-seeking abandon. Pushing me closer and closer to the edge of that cliff of control and the treacherous chasm beyond.

I focus on my frenzied desire for her, watch fascinated as she gives me head I'll remember for the rest of my life. I should have known that, even while I try to manage this thing between us, she'd bring me to my knees. She's a siren and I'm battling overwhelming currents.

But this is better than digging through the past.

I cup the back of her head as she bobs over me, her tongue working my shaft and hitting all the right places as she watches the pleasure I can't contain contort my face.

'Brooke,' I growl in warning as my balls rise up and fire builds in my groin. My valiant attempts to contain the rapture tense every muscle in my body, and I'm all but spent.

She smiles, perhaps at my use of just her first name, and shakes her head. Eyes that are glassy with arousal widen in warning. Her sucking grows stronger. Her hands grip my thighs, telling me she wants this almost as much as I do. There's no place to retreat, even if I could.

I grit my teeth, staving off the inevitable. I'm going to come in her mouth and I don't think I'll be able to hold all that euphoria inside. She's tearing me apart, strip by strip, and part of me—that part already addicted to Brooke Madden—wants to explode for her, spill out all my ugliness and be done with the endless, lonely and soulless fight.

She moans out encouraging noises. The erotic sound, muffled by her full mouth, vibrates through my cock.

I curl my hand into a fist in her short hair as bliss grips me, slamming into me harder than ever before. And with a roar I'm not even aware of, until it echoes back from the shower walls in shockwaves, I release myself in racking spasms down her throat.

I gasp, fire streaking along every nerve. I open my eyes and she's still sucking me, triumph glittering in her pretty eyes, deservedly so. I'm undone, physically demolished.

And emotionally I feel like, where this woman is concerned, there's nowhere left to hide.

CHAPTER TWELVE

Brooke

MY BREAST CANCER charity work is important to me, especially since my mother's diagnosis. But today I am distracted as I talk with survivors of this common and often devastating disease. I paste on my smile, and pose for the photographs that will launch my new fund-raising lipstick range in collaboration with the charity.

I leave the Breast Cancer Awareness building in central Milan feeling drained and duck into the car. Nick and I made some huge progress yesterday. My head is still fuzzy with everything he confessed. My chest aches for his dreadful and tragic loss. One that I'm sure the passage of time can't diminish. But stronger still are my feelings for Nick.

Complex feelings.

I care that he's hurting. I want to hold him until he stops punishing himself. To absorb the blows he thinks he deserves and give him a moment's reprieve from his pain. I want him to know that I'm here for him, to feel that he's not alone.

But how can I do that when he's still holding back? Obviously his physical withdrawal reflects his emotional distance. Can he ever overcome such a long, self-inflicted sentence of punishment? Last night proved that, where I'm open to our deep physical connection, Nick is way behind. Thanks to Dave's cruel betrayal, I struggle with trust. But Nick clearly doesn't trust me. If he did, he'd let go, let us happen. He'd see that I'd be there to catch him. That I'm not going to use his vulnerability against him.

I'm silent as Nick pulls into traffic.

'Are you okay?' he asks, heading north out of the city. The three-hour drive to Saint Moritz will take us just over the border into Switzerland, one of my favourite places in the world. My parents would hire a lodge every year of my childhood. I have memories of fun and crisp alpine air and cosy hot chocolates…

I nod, aware of this man in whole new ways. His beautiful conker-brown eyes still carry that haunted look of last night. I want to reach out to him, but I'm also wary of my growing emotional entanglement.

I offer him a grateful smile. 'I'm just feeling a little wobbly. I met a lot of brave women today. Women fighting a horrible illness. Women like my mum.'

He glances sideways, remnants of his former guardedness shielding his expression. 'Your charity work must be sometimes gruelling. It's natural for it to take its toll.'

I ache to hold him. To seek out and to offer comfort. Because physically we click, at least for me. But there's new risk. Our closeness is a brittle and fragile thing. I shake my head to clear the images of Nick's heartbreak last night when he spoke about the loss of his baby, although my throat aches with trapped feelings. 'It certainly puts some of the things I worry about into perspective.'

'Such as?'

I inhale deeply. 'Sometimes I feel like a fake because I'm always projecting an image. I feel like I've been acting my whole life, slipping on the mask the public sees in order to protect myself and my family. When we were little girls my parents would take my sister and I to places they knew there'd be cameras. We'd be excited to dress up, but terrified we'd put a foot wrong and the world would see. Terrified of the wall of lenses and flashing lights. Terrified we'd let our parents down in some way.'

I lean back against the head rest. 'Days like today make me realise that perhaps I've forgotten what's real and important. What matters.'

People. Loved ones. Him.

'I can understand how you feel, but there's nothing fake about you. You're the most real person I know.' His hand covers mine in my lap. It's such a normal yet intimate gesture that, for the first time, I feel like maybe we could have something real when this trip is over.

The thought should bring me contentment. Excitement. Instead my mind throws up roadblocks. Nick has spent years protecting himself from his past pain, avoiding meaningful attachment. The depth of his issues scares me. Yes, we're similar in some ways, although I haven't experienced anything like his degree of personal devastation. But we're both struggling. Me by trying to separate my private life from the media interest I attract for fear of hurting my loved ones. Fear that I'll misplace my trust and be humiliated and hurt again.

Maybe it's time for us to stop fighting so hard.

I drag in a shuddering breath. Being emotionally open is terrifying. I know the consequences. I've felt the sting of that exposure and I've spent the past year recovering from its harshness.

Nick glances my way and then merges onto the motorway that will take us north towards Switzerland. 'Just because you have parts of your life you don't share with the world doesn't mean you're acting. Everyone is entitled to a private life. And you brought happiness to those women today—laughter and lipstick. That's a real skill. That relatable connection is your gift.'

That he sees me so deeply and understands what I'm trying to achieve brings tears to my eyes. I blink them away, my mind restless with doubts.

'I'm sure when you've been through something life-changing like those women have, like your mother has,' he continues, 'looking and feeling good about yourself again is a vital part of recovery.'

'Yes, it is. It's so much more than lipstick.' A lump settles in my throat. 'I'm not sure what's wrong with me today—perhaps I just need to speak to my mum. Hear her voice. Feel her love…'

Perhaps that's part of the answer for him, too. Perhaps if Nick talked his emotional regrets through with his mother he'd discover that she doesn't blame him the way he blames himself. Maybe then he could learn to forgive himself. Be open to healing rather than pushing people away because it's too painful to feel.

'Can I ask you something?' I hold my breath. Beyond our physical connection things are delicate. Complicated. Uncertain. But I'm starting to care about him; I realised that the moment I opened my eyes this morning and instinctively reached for him in my empty bed.

We returned from Club Vivace in the early hours and Nick insisted that I needed some quality rest before my busy schedule today. In truth, I think he needed space after his confession. He's not the big tough guy he projects. Well, he is, but he's so much more than that cliché.

He's considerate and loyal and harbours strong regrets that have broken parts of him. Anyone who has that capacity to feel as deeply as he does also has the capacity for deep and lasting commitment. But for my own sake I need to tread carefully. I can't get ahead of myself. Falling for someone like Nick, or anyone after Dave, is risky. The fact that I haven't dated in a year tells me I'm still recovering.

'Sure.' He shrugs, the wariness back.

'Have you ever talked about your feelings with your mother?'

His body tenses. 'No. Why would I remind her of what a disappointment her son is?'

My heart clenches, each beat painful. 'What if she's not disappointed? You're a thoughtful, trustworthy and dedicated man, Nick. You don't have to punish yourself for ever over one mistake you made as a teenager.'

His mouth flattens into a stubborn line. 'It's... complex. My child died,' he bites out.

'I know,' I whisper, because I'm in no way diminishing his past trauma or claiming to understand that kind of loss. 'And I'm sorry. We don't have to talk about it if you don't want to.'

I fall silent, so I'm shocked when he volunteers more information.

'Julia was twenty weeks when the bleeding started. The baby was too young to survive. But the stress I put her through must have contributed.'

He pales, and guilt lances my chest. I've taken him back to memories that cause him pain.

'Before I went inside, we'd made plans. We had a list of names... I hadn't realised until she told me she was expecting how much I wanted to be a father. To do a good job and always be there for my kid. Always. I never knew my father, so it was important to me that I be the total opposite to my own child.'

His hands grip the wheel so tightly I feel sick for putting him through this.

'Julia almost died, too. She bled so much… And I wasn't there—not for her or for my son.'

I'm so choked up I have to grate out the words. 'That would have been terrifying…distressing for you. Didn't the prison service give you any dispensation at all?'

He stares at the road ahead, his face grim. 'I was released in time for the funeral.'

I shouldn't have brought this up. But he's punishing himself, and seventeen years is a life sentence. Part of him will always have regrets, but he needs to forgive himself too. He's a good man who made one bad decision, and he's paid the ultimate price with his loss.

'Julia was too devastated to speak to me. Her parents were hostile and blamed me—I could see it on their faces. My mother had also been supporting Julia when I couldn't, so they were united in their grief. It would have been better for everyone if I hadn't been there.'

So he felt shut out. Alone. My throat is scratchy with unshed tears. 'But not better for you,' I whisper. 'You had the right to say goodbye too. The right to grieve for what *you'd* lost. Your feelings are as valid as anyone's Nick. It's tragic and painful, and I know these things happen every day. It's no one's fault.' I take a deep breath. 'I think if you talked about it you might discover that no one else blames you.'

'It can't change anything.' His lips thin.

'No…but perhaps your mum wanted to be there for you too. It might help you to forgive yourself.'

His expression turns blank. I've over-stepped the line. But I can't stop, after my emotional morning. After last night. After waking with feelings that scare me.

'I care about you, Nick. I'm not trying to interfere. It's just that after talking to those breast cancer survivors today, and then thinking about my mum, it confirms that life is short and precious and sometimes there's little love to be had. Which means we should grab whatever love, whatever human connection, we can and never let go.' I grow impassioned, my voice urgent with emotion. If I can just help him to see that he deserves good things, maybe he'll allow someone to be there for *him*.

'I guarantee your mother loves you and would welcome the opportunity to tell you that. You think she blames you for the past…but what if she doesn't?'

He huffs, frustrated. 'I should have kept my secrets locked away.'

I gasp at the bitterness in his voice. 'Why? Because confiding in me has forced you to consider the possibility that you're not as content as you think? That all your precious control does is push people away and anaesthetise you from feeling?'

Nick's face might as well be carved from granite. 'Thank you for your concern, but your caring is misplaced. In two days we'll part ways. Perhaps we should just leave this conversation here before we say something we can't take back.'

Just like that, any progress I imagined had been made between us disappears. Of course he would shut down after being vulnerable. I understand that. And it's a timely reminder for me, too. I'm getting close to a man I hardly know because he won't allow anyone near. Having naively trusted the wrong man before, and ended up with a tattered, exposed heart for all the world to see, I need to keep my guard up. I trust Nick with my safety and my body.

But my heart is another matter entirely...

CHAPTER THIRTEEN

Nick

I KNOCK ON the door to Brooke's suite, my insides knotted with anticipation and regret. It's only been a few hours since our tense exchange in the car, but despite having survived without it for the past thirty-five years, I somehow can't breathe unless I'm basking in the warmth of her smile. I need to make things right.

I drag in a ragged breath. How the hell did I wind up here? Not the penthouse floor of Saint Moritz's most exclusive hotel, which has the best views of the lake and surrounding alpine peaks, but temporarily incapacitated by need for this woman. Because it has to be temporary...

There's little love to be had. Which means we should grab whatever love we can and never let go...

Her words ring through my head. Since my first foray into love, when I gave everything and lost everything, I've sworn off feelings, even trying to control physical intimacy so I don't get too close.

Last night clarified things. Because the club, the sex, confirmed that, no matter how addictive Brooke is right now, it can't lead anywhere. One time inside her and I feel prised open, the emotions I've tried to bottle up most of my adult life bursting free like shaken champagne.

And this violent craving burning me alive, the constant physical need for her, scrapes away the numbness I've cultivated for protection. She's made me want things. Impossible things that I *can't* want. Can't have. All I can do is hold on to my shit until I can achieve some physical distance. Maybe then the emotional distance will follow. It's always worked for me in the past.

Except, not only is Brooke spiking my blood like heroin, she's urging further emotional catharsis. The idea of talking to my mother about the past has opened another floodgate. What if Brooke's right? What if there's a way to live without my harsh defence mechanisms? Seeking the forgiveness she talked about feels like climbing the mountains outside in bare feet. But what if the pain is less than the burden I already carry? What if I reach the far side of those snow-draped mountains and can finally breathe the pure alpine air without shame and regret?

After what feels like hours, but can only be seconds, Brooke swings open the door. She's wearing the work-out clothes I suggested in my text. Her flushed face is free of make-up, her hair damp from the shower. She too is a little breathless, as if she's been waiting to see me as much as I have her.

My eyes burn at the sight of her. I'm dazzled, my chest thumping with that now familiar thrill. How can I have been so rude and dismissive?

'I'm sorry,' I blurt out. 'I don't want us to fight.' I behaved like a dick. None of this is her fault.

She shakes her head. 'Neither do I, and I'm sorry too.'

And then she smiles.

Yep, there it is, the sunrise striking me full in the face and warming up all my frozen corners.

I step into the room and allow the door to swing closed at my back. Wordlessly I cup her face, press my lips to hers, breathing in deeply as if I can suck her very essence inside and hold onto it as a keepsake. She melts into my chest, her soft lips pliant and then demanding under my kiss so I feel her forgiveness. My turbulent mind blanks. I allow myself to feel pure, physical sensation. She fits in my arms like a puzzle piece. My feet feel more solid under me with her touch. Her kisses leave me restored, as if she's all I'll ever need.

We part for air. Reluctant. Panting.

Her eyes are glazed with the same passion that's led me to forget why I'm here apart from to lose myself in this woman again and again. Our disagreement was a perfectly timed reminder that relationships, beyond those one-nighters that I've perfected, involve feelings. Expectations. Compromise.

And maybe if I was a different man I could change for her. If ever there was a woman to make me want more, it's *this* woman. But it's been so long. I'm incapable. I'm just not made for the light, for everything that degree of soul-searching involves. The well of bottled-up feelings in me is just too enormous. I couldn't survive the pressure if the cork were ever to fly off.

'What's going on?' She breathes. 'I thought we could have a quiet dinner overlooking my view.' She indicates the wall of windows the suite offers. The idyllic, panoramic, snowy mountain vista is one of the main reasons tourists flock here. But its beauty is nothing compared to this woman, who gives and gives and gives and then worries about keeping a tiny piece back for herself. The woman who sees something in me that's redeemable. Sees a future I can't make out myself. The woman I could care for if I was able to care for anyone.

If I can survive the next forty-eight hours until I drop her back at her home in London, then I can retreat and repair the damage of allowing her too close. Closer than I've allowed anyone in years.

Because, whatever the future holds, it will always carry the past.

'You wanted to learn some self-defence moves.' I push the hair back from her forehead so I can see the excitement flare in her luminous eyes. 'So let's go.'

It won't help safeguard her against press intrusion or social media trolls, but everyone should know how to defend themselves. She brings out my protective urges. I can't walk away until I know I've taught her enough that I'll be able to sleep at night.

'Really?' She smiles. 'Thanks, Nick.' She grips my arm, and I fight the temptation to spin her onto the bed and take us both to the place where we forget all the ugliness in our worlds.

Instead I take her hand and tug her after me. Her suite is big enough to work in, but I've hired out the hotel's gym for an hour so we can do this properly. There's a matted area surrounded by mirrors, which is perfect for her to learn the few simple moves I plan to teach.

In the gym we do a few warm-up stretches and then I switch into teaching mode, which means trying my best not to drool over her black-Lycra-covered body. But, beyond the urge to peel her out of her clothes and block out all the things I can't have, there's another weight sitting on my chest. I'll have to put my hands on her in a way that represents that of an attacker, when all I want to do is caress, stroke and embrace her until I put that look of flushed ecstasy on her face. Until I remind myself that this thing between us is about sex and nothing more. Until I take all the stirred-up feelings and bury them back where they belong.

I clear the ache in my throat, aware she's waiting.

'The best way to get out of a bad situation is to run.' Tension hitches my shoulders at the idea of

Brooke in danger. 'So I'll show you how to get out of the most common attack holds.'

She nods, taking this seriously when it's all I can do to stop myself from dragging her into my arms and kissing her until I feel calm. But will I ever feel that again? Because I have to walk away. I can't run security for her personally now I've crossed the line. I'm too invested. So consumed by her that I've started to think what ifs…

I want to be the one to keep her safe—always. But that can't happen. Brooke is heroin, and I need to give her up.

I latch onto the lifeline of her sparkling eyes shining with trust and affection I don't deserve after the way I pushed her away earlier. But it's like she said. That's what I do.

Why is she still here? Still trusting and giving and open?

'First, the arm-grab,' I say, taking her wrist. The bones feel delicate under my fingers, which detect the vital beat of her pulse. It reminds me of that first intimate touch after her fashion show in Milan, when I'd been powerless to maintain my distance.

Yeah, you've been kidding yourself ever since…

I tighten my grip, making this as realistic as I can without causing her pain. My body rebels, my brain demanding gentleness, my limping heart clamouring to hold her with care and passion and never let go.

'So, pulling your hand away won't work,' I explain, my voice sounding tight. She tries the reflex move, which only makes me grip all the more and brings my body closer to hers.

Brooke's eyes go wide, and I want to stop this. The idea of someone hurting her makes me want to drive into the mountains with her and hide away for ever.

I swallow hard, focus on the instruction the way I would with my students. 'Instead, lift your elbow until it points to the ceiling.' I direct her arm into position. 'And then slice that arm downwards using your core muscles.'

She nods, performing the move as instructed and knocking away my grip with ease. Her grin of surprise and triumph shifts something in my chest.

She flings her arms around my neck and presses a quick kiss to my mouth. 'I did it.'

I extricate myself from her arms when all I want to do is kiss her again and not think about the number of hours I have left to be free to do such a thing. Because every time we touch I feel rejuvenated, as if I'm building myself a new cage. But, where the old one was steel and chains, this one is made of glass to let in the sun.

'And now the most important part of the move,' I say. 'You'd run.'

She nods. 'Got it.'

We practise the technique a few more times until her confidence is high and I feel less strung out with the strange restlessness. I tell myself it's just the vile idea of Brooke needing to defend herself for real.

But also, a part of me wants to impress her. Part of me is honoured that I can teach her something and that she's determined to learn to take care of herself.

'Next, the grab from behind.' I stand behind her and hook my arms around her waist, gripping my wrists in the centre of her stomach. I'm conscious of my physical advantage and how easy it would be for a man like me to hurt a woman like her. Then I recall the same position last night, when I was buried inside her, ripped to shreds by the feelings struggling to fight free. How easily she dismantled my defences in the shower, until it was all I could do to keep breathing. How again in the car journey today she prised me open with her gentle insight and caring.

Physically, she's vulnerable, but emotionally she's so strong. Stronger than I'll ever be.

Her body is tight against me, her eyes trained with trust on mine in the mirror. For a few seconds I imagine what it would be like never to let go. To try and keep her in my life back in London. Yes, we're complete opposites, but we're also similar.

It could work…could be wonderful. But it could also open up a world of pain for us both. I have an ugly past and she makes me want to examine it. To pick over the bones and see if anything can be salvaged. But what if she's wrong? What if I can't be whole? She deserves better than half a man.

'So, to get out of this, hold onto my arms and bend at the waist.' I focus on teaching to stop the creep of foreboding over my skin. Once we return to London and I walk away for good, protecting her won't be my problem. The next time I see her will be on a billboard or on TV, perhaps with someone else.

The thought should give me peace of mind, a sense of my life soon returning to normal. Instead I'm hollowed out. Frantic. Filled with the sense I've forgotten to do something vitally important.

'Nick?' she asks.

'Sorry.' I snap from my daze to see she's still staring at me in the mirror. 'I zoned out for a second. Okay, make a fist and slam it backwards into my groin—but please don't make contact for real. I'm kind of attached to my balls.'

She laughs. 'I kind of like them myself, don't worry.' She blows me a kiss and then performs the move at half-speed. I release her and clutch my junk as if I've truly been struck in the balls.

'Now it's time to finish me.' I hunch over. 'Lock your hands behind my neck and drive your knee up into my groin.'

She follows my instructions, giving me time to dodge the blow for real, her eyes glittering with the excitement of feeling empowered. I wish I had all my equipment so she could really go to town on overcoming a man my size.

'And now you'd—'

'Run,' she says with a huge grin. 'I get it.'

We practise a few more times, a warm sense of pride settling in my chest. 'Okay. Last move—the choke-hold.' Understandably, she looks a little nervous as I place my hands loosely around her neck. I feel her pulse fluttering against my palm and smile, my face twitching with tension. All I want to do is drag her mouth to mine.

I've taught these moves a hundred times. But it's different now, because she's different. Because I care. I've let her in, and until I can get away, get some distance, I'm fucked…

Her crystal-blue eyes seem huge as she looks up at me, waiting, full of trust.

I know before I speak that my voice is going to crack. 'Lift one arm up… Turn your whole body to the opposite side.' I want this session over and done. All the physical contact in this context is torture. Because I want so many things, I'm crushed under their weight. But what I absolutely don't want is to hurt anyone, especially Brooke. My brain is just tricking me with all this pseudo-aggression.

'Crunch down your upper body. See how you've trapped both of my hands?'

She nods. 'Now what?

'Strike up at my face with your elbow.' When she does, I fake a stumble back, as if she's made contact.

'And now I'd run,' she says, beaming.

I nod, helpless to a flicker of a smile. 'Well done. You picked it up very quickly.'

I should feel satisfied that I've helped her be less vulnerable. Instead bile swirls into my throat. I care. She's chipped at my defences with her compassion, her bravery and her light. And I need those barriers, because without them all the wants in me are snarling to escape years of confinement.

'I have a good teacher.' She winks, stepping closer. 'Thank you, Nick.'

'You're a good student. I just hope you'll never need to use any of this.' I take her hand and rub my thumb over her knuckles to stop me tugging her into my arms and holding her until the solid beat of her heart reassures me that all this is make-believe. That neither of us is actually at risk. But the emotional peril is overwhelming.

We fall silent, eyes locked. Face to face. Surrounded by our reflections in the mirrors, every feeling in me is amplified. We're both breathing harder than we should—we haven't exerted that much energy. But she must see the desperation on my face. Sense how close I am to disintegrating into a million pieces.

'I'm here, Nick.' Her voice is a whisper, her eyes aglow with her passion. 'I see the real you. I see your integrity and your generosity and your calm strength. It's okay…'

Her words all but buckle my knees. Could this slight and delicate woman have what it takes to hold me together? I want to bear my soul, knowing she's strong enough to take all of me.

'Brooke…' I start in warning, although I don't know what I want. To push her away or to drag her into my arms. I need to reconnect after acting as her attacker because I feel more alive than I have for years when I'm with her—as if her light has shocked my heart back into rhythm.

'I'm here. I feel it too.' Her small smile slashes me.

She *does* see me. Perhaps clearer than I see myself. The watcher has become the watched.

Uncontrollable fire rushes through me. I pull her into my arms, desperate. She kisses me hard. I scoop her feet from the floor as I kiss her back with all my awakened emotions. Emotions I don't want but can't stop. Not while I'm with Brooke. I let them flow through me, twist them into fear for her safety and the lust that just can't be denied. Because those are easier to deal with than my bigger issues of once more caring enough to do something stupid and reckless.

When we start tugging at each other's clothing, she comes to her senses and takes my hand, dragging me back to her suite at a brisk pace. Inside, we shed clothes as rapidly as we can while walking to the bedroom and kissing. There's no teasing or flirtation, no restraint or denial. Only the urgency that seems to have us both powerless in its grip.

Her hands roam everywhere, branding my skin, tugging, demanding with frenzied need. And I feel it too, my foggy brain vaguely aware of the need to locate a condom before collapsing on top of her on the massive, sumptuous bed.

'Hurry, Nick.' She grabs the condom from me and tears it open.

There's nothing controlled about this coupling. It's frantic. Furious. Need roars through me, driving me to get inside her as quickly as I can, as if life on earth depends on it. And in a way it does. She's my salve. My balm. The ultimate distraction from facing my feelings, even when she's the one bringing them to the surface.

I work the condom on and settle my hips between hers, probing her entrance and then pushing inside in one sublime glide.

She cries out. I rest my forehead against hers. Our breaths gust. I search for some remnant of my former restraint, try to master the needs in me that this woman has awoken so this isn't over in seconds.

How can she do this to me? I feel like an animal desperate to rut. To claim her as mine. To mark her and change her, as she's artlessly altered something in me that I have no hope of ever repairing.

For seventeen years I've commanded my body, my desires, my very essence. In a few days, Brooke's destroyed the man I thought I was, tearing me apart and rebuilding me in another form, one spiralling out of control for this woman and the way she makes me feel redeemed.

'Nick, I need you.' Brooke crosses her ankles in the small of my back and grips my shoulders, urging me to move. I tunnel my fingers into her short, silky hair, wrap my forearms around her slender shoulders and press a kiss over her parted lips. Our stares lock as my hips move. No speech is required. No rules, bargains or safeguards. It's just us, incapable of avoiding this violent connection.

Have I ever felt so at one with someone? There's no kinkiness, no gimmick. Just simple old missionary position. But I've forgotten this sensation of true intimacy. Maybe it's even a first for me…

Because somehow she sees all of me.

Her heart thuds against my chest. Her stunning eyes penetrate mine, as if searching the deepest recesses of my tattered soul. Her gentle hands cup my face, stroking my hair as she speaks to me with her body, mind and soul.

I kiss her then. I can't keep my mouth from the softness of hers any longer. And, as our tongues touch, she shatters under me, her cries muffled against my lips, her eyes pleading and, her arms and legs clamped so tightly around me that I feel as if without her I'll never be whole again.

I push back, lock my elbows so I can see all her beauty laid beneath me. My chest aches. I'm humbled that she's given so much of herself to me, a man too broken to offer much in return.

But that's Brooke.

She cups my face once more. Her fingers tunnel into my hair, fingernails scraping my scalp as she holds me captive.

'I've got you, Nick. I'll catch you. Let go.'

My orgasm rises up to engulf me in heat, like the explosions on the sun's surface. A harsh shout rips from my tight throat as I come, pumping into the condom, safe in the knowledge that Brooke is holding me tight, anchoring me to the earth. And while I'm in her arms, while we're connected like this, nothing bad can happen.

As soon as I collapse on top of her, crushing her beneath me on the rumpled white sheets, I have the absurd urge to go again and again, every hour until we part. And one single, terrifying thought pounds in my temples.

What if wanting her never stops?

CHAPTER FOURTEEN

Brooke

As APRÈS-SKI GOES, lying naked with Nick wins hands-down. The bedroom curtains are open to let in the twinkling lights of Saint Moritz, nestled in the bosom of the imposing Swiss Alps at dusk.

My body is tired from a day spent on the slopes, my nose tingling with a hint of sunburn. With our experienced local mountain guide, we went off-piste in search of powder, and then had lunch on the sun terrace of a mountain restaurant. A visit to a stunning thermal spa, with mountain views from our own private mineral pool, rounded off a day that feels more like a week. I sigh in contentment, running my hand down the valley of Nick's muscular back to the top of his steely buttocks.

'I ache,' I whisper. 'We should have just scrapped the skiing and done this all day.' I try to forget the clock ticking in my head. Try to not resent the hours spent outdoors or in public when each precious moment inches us closer to departure. The end of the holiday, and the end of us.

'Then we'd still ache, just in different places.' He raises his head from his folded arms, leans over and kisses me. His unrestrained contact is still such a revelation that I could cry. I've had no time to get used to him as a lover, to learn all the things I want to know, and now our time is almost up…

'Good point.' I blink, battling the sting behind my eyes. 'Although, that's a price I'm willing to pay.'

Nick rests his head on my chest, falling still and quiet.

I play with his hair, my throat tight. I don't want this to end. I want to see him again. Not in a professional capacity, but like this. Since we left, Milan he's been different. Spontaneous. As desperate for me as I am for him. Despite my reservations that he's too damaged to allow anyone in, despite our disagreement, it feels as if we're finally moving closer than ever.

Could we continue our journey together if we had more time…?

I try to keep my breathing steady while butterflies collide inside me. For the first time in a long time I see myself having the kind of relationship I crave. The kind my friends have. Safe. Real. Equal.

But what if I'm wrong again? I know Nick's avoided commitment to protect himself from the pain of his past, but I have my own reasons not to rush back into a relationship. The damage Dave inflicted left me worried about more than sex scandals and sold secrets. Perhaps my instincts are awry…

Can I trust a man who has held back from commitment for seventeen years with my bruised heart?

But surely this can't just end?

Every time we touch I feel closer, even when I'm nervous that it's an illusion I've created. In every experience we share, such as the self-defence last night and the skiing today, I see new sides to him, learn more about his mind, his sense of humour and his dedication. And of course his deliciously deviant side. He has a big heart that feels things to the core of his being.

But could he feel things for me, and could I trust that it was enough?

Just as on the ski slopes today, one person has to go first to forge a path for the other to follow. Nick isn't Dave—our relationship had had issues before Dave sold me out. I'd never willingly have asked him to take nude pictures of me. Some sixth sense knew Dave had dubious scruples.

But I trust Nick. He's taught me to defend myself. He's accepted the real me. He's shown me his vulnerabilities. Perhaps I just need to nudge him further by leaping first into the scary unknown…

'Nick?' I say, like an impatient kid on a long road trip.

'Hmm?' he murmurs, sounding sleepy, although his fingers haven't stopped swirling over my skin since we collapsed onto the bed, spent.

'Remember how you said you liked to look at photos?' I slide my fingernails along his back. 'Will you…photograph me?'

His head shoots up, confusion pinching his brows into a frown. 'What…? Why?'

My heart thumps with fear and longing. It's bad, but in a good way.

'We're going back to London tomorrow.' Yeah, bad wins as my stomach lurches. 'I want you to have something to look at, you know?' I chew my lip, sudden nerves making me stammer. 'So…so you don't forget me.'

Perhaps with reminders on his phone he won't be able to go for one day without needing to see me. Perhaps he'll work through some of his issues and decide he's ready for a relationship. It's risky but some inner part of me knows, just knows, that Nick would never betray me like Dave.

One arm encircles my waist and Nick drags me under him, his weight crushing me into the mattress so I feel surrounded and protected. He's erect again. My idea excites him. And me too. I'm wet between my legs at the idea of Nick losing the battle to jerk off over a picture of me.

'Brooke…' He knows what this request means to me. The unspoken message.

'Oh no, not the scary face,' I tease. 'It's your fault—I think you've turned me into a pervert too.' I smile my smouldering Brooke Madden smile that

I use for the camera and bat my eyelashes in an exaggerated fashion.

He laughs and my insides twist, bittersweet. I want to see more of that smile. Hear that laugh daily. I want him to be helpless to wait five minutes after walking away from me before he takes out his phone to recall our time together in Europe. I want him to question everything he thinks he knows about himself until he can't stay away. Because I'm certain, once we part ways, I'll second-guess not having taken more of a risk with him. Bit I can't voice the direction of my thoughts. It might scare him off.

'I won't forget you.' He presses his mouth to mine, his tongue pushing inside in a lazy, languorous glide. Then he licks his lips. 'You can never forget how delicious chocolate is, right?' He quirks one eyebrow, his beautiful mouth twisted in that sexy half-smile of his that is so rare it makes my breath catch.

I laugh, although I'm hot and breathless with longing. 'So, I'm chocolate in this scenario?'

He nods, his head swooping to take one nipple gently between his lips. 'You're delicious.'

He worships my nipple with his mouth as if we have all the time in the world to enjoy each other's bodies. Not the handful of hours that is our sickening reality. Before I get lost in him again, I reach over and fumble for his phone on the bedside table.

'Please…' I shove the device at him and grind myself against his erection as an extra layer of inducement. 'Photograph your favourite delicious bits, as a memento…'

He sighs, abandoning my nipple. He takes his phone and looks down at me with a small frown.

I lie there, my heart thudding, because as much as I want him to do this it's a reminder to us both that this holiday fling is coming to an end. It's also a form of communication, one I know he won't want to hear aloud and one I'm too scared to verbalise: I trust you with all of me.

My ribs pinch as I look at Nick's handsome face staring down at me. I'm not ready to let him go. I want to be there for all of him. I want to know if he takes my advice and talks to his mother. I want to show him the baby's cardigan I'm close to finishing for my nephew. I want to introduce him to my parents and my sister.

I want him in my future. But, until he believes he deserves the kind of future where he can once more open his heart, I'm knocking at a closed door. He's not ready to hear my developing feelings. He has to want me in return, otherwise I'll be making the same mistake I did with Dave.

He sits up and fires off his first shot—me simply looking up at him, trying not to display the panic that we may never have more than these few stolen days.

He shows me the photo he's taken, and something close to uncertainty flickers in his dark eyes. It's a head and bare shoulders shot. Perfectly PG. I look away from my own facial expression immortalised on the screen—scared and aroused, desperate and satisfied, all at once. I look like a woman precariously close to falling in love.

I swallow the lump in my throat, praying Nick's observation skills are less well-developed. 'That's very tame. That all you got, Big Guy?'

He stares for a beat or two, his intense eye contact making me want to hide under the sheets. And then he aligns the camera over my breast, which is reddened from the scrape of his facial hair, and fires off a close-up shot of my erect nipple.

I feel a tingle there, as if he's touched me. And then my breath catches as Nick leans close, presses a kiss to the curve of my breast and captures the moment with the phone. Silently he shows me the photograph.

It's a little blurry, but still breathtakingly intimate. His thick, sooty lashes are curved in a crescent on his cheek. His soft lips pursed against my skin.

I shudder, too moved to speak. Too full of longing to do anything but lie there and watch. Nick has taken what started out as a risqué suggestion, a display of my trust, and turned it into some sort of tribute to how he feels about my body. And perhaps more deeply—how he feels about me...?

The room is tense with reverent silence as he tilts my head to the side, kissing the slope of my neck before taking another close-up shot of my clavicle. He wordlessly encourages me to roll over onto my stomach, his hands gentle, stroking. His quiet intensity reminds me of the Nick I thought was too closed down, too withdrawn for intimacy. But this is one of the most profound and erotic moments of my life. Nick shows me what he loves about my body with an adoration that makes me forget that I'm vulnerable to exploitation and exposure by him, if he so wished.

But I know this man.

Shot after shot he photographs my body in close-up—the small of my back, the crease under my buttocks, the back of my neck—each time pausing to show me the toils of his worshipful labour.

By the time he turns me over again, I'm panting, my head spinning with oxygen deprivation. My feelings fight to push free, but Nick's not done.

He snaps a close-up of my belly button and then he shoulders his way between my legs, spreading my thighs open until he's happy with the angle. He photographs himself kissing my thigh and then my mons.

I'm on fire. My limbs are leaden with paralysing arousal. My head is full of this man who has so much capacity for love. So much to offer. I can't decide if I want to straddle him and feel the sublime bliss of his penetration, or fall into his arms and confess every terrifying feeling blooming in me.

Just when I think I'm going to have to snatch the phone from him and do something, anything, to chase away the need raging in me, he angles the camera between my legs and takes some close-ups of my pussy.

He looks up, his face a study of rapt focus and fiery desperation. We stare, no words necessary, because surely he feels this too? I can't be alone. It's more than the best sex of my life. It's more than lust and kinkiness and…

My thoughts shatter as Nick pushes a finger inside me and fires off another round of shots. My muscles clamp around his finger, and I bite my lip to hold in the cries of pleasure. I don't want to disturb him. I want him to photograph every inch of me so I never leave his head. So he's as consumed by me as I am with him.

Through the pleasure, I watch him. His jaw is bunched as he watches his finger slide in and out. His nostrils flare as he abandons the phone with a careless toss, removes his finger and then covers my clit with his mouth.

I gasp at the incendiary sensations of his tongue laving and flicking but, before I become too lost to my building climax, I rummage on the bed for the phone and capture a few shots of his mouth on me.

'Those are for me,' I say, and then speech deserts me for good. Because, beyond the rapture, one thought lingers. If I can't be brave, and Nick doesn't change his mind about commitment, all we'll have is this handful of memories.

CHAPTER FIFTEEN

Nick

SHE'S ONCE MORE sprawled over my chest, a place I now think of as her spot. But perhaps I should slide her off. My heart is beating so fast, I'm worried she'll know exactly what that little photographic exercise cost me—the last shred of any pretence that I have a handle on this thing between us.

And my very sanity…

Today has driven me crazy. When she's not working, Brooke still displays her vibrant energy and dry sense of humour. Skiing is something I've only come to in the last five years, so I'm not an expert like her. But she made every moment memorable. I forgot that I occupied her world. Forgot that she's famous. We were just a man and a woman—laughing and talking about everything and nothing. The world-class views and elite ambience faded away. The decadent lunch of caviar and Cristal could have been burgers and beer. The private rejuvenating spa with a mountain vista could have been the local leisure centre.

The key was Brooke.

I force a swallow, trying not to count down the hours until we return to London tomorrow and this job officially ends. How will I go back to not reaching for her? How will I return to famine after sampling the feast has become second nature? We barely made it back into the suite earlier before I fell upon her, slaking the out-of-control need I have for her on the floor. And then in the shower. And then on the chair. But soon all I'll have is a cold bed and a phone full of second-rate keepsakes.

Those photos aren't enough when compared to the real thing. It's like seeing the Swiss Alps in a snow globe versus breathing in the crystal-clear air while blinded by the azure sky and warmed by the brilliant white sunlight.

Every click of the camera as I captured shot after shot of her exquisite body felt like a six-inch nail to my chest. Because I don't need the visual reminder of her to remember. She's in my blood. A part of my soul.

I curl my hands around her backside and press her to my aching cock, needing an outlet to slake this wild, frenzied feeling crushing me. The overused appendage grumbles but of course rallies.

'I have to say, for a man who likes to watch, you've become very handsy,' she quips, looking up at me with humour in her breath-taking eyes. 'What happened to Mr Control?'

I groan, ignoring her, instead filling my hands

with her perfect breasts and rolling her nipples between my thumbs and forefingers until she gasps. 'I have control. Putting my hands on you is an active choice, Lady.'

Liar. I could no more stop than I could shift those shadowy mountains out there in the dark with my bare hands. Who cares when the clock is ticking?

'Oh, no, no, no...' she says, straddling me. 'I think we need some rules if this is going to work. You can't have all the power...'

Her words mimic our deal, from back when I believed I could resist her brand of magic. Back when I thought one taste of the sumptuous banquet that is Brooke Madden would satiate me...

Idiot.

'Trust me,' I say, nuzzling her neck and sucking in her delicious scent. 'You still hold all the power.'

'Well, in that case...' She kisses me before clambering from the bed with a playful grin.

I roll over to watch her—my favourite thing. I soon find out what she's up to when she locates her prize: my jeans.

'Yes, this is what we need.' She tugs the belt free of the denim loops, her eyes full of challenge and spark.

My heart bangs with excitement. How did I ever think those exquisite features formed the face of an angel? She's devious and debauched. And perfect...

She grabs a chair and carries it closer, while I watch her body's slow sensual movements, because I can't keep my hands, my eyes or my mind off her.

'Do you trust me?' she asks, her voice hesitant all of a sudden at the loaded question.

I want to unleash my reflexive *yes*, shocked by its certainty. Instead I hold it in and pray for the strength to survive whatever she has in mind.

'Brooke…' My voice is tight with warning. But I can't deny that I want to worship at the altar of whatever plan she's concocting. I can't deny her a damned thing.

'You can't touch me if you're tied up, Nick. You'll be forced to watch.' She bites her lip and slides the leather belt through her hands. 'Your favourite pastime…'

There's so much blood headed south that my head spins as I stand. My cock weeps, straining for her along with every other cell in my body. Every scrap of fight departs. I lower myself into the chair, my head full of depraved acts of retribution. She makes quick work of tying my hands together, and then securing them to the back rails of the chair for good measure. Then she steps away, examining her improvised shackles.

I watch with a kick of satisfaction when she shivers. She knows there'll be payback and, from her restlessness, she's looking forward to it.

I'm breathing hard as she approaches. She steps between my spread thighs and traces her fingertip up the shaft of my cock, which rests against my taut stomach.

'I should have had this idea long ago,' she murmurs, her voice laced with hunger. 'You look delicious too.'

I try to lunge forward to press my face to her stomach, to make any skin-to-skin contact I can, but she steps out of reach. With a small laugh, she collects my T-shirt from the floor and slides it on, covering all the irresistible nakedness from my greedy stare.

'Get back here now, Lady, or I promise you'll regret it.' I grit my teeth, seeking any remnant of trusty patience. She rests her hands on my thighs and bends forward so I'm gifted a clear view down the neck of the shirt.

'Like what you see, Mr Rivers?'

I all but swallow my own tongue. Somehow coy flashes of Brooke's delicious body are twice as gratifying as the sight of her completely naked, if that's possible. This way is akin to eating a cake one slice at a time rather than face-planting the entire thing in one go. Although, right now, both approaches have merit.

'I like you better wrapped around me.' I strain against the belt.

She captures my mouth, kissing me long and hard until it's unclear which of us is more worked up. Then she straddles one of my thighs, standing over me and tugging my head back by my hair until our eyes connect. I make fists, close to ripping myself from my bonds and fucking her until we both die of exhaustion. Until time stops and we're trapped here in this hotel room for ever.

Her soft kisses trace my jaw, then move down my neck to my shoulder. Everywhere her lips glide is bliss and torment. Like a branding iron searing my skin.

My body jerks, bucking against the chair and the makeshift restraint. 'Brooke,' I warn again, or perhaps it's a plea. I'm approaching my limit.

It seems to do the trick. With a small smile, she lowers herself to my lap, her slick centre scalding my thighs. She's so wet for me. She grips my erection and works her hand up and down in slow, taunting sweeps.

Fuck, I'm hers. Completely at her mercy.

She rises up over me, and with a whimper of need bends her knees so the head of my cock slides between her legs. Her wet heat swallows the tip. I grunt out my frustration, feral need gripping me and causing involuntary thrusts of my hips in the chair. I need to get closer, get inside her. Just a few more inches… My balls contract along with every muscle in my body, urging me to fill her. To spill inside her and never, ever stop.

'I ache inside for you,' she says, flicking her tongue over my earlobe. Then she pulls away. 'Don't go anywhere—I need to find a condom.' She strips off my shirt so she's once more naked and I breathe a partial sigh of relief. No more teasing. But any delay fuels the fire in me.

'Fuck the condom,' I croak out, my voice strangled. I'm wild, past the point of control. For the first time in seventeen years I'd willingly forgo protection. 'Untie me.'

She shakes her head, still enjoying her power trip. 'Not yet. Good things come to those who wait, and I'm enjoying myself.'

At that moment there's a knock at the suite door.

I freeze. A burst of adrenaline hijacks my pulse.

Brooke glances at the clock. 'It's okay—I ordered room service, remember? We never got to have our candlelit dinner yesterday.' She scoops her robe from the chair, wrapping her beautiful body in thick, fluffy cotton.

'Untie me, Brooke.' I'm deadly serious now, tension and dread replacing all the intense desire of seconds ago. I don't want her answering the door alone.

'No way—I'll be back in a second and we'll pick up exactly where we left off—which was a very interesting place indeed.' She kisses me and then heads for the living area, tugging the robe's belt tight.

The minute she's out of sight, panic explodes like shrapnel in my head.

'Brooke!' I yell, and then freeze again so I can hear what's going on in the other room.

It's not safe. She's not safe. I'm supposed to keep her safe.

The click of the main door ricochets like a gunshot. I strain to listen, my heartbeat one continuous lurch. Impotence tenses every muscle in my body.

Perhaps I'm overreacting. Perhaps it's just as she said—room service. Yes. This is an exclusive hotel.

It's hard to get beyond the lobby without a room card. But flames of foreboding lick at my skin. How can I have been so stupid? How can I have allowed her to get so close that I've forgotten to do my job? How can I have relaxed so much that I'm tied to a fucking chair in another room from my client?

But she's not simply a client any more. I've let her in. Developed feelings for her. Dangerous feelings. And I've grown sloppy. Lost sight of what's important. I've indulged that locked down part of myself, allowed emotion back into my decision-making process.

The last time this happened...

I taste blood where I'm biting my cheek. I hear muffled voices, Brooke's higher pitched, and the deeper voice of a man. They're both speaking Italian, so I have no idea what the conversation is about. I'm helpless, reliant on tone of voice alone to interpret what's being said.

What if he touches her? Hurts her? Bile hits the back of my throat. I struggle with the belt around my wrists, desperate to intervene, to get to her in case she needs me. Needs protecting. No longer because it's my job, but because I'll die before I let my stupidity and recklessness put her in danger.

The seconds tick by while I fight with the leather. The tone of their conversation changes. I can't make out individual words but, whereas Brooke has gone quiet, the man dominates with rapidly spoken Italian, his voice growing in urgency.

He's not simply delivering room service, or he would have been and gone by now. He could be threatening her, taking her hostage, even assaulting her.

I've heard enough.

The need for action pounds through my body. I rise to my feet, bent double where I'm still attached to the chair. Red-hot rage builds, giving me added strength.

I struggle and twist, the belt cutting into my skin. Then, with a final frustrated growl, I swing the chair against the wall, cracking it in two. I disentangle myself from my restraint, toss the tattered chair and grab my jeans. I'm stumbling into them as I head for the other room.

I burst in just as Brooke closes the main door, her nocturnal visitor having departed. In two strides I'm in her face. I grip her shoulders, my stare completing a quick scan of her from head to toe. No obvious injuries.

'Are you okay? What the fuck? Who was that?' I want to chase the guy down the corridor, but I'm not ready to let go of her yet. Not until I'm certain that she isn't hurt, traumatised or scared.

She looks sheepish, pale, shaken. 'I'm fine. It was room service. The guy...' She swallows, shakes her head, as if clearing her thoughts.

When I realise I'm so tense my fingertips are digging into her skin, I drop my hands to my sides. 'Did he hurt you?'

'No.' She drags in a shuddering breath. 'He just wanted to tell me he's a fan. He was a bit over-excited and wouldn't stop talking and for a second or two…' she swallows, struggling to hide the shock from wide eyes, 'I couldn't make him leave…'

'Fuck,' I say, scrubbing at my face. I stride back into the bedroom to locate my T-shirt and boots. 'Did he lay a finger on you?' I ask, my voice so icy-calm it shocks us both. Rage freezes the blood in my veins so I'm almost disassociated from myself as I dress.

'No, of course not. I'm fine.' She sits on the bed. Her hands fidget with the belt of the robe. 'I'm sorry. I should have untied you.' Her smile turns watery, as if she's finally realised it could have been a lot worse. 'I knew it would be safe. This hotel is lock-tight.'

She sounds as if she needs reassurance. And I want to oblige. I hate the look of fear in her eyes. Hate that I'm responsible for putting it there. Hate that it calls to the wild spinning of my own unstable thoughts.

Anything could have happened to her…

I look away. Breathe. Try to hold on to my stomach. Reproof after reproof dies on my tongue. I'm struck dumb with self-hatred. A blessing, because I need time to calm down.

Her wide eyes slash into me. I should stay and make sure she's okay after the shock. But I need to punch something. A wall. Myself. At the very least I need to ensure that this never happens again. Not in this hotel and not on my watch.

'Where are you going?' she asks, her voice timid.

'Downstairs to speak to security.' I grab my phone from the bed and spin on her. 'Please do *not* leave this room.' I bite out each word, my face so tense I feel like I'm wearing a steel mask.

She shakes her head. 'I won't. I promise.' Then she reaches for me, her hand falling to her lap when I step back. 'I'm fine, Nick. I really am.'

Chills flood my body. I can't accept her touch right now. I'm strung too tight. And her touch makes me weak. Forgetful. Careless. The type of man I never wanted to be again...

'I'm glad one of us is fine,' I say and then leave to ensure history can never repeat itself.

CHAPTER SIXTEEN

Brooke

IT'S MIDNIGHT BY the time he returns to the suite. He shrugs out of his jacket, his face ruddy, as if he's been outdoors. He's wearing his withdrawn mask, his big, beautiful body carrying tension from head to toe.

I've been staring at the inky sky, the shadowy mountains and the sparkling town, waiting for answers.

'What happened?' I ask, a fist of fear squeezing my throat at the idea I've caused him trouble with my naivety. My stupidity.

'I texted you that I'd dealt with the situation.' His voice is flat. 'The staff member has been sacked.'

I wince, hating that I'm responsible for someone losing their job. But establishments like this one cannot afford to have starry-eyed staff on the payroll. I'm not the most famous or high-profile person ever to stay at this hotel. And we pay a high price-tag for discretion. For anonymity.

My mouth feels dry as I speak. 'I'm sorry about that. I feel…terrible.'

'Don't,' says Nick. 'He broke the hotel's policy. It's his own fault.' I shudder at the cold distance in his voice.

He won't look at me. He's holding back, as if he has more news to deliver.

I want to go to him with my touch. To rediscover all that lovely trust and deep connection we shared today—a magical, sparkling day where anything seemed possible. Did I imagine it? Perhaps it was as fragile as ice crystals, now melted away.

Instead I twist my fingers together with dread. 'You've been gone ages.' Long enough for me to pace and pine and stare out at the night, examining just how far we've travelled together this week, and how much I've come to care. No, it's more than that. I'm stupidly in love with him.

I've fallen for a man who understandably wants nothing to do with emotions. A man who's locked himself down for seventeen years. A man who warned me that he wasn't interested in commitment and couldn't make me happy.

Nick nods, his eyes darting away to the view from my window. 'I posted the hotel's security guard outside your door. I needed some time to think, so I took a cable-car ride.'

I wait, pressure building inside me at the silence, awkwardness and my own foolishness. Just because I trust him, just because our five-night getaway has taught me so much more about this man… I should have taken extra care to stop my own feelings. Because they too are fragile, forged from the ashes of my past betrayal. What if Nick can never love me back and I'm hurt all over again?

I swallow down the panic. I'll bide my time. Keep my feelings a secret until he's ready to hear the truth.

Nick has better stamina than me, because I cave first. 'Nick, I'm sorry. You were right.' I blurt out things I've wanted to say for the past three hours. 'It was stupid to answer the door without you. I should have untied you first. I just got carried away with our little game, and—'

'No. It was my fault.' His voice is calm, his control returned. He clasps his hands at his back. His broad chest, a place where I know every contour, is rigid. 'I take full responsibility. I know better than to behave so…carelessly.'

I go to him, crossing the chasm of fraught distance.

'Can we put tonight behind us?' I ask, my heart thumping out a countdown of doom at the blank look on his face.

He doesn't answer directly. 'I should never have let down my guard.' Cagey, resigned, taking the blame.

He winces. 'You could have been—'

'No, Nick. It's not your fault.' I shift my weight from one foot to the other, needing to move but too scared to step closer in case it forces his hand. I need time to salvage this. 'This is my life. I'm used to things like this happening. Over-eager fans. It's just part of the fame thing.'

He snorts. 'If you believe that's all that happened here tonight, you're more naive than I thought, Lady Madden.'

I wither a little inside. After everything I've confided, him calling me out, reminding me of the power I gave Dave, stings like a slap. But we can repair this. *I* can make it right.

'Perhaps we blurred the boundaries a little too much,' I concede. 'Perhaps the after-hours demarcation wasn't enough. The next time I need personal protection, I'll employ another firm. Perhaps you can recommend someone?' That way he won't need to feel conflicted. When we're together we can focus on us. He can relax.

'I think that's for the best.' He offers a stiff nod.

Silence falls once more. My mind fills with all the things I want to say. I feel him withdrawing. Beating a retreat. He looks as though he's preparing to walk out and never look back.

The true depth of my feelings for him explode and expand.

Panic trembles through my body.

'Maybe we can start afresh…back in London?' I feel him stiffen. See the answer written over his grim face. I expected his hesitance. But surely he can't just walk away from what we've shared this week?

I haven't imagined our connection or the lowering of both his barriers and mine.

'I don't think that's a good idea.' He looks at me finally, and I feel like a collapsed paper bag. His dark eyes are chilly. I'm losing him. 'I haven't dated in seventeen years. Tonight has proved that I still can't trust my emotions. This was…a mistake.'

My jaw is weighted with shock. How can we have gone so off-track so quickly? Perhaps for him, what we shared was nothing special. Perhaps he sees me as some naïve, privileged socialite who's once more given all her trust to the wrong man.

I move closer, hating our physical distance. 'Look, I accept we played with fire, mixing business and pleasure. But I don't have to employ you any more. We can just see how this goes when we're just a woman and a man who met through work. When we're back in London and there's no power imbalance between us. No need for you to worry about protecting me.'

'That's not the issue.'

He's unmoved, so I plough on, needing him to understand that the kind of trust we've shared doesn't come along every day for everyone. It's special.

'Are you worried that my life is too complicated because of the constant scrutiny? Because I'll do everything in my power to keep our relationship out of the media, to protect you from gossip and speculation, if that's your concern.'

'It's not, but you raise an excellent point. If it ever

got out that I sleep with my clients and forget to pro-tect them, it could be disastrous for my business.'

'I understand that, and I'll do everything I can to prevent that.'

He shakes his head. 'It's irrelevant. That's not why we're a bad idea. I think it's best if we part tomor-row and leave it at that.'

I gasp, helplessness leaving me light-headed. 'I don't want that—I thought we'd overcome this dis-tance. I care about you, Nick. I'm falling for you. I want to see you again. I thought you felt the same way. Don't kid yourself that you'll be doing me a fa-vour by running away from this.'

Horror slashes his tight expression before he reins it in. 'This *is* for the best, Brooke. I'm too close. Can't you see that? I made a mistake tonight because I re-laxed too much. I let go of my control.'

'So what? You can't control feelings, Nick. You can't control love. All you can do is acknowledge it and be kind to yourself. Supressing emotion is just another way of invalidating what it is that makes us human. So you relaxed, opened up to me—that's supposed to happen when people connect like this. I did the same with you. That's what's real and hon-est and special about us—we can do that with each other. Just be ourselves…'

'No. I don't want it. I don't want to feel out of con-trol.' He bites the words out past his clenched jaw. 'I failed to do my job tonight.' His hands curl into fists at his sides. 'I saw red.' He stares at me now, his eyes anguished with all his internalised pain. 'I wanted to damage another human being just for placing you at risk. If I hadn't been tied to that chair, I would have.'

'No, you wouldn't. You'd *never* do that.' My voice echoes across the room. I've never been more certain of anything in my life. He's strong. Protective But not violent. 'You taught me to run, and that's what you'd do. We'd run away together...'

'I can't be that reckless man again. I can't make another mistake.' His breath pants out with conviction. 'Not even for you.'

His final sentence is a mortal blow. I absorb its shock. But I still ache to touch him. To hold him. To show him that it's okay to feel scared. That the challenge is not to allow that fear to rule your life above all else. 'You're just wary of feeling because you've been terribly hurt in the past—I understand.'

His eyes seem to soften a fraction. 'You're right, in part.' But then they shift back to flintiness. 'But I'm more scared of hurting you. Look at us, Brooke. You've given me everything—your trust, your vulnerability, your confidences, not that I asked for them—but you laid yourself open to the wrong man again. One who'll let you down, because that's what I do. What I've done tonight. I put you at physical risk, the very opposite of what you're paying me to do. Why would you trust me with your emotional risks?'

His reasons feel like repeated blows, because of course I did give him all those things. Because I thought he was different. I thought I could finally be my whole true self with him and be safe. But he's thrown it all back in my face so he can keep hold of his blasted detachment. His emotional distance. His fear.

'Maybe I have been foolish again,' I say. 'Because I thought *you* were different to anyone I've dated in the past. I thought that I could be myself without fear. I thought what we shared was unique and liberating and precious.' My throat threatens to close, it's so clogged with tears. I fight them off. 'Maybe I have put my trust in the wrong man again. Because there are many forms of cowardice, Nick—yours is that you're too scared to forgive yourself. And until you do you're always going to push away the possibility that anyone could love you.'

Despite the crack in my voice, my words fall on deaf ears. His expression stays locked down, guarded, unflinching, as if he's made of ice. We stare for a handful of painful heartbeats, silent recriminations passing back and forth. For a few heady and illogical seconds, I truly believe he's going to snap out of it, admit he's being silly and scoop me into his arms.

But that's naïve and wishful thinking.

CHAPTER SEVENTEEN

Nick

I SIP MY coffee and stare at the brown paper parcel. I should have left it in the car, on the passenger seat where Brooke placed without explanation last night when I dropped her at her home in Kensington. It mocks me. The bland paper burns my eyes. The unknown contents are a reminder of my failures.

And, just as I couldn't bear to unwrap the mysterious gift when I returned to my dark, empty house in Fulham, I also couldn't bear to unpack my feelings around what happened in Switzerland. I still can't this morning. Examining the contents of my head causes the actual physical pain of a million darts. And also involves facing the possibility that Brooke was right: I am chained by fear.

Have I made the most monumental mistake of my life? Thrown away the rarest gift. Turned my back on life-giving sunshine…?

What could she possibly have given me after the way we parted?

I abandon my tepid coffee and prod at the parcel, my curiosity rampant, but still I resist. My stellar display of restraint brings me no pleasure or even satisfaction. It's as if all my past coping techniques, all the things I thought made me who I am, no longer work.

Everything's changed. Everything is Brooke.

I swallow past the crushing pressure in my chest.

I've developed feelings for her. That's what this rampant, uncontrollable restlessness is. It's ripped me in two so there's nowhere to hide, no matter how much I want to wrap up these terrifying emotions in brown paper and ignore them.

Brooke was right—I've been punishing myself for so long. Pushing people away. Trying not to feel anything in order to avoid the guilt and the pain and the helplessness of my past. But all I've done is delay dealing with those things. I've bottled them up and now they've resurfaced with freshly sharpened claws. Because, without realising, I let Brooke behind my guard to the very heart of me.

I peel off my running gear and head for the shower, seeking solace from my own thoughts and recriminations. But, just like my other coping techniques, silence and solitude no longer work either. How could I have believed that I had everything under control? How could I have been so content with so little for so long? Because where today there's chaos, and the clutter of so many emotions, the release is also cathartic.

Because I'll never be able to extricate Brooke

from my heart and soul, and I don't want to. She's melted all that's been frozen inside me. I deserve to bask in her warmth.

I'm falling for you, she said in her candid and fearless way.

Is it too late to repair what I did in Switzerland? Can I take back what I said and fling myself at her feet and beg for her forgiveness? Because I'm falling too.

But that's not enough reason to beg her to reconsider. She deserves a whole man. An emotionally mature man, one she never has to doubt. I can't undo seventeen years of self-inflicted damage during twenty minutes of shower therapy, but I can start today. Stop hiding. Face all the things that have been holding me back.

With my towel wrapped around my waist and dripping water onto the tiles, I stride back into the kitchen. I tear into the brown paper parcel as if it's the lifeline I need in order to breathe again. The paper yields and for a split second I can't compute what I'm seeing, what I'm holding in my hands. But then my index finger traces a hole, and a burst of laughter splits the silence of my quiet home.

It's a bobble hat. Hand-knitted. Black.

My grin makes my cheeks ache. I pull it on. It's a little too big. I search the discarded paper for a note or a card like a starving man. Disappointment slugs me in the gut. There's nothing. But hope surges through me in electrifying currents.

She made this with her own two hands. For me.

I've seen how slow her progress is. It's painful to watch. This must have taken her hours. I've been with her every minute of every day and some of the nights for the past five days. When did she have time? She must have worked on this while I slept.

Before I even know what I'm doing, I grab my phone and dial a number I know by heart. One I haven't used nearly enough. My head pounds, uncertainty crawling over my bare skin like an uncontrollable itch. The phone answers after one ring.

'Nicky?'

I clear the tightness from my throat. 'Hi, Ma. I just wanted to wish you happy birthday for tomorrow.' My voice is thick with emotion, but instead of cowering from that, rejecting it, I embrace it. Allow it to flow through me so I feel every heart-pounding inch.

'Thank you, son. It's been a while. How are you?'

I haven't spoken to my mother in months. Haven't seen her for longer. Is it my imagination, or does she sound older…?

'I'm good, Ma. Getting there, anyway.' Relief floods through my tense limbs and I collapse onto a bar stool. I already know from the tone of her voice and her obvious delight at hearing from me that Brooke was right. This woman loves me. She always has and likely always will. That's how parents feel for a child. That's how I feel for my little boy. I've just blanked out the knowledge for years. Another coping mechanism that prevented me from feeling.

But now it's as if all I am is emotion and sensation,

splintering apart with the pressure of being so full. Is this what happens when you stop fighting and allow feelings to take over? When you open your heart?

'You're a good man, you know that, right?' my mother says. 'A good son. I miss you.'

My swallow tastes acidic with guilt. But there must be truth to her words. Brooke is the best person I know, and she sees something in me worthy of her trust and feelings. But have I pushed her away one time too many?

'I miss you too. If you're free tomorrow, I'd like to meet up for a catch-up.' I grit my teeth, ashamed that by trying to protect myself and those around me I might have neglected my relationship with the woman who gave me life and raised me. A strong, compassionate woman. A woman who, it seems, accepted me when I wasn't ready to accept myself.

Just like Brooke.

'I'd like that,' she answers, with the quiet assertion that tells me we're going to be okay.

We talk for a few more minutes, arrange a venue for tomorrow and, just as we're about to hang up, she says, 'Nicky, are you…happy?'

Blood roars through my head with the yearning for the one thing that will enable me to say yes. The one thing that's been missing from my life. 'I'm working on it, Ma. I'll update you tomorrow.'

I say goodbye, hang up the phone and jog to my wardrobe to choose clothes that will complement my hat.

I've never dressed more hurriedly.

* * *

By the time I arrive, Regent Street has been cordoned off in preparation for the annual turning on of the Christmas lights. The iconic street has been pedestrianised from Piccadilly Circus to Oxford Circus. The world-renowned shopping destination is awash with onlookers, tourists and families, the festive atmosphere high. There's live music and food vendors and giant screens displaying the action on the stage.

But all I see are obstacles and barriers to me finding Brooke.

A quick search of her website and social media accounts once I'd thrown on some clothes had told me where I could locate her tonight. She's pressing the button that will illuminate Regent Street with the impressive Christmas lights, the largest festive installation London boasts. How fitting that they chose a woman who could illuminate the whole city with just her smile…

I wanted to call, to speak to her, but I can't tell her how I feel over the phone or in a message. It's too huge. I need to be able to see her when I lay myself bare. When I tell her that I need her and want to be worthy of her.

Refusing to believe that I've missed my chance, I dodge the stream of bodies aimlessly shopping and milling around. I duck frantically through the buoyant crowds to get as close to the stage as possible. A sense of urgency drags the frigid November air into my lungs in great gusts.

What If I'm too late? What if my rejection proved

to her that she was wrong to give me her trust? That I'm just like the ex who betrayed her? Taken her wonderful gifts—her wicked, playful humour, her astounding bravery and her enormous capacity for compassion and love—and used them against her.

Time ticks in my head, growing louder with each second. I fight my way closer to the stage, listening to the talk on the PA system for the sound of her voice as panic flies through my bloodstream.

Then I'm slapped in the face by a glimpse of her. She's glowing, wrapped up against the cold in a woollen coat and matching *faux* fur hat. My other senses shut down as I watch her smile, laugh and wave. When my hearing returns, the countdown is coming to an end. The entire street overhead lights up with a million tiny bulbs woven in intricate patterns. Fireworks erupt against the black sky. The crowds cheer and clap and children gaze in wonder.

But I only have eyes for Broke.

I need to get to her, but I'm trapped where I am by the crush of bodies and the weighty sense that it's too late. She'll leave the stage and I'll miss my chance.

I fight the panic, searching my mind for logic. Brooke won't hang around. She'll be whisked away as soon as her job is done. I scan the closest side streets for a sign of her car. Nothing obvious. But I have a split second to decide which street to choose. To go left or right.

She's waving goodbye to the crowds. Heading for the stairs at the back of the stage where, if they have any sense at all, the security team will quickly bundle her away into the night.

Of course, I know where she lives. But I don't want to wait another second to tell her that I'm ready to stop punishing myself. That I made a mistake, perhaps the biggest of my life, in letting her go. That I'll work on my issues every moment of every day just to be worthy of her love.

Taking my life in my hands, I dive right, weave my way through the mass of bodies until I'm only a few rows back from the cordon facing backstage. There are fewer people here, because the view to the stage is obscured. But enough people have twigged that this is the best vantage for celebrity spotting. They're lined up against the barriers with their phones out ready to snap a picture.

Then Brooke emerges. My heart lurches against my ribs. I instinctively raise my arm, trying to win her attention. But I'm not the only one who's spotted her. I'm not the only one clamouring for her breathtaking smile. I'm just another face in the crowd.

Several people call her name, their phones clicking in her direction. Flanked by two guys dressed in black overcoats, she waves over as the men usher her towards a car idling at the kerb in the nearby side street.

Her name is trapped in my throat. The vision of her so blinding I actually close my eyes against the glare. But they're open again a split second later. I rise up to my fullest height, craning onto the balls of my feet, and wave once more. I've never been more grateful for my height.

She sees me. Our eyes collide. The noise of the crowd disappears. A thread of connection arcs between us across the space. But the beam of her smile falters a fraction, her eyes dimming. And then she turns away and ducks inside the car, speaking to one of the men before the door closes.

A part of me withers. Dies.

I know she saw me. I felt the pull as surely as if she'd tugged on that connecting thread. I know, because the end of it is coiled between my ribs and wrapped around my vital organs.

I watch the tail lights of the car disappear around the corner, my stomach somewhere in the vicinity of my size-eleven boots.

Then my phone vibrates. I yank it from my pocket, my hands trembling as I read the text.

Pick you up at Golden Square.

I set off at a run in the direction of the small public garden, one of London's many historic squares located near Regent Street. When I see her car parked in a no-parking zone, I almost collapse with relief. Her driver opens the rear door as I approach and I slide inside, bracing myself for the dazzling vision of Brooke, once more up close.

She's more exquisite than I remember, although it's only been twenty-three hours and forty-seven minutes since we parted.

'Hi,' she says with a tight smile as we pull out into traffic.

I open my mouth to speak and then close it again. There's not a single word in my head, though I've waited for this moment, the chance to allow everything I want—no, need—to say to burst free.

She's removed her hat and unbuttoned her coat. The car interior feels stifling, perhaps because I sprinted like a man running for the last train to the rest of his life.

I pull the bobble hat from my head and Brooke smiles. 'It more or less fits,' she says. 'I'm sorry about the holes, but…' She shrugs. 'You know me. What I lack in skill, I make up for in enthusiasm.'

I'm still agape at her beauty. Humbled anew by her gift and, for a big tough guy, struck strangely mute.

'Did you come to see the lights?' She slides her hand along her trouser-clad thigh in a gesture that hints that she's nervous.

I'm almost apoplectic with my own nerves. I exhale a sigh. 'No. I came to see you. I need to apologise—'

'No, you don't,' she interrupts. 'I overstepped the mark. I should mind my own business and examine my own behaviour before I go around finding fault with others. I'm sorry for all the trouble I caused you, Nick.'

A band tightens around my ribs. It feels as if we're strangers again. But, even if she can, I can't go backwards.

'You're perfect, Brooke. Your gift is perfect.' I clutch the woollen hat in my fist for luck. 'I'm the one who should be apologising. I said horrible things—lies. You were right. I've been punishing myself for years. Hiding, pushing people away to avoid facing the pain of what I did, and then the pain of the consequences…losing my baby. Being with you these last few days—it's woken me up to a lot of things.'

She stares, her big eyes catching the reflection of the many city lights outside.

'I thought my mistake, the past, defined me. That I could never be accepted again because I didn't deserve happiness. But I felt it with you. As if I was capable of finding it if I was only brave enough to open my eyes and see.'

'Nick—'

'No.' I shift a fraction closer to her on the seat. 'I'm falling for you, Brooke. I can't even put it into words yet. I have a lot of work to do on myself, but I want to keep seeing you, as you suggested. Try dating. Those people back there screaming for you don't know you. But I do. And I want the real version, the knitting version the most.'

Tears glisten on her lashes and I touch her then, dropping my precious hat and sliding my palms against her smooth cheeks.

My thumbs gently brush away the first drops to fall. 'Don't cry, Lady. Just tell me it's not too late. Tell me you still mean all the wonderful things you said yesterday, because I'm ready to hear them now.

I'm ready to feel again. I can't help myself—you've jump-started my heart with your sunshine.'

She looks up at me with those trademark eyes of hers and I search for all the things I saw there when she was open and trusting. 'I know it's a risk for you. I'm a risk,' I admit. 'But I'm ready to be open to my feelings. For you.' I grip her face and search her sparkling eyes. 'Say something…'

'Nick…' Her voice breaks and I shrivel inside. She's going to rebuke me. I've messed up and she's done.

The panic and desperation must be etched into my face, because she slides her hands over mine and holds them to her cheeks. 'You feel things so deeply. You're an all-or-nothing kind of guy. I understood that the first time you made me sign the security code of conduct that first time we met.' A smile dances on her beautiful mouth and the urge to kiss her overwhelms me.

I stop fighting it. Pull her close. Brush my lips over hers in a whisper-soft caress. 'Is that a bad thing?'

She laughs. 'No. It's wonderful because I know that, just like everything else you do, you love intensely too. So I know that, if you ever love me, it will be worth waiting for. I was never going to give up on you. You may have noticed that I'm fairly persistent when I want something.'

I grin, shrug, pull her mouth back to mine, properly this time. She climbs astride my lap and we kiss and kiss and kiss. I try to show her how I feel with my lips, my grip and the way I seem to need her air. It leaves me splayed open so that, when we pull apart for breath, I have to rest my forehead against hers while I seek composure.

'I'm sorry the hat wasn't a better gift,' she says, her fingers stroking my hair.

I shake my head, gripping her tighter. 'It's perfect, just like you.'

She snorts in disbelief. 'It's riddled with holes.'

I lean back. Lock eyes with her. 'Mistakes are what make us human.' I blow out a prolonged exhale, my heart fighting to escape my chest. 'I'm not going to lie, Lady Madden. This emotional stuff has me feeling seriously off-balance.'

This time her smile is wide and uninhibited—a private smile, just for me. I'll never tire of witnessing that privilege. 'It's meant to feel like that,' she says. 'Life-changing. That's how we know our connection is the real thing.' She presses her lips to mine. 'I'm not going anywhere.' Another kiss. 'Think you can handle that, Big Guy?'

I grip her waist, crush her to my chest and suck in the comfort of her familiar Brooke scent.

'For you I can.' The steady beat of her heart thuds under my cheek.

'Good. Then it's all settled.'

And just like that a bad decision becomes the best one of my life.

EPILOGUE

Seven months later
Brooke

SUNDAYS HAVE BECOME my favourite day of the week. A day where we hide away at home. Sleep late and make lazy love. Venture out to Covent Garden for brunch and spend the evening on the sofa together. Which is where I find myself now, sprawled next to Nick, relaxed and content while the summer sun sets over London.

'Oh, let me read you this,' I say, folding up the Sunday newspaper so I can hold it with one hand while I tangle the other in Nick's hair. His head rests on my chest as if I'm his favourite pillow.

I clear my throat. '"Rumours abound this week that, in what is believed to be a highly secretive ceremony attended by only close family and a few select friends, Lady Brooke Madden, daughter of Earl Madden and Countess Madden, better know as the actress Lori Colt, is thought to have married her former bodyguard, Nicholas Rivers of Rivers Security".'

He shifts against me. Mumbles. Wraps his arm around my waist more securely.

"'The pair have been regularly spotted around London in recent months and, while they have made no secret that they are a couple very much in love, no official announcements have been forthcoming from the top model's team".'

Nick lifts his head, presses his mouth to mine and then trails kisses across my cheek and down my neck.

I grow breathless but keep reading. "'Sources close to the couple confirm that the nuptials took place in an intimate twilight ceremony at an undisclosed location in the playground of the rich and famous, Saint Moritz in Switzerland".'

'Blah, blah, blah…' says Nick, his voice sleepy but husky with desire. 'They know nothing.'

I spread my legs to accommodate his thick thigh so that it's where I want him most. He pops the first button on my shirt and presses kisses to my collarbone and the valley between my breasts.

'They certainly don't know what a kinky bastard I married,' I finish, tossing the newspaper so my hands can glide up his warm back under his shirt.

I feel his smile against my skin. Catch the low rumble of his sexy chuckle. With one hand he pops the back fastening of my bra and tugs the garment down so my aching breasts spill free. Each nipple gets some of his divine and very through attention, and then he says, 'They also don't know how delicious my wife is.'

His hand moves south and his weight shifts so he can press his mouth over my stomach. 'And they have no idea who's in here.'

I look down at my husband, his handsome face transformed by love. Once he stopped punishing himself, Nick's defensive barriers crumbled one by one. I never once doubted his love—I could see it written in his expressive conker-brown eyes, eyes I hope our baby inherits.

'No…that's our secret,' I agree, tangling my fingers in his thick, luxurious hair.

Nick pops the button on my jeans and I lift my hips so he can shimmy them and my underwear down my legs. Then his eyes meet mine. 'I don't care anything apart from what I know.'

He strips off his shirt and drops it on the floor before shoving down his jeans and boxers.

'And what's that?' I pant as he takes my hands in his and then pushes inside me, as if he's coming home.

'That I love you.' His kiss steals my air and another little piece of my heart. 'That I love our baby. That I love our family.'

'I love you too,' I say. 'That's a lot of love, Big Guy.'

He nods, freeing his beautiful smile. 'It's only what we deserve.'

And there's no arguing with that truth.

* * * * *

COMING SOON!

We really hope you enjoyed reading this book.
If you're looking for more romance, be sure to
head to the shops when new books are
available on

Thursday 26th
November

To see which titles are coming soon, please visit

millsandboon.co.uk/nextmonth

MILLS & BOON

LET'S TALK

Romance

For exclusive extracts, competitions
and special offers, find us online:

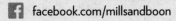 facebook.com/millsandboon

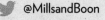 @MillsandBoon

@MillsandBoonUK

Get in touch on 01413 063232

For all the latest titles coming soon, visit
millsandboon.co.uk/nextmonth

MILLS & BOON

THE HEART OF ROMANCE

A ROMANCE FOR EVERY KIND OF READER

MODERN

Prepare to be swept off your feet by sophisticated, sexy and seductive heroes, in some of the world's most glamourous and romantic locations, where power and passion collide.
8 stories per month.

HISTORICAL

Escape with historical heroes from time gone by. Whether your passion is for wicked Regency Rakes, muscled Vikings or rugge Highlanders, awaken the romance of the past.
6 stories per month.

MEDICAL

Set your pulse racing with dedicated, delectable doctors in the high-pressure world of medicine, where emotions run high an passion, comfort and love are the best medicine.
6 stories per month.

True Love

Celebrate true love with tender stories of heartfelt romance, fr the rush of falling in love to the joy a new baby can bring, and focus on the emotional heart of a relationship.
8 stories per month.

Desire

Indulge in secrets and scandal, intense drama and plenty of siz hot action with powerful and passionate heroes who have it all: wealth, status, good looks…everything but the right woman.
6 stories per month.

HEROES

Experience all the excitement of a gripping thriller, with an int romance at its heart. Resourceful, true-to-life women and stron fearless men face danger and desire - a killer combination!
8 stories per month.

DARE

Sensual love stories featuring smart, sassy heroines you'd want a best friend, and compelling intense heroes who are worthy of t
4 stories per month.

To see which titles are coming soon, please visit
millsandboon.co.uk/nextmonth